SILENT ENEMY

ALSO BY THOMAS W. YOUNG

FICTION

The Mullah's Storm

NONFICTION

The Speed of Heat:
An Airlift Wing at War in Iraq and Afghanistan

SILENT ENEMY

THOMAS W. YOUNG

G. P. PUTNAM'S SONS | NEW YORK

PUTNAM

G. P. PUTNAM'S SONS
Publishers Since 1838
Published by the Penguin Group
Penguin Group (USA) Inc., 375 Hudson Street, New York, New York 10014, USA • Penguin Group (Canada), 90 Eglinton Avenue East, Suite 700, Toronto, Ontario M4P 2Y3, Canada (a division of Pearson Penguin Canada Inc.) • Penguin Books Ltd, 80 Strand, London WC2R 0RL, England • Penguin Ireland, 25 St Stephen's Green, Dublin 2, Ireland (a division of Penguin Books Ltd) • Penguin Group (Australia), 250 Camberwell Road, Camberwell, Victoria 3124, Australia (a division of Pearson Australia Group Pty Ltd) • Penguin Books India Pvt Ltd, 11 Community Centre, Panchsheel Park, New Delhi–110 017, India • Penguin Group (NZ), 67 Apollo Drive, Rosedale, North Shore 0632, New Zealand (a division of Pearson New Zealand Ltd) • Penguin Books (South Africa) (Pty) Ltd, 24 Sturdee Avenue, Rosebank, Johannesburg 2196, South Africa

Penguin Books Ltd, Registered Offices: 80 Strand, London WC2R 0RL, England

Published simultaneously in Canada

Library of Congress Cataloging-in-Publication Data

Young, Thomas W., date.
Silent enemy / Thomas W. Young.
p. cm.
ISBN 978-0-399-15779-0
1. Soldiers—Fiction. 2. Afghan War, 2001—Fiction. 3. Taliban—Fiction. 4. Afghanistan—Fiction. I. Title.
PS3625.O97335S55 2011 2011007378
813'.6—dc22

Printed in the United States of America
10 9 8 7 6 5 4 3 2 1

Book design by Gretchen Achilles

IN MEMORY OF MY GRANDFATHER MORGAN DANIEL,
OF THE LEGENDARY EIGHTH AIR FORCE

SILENT ENEMY

1

The world went away, and every part of her hurt. But nothing made any noise. Silence rang pure as the thoughts of the dead. Sergeant Major Gold knew only that some power threw her in every direction at once, flung projectiles against her in the darkness. She was so close to the explosion the sound never registered.

A moment before, the lights had been on in her office. Now her office no longer existed; nothing existed but blackness and force. No room even for fear, just shock and confusion. Then Gold's senses began to return. Dust, grit, smell of burning. An odor like nitric acid.

The fragments of her consciousness reconnected; her mind started to function again. For an instant, she thought with purely professional interest, *So this is what it's like to die in a bombing.* Pain behind her eyes, a keening in her ears. What was that sound? Screams.

Gold moved her fingers. Twitched her foot. Bent a knee. Everything hurt, but it all worked. She couldn't imagine how that was possible.

She eased up into a sitting position, checked for injuries. Maybe not bad, nothing broken. She coughed, and that hurt worse. Cracked ribs, maybe. Probably a concussion. Lucky. But what about everybody else?

Gold felt for her helmet and rifle. The helmet had disappeared, but her fingers found the M-4. She wanted to fight, but she knew whoever did this was either long gone or dead with his victims. She used the weapon as a crutch to pick herself up from the floor. Then she struck her head on a collapsed beam.

This day had always been coming, she knew. The Afghan National Police central training facility in Kabul made an obvious target for the Taliban. Gold helped run the literacy program; her office on the west end of the first floor was as far from the main entrance as it could have been. That was the reason she wasn't burned or crushed.

She coughed again, spat phlegm. Squinted through smoke, looked for the door. No door remained anywhere. But she found a gap in the wall.

Outside, Gold took a clean breath. She inhaled once more, and that felt better. Still some pain in the chest. She staggered along the wall until she reached the front of the training center.

The explosion had ripped open the concrete building, side to side, top to bottom, all four floors, like some monstrous shovel had torn an oval scoop from the front of the entire structure. A burned mass of steel lay on the ground near the blast crater, the engine block from what must have been a truck bomb. Moans, shouts, and curses came from within the rubble in Pashto, Dari, and English. Gold picked her way through broken masonry and twisted beams. She found part of a hand, with three fingers. A bloody scrap of uniform. A boot with a foot inside.

A lone fire truck sputtered into view. Its horn blared in deep, staccato bursts. Afghan and U.S. flag decals marked the new Ford with labeling that read in three languages FIRE AND RESCUE STAY BACK. A second truck arrived. Firefighters clung to the side of the vehicles, bands of yellow reflective fabric across the backs of their turnout coats.

The men pressurized a hose and opened its blast onto flames flickering thirty feet from Gold. A black spray of water and soot spattered her face. She fought tears, called names: "Hamid? Hikmatullah?" No answer but indistinguishable cries from victims hidden within the scene of destruction around her. The fires, crater, smoke, and screams made it seem hell itself had ruptured and burst up through the ground.

Gold found her way to the rear of the training center, where an exterior wall stood intact. She pulled open a door, entered the part of the building where her classroom used to be. Little remained to distinguish one room from another. Each was open to the street outside, like a dollhouse with the front removed.

"Ma'am," called an American voice. A man in firefighting gear, maybe a civilian adviser. "Stay out of there!"

Gold ignored him. She climbed stairs exposed to the sky. The thump of helicopter rotors began to build, grew louder. A Black Hawk settled onto the grounds of the police center.

She shouted names over the noise. No reply. Water trickled from a broken pipe. Odor like car exhaust and trash fire. Then she heard a familiar voice.

"Maalim, maalim." Teacher.

The young man cried out again, and she found him. Mahsoud lay on his back in the remains of a hallway. Dust covered him, but Gold could see that his face was badly burned. He looked at her through reddened eyes. A section of wall had fallen across his legs.

"Daa kharaab dai," he said. It is bad.

Seeing him like that made her want to rage, to cry, to strike out. Be professional, she told herself. ABC. Airway. Breathing. Circulation. If he can talk to me, then he has the *A* and the *B*. She felt the carotid artery. Pulse fast but weak. The *C* could be better.

Gold tried to remove the concrete slab on his left thigh. She pushed so hard she thought her spine would crack. No movement. She pushed again. The slab moved a quarter inch, and Mahsoud screamed.

"Zeh mutaasif yum," she said. I'm sorry. Then she shouted, "Medic!" The helicopter had shut down now. Gold assumed it carried medical help.

She could not lose Mahsoud. Her favorite student. Unlike many young men his age, he had somehow managed to learn to read during Taliban rule. So Gold was teaching him English while she taught the other police recruits to read their own language.

He reached out to her with his left hand. His right was mangled. She took his hand, and he squeezed so hard it hurt. The grip of a blacksmith, his father's occupation.

"You're going to be all right, buddy," she said.

He took two labored breaths, then said, "What is this word you call me?"

"Like friend. Companion."

"This is good English word."

"Medic," Gold yelled. "Now!"

A Navy corpsman appeared and kneeled beside Gold and Mahsoud. The petty officer put a stethoscope to his ears and listened to Mahsoud's chest. Shone a light into his eyes. Felt his abdomen, arms, ribs.

"Does it hurt to breathe?" asked the corpsman.

Gold thought Mahsoud would understand, but she repeated the question in Pashto, anyway. Mahsoud nodded.

"Do you have other pain?"

Mahsoud nodded again. The corpsman uncapped a needle, gave Mahsoud an injection. Then the corpsman shone his light under the concrete that trapped Mahsoud. Gold leaned to look. When she saw, she hoped Mahsoud did not notice her shock.

His lower left leg was bent back toward his thigh at an impossible angle. A section of rebar, twisted and sheared into a meat hook, had spiked the knee. A horror of torn flesh. But not much blood.

"Can we get this concrete off him?" Gold asked.

"Even with the right equipment, this would be a tough extrication," the corpsman said. "That concrete is trapping him, but it's also keeping him from bleeding to death."

"He can't stay here forever. What are you going to do?"

"I'll have to let my skipper handle this. He's a surgeon."

Gold didn't like the sound of that. "Will he amputate?" she asked.

"If you put aside the problem of moving the patient, that leg still looks bad. I think he has some lung injury, too."

He's not "the patient," Gold thought. He has a name. He wants to help his fellow Afghans. God knows, their police need people who are trainable and honest.

"What about my leg?" Mahsoud asked in Pashto.

"They will do all they can," Gold said.

"You must not let them take my leg. You know I want to be a policeman."

The corpsman's radio barked. The man pressed a TALK switch and said, "Yes, sir. Second floor. Be careful coming up. Severe trauma to the left leg, probable smoke inhalation. Entrapped patient, conscious and alert."

Gold surveyed the mess around her. Smoke still rising here and there. Tangled pipes and conduits. Pools of reddish water. Wailing of the wounded. Lives ruined by terrorists who thought they would launch themselves to paradise on a load of fertilizer and diesel fuel, or maybe a trunk full of daisy-chained 105s. Again.

The corpsman kneeled, twisted open a water bottle. He dribbled water onto the burned part of Mahsoud's face. Then he tore open a foil package and took out a dressing wet with some compound. Placed it across Mahsoud's cheek.

The doctor arrived, peeled off bloody latex gloves, and put on fresh ones. He clicked on a light to see Mahsoud's leg. Looked around at the fallen concrete. Sighed hard.

"Tell him I'm going to have to take off that leg," the doctor said. "I'm sorry."

"He understands you, sir," Gold said.

Mahsoud began to cry. "I was going to be a bomb technician," he said. "Now I will become a street beggar."

"I do not know what you will become," Gold said in Pashto. "But you will never be a beggar."

"I wanted to help stop these apostates."

"You will, my friend. You will find another way."

The surgeon scissored Mahsoud's trousers. Then he injected three syringes and waited for the anesthetic to take effect.

"Look at me, Mahsoud," Gold said. "I want you to look at my face." Look at anything but the cutting.

"Do not let go of my hand, teacher."

"I won't. I'll stay right here."

The surgeon opened a case and took out a long stainless steel knife.

AT BAGRAM AIR BASE NORTH OF KABUL, Major Michael Parson peered out the cockpit windows of his C-5 Galaxy. He was waiting for aerial port to load several old Humvees into the aircraft's cargo compartment. The worn-out vehicles were supposed to be going back to Al Udeid Air Base, in Qatar. Parson wanted to take off as soon as possible. Get the hell out of this godforsaken country. But when he'd checked in at the Air Operations Center, the intel guys were talking about a major explosion nearby. There was no telling how that might affect flight operations.

Static crackled from loudspeakers on the steel lamp poles along the ramp. Then, an announcement on Giant Voice: "Attention on base. Bagram is at Force Protection Condition Delta. MASF personnel stand by for a mass casualty event."

The flight engineer, Sergeant Dunne, sat at the engineer's panel. He wore his headset over salt-and-pepper hair a little longer than regulation. He unwrapped the foil on a stick of Wrigley's and chewed it with a frown, as if the gum tasted strange. Dunne took off his headset, interrupted his preflight checks.

"What the hell's going on?" he asked. "There's all kinds of chatter on the tower frequency."

Parson looked out the cockpit windows. A pair of F-16s launched, the streak-scream of their takeoff rumbling over the base in waves. The jets rode the orange-and-blue flames of their afterburners in a near-vertical climb, and they vanished from sight as they soared higher.

If they're putting up fighters for a combat air patrol, Parson thought, this must be bigger than the usual suicide bombing. Coordinated with other attacks, maybe? He looked to the south, where the fighter jets had disappeared.

"Just keep your preflight going," Parson said, "but watch your back."

"Will do," Dunne said.

"I'll check in at ops and see what's happening."

As Parson jogged across the ramp, he heard the whine of aircraft turbines, then felt the wind from helicopter rotors. On the Army flight line, blades spun on three H-60s, red crosses on their sides. One by one, the Black Hawks lifted off, hover-taxied from the apron, and fluttered away to the south. Going to pick up wounded, Parson guessed.

Inside flight ops, the babble of voices mixed with the squelch and pop of radios, the jangle of telephones. Parson found the air base commander, a full bird colonel. The sleeves were rolled up on his ABU fatigues. Beretta in a holster across his chest. Handset to his ear.

"At the police center?" he said. "Yes, sir. We have an aeromed team ready to go. Yes, sir, I'll hold."

"Colonel, I'm the aircraft commander of Reach Three-Four-Six," Parson said. "Is my mission on schedule?"

"You're not a Reach call sign anymore," the colonel said. "We're putting you on an Air Evac mission to Germany. We're going to get a shitload of patients. Most of them will need to fly to Landstuhl."

There had to be some mixup. Other planes, like the C-130, were far better configured for patients. Easier to get the wounded on and off. More reliable pressurization. Parson had done plenty of aeromedical flights during his days as a C-130 navigator. But this was his first mission as a C-5 aircraft commander. The last thing he needed was a task neither he nor his crew had ever done on a C-5, a plane never meant for air ambulance flights.

"I want to help," Parson said, "but are you sure this is a good idea?"

"We don't really have a choice," the colonel said. "You're all we have to work with at Bagram. There are some patient support pallets in storage at one of the hangars here. Once your loadmasters install them, the aeromeds will take it from there."

Not ideal, Parson thought, but we can make it work. Install the pallets, run some drop cords to power the aeromeds' equipment, and we'll have ourselves a flying hospital. A damned big one, too. Parson was proud to fly the largest aircraft in the Air Force fleet. Nearly two hundred and fifty feet long, with a max weight of more than four hundred tons, the C-5 could transport outsized cargo that nothing else could carry. But the A-models were older than many of the crew members who flew them. And with all those miles of wiring and tubing, in a mix of technology from two different centuries, a lot could go wrong.

When Parson got back to the tarmac, choppers were already returning with wounded. Dust and exhaust mingled in their rotor wash, stung his eyes, abraded his throat.

At the C-5, his four loadmasters were sliding the patient support pallets into place. Each pallet had stanchions for mounting stretchers. The loadmasters had expected to chain down ten Humvees, but now they were setting up for about forty wounded.

"Do you guys have everything you need for this?" Parson asked the senior load.

"I think so, sir. We had to break out the books to make sure we did this by the T.O. I used to carry patients on the C-141 all the time, but I ain't never done it on this thing."

Parson watched the crewmen slide the last pallet across the rollers. The loadmasters flipped cargo locks up from recesses in the floor, kicked the locks into place. An industrial scene of clanking metal, grease-stained checklists, commands shouted over the whine of the auxiliary power units.

Once the aircraft was configured, a bus with a red crescent on the side backed up to the open aft ramp. A loadmaster stood on the ramp, guided the bus driver with hand signals. The loadmaster crossed his fists, and the bus stopped next to a stair truck positioned against the ramp. The aeromed team—two commissioned flight nurses and three enlisted flight medics—began hoisting their litter patients up the stairs.

Other crew members continued their preflight checks. Dunne stood under the number four engine, looking up at the cowling.

On the way into Bagram, the MADAR computer had spat out a fault code for abnormal vibration on number four. Parson had thought he was going to have to shut down an engine and declare an emergency. Turned out not to be necessary, but now he was suspicious of that engine.

"Is that one going to be all right?" Parson asked.

"As long as you keep her out of the vibe range," Dunne said.

Of course I'll keep it out of the vibe range, Parson thought. Flight engineers seemed to think all pilots were idiots.

With his flight suit sleeve, he wiped sweat from his face. Unlike his last trip, today it was hot at Bagram. Clear and a million, too: unlimited visibility. You could see all the way into the Panjshir Valley. Bagram lay in the flat part of a bowl: scrubby vegetation dotted rocky soil that stretched into a rim of gray mountains.

It would be cooler at Ramstein Air Base, Germany, Parson's new destination. Close to the military's Landstuhl Regional Medical Center, one of the few hospitals in the world prepared to handle so many trauma patients at one time. Poor bastards. Most had probably never been out of Afghanistan. They had to get blown up and burned in numbers beyond what Afghan hospitals could handle to get out of this hellhole.

Parson climbed the crew ladder into the cargo compartment. The aeromeds hovered over their patients, some hooked up to monitors, a few with chest tubes, some apparently unconscious, many wide-eyed with apprehension. Human wreckage. A medicine smell like rubbing alcohol overpowered the usual airplane odors of grease and hydraulic fluid.

He found the medical crew director and introduced himself. Her flight suit bore the wings of an aeromedical nurse and the insignia of a lieutenant colonel. She wore rimless eyeglasses with a lanyard attached to the stems.

"Ma'am," Parson said. "My crew isn't used to this kind of thing, but we'll do the best we can." Though Parson was the aircraft commander, he still owed courtesies of rank to the MCD.

"And we're not used to this airframe," she said, "but a lot of these patients are in very bad shape, and they need to fly out on anything that's available."

She sounded as though she didn't like the arrangements any

more than Parson did. But sometimes in war you had to improvise, make do with the resources at hand.

A loadmaster handed Parson some paperwork.

"Form F and manifest, sir."

Parson signed the weight-and-balance sheet, then scanned the passenger-and-patient manifest. Afghan names, mainly, blanks for Social Security numbers. A few Western names, perhaps advisers and trainers. He stopped on one: GOLD, SOPHIA L. SGT. MJR. No, not her—please. Not blown up, too, after everything else she'd been through. He had not seen her since that day at the Pentagon when they'd both received Silver Stars.

"Is this one of your patients?" Parson asked the MCD. He showed her the form.

"No. Her injuries are minor. She's just traveling with some of the Afghans."

Parson stuffed the paperwork into a thigh pocket of his flight suit. He hurried through the cargo compartment, edged between litters, stepped over cords. Looked for anyone in ACUs. She wasn't down here. Maybe upstairs, then. The C-5 had two levels: the flight deck and troop compartment were above the cargo bay. Parson climbed the steps to the troop compartment three rungs at a time.

She was sitting in the first row. She looked up from her book, which appeared to Parson just a jumble of squiggly lines. She stared for a moment. Then, for the first time ever, Parson saw her smile broadly. He noticed her rank insignia. The last time he'd seen her, she'd been a master sergeant.

"Congratulations on your promotion," he said.

"Thank you, sir."

She stood, offered her right hand, and Parson shook it with both of his. She winced in pain, and Parson let go. He wanted to embrace her, but not if it would hurt.

"I'm sorry," he said. "Are you okay?"

"A couple cracked ribs. Nothing serious."

Parson noticed scrapes and minor cuts on her face and cheek. He decided not to ask her about it. He caught her looking at the fingers of his left hand. The tips of three of them had been lost to frostbite. The same with two fingers on the other hand, and four of his toes. A memento of his last trip to Afghanistan, with her. Because of his injuries, it had taken a medical waiver to let him go to pilot training.

"What are you doing here?" he asked.

Gold explained about her literacy program, her students, Mahsoud. Her smile vanished. She seemed beaten. Or was it just worry? Plenty of reason for that in Afghanistan, any damned day of the week.

"I promise I'll get you to your destination this time," Parson said.

"I'll hold you to that."

"But you're not riding back here in coach."

There was no direct access from the troop compartment to the cockpit, so Parson led her downstairs and through the cargo compartment. On the way, she stopped at one of the patients, an Afghan missing a leg. A DD Form 602 Patient Evacuation Tag hung from one of his buttonholes. He seemed to be sleeping or doped out. Gold spoke to him, anyway. She touched his arm and whispered in Pashto.

"How's he doing?" Parson asked. In the 602's Diagnostic block, it read LEFT LEG AMPUTATED IN FIELD, CRUSH INJURIES TO RIGHT HAND, SMOKE INHALATION, BURNS.

Gold shrugged. "If there's any hope for this country, it's in guys like him," she said. "And look at him now."

Parson was surprised she used the word "if." He decided not to have that conversation. Her friends had just been blown up.

On the flight deck, Parson showed her the cockpit, explained how he'd cross-trained from navigator to pilot. Then he led her down a narrow hallway to the relief crew area, with its seats and bunks.

"This is Sergeant Major Gold," he told his crew. "She's going to ride up here with us. Give her anything she wants. There's coffee in the galley. And, Sophia, you're having dinner with us, on me, when we get to Ramstein."

Parson left Gold in the aft flight deck. He planned to let her visit the cockpit after takeoff, but for now he wanted to put her in a more comfortable seat, near the coffee and food. For a moment, he kicked himself for using her first name in front of the crew. First names were common in the Air Force, at least when away from wing commanders and check ride evaluators. But it wasn't the Army way, certainly not Gold's way. She allowed few people to call her "Sophia," and she tolerated "Sophie" from no one. He figured she'd understand he was just excited to see her.

As he settled into the pilot's seat, he felt the warmth of meeting an old friend, but with a twinge of regret. How great to run into her again, but what horrible circumstances. Such a small world in the military. Dunne handed him TOLD cards, and he posted them on the instrument panel where he and his copilot, Lieutenant Colman, could see the takeoff speeds.

Colman entered the flight plan into the FMS. Colman, just out of flight school, took forever to check the waypoints. Parson let him finish, resisted the urge to take over the job. You couldn't blame a new copilot for acting like a new copilot.

"Before starting engines checklist," Parson called.

His crew began the clipped ritual: terse commands, the snap of switches, the whine of pumps and fans. Parson appreciated the choreography, felt like an orchestra conductor. *His* crew.

One by one, the four TF-39 engines came on speed, thunderous even at idle. Parson taxied for departure, left hand on the steering tiller. When he received takeoff clearance, he turned onto the runway and said, "Advancing throttles now."

From the corner of his eye, he saw Dunne punch a clock on the engineer's panel. The aircraft inched forward, thousands of pounds of thrust fighting the inertia of tons of steel and fuel. The jet moved at walking pace, then accelerated more quickly until the airspeed indicators came alive, then hurtled down the centerline like a gigantic missile.

"Fifteen," Dunne said. "Twenty. Time."

"Go," Colman called.

With three fingers, Parson pulled at the yoke, and his airplane, the size of an apartment building, lifted into the air. There was a hammering roar from the General Electric turbofans. The plane's own shadow chased it along the runway, grew smaller, vanished.

"Air Evac Eight-Four, Bagram Tower," called the controller. "Contact departure. Have a safe flight."

Parson pitched for climb speed, enjoying the smooth air. When the landing gear came up, he said to Colman, "Warm up the autopilot for me, will you?" Built in 1970, the plane still had some Vietnam-era electronics.

The crags and ridges of the Hindu Kush dropped away as the aircraft climbed. Parson looked out his side window at the ground where he and Gold had suffered through so much. Gold had been a passenger on his C-130, escorting a high-value Taliban prisoner. After they were shot down, the two of them went through a winter hell and back to keep that prisoner in coalition hands. And then they'd parted. But the experience had imbued Parson's spirit in permanent ways, like metallic changes in the turbines of an overtemped jet engine. Little difference to the eye, but an altered chemistry that could never be put back the way it was before.

Now the sky seemed to open in front of him, a cerulean infinity. Pale disk of moon over the mountains. No clouds but the wisps of horsetail cirrus in the upper atmosphere. Sunlight glinting off the windscreen. He found his aviator's sunglasses in his helmet bag and put them on.

At that moment, a screeching warble sounded in the cockpit. Parson tensed, felt his palms grow slick and his throat turn dry. Then the fear passed and left jangled nerves in its wake. Not a missile warning, just a stall tone. False alarm, since the plane was flying well beyond stall speed.

He reached overhead and clicked off the two toggle switches for the pilot and copilot stall limiters. The noise stopped. He looked to his side panel and saw the STALL light. So it was his side that had malfunctioned. He reached up and turned the copilot's stall system back on. Felt the sweat on his upper lip and under his arms.

Whoa, boy, he told himself. Don't let coming back to Afghanistan spook you. Just a nuisance warning. The airplane is old. These things happen.

"Maybe we can get that fixed at Ramstein," Parson said.

"If they have the parts," Dunne said.

The flight engineer had a point. Last time Parson and crew had broken down at Ramstein, they'd had to wait several days for a fuel control. One night during the layover, Parson came back from the officers' club to find Dunne in the lobby at billeting, strumming a weird all-metal guitar. Dunne played it with a slide, and he called it a National Steel. Not your typical hobby for a flight engineer, Parson thought, and the guy turned out to be a pretty darn good musician.

Now Parson cracked the throttles back from the takeoff setting to normal climb thrust. He hoped Colman and Dunne didn't see that his hand was still shaking. Then he moved his hand down to the center console and pressed VERT NAV, engaged the autopilot.

When the airplane leveled at thirty-four thousand feet, Parson felt better. Germany was just seven hours away. And today would be a short day by C-5 standards. With only one hop to fly, the gear handle was the hotel switch.

"Tell the sergeant major she can come up here and look around," Parson said over the interphone. Unlike with civilian passenger planes, the C-5 had no secure cockpit door. Most people with any business on a military transport would have a security clearance or some other form of background check. Letting friends and VIPs ride in the cockpit remained a frequent courtesy.

Gold came forward and sat at what used to be the navigator's seat. C-5 navigators had been replaced by inertial navigation units, three black boxes in the avionics bay, so now there was an unused seat on the flight deck. Dunne handed her a spare headset, and when she put it on she said, "Nice view."

Parson turned to look at her. Four years had made little difference. She was still fit, still looked like she'd be attractive in civilian clothes. No gray yet in the blond hair. Lines around her eyes a little deeper, though. She didn't seem especially awed by the cockpit.

"Feel free to take pictures," Parson said. He couldn't wait to get a chance for a real chat with her. If he got a day or two off at Ramstein, maybe he could rent a car, pick her up at Landstuhl, and do some touring. That wouldn't be fraternization, he figured—just giving her a break if she got stuck at the hospital without wheels.

Before Parson could continue the conversation, Dunne said, "We have a satcom message." Dunne tapped on a Toughbook bolted to the flight engineer's table, accessing what amounted to an e-mail transmitted through space. "Now, that's damned strange," he said. He printed the message, tore off the strip of thermal paper, and handed it to Parson.

The message read MAINTAIN ALTITUDE. DO NOT CLIMB OR DESCEND UNDER ANY CIRCUMSTANCES.

2

Parson had seen some strange messages and requests from the Tanker Airlift Control Center at Scott Air Force Base, but nothing like this. Something screwed up with routings and clearances, maybe. Who left the fuckup switch in the autofuck position? Nothing for it but to call and ask.

"Your airplane," Parson told Colman. "I got the radios." Then he spun a frequency into the HF, pressed his TALK switch, and said, "Hilda Contingency Cell, Air Evac Eight-Four." It was a long way from the skies of Central Asia to a windowless room in Illinois. Parson hoped he'd make contact. He looked back at Gold and said over the interphone, "Sorry. I'll talk to you once I figure this out."

Then he got his callback: "Air Evac Eight-Four, Hilda."

"Received your message on L band," Parson said. "What's going on?"

"Eight-Four," the flight manager said, "there's no good way to tell you this. There's a bomb threat against some of our aircraft, including yours."

What kind of nonsense is this? Parson wondered. We're flying, aren't we? Some Chicken Little in intel, probably. Typical Air Force. We make more problems for ourselves than the enemy does.

"Where is this coming from?" he asked.

"Jihadist websites are claiming that bombs have been planted on U.S. aircraft that departed Bagram today."

Well, Parson thought, you could scare yourself to death if you sat around reading those websites all the time. "They make all kinds of claims," he said. "Why are we paying attention to this one?"

"Because of its specificity. They say they had help on the base at Bagram."

"So why can't I climb or descend?" he asked. Terrorists can say anything. Give me a break.

"If there are any bombs, we don't know the trigger. They could be on timers, or they could be barometric."

Or they could be in somebody's imagination, Junior. And the timer, if there's a bomb at all, could be set for any time. For now. Or in ten minutes. Or four hours. But if it was barometric, well, what then? Parson knew the bomb that destroyed Pan Am 103 over Lockerbie, Scotland, might have had an aneroid barometer trigger. The 747 climbed through a set altitude and into eternity.

But we're already at flight level three-four-zero, he thought. We're probably fine, and more than likely the whole thing's bullshit.

"Hilda," Parson called. "We'll conduct a search. Call you back."

"Roger that, Eight-Four. If you find something, don't move it."

Don't move it, my ass, thought Parson. If we find something, we're going to chuck it out the damned door. But we're not going to find anything because there's nothing to find. No one has ever attempted to hijack a U.S. military plane, and planting a bomb on one would be just as hard.

"Eight-Four, do you copy?"

"Yeah, Eight-Four copies," Parson said.

"We'll be here for you, Eight-Four. Army liaison's working on getting some EOD expertise on the line. We'll also get a tanker set up to buy you some time."

"Thanks, Hilda," Parson said. "Air Evac Eight-Four out."

A tanker to buy us some time, Parson thought. Not a bad idea if they're going to insist on making us bore holes in the sky until everybody calms down. Won't be the first time we've burned a lot of fuel for nothing.

"All right, crew, you heard it," said Parson over interphone. All the aircrew members on headset could monitor the radios. "We're going to search every millimeter of this aircraft. I want one loadmaster checking the troop compartment, two for cargo, and one for the aft flight deck."

Parson looked at Gold again. She had her head in her hands, elbows on the nav table. Too bad she had to hear this nonsense. Probably hard to keep it in perspective when your building's just been blown up for real.

"Sergeant Major," he asked, "are you all right?"

She looked up. "What can I do?" she said.

"Tell the patients," Parson said. "Then help us look around, I suppose."

GOLD WONDERED IF IT WAS A GOOD IDEA TO TELL THEM, then decided not to argue. Parson had enough on his mind. And it wasn't fair to keep the Afghans in the dark. Besides, one of them might have noticed something.

She took off her headset and descended the steps to the cargo compartment. From above, on the ladder, the scene looked like an emergency room hastily set up in a metal warehouse. She found Mahsoud still asleep, a medic monitoring his vitals.

"How's he doing?" she asked.

"Stable for now," the medic said. "We're keeping him on oxygen because he has smoke and heat damage to his lungs." Gold looked at the plastic tubes leading to a cannula in Mahsoud's nose.

"Do you know what's happening?" she asked the medic. He looked about twenty, with close-cropped black hair. His name tag bore his wings, and it read JUSTIN BAKER, A1C USAF. On his right sleeve he wore the patch of the 455th Aeromedical Evacuation Squadron, embroidered with the word "EVACISTAN."

"The MCD told me," he said. He seemed worried. When he wasn't checking Mahsoud, he kept smoothing the fabric on the legs of his flight suit, as if he couldn't decide what to do with his hands.

One of the American patients stared up at the ducting and wires in the ceiling, breathed hard. Just three of the Afghans were awake, and she told them in Pashto what was going on. One of them said only, "*Wali?*" Why? Another began to recite the Shahadah. The one who had lost both legs and an arm did not seem to care.

At the front of the cargo compartment, two loadmasters began breaking down a baggage pallet, apparently following Parson's orders to search for anything unusual. Gold found her backpack and pulled her flashlight from a side pocket.

"I'll help you look," Gold said.

"Thanks, Sergeant Major," a loadmaster said. "You don't mind if we search your bag?"

"Not at all."

The loadmaster unzipped the backpack, paused to note the patch sewn onto the outside: the AA of the 82nd Airborne. Gold supposed he hadn't seen a lot of women who were jump qualified. He pulled out Gold's spare ACU uniform, a pair of jeans, a civvie sweater. Running shoes. Underwear, toiletries bag.

"Sorry, Sergeant Major."

"You're just doing your job," Gold said.

Then he found one of her books in Pashto. *The Diwan of Rahman Baba.* He looked at her without smiling.

"Is this a Quran?"

"It's a book of poetry," Gold said. "I'm a translator."

"Oh."

He thumbed through the pages as if looking for a razor. Then he put it back, replaced all her clothes, zipped up the backpack.

"No bomb in there," he said.

Guess he thinks I've gone native, Gold thought, or maybe that I've switched sides altogether. Doesn't matter what he thinks.

Gold helped the loadmaster look through the rest of the bags. It felt strange to examine the mundane details of every life on board.

The traditional clothing of the Afghans. Little else in their U.S.-issued bags. In the luggage of the Americans, hints of their tastes and lifestyles: an electric shaver, *Men's Fitness* magazine, an iPod. PDAs and computer games. A bundle of letters from Alabama. Nothing out of the ordinary.

After they had searched all the bags, the loadmaster paused to listen to his headset. Then he shook his head, keyed his mike, and said, "Yes, sir." Unstrapped the baggage pallet again.

"Major Parson talked to an EOD guy at Scott," the loadmaster said. "He wants us to check all the electronic devices. Anything that doesn't work could be a disguised bomb."

They dug through the bags again. Gold tested four portable DVD players, a half dozen MP3s, two laptops. All powered up okay.

She wondered if the next ON switch would send her and everyone else to oblivion, but figured that probably was not how the bomb would trigger.

"Well, it isn't here," the loadmaster said finally.

Gold looked around the cargo compartment. Plenty of other places it could be, behind all the panels and tubing and wiring. A crew chief shone a light under a walkway along the left side of the aircraft, inched along on his knees.

"I need to go check on someone," Gold said.

Mahsoud lay awake now. He gave a thin smile as Gold approached him.

"My friend," Gold said, "we have another problem." She told him about the bomb threat.

"Is it real?" Mahsoud asked.

"We don't know."

Was it real, indeed? Gold wondered. Parson seemed to think not, though he was doing a good job of making sure. Bet he'd feel differently if he'd been in my office a while back.

"Were I not a useless cripple," Mahsoud said, now in Pashto, "I could help you."

"You are hardly useless," Gold said, "but now you should try to rest and let us deal with this."

"I have studied these matters."

"I know, friend. Sleep."

"I cannot."

Gold considered what she might do to ease Mahsoud's mind if he was too fretful to sleep. Nothing, probably.

"If you're wide awake, do you want to see outside?" she asked.

"I would like to see the sun," Mahsoud said.

The cargo compartment had few windows, and they were round and narrow, not much bigger than a dinner plate. They reminded Gold of portholes on a ship. A nylon shade attached by Velcro covered each one. Gold pulled the shade from the window just above Mahsoud's litter. It came loose with a ripping sound.

Just outside, she saw a jet engine bigger than the cab of an Army deuce and a half, and another engine like it farther outboard. Plumes of heat and gases shimmered from the exhaust cones. Beyond the wing, the earth met the sky at an indistinct, hazy horizon.

Gold kneeled to look out from Mahsoud's angle. No direct view of the sun, at least not yet, but a good wedge of blue along with a chunk of the right wing. A beam of daylight shafted down from the window onto the green blanket that covered what remained of Mahsoud's legs.

The search continued throughout the aircraft. The MCD gave commands Gold could not quite hear. But Gold saw the aeromeds begin searching the patients, lifting blankets, checking clothing.

Under the covers, bloody bandages wrapped over stumps of limbs, dressings over burns. Fractures and lacerations and sutures. But no bomb. After all these victims have suffered, Gold thought, now the indignity of suspicion. She hoped they understood it was just procedure. She debated whether to go explain that to each one, but then she thought, No, they'll get it. Leave them alone and let them rest; don't do harm with good intentions. Any more than you already have.

The waterfall roar of the engines dropped an octave. Gold knew little about airplanes, but she guessed Parson had pulled back the throttles a bit to slow down. No sense rushing to Germany at top speed if we can't descend until the search is finished. She imagined

Parson was on the radio, trying to get more information to make decisions, probably using every resource at hand. He had certainly made the most of terribly limited resources when they had been shot down together. Her life should have ended when the Taliban dragged her away. Captured Americans usually made one or two video appearances on extremist websites, then met an awful end. But Parson would have none of that. He gave her captors the martyrdom they claimed to seek, delivered through the barrel of his rifle.

Now she and Parson faced a very different set of problems. Gold resolved to stay busy. Tasks could keep her from dwelling on things she couldn't change. She switched on her flashlight again to help the crew chief. Then she lowered herself to her hands and knees to peer into what looked like a gutter along the floor on each side of the aircraft. She saw a jumble of cables and hoses, valves and junction boxes.

"Is that wire supposed to be there?" Gold asked.

"Yes, ma'am," said the crew chief. "That's okay." From the crew chief's name tag, Gold saw his name was SPENCER. His uniform bore what she assumed was the badge of an aircraft maintainer: a wreath surrounding an eagle holding weapons in its talons.

In spots along the gutter, pools of red liquid rippled with the vibration of the airplane. Whatever it was, hydraulic fluid or a strange kind of oil, Spencer didn't seem concerned. But it put Gold in mind of some huge animal bleeding internally.

When she came to the aft end of the cargo compartment, Gold stood to stretch her legs, and she peered through the window in the troop door. From that angle she saw the rear aspect of the wing. It was not a solid sheet of metal but made of segments and panels in a geometry Gold did not understand. To a paratrooper, airplanes were just a platform to jump from. Beyond the wing, a line of clouds looked like a mountain range blanketed in snow. The ground a dark mist beneath them, a mere suggestion of a solid earth.

She wondered if anyone down there could see the plane. Gold supposed it would appear as a gray dart pulling a white contrail, traversing the sky in utter tranquillity.

One of the wounded moaned loudly enough to be heard over the slipstream and the turbines. Gold could not tell who it was. Perhaps a soul in the depths of morphine or Vicodin, imagining some horror or recalling one that had been realized.

As Gold made her way up the other side of the cargo compartment, she heard snatches of conversation between aeromeds and the English-speaking patients who were awake.

"It's nothing," one medic said. "We're gonna drag our asses around the sky all day and then we're going to land and be fine."

"Yeah, they're probably just screwing with us."

Another patient was sobbing openly. Gold thought maybe he was the one who had been moaning. By the unbandaged side of his face, he looked like a Westerner. There was gauze over the top of his head, an IV tube in one arm.

"Just point this thing at the ground and get it over with," he shouted. He had an American accent.

A nurse caressed his hand and whispered, "Rest, Sergeant. We've all heard bomb threats before. How many are real?"

"I know one bomb that was real. Don't tell me these things aren't real!"

Then the nurse conferred with the MCD. Gold didn't catch it all but heard: "I can't give him any more now."

When Gold reached Mahsoud's litter again, he held his bandaged hand against his good hand, both cupped in prayer. She kept a respectful distance until he finished.

"How do you feel, buddy?" she asked.

"There is that name again. Bud-dee."

He seemed to enjoy the sound of a single word. He had the heart of a Pashtun poet. Good thing he likes words, Gold thought, because we can offer him precious little else right now.

"Do you want something to eat?" Gold asked.

"Perhaps later."

Gold felt grateful that he wasn't panicked like that sergeant. But then, life could be cheap in Afghanistan. Mahsoud was probably used to the idea that it could end quickly and violently or worse. He wasn't old enough to remember peace.

3

While Parson waited for the loadmasters and crew chief to report back on their search, he pondered his next move. When we get to Germany, he thought, the controllers will probably put us into holding at Saarbrücken until they decide what to do with us. But I won't hold forever. These patients need to get to a real hospital, and we're not going to keep flying around in circles playing games. I'm in command of this aircraft, not some European air traffic controller or a clock-watcher at Scott.

The radio interrupted his thoughts: "Air Evac Eight-Four, Gunfighter One-Zero." A voice distorted by the suctioned acoustics of an aviator's oxygen mask.

Parson squeezed a TALK switch on his control column: "Gunfighter, Air Evac Eight-Four, go ahead."

"Gunfighter's a flight of two F-15s. We're going to come up on your right side. You probably want to put your TCAS on standby."

Somebody sure was taking this thing seriously if they were launching fighters. Terrorist threats didn't usually get this kind of response. Parson pressed buttons on his CDU to silence the traffic collision avoidance system.

"We're set, Gunfighter," he said. "Come on up."

The two Eagles slid into view out the right windows. Swept angles and sharp points of supersonic aircraft. Flying cutlasses. Faces of the helmeted pilots invisible behind oxygen hoses and black visors. Needlelike shapes under the wings: Sidewinders.

"Makes me feel better to see those boys," Colman said.

"They aren't here to do us any good," Parson said. "They're here to blow us away if they think we're hijacked."

"How you doing over there?" called the lead fighter.

"I've had better flights," Parson said. Go fuck yourself.

"Roger that. Sorry to have to ask this, but can you authenticate Tango Four?"

Colman picked up a classified comms table, read across the columns and rows.

"Don't get it wrong," Parson said. He watched Colman run his finger down a row of code letters until he stopped on one.

"It's Bravo," Colman said over the interphone.

Parson leaned across the center console to double-check.

"Gunfighter, Air Evac Eight-Four," called Parson. "Bravo."

"That checks."

So at least the fighters won't open up on us yet, Parson thought. He looked out at them, watched them holding close formation, then looked past them. Dust hung in the air below the aircraft, giving that part of the sky a beige tint more like a painting than reality. A temperature inversion, he guessed, kept the dust from rising above a certain altitude. The effect created a line along the horizon like a layer of smoke.

"Anybody find anything?" he asked over interphone.

A loadmaster called from downstairs: "Negative."

"Nothing up here, either," came the answer from the troop compartment.

"Engineer," Parson asked. "You guys did a thorough preflight, didn't you?"

"We did," said Dunne. "I'm sure there's nothing in the wheel wells. The scanner and I both looked."

That was good. If it were in a wheel well, they couldn't do anything about it. No access from inside the plane. Parson decided to check in with TACC again.

"We're negative on anything suspicious so far," he said. "We'll keep you advised."

"Roger that," the flight manager said. "Also, we have a tanker launching from Manas to refuel you. And the DO says he'll waive crew duty day limits."

Parson rolled his eyes, pressed his TALK switch. "You think?" he said. He usually tried not to use sarcasm over the radio, but this was asking for it.

"Hilda out," came the response.

Good, thought Parson. Talk to me when you're not going to say something stupid. Sounds like things are more in control up here than they are down there.

He felt he could afford to let his guest come back upstairs. "Cargo," Parson said, "what's Sergeant Major Gold doing now?"

"She's talking to that Afghani guy."

"When she finishes, tell her she can come up here."

"Yes, sir."

Perhaps her presence would keep his thinking clear. It certainly had four years ago. Back then, at a moment when rage had overcome his reason, he'd nearly killed a valuable Taliban prisoner. Gold had prevented it, by a swift blow to Parson's cheek with the stock of her weapon. Getting your ass kicked by a girl wasn't something you bragged about, but it had kept him focused on the mission.

When the flight deck door slid open, Gold sat at the nav table and put on the headset Dunne had loaned her.

"Thanks for coming, Sergeant Major," Parson said.

Gold leaned forward and patted the headrest of Parson's seat. She didn't actually touch him, just his crew station. But it seemed to say what Parson wanted to hear: *You were there for me, sir. I was there for you. If things turn bad, we can do this again.*

She pulled up the hot mike switch on her comm panel and asked, "Any new info?"

"Negative," Parson said. "Except that we have company."

Gold looked out the windows at the F-15s. Her face darkened, and Parson knew she understood their real purpose.

He scanned his instruments, tried to think. No warning lights or OFF flags. Mach zero-point-six-two. Vertical speed: zero. Flight level: three-four-zero. More than six miles above the earth, where the temperatures are always below freezing. Getting a little cold inside, too. Parson hated to be cold.

"Engineer," he said, "can you throw another log on the fire?"

Dunne twisted a rheostat on his panel toward HOT. Parson nodded to him in thanks. Think about the crew, Parson told himself. Some of them are pretty young and haven't seen much action. They could be letting their imaginations run away with them.

"Crew," Parson said, "this could turn into a long day. I want everybody to eat at least a little something for lunch. Stay hydrated, too. We don't know how long we're going to be up here now, and I need all of you at the top of your game."

Parson knew he'd better be at the top of his own game, too. Everybody would expect him to know what to do, to have a plan. Always, no matter what. Up until now, he had been a crew member, responsible for knowing his job and providing good suggestions to the aircraft commander. Now he was in charge. He'd once heard someone say, *To command is to serve.* He couldn't remember where that quote came from, but he felt its truth. Yes, he was the leader; people answered to him. But he answered for their fates. If you didn't want this burden, he told himself, you shouldn't have asked for it.

"Engineer's going off headset," Dunne said. "I'll bring us some stuff out of the galley."

Dunne returned with a six-pack of Pepsi, cans lettered in English and Arabic. From the chow hall at Balad. A jar of Spanish olives, from outside the base at Rota. Wurst and crackers from the commissary at Spangdahlem. All stops before arrival at Bagram.

Parson had no appetite at all, but he decided to set an example and follow his own order. He drew his boot knife and, with paper towels in his lap, cut a few slices of the wurst. Wiped the blade on the sleeve of his flight suit. Passed some of the meat and crackers to Gold and his crewmates.

GOLD TOOK AN OLIVE, offered on the tip of Parson's knife. Ate it without tasting. She watched the F-15s float alongside like Grim Reapers in solid form. Death itself, always there, never far away, only now you could see it.

She had thought the most dangerous part of her career was over. No more translating for combat patrols, no interpreting for interrogations. She had a school to run. A way to help undo the damage from a regime that had banned learning from the time it took power in 1996 until the U.S. military blew it away in 2001. The Army, of all institutions, had introduced her to the life of the mind. Educated her in a foreign language. Funded additional courses in a culture and history so rich she could study it all her life and not learn it all.

But what had it gotten for her and her students? Fire and pain, fear and loss. More of the same if there was anything to this bomb threat.

She knew she had to change her line of thinking. Fear was like a virus. It could always find its way in, but it hit you harder if you allowed yourself to become vulnerable. And it was contagious. You're a senior NCO, she told herself, and you're supposed to set an example.

Parson and his men still seemed pretty focused. They were lucky they had things to do, Gold thought. Something to keep their minds from wandering. Tweaking knobs, examining charts, checking weather sheets. Their instrument panels, with yellowed lettering and round gauges covered by scratched glass, looked old enough to belong in a history museum. The engineer had some book of graphs with lines like spaghetti, and he kept running his pencil through the graphs and worrying at his calculator.

That's what she needed: a job. When she and Major Parson had trekked through the mountains of Afghanistan, her language skill had made her a functional leader despite rank. Among the Afghans, she had been in her element while Parson, a grounded flier, was robbed of his. Now those roles were reversed, and Gold felt useless.

"Can I help with anything?" she asked.

"If there's still coffee in the galley," Parson said, "I could use a cup."

"Me, too," Dunne said. "Appreciate it."

Waitressing wasn't what she had in mind, but it was better than nothing. She took off her headset and went aft, down the hallway to the relief crew area. The galley had a small oven and a refrigerator. Overhead cabinet, cup dispenser. She found the coffeemaker against the galley's back wall, poured two cups and brought them to the cockpit. She placed Dunne's on the engineer's table, handed Parson's to him. When he took the cup, for an instant she saw herself reflected in his sunglasses. He expects me to be professional, she thought. Don't let him down.

She regarded him as he sipped and spoke inaudible words into the boom mike on his headset. Beige desert flight suit, like the one he had been wearing four years ago, only this one was clean. American flag on the left shoulder. Below the flag, another little patch, one that had to be unauthorized. It showed a gauge with ranges in green, yellow, and red. The needle pointed into the red. The label said SUCKMETER. Some of these Air Force flyboys personalized their uniforms in ways you could never get away with in the Army.

So this is Major Parson's world, she thought. His machine and crew far above the ground, nations and cultures passing underneath his wings by the hour. She had come to know him in vastly different circumstances, fleeing from the enemy during the worst blizzard Afghanistan had ever recorded. Parson saved her life with his outdoor skills and marksmanship, talents not always associated with fliers. She gathered that he'd spent a lifetime hunting, fishing, and camping. Elemental pastimes, she supposed, that helped him escape the technology filling his working hours. She wondered if he still liked to hunt after all that had happened.

Gold went back to the galley. She found a Ziploc bag filled with sugar packets, creamer, and coffee. It also contained a few tea bags. That gave her an idea for something she could do for Mahsoud and the others.

She looked around until she noticed the watercooler behind her. Gold filled the galley's hot cup and plugged it in, scanned the knobs and switches until she found the timer for the hot cup, then turned the dial to set it for five minutes.

While she waited, she climbed halfway down the cargo compartment ladder so she could see her students. Mahsoud and Baitullah were awake; the others were asleep or unconscious.

Back at the galley, she put tea bags and sugar into two cups. Not the chai the Afghans were used to; Lipton would have to suffice. When the timer stopped, she poured the hot water. Once the tea had brewed, she took one of the cups and eased down the ladder, holding on with her other hand. The retractable ladder creaked and shifted; it occurred to Gold that if she weren't used to jumping out of airplanes, simply descending these steps would seem dangerous.

She carried the first cup of tea to Baitullah. He smiled at her, but he looked rattled. No wonder. He was two litters away from the American sergeant who had been shouting and moaning. Now the sergeant was whispering, "I have to get out of here . . . I have to get out of here."

Gold knew Baitullah spoke not one word of English. But to understand the sergeant's mental state, he wouldn't need to. Gold patted Baitullah's shoulder and wished she could move him. But the aeromeds had him hooked up to monitors, and he was missing both feet.

After another trip up and down the ladder, Gold brought tea to Mahsoud. He had raised up on one elbow, perhaps to see better out his window. Blue sky above, but the weather had changed below. A cloud layer like rumpled linen obscured the ground completely. There was no sense of distance or perspective, as if the planet consisted of nothing but its atmosphere.

"How do you feel?" Gold asked in English.

"It hurts to—" Mahsoud looked puzzled, made a sweeping motion across his chest.

"Breathe," Gold said.

"Yes. It hurts to breathe." Mahsoud adjusted the cannula in his nose, took the foam cup. "Thank you," he said. He took a sip, and Gold could tell from his expression that he wasn't impressed. Or maybe he was just too uncomfortable to enjoy tea. He drank again, and seemed to watch the steam rise from the cup.

Gold thought about what she might do to ease his mind. Things for her were hard enough, but she could at least move around. What if you were confined to a litter with nothing to do but wonder if the end was . . . soon? Or now?

She went to the baggage pallet and found her pack. Gold considered giving Mahsoud her book of poetry, but he had already read it. Three times, that she knew of. She had another book, one about which she had once written a term paper. She'd even thought of it as a topic for some future master's thesis.

It was a Falnama, a book of omens. Not a holy book like the Quran but something perhaps once appended to the Quran, containing Muslim lore and legends consulted for advice and predictions. Gold had a reprint of one from the Safavid dynasty, during the sixteenth century.

She dug the Falnama from her backpack and opened it. The pages fell to fortune-telling so ironic it made her shake her head:

If you have taken this augury for travel or trade, prospects are good.

No help there. Gold leafed through the book, unsure of what she was looking for. She stopped on another augury:

Beware, a thousand times beware, not to let trouble reach you.

Well, it's a little too late for that, she thought. Trouble certainly reached us at the training center. And it may not be finished with us yet. So much for the Falnama. She left it in her baggage and took her book of Rahman Baba's poetry to Mahsoud in case he wanted to read it a fourth time. He thanked her in Pashto. Going through the motions of politeness, Gold supposed, but he was probably beyond any morale boost she could offer. Failed again.

Gold decided to leave him alone so he could rest. She climbed the ladder to the flight deck and slid open the door. The crew appeared in deep discussion, but without her headset she could not hear their words. The flight engineer had his computer on a page that looked a lot like common e-mail. Gold bent to see the message:

TO: ALL MOBILITY ASSETS

FROM: 618 TACC

A C-130 THAT DEPARTED BAGRAM HAS EXPLODED

EN ROUTE BAHRAIN.

4

Parson swallowed some of his coffee, felt the heat all the way down. So this shit is for real, he thought. He felt his palms go clammy.

He started to imagine what it would feel like at the moment of explosion. Thrown down in a fury of smoke, flame, and debris like a fire bucket of charcoal dumped from a high place. Then he told himself, Stop this. You don't have the luxury of falling apart. The citizens of the United States have entrusted you with the lives of fifty-seven souls on board.

"Souls on board." One of the aviation terms borrowed from the older traditions of mariners. Rescuers used to refer to people on a foundering ship as "those poor SOBs." For public consumption, the phrase got changed to a more palatable version. Well, we're not dead yet, Parson thought. He felt his pulse in the crook of his thumb as he held on to the yoke.

Parson wondered if there was anything he could do, anything more he could learn about his situation. He turned his wafer switch to HFI.

"Hilda," he called, "Air Evac Eight-Four."

"Eight-Four," came the reply. "Go ahead."

"Received your latest on the C-130. What happened?"

Long pause. Then: "ATC says it disappeared from

radar as it descended through ten thousand feet. They got down to minimum fuel."

And that model of C-130 couldn't take fuel in the air, Parson knew. Probably a barometric bomb, then. So descent was the enemy and not time. At least he could refuel in flight, unlike that Herk. And if the bomb was set to go off at ten thousand feet, he could still drop to rendezvous altitude when it came time to get gas. He'd meet the tanker at around twenty-five thousand.

"Hilda," he called, "do you know where that C-130 was based?"

"Affirmative, sir. Al Udeid."

"No," Parson said. "I mean, its home base."

"Dyess, I believe."

Parson swore under his breath, shook his head. He had done a tour at Dyess Air Force Base in Abilene, Texas. He wondered if anyone he knew was on board.

He looked around at his own crew. Dunne seemed all right, but he tapped his pencil on the engineer's table like he was ticked off. Colman looked pale. Gold had put on her borrowed headset and sat again at the nav station. Parson knew that stricken look in her gray eyes. He'd seen it before, right after he'd killed the insurgents who held her hostage. She was the strongest woman he knew, maybe the strongest person he knew, but everybody had a limit. Parson felt glad to see her back on the flight deck and sorry she was on board at all.

"Sounds like they set the bombs to throw debris onto whatever place the planes were flying to," Colman said.

That made a sick kind of sense to Parson. Bombs set to blow on descent might cause ground damage in countries supporting the war effort. The terrorists would get the airplanes, and maybe more.

"Reminds me of the Bojinka plot," Dunne said.

"The what?" Colman asked.

"Back in the nineties, al-Qaeda had this plan to blow up a dozen airliners over the Pacific. I think they got a bomb on one plane, and the plotters were arrested."

"When they get an idea they like," Gold said, "they tend to stick with it. I was thinking of Bojinka, too."

So up to twelve planes might have bombs on board? We're going to lose a lot of friends today, Parson thought.

He was glad a tanker was on the way. No telling how much gas he'd need now, and the aerial refuel would keep him and the rest of the crew busy. With too much time droning on autopilot, his mind was beginning to wander, to think about things he might never experience again: the fragrance of a woman's hair, the smell of autumn woods on opening day of deer season, the smoky burn of single malt when he bought a round for the crew.

None of that, he told himself. You're about to fly tight formation with another big airplane at about three hundred miles an hour. Keep your mind on what you're doing, your eyes on your instruments.

"Crew," Parson called over the interphone, "still not finding anything?"

"Negative in the troop compartment."

"Negative, aft flight deck."

"Cargo's got nothing."

Maybe we're all right, Parson hoped. But if the terrorists were hitting planes departing Bagram today, it was hard to imagine they'd overlook the biggest thing on the ramp, the thing with the most hiding places. Where else could it be? If Dunne said he'd checked the wheel wells, he'd checked the wheel wells. And nobody has found anything inside.

Parson tried to think of any other part of the plane where bad guys might plant a bomb. Mentally, he walked the flight deck, the cargo compartment downstairs, the troop compartment upstairs. The lavatories, galley, closets. The loadmasters had checked all that. Where else? Oh, shit. The back end of the airplane, in the tail cone.

"All right, crew," Parson said, "listen up. We're about to conduct an aerial refuel. To do that, we're going to descend to two-five-oh. While we're down there, we're going to check the tail cone section. I need a volunteer to go through the negative pressure relief valves and look around. It's going to suck because it'll be loud and cold."

"How can somebody get back there in flight?" Colman asked.

"After we take on gas," Parson said, "we'll depressurize. Then you can open those valves."

Parson knew that even inside the manned sections of the plane, depressurizing at that altitude would be no fun. Ears would pop, sinuses would hurt. Everybody would need to be on oxygen. Normally, if you depressurized in flight for something like an airdrop, you did it at a much lower altitude, and even then you might prebreathe pure oxygen. However, descending farther was out of the question if planes were exploding at ten thousand. Parson wanted as wide a margin as possible above any bomb's trigger altitude. Even if one bomb had been set for ten thousand, another might be set at eighteen thousand. And at two-five-oh, you could probably avoid decompression sickness as long as you prebreathed.

The interphone broke into his planning.

"Pilot, MCD."

"Go ahead, ma'am," Parson said.

"Did I understand you to say you're going to depressurize at twenty-five thousand?"

"Yes, ma'am."

"You can't do that. I have two patients with head injuries. If the air expands inside their cranial cavities, it could kill them or cause permanent brain damage."

Parson hadn't transported wounded since his C-130 days and he'd forgotten how complicated that could get. It took a few minutes to get his mind around the enormity of the decision facing him. Perhaps sacrifice two lives to save the other fifty-five. This wasn't taking the life of an enemy; it was killing someone who had served honorably and suffered for it enough already. He didn't know if those two patients were U.S. or Afghan, but it didn't matter. They were either Americans or allies.

He wondered what it was like to die of an embolism inside your brain. And what if there was nothing back in the tail? How likely was it that a terrorist would know enough about airplanes to put something in the empennage section of a C-5? Well, terrorists had learned to fly once upon a time.

Damn it all to hell. Parson knew firsthand how military service could put a crushing burden of responsibility on certain people. Sometimes it was unpredictable, like right now. Sometimes it came all out of proportion to rank, like right now. I'm a major, he thought, not God.

I'll just think about it for a while, Parson decided. First we'll get through the AR and then we'll either depressurize or not. One crisis at a time.

He entered a frequency on his CDU for the tanker's beacon. As if on cue, the tanker called up on UHF.

"Air Evac Eight-Four, Shell Two-One."

"Shell Two-One," Parson called, "Air Evac Eight-Four. Go ahead."

"Shell Two-One is a KC-10 standing by for an emergency AR. How do you want to do this?"

"Let's set up a point parallel at two-five-oh," Parson said. "We'll take about a hundred and fifty thousand pounds if you have it." Hell, why did it have to be a KC-10? The tail-mounted engine on that monster always beats you to death with its jet wash, Parson thought. It was tricky enough to stay in position behind a KC-135. But at least the KC-10 should have plenty of gas.

"Roger that, Eight-Four," the tanker pilot called. "See you at two-five-oh."

Parson entered 25,000 into the altitude alerter and hooked his fingers over the throttles. Eased the power back until the vertical speed indicator showed a gentle descent. Hoped he wouldn't make the wounded too uncomfortable until he moved into precontact behind the tanker. Then there wouldn't be anything he could do about the bumps. By the time we climb again, he thought, I'll have made a life-and-death decision.

During his cross-training to the pilot's seat, Parson had experienced all manner of emergencies in the simulator: fires, missile strikes, hydraulic losses. On a night flight, he had suffered an electrical failure that darkened the cockpit. Made an instrument approach with a penlight in his mouth. But there was no sim scenario, no regs, no guidance whatsoever for a bomb on board. He thought that was because no one expected it to happen to a military plane. Or maybe because if it did, the only procedure was to kiss your ass good-bye.

GOLD LOOKED OUT THE COCKPIT WINDOWS, over Parson's shoulder, as the airplane descended. The undercast had broken up enough to reveal what appeared as a sheet of iron down below. The Black Sea, she guessed. Above the water, higher clouds rose many thousands of feet. The airplane flew through towering cumulus that rocked the jet with turbulence. Bulbous fists boiled out from the main body of each white mass, seemed to punch the aircraft. The cloud formations were so laden with moisture that they sprayed the windscreen like ocean spume. The droplets froze when they touched the glass, then dwindled away. The blast of cold, high-speed air sublimated the ice directly into vapor.

She had never seen a view quite like this. When she traveled on military transports, it usually felt like a subway ride. Few windows where she rode, and small ones at that. Even when she jumped, it was from a much lower altitude, and she had other things on her mind: check the canopy, pull the risers apart if the shroud lines were twisted, aim for the drop zone.

But this must be what God sees, she thought. So does He see us now? Could He help us now?

Thy will be done. She left the prayer at that. Didn't know what else to say. He already knows we want to live. Why state the obvious? Gold believed in prayer—but prayer for its own sake, to let your Maker know you were paying attention. Praying for a sick person, for example, was well and good. But did it actually change the outcome? If it did, that implied God needed man's help. Impossible.

Gold accepted that was a question she wasn't meant to answer. She was a finite being, not programmed to comprehend the infinite. Right now the biggest question was whether she and her students would get off this plane alive. She felt she had a right to know. And she knew that question had no answer yet.

Parson was pointing back toward the nav table, and Gold realized he was talking to her. "Put on that oxygen mask," he said. "Dunne will show you how to hook up your headset to it."

"Sorry," Gold said.

"Crew," Parson called, "I want everybody to put on a mask and prebreathe on one hundred percent in case we depressurize."

"I have two patients who might not live through that," the MCD said.

"Understood," Parson said. "But I have to make the decision, ma'am. I'll keep you advised."

Dunne helped Gold don the mask that hung from a clip over the navigator's station. Her headset went silent when he unplugged it, but after Dunne reconnected it she heard Parson continue with his orders:

". . . Aft flight deck, go ahead and drop the passenger masks."

"Yes, sir." Then, after a moment, "All right, we got the rubber jungle back here."

"Good," Parson said. "Now everybody listen up and stay on your toes. We have a lot to do. Rendezvous checklist."

Gold breathed through the mask and tried to follow the commands and responses as Parson and his crew set up the jet for refuel. The pure oxygen she was inhaling felt good going down, a little cold. Like walking outside on a snowy New England morning and taking that first deep breath.

Eventually, Parson and Colman began to point at something outside the windscreen. Gold leaned forward to look, and she saw a gray speck up ahead. As the distance narrowed, the speck took the form of an airplane. Not as big as the C-5 but as big as a heavy airliner.

Dunne flipped rows of switches on the flight engineer's panel, read from his checklist.

"Air refueling door," he called.

"Clear to open," Parson said.

As the crew members spoke, their oxygen masks covered most of their faces. Gold had only their eyes for clues to their emotions. Not much there. This high-speed aerial ballet seemed routine to them.

Dunne moved another toggle switch, and the whisper of the

slipstream rose like the swell of orchestra strings in some mournful adagio. Gold noticed two lights illuminate on Dunne's panel: DOOR NOT LOCKED and READY.

The airplane began to shudder. It felt different from the jolting ride inside the cumulus clouds several minutes earlier. A steadier shaking. The motion reminded Gold of speeding along one of Afghanistan's washboard dirt roads in a Humvee. But with no visual cues to help make sense of the vibration, it made her a little sick.

When she looked outside again, what she saw made her grip her armrest. The tanker filled the windscreen, impossibly close. A refueling boom extended from the KC-10's tail section, seemed about to spear through the glass.

"Air Evac Eight-Four," called a voice on the radio, "you're cleared into position."

"Cleared into position," Parson answered as he pulled on his flight gloves.

He put his hand on the throttles but seemed barely to move them at all. The tanker grew larger in the windscreen; collision appeared imminent. Then the two airplanes stabilized, locked into position with little relative motion except for the constant chop of rough air.

Something banged into the C-5, directly over Gold's head, and startled her. Was that supposed to happen? None of the crew seemed concerned.

"Latched," Dunne said.

"Contact," called a voice on the radio.

"I have pressure—and flow," Dunne said.

No one said anything for a few minutes. Parson seemed deep in concentration, left hand on the yoke, right hand on the throttles. Hissing roars all around: the rush of air and the flow of fuel.

Then Dunne spoke again. "Shell Two-One," he called, "Air Evac Eight-Four. Can you cut back your pressure? You're approaching my manifold limit."

"Roger that. Sorry."

"Guess they want to off-load the gas as soon as possible," Colman said, "so they can get the hell away from us."

"I'd want to get away from us, too," Parson said.

When Gold looked outside again, she saw the two fighters, smaller now that they were keeping distance during the refueling. Twin steel arrowheads slicing through the sky. She wondered how long they would follow the C-5, waiting to pull the trigger to take it down. One of them called on the radio:

"Shell, Gunfighter. We're almost bingo fuel. Can you gas us up next?"

"Affirmative. Two hundred and sixty thousand pounds on board."

"We heard about the C-130 that blew up. You guys have any other word about what's going on?"

A few moments of static. Then: "Before we left Manas, command post said a C-17 was overdue."

Gold held her breath, saw the blinker on her oxygen regulator flip from white to black. Thought about prayer again. *Deliver us from evil.* The police center bombing, followed by all this. It was starting to remind her of September 11th. Simultaneous attacks, something clearly planned for years.

"I wonder if they got another plane," Dunne said.

"Sounds like it," Parson said. Gold watched him clasping and unclasping his gloved right hand over the throttles. The flight glove looked new, and the sun's angle gave it a sheen that made Gold think of chain mail.

She considered the C-130 that had exploded, the C-17 that had likely suffered the same fate. Perhaps their crews didn't know of the bomb threat; perhaps they could not refuel in the air. Gold realized the same thing might have happened to Parson if he'd not been delayed by the change in his mission and destination. The time it took to reconfigure the airplane for a medical flight had bought him the knowledge of what he could be facing.

After a few more minutes, a voice on the radio said, "Air Evac Eight-Four, off-load complete. One hundred and fifty-one thousand pounds."

"Copy that," Colman said. "Request disconnect."

The LATCHED light winked out, and the tanker seemed to creep forward.

"Post air refueling checklist," Parson said.

More commands and responses as Dunne read the checklist. The slipstream's roar quieted to a murmur after Dunne closed the AR door. Parson was still clenching and opening his fingers. Gold wondered what was going through his mind. When Dunne declared the checklist complete, Parson sighed so hard Gold could see his shoulders move against his harness straps.

"We haven't finished searching the airplane," Parson said. "MCD, are the patients prepared?"

"They're as sedated as much as we can, but it won't make much difference."

"Ma'am, I think we need to do this."

"Major," the MCD said, "either there's a bomb on board or there isn't. If there is, you can't do much about it."

"We won't know what we can do about it until we find it," Parson said.

"I've told you what could happen if you depressurize. If you do and there's nothing in the tail section, God help you."

No one spoke for several seconds. The KC-10 was banking away far to the right, the two F-15s lining up behind it. Faint smudges of exhaust trailed from their engines. Clouds threw shadows like dark stains on the sea below.

"What do you want me to do, sir?" Dunne asked.

"Engineer," Parson said, "depressurize this aircraft."

5

Parson turned to see Dunne flip the pressurization master switch to RATE DEPRESS. At first, Parson felt no change, but then the air inside his ears began to expand. He swallowed, heard the pop inside his eustachian tubes.

Dunne was being careful. Maybe this slow rise in cabin altitude would make it easier on the patients. At two or three hundred feet per minute, it would take the better part of an hour to depressurize. With some luck, perhaps their ears, sinuses, and wounds could adjust.

Parson knew the easiest course would be to call the search complete right now and try to land. No one would blame him for that. If he did anything else, investigators might spend weeks and months second-guessing decisions he made in minutes. But what if something detonated on descent? He'd leave this world knowing he let people down because he didn't do enough. Because he shrank from making a tough call.

After several minutes, the CABIN ALT warning light came on. As the aircraft depressurized, the thinning atmosphere inside it was above ten thousand feet now. Fifteen thousand to go to reach ambient outside pressure.

"Everybody all right?" Parson asked. "Crew, check in."

"Copilot's good."

"Engineer's okay."

"Cargo."

The rest of the crew called in from the aft flight deck's rest area and the troop compartment.

"Thanks, guys," Parson said. "Keep an eye on yourselves and each other. Remember the signs of hypoxia from your altitude chamber training." Tunnel vision and grayout, slurred or irrational speech, lips turned blue from cyanosis.

During Parson's days in the C-130, he had done a number of high-altitude airdrops, letting out SEALs, Green Berets, or PJs so high up the jumpers had to breathe from oxygen bottles during their free fall. The airmen who flew those missions ran cabin altitude checklists to monitor one another, to make sure no one passed out from a loose oxygen mask or a bad hose connection. It all became second nature.

But to this young C-5 crew, that kind of thing was exotic special ops. You wouldn't normally operate a Galaxy this way, and Parson knew he'd need to talk them through every step. He was in his late thirties, and that copilot Colman looked about twelve. Decent stick-and-rudder skills, and smart enough, but certainly not ready for anything like this. An Academy grad who bled Air Force blue. He seemed to get a haircut every week. The guy even kept the tabs on his flight suit zippers tucked under the fabric so they wouldn't protrude.

Dunne was older, around forty-five. An activated reservist. Parson seemed to recall Dunne had put in twenty years with the regular Air Force before going back to the family cattle business in Tennessee. Thank God, they gave me an experienced flight engineer, Parson thought, since I have so little time in this plane. And the loadmasters were all kids. Parson had to check the flight orders to remember their names.

Unlike his old C-130 crew, they were not his brothers. He did not know how they would react in any given situation. He could not communicate with them merely by a wave of his grease pencil or a double click of his interphone switch. The only crew he had ever known that well had gone down with him in Afghanistan, and he was the sole survivor.

These crew members were his responsibility, but they were not his family. At least not yet.

Gold was something different. She had seen his best and his worst. She was the only person in the world who knew exactly what he'd been through, how it had changed him, and how it had cost him. Parson had a hard time defining his feelings for Sergeant Major Sophia Gold, U.S. Army.

As cabin altitude rose, a warning tone blared through the cockpit. Colman looked around the flight deck, seemed unsure what to do.

"It's above you," Parson said.

Colman moved his index finger toward the switches and rheostats on the overhead panel.

"No," Parson said. "Farther right."

Colman pushed the SILENCE button, and the tone stopped.

"Everything okay?" called a loadmaster from downstairs.

Parson pressed his TALK switch and said, "Affirmative. Just a warning horn because we're depressurizing. How are the patients doing?"

"I don't know. The aeromeds are working on one of them."

"MCD," Parson said, "what's the status?"

No answer.

"She's off headset, sir," the loadmaster said.

Parson heard commotion in the background when the loadmaster pushed his TALK switch. Then someone shouted. Parson heard it all the way from the cargo compartment without benefit of the interphone system.

"One of the patients is freaking out," the loadmaster called.

Another shout. Then a full-throated scream.

Clicks and hiss on the interphone. A voice said, "Get him—"

"Sergeant Gold," Parson said, "look down there and tell me what's going on."

Gold got up from the nav table and slid open the flight deck door, next to her seat. She disappeared down the steps, went as far as her oxygen hose and interphone cord allowed.

"It's that American sergeant," Gold said. "They have him on the floor."

"Is he one of those with a head injury?" Parson asked.

"I think so."

So it's happening, Parson thought. I'm killing him. Just as surely as if I went down the ladder and shot him. And that would be more merciful. Dear God, what if this is the wrong decision?

"Do you want me to level off the cabin pressure?" Dunne asked. He put his hand on the master switch.

That sergeant has a mother, Parson thought. A girlfriend or a wife. Maybe children. Parson felt as if his moral compass had spun, could not find its cardinal headings.

"Sir?" Dunne said.

Everyone on board has a family, Parson told himself. The chaplains will be visiting; it's only a question of how many.

"Negative," Parson said.

He checked his radar display as if it held answers. But it told him only that there were light scattered showers ahead and below. Green splotches across a cathode-ray tube. Outside, the sun lit up the nimbus clouds like they were incandescent, and in places the light refracted into colored bands.

A squeal and a pop came over the interphone as someone plugged in an audio jack.

"MCD back on headset," the lieutenant colonel said. "We have a patient restrained."

"What about the other one?" Parson asked. "Weren't there two with head injuries?"

Seconds ticked by with no response. Nothing on interphone but electronic hum.

"That one's already dead."

GOLD SAW THAT DUNNE WAS CONCENTRATING on a gauge in the middle of his panel. It had large and small hands like a clock, but this was different. The big hand crept toward zero while the little hand reached twenty-five thousand.

"Almost there," Dunne said. "All right, zero differential. We're depressurized."

"I still need that volunteer," Parson said.

"Can I do it?" Gold asked.

"Thanks," Parson said, "but I need someone who knows the airplane."

"I'll go," Dunne said. "Just get the scanner to watch the panel for me."

"Good," Parson said. "Bundle up, if you can."

Not much to do that with, Gold thought. I'd offer him a coat, if I could, but who carries a coat around during warm months in Kabul?

"Hey, Gold," Parson said. "There is something you can do. Go with Dunne and keep an eye on him."

"Yes, sir," Gold said.

"Don't follow him into the tail section. Just watch him from those negative pressure relief valves. You'll see what I mean when you get there. Take my flashlight."

Parson reached into his helmet bag and pulled out a Maglite, passed it to Gold. It felt substantial in her hand, loaded with D cells. The kind police carried because it could double as a blackjack.

From the bulkhead behind his seat, Dunne lifted a yellow metal bottle with a mask attached to it.

"Do you know how to use these MA-1 cylinders?" he asked.

"No," Gold said.

"There's one for you in front of the nav table. Take off the mask you're wearing now and use the one on the walkaround bottle."

Gold found the MA-1 bottle and switched masks.

"Disconnect your headset," Dunne added. "When we get back there, you can plug into the interphone with this." Dunne showed her the audio connections on the oxygen bottle's mask. Then he pointed to a gauge on the bottle and said, "Keep an eye on this needle. When your oxygen gets low, refill it like I show you."

Dunne detached a silver hose mounted on the cockpit wall, plugged it into a port on the bottle. Gold heard a pneumatic hiss, saw the pressure needle rise.

"This refills it from the ship's supply," he said. "We got plenty of liquid oxygen on board."

"Is that liquid in the bottle?" Gold asked.

"No. It turns to gas before it gets that far."

Gold found that her bottle had a nylon strap. She put the strap across her shoulder, leaving her hands free to carry the flashlight. Dunne pulled on his flying gloves, donned what Gold supposed was a summer-weight flight jacket. Then he went aft to a crew bunk room and came back with a green U.S.-issued blanket.

"Are you ready to do this?" Dunne asked.

"I think so," Gold said.

"You guys be careful," Parson said. "Sergeant Major, all you need to do is watch him, and let us know if anything's wrong."

"Yes, sir," Gold said. "Hooah."

Parson looked at her strangely, and she reminded herself these flyboys spoke a different language. Maybe they didn't know what HUA meant: Heard, Understood, Acknowledged.

"If you find something," Parson said, "don't move it. At least, not yet."

"Don't worry," Dunne said.

Dunne led the way down the flight deck ladder to the cargo compartment. Downstairs, Gold saw that a blanket covered the face of one of the patients. And the wounded sergeant lay still and quiet now, Flex-Cuffed to his litter. At least he'd survived the depressurization. Blood stained the bandage around his head.

When they passed Mahsoud's stretcher, he looked at Gold as if to say *What on earth are you doing?* Gold touched his arm as she walked by, but she didn't stop to speak to him. It was too hard to yell through the mask at someone not on headset.

At the aft end of the cargo compartment, Gold and Dunne climbed another ladder to the troop section. At the back of the troop compartment, Dunne moved aside an aluminum cage that guarded two circular hatches in the wall, each big enough for someone to crawl through. They had hinges at the top, so they could swing open vertically. What the crew had called valves looked more like round doors to Gold.

Dunne flipped a wall-mounted toggle switch marked EMPENNAGE SERVICE LIGHT and raised the lower door. Cold air rolled from it like he'd opened a freezer. When the frigid air mingled with the warmer atmosphere of the troop compartment, fog swirled as if some malevolent specter haunted the aircraft.

"These are the negative pressure valves," he said. "They just lift open now that we're depressurized. Hold this one for me, please, and you can watch from here."

Dunne took an interphone cord from the wall and connected it to Gold's mask. Then he wrapped himself in the blanket and snapped on his flashlight. Gold held the pressure valve as he squeezed through it.

He passed into a hollow dark opening big enough to contain two Army trucks. Inside the tail cone, the plane's structure rattled and shook. With no insulation or noiseproofing there, the slipstream raged like a hurricane tearing at a tin shack. A service lamp trembled in its mounts and cast a dim, pulsing glow on cables, wiring, endless rows of rivets.

This strange section of the aircraft amounted to a tunnel about eighty feet long. At the entrance, by the pressure valves, it was about thirty feet wide, but it narrowed toward the end of the tail. The area contained no seats or steps; it was obviously not intended for access in flight. The metal cavity was larger than the interior of some passenger planes Gold had seen, but in this aircraft it served only as the aft tip of the tapered fuselage.

Gold watched as Dunne made his way down a catwalk, cradling his oxygen cylinder in one arm. He steadied himself against the vibration with the other arm, found handholds among the braces and formers. To Gold, he looked like a coal miner descending a contaminated shaft during an earthquake. She found her TALK switch and pressed it.

"He's in the tail," she said.

"Roger that," Parson said. "How's he doing?"

"I'm sure he's freezing, but he's moving around okay."

Dunne swept his flashlight beam, a pool of light playing against the cold, buckling metal. So many hiding places, Gold thought. She shone Parson's Maglite at Dunne's feet, hoped she could at least help keep him from tripping.

He came to a ladder at the aft end of the tail cone. Pocketed his flashlight, ascended the ladder. His boots disappeared as he climbed out of sight.

"He's headed up some kind of passageway," Gold said. "Where's he going?"

"That leads up into the vertical stabilizer," Parson said. "The maintenance guys use it."

"I can't see him now."

"He shouldn't be gone long."

Seconds ticked into minutes, and Gold began to worry. Still no sign of the flight engineer. Had he gotten stuck up there? Passed out?

"I still don't see him," Gold said.

"Keep me advised," Parson answered.

Gold wanted to go back and look, but Parson had specifically told her not to do that. The pressure on her bottle was dropping, and she knew Dunne had to be low on oxygen, too. Gold wasn't an aviator, but common sense told her that since Dunne was exerting himself and he was a big guy, he was probably using up oxygen faster than she was. And there certainly wouldn't be any refill hoses where he had gone, in a part of the plane never meant to be manned.

She stood and refilled her own bottle from a recharger hose on the troop compartment wall. The effort brought a stitch of pain in her ribs. She watched the oxygen pressure needle climb back to 300 psi. Then she kneeled by the pressure valves and looked around for Dunne. Still nothing.

Another oxygen cylinder stood in a bracket nearby. Gold took it, checked its pressure. Full. She scanned the tail cone again with the flashlight.

Dunne's boots appeared on the ladder, first his left, then his right. He seemed steady enough on his feet.

"I see him," Gold said. "He's coming back down."

"Copy that," Parson said.

Dunne reached the catwalk, began walking toward Gold. Now he appeared to move with effort, as if his boots were sticking to the metal. Then he sank to his knees, fell forward as if shot. Motionless.

Gold took off her headset and scrambled through the lower valve, pointing the flashlight so she could see where to step. The strap on the extra oxygen cylinder caught on the lip of the valve opening, and Gold jerked until it ripped free. A stabbing pain spread through her torso, but she tried to ignore it. Dropped the flashlight. Gold fumbled in the shadows cast by the weak service lamp overhead and found the flashlight underneath the catwalk. She grasped for it with ungloved hands, the catwalk's steel so cold it seemed to burn. As she raised herself back up, she grabbed a cross brace for support. Her sweating palm stuck to it. She yanked her hand away, left a strip of skin frozen to the steel.

When she reached Dunne, she cradled her flashlight between her knees and rolled him over. No response, like moving a corpse. His eyes were closed, face ashen. Pressure on his oxygen bottle was zero.

Gold disconnected his mask from the empty bottle, plugged the hose into the spare, and felt it seat into the receptacle with a click. Dunne opened his eyes, blinked. Gold could hardly believe one breath would make him recover so quickly. Though she was a paratrooper, she had never been free fall qualified, so she had no training in high-altitude physiology. Now she just hoped Dunne could get up. She thought she could drag him to the pressure valves if she had to, but it would hurt like hell. Pulling him all the way through one of the valves would be impossible.

Rays of sunlight filtered through a louvered panel on the floor. Blue segments shining from some kind of access hatch, hints of clouds and sea below.

Dunne staggered to his feet, tried to shout something. Gold could not understand him above the roar. She put his arm around her neck and helped him to the pressure valve. He went down on his knees and crawled through. When Gold followed, she found him shivering on the troop compartment floor, still clutching the blanket around him.

He yelled again through his mask. Unintelligible.

"What?" Gold said.

He grabbed his oxygen mask by the hose and pulled it far enough from his face to speak.

"There's something back there," he said.

6

Too much time had passed since Parson had heard anything from Gold and Dunne.

"Sergeant Gold," he called, "are you still on headset?"

No answer. Parson cursed himself for not briefing her that you always checked with the aircraft commander before you went off headset. She's bright, he thought, but don't expect her to think like aircrew.

Then he heard clicks on the interphone, the whine of audio feedback, Dunne's voice. Sounded out of breath: "Pilot, Engineer. We got problems."

For a moment, Parson said nothing. The objects around him seemed to blur, as if imagined in some dreamlike state. Switches and instruments faded, their purposes forgotten. His mouth had a leaden taste in it that made no sense.

Parson knew of a C-130 crew years ago that had made a navigational blunder on a low-level training flight. They flew into a box canyon and found they had neither the turning radius to reverse course, nor the power to climb over the rim. Was this how they felt in those moments before they hit the canyon wall?

Focus, he told himself. Function. Face whatever comes. He took a deep breath, pressed the TALK switch.

"Tell me what you saw," he said.

"There's a duffel bag up in the stabilizer." Dunne's voice shook. Probably still shivering, Parson guessed. "It has wires attached," Dunne added.

So there it was. Nothing theoretical about the threat now. Parson's universe narrowed, tunneled, consisted only of the airplane, its crew and passengers, fuel, sky, and high explosive.

"Can you remember anything else?" Parson asked. "We need to describe it to TACC."

"There's more than the bomb," Dunne said. "Pasteboard boxes and black plastic bags. Maybe a half dozen. I didn't see any wires in those."

What the fuck? Parson thought. Then he understood. A dirty bomb. Or worse. Anthrax spores. Sarin. Mustard gas. Or VX.

"You didn't touch any of it, did you?" Parson said.

"Negative."

"Good. God only knows what that garbage could be."

"Yeah, but I got a vague idea."

No wonder the bad guys set these things to go off on descent instead of climb, Parson thought. Scatter that shit all over Germany and punish them for helping the U.S.

Down below, the edge of the Black Sea hove into view. Romania. The shoreline passed under the wings, the ground a patchwork quilt of green forests, brown fields, crops in corduroy furrows, hedgerows embroidering the borders.

The stamping of boots up the ladder announced the return of Dunne and Gold to the flight deck. Gold's blond hair had tangled into her headset. Dunne's cheeks, the part of them not covered by his oxygen mask, were red. He coughed into the mask as he strapped back into the engineer's seat.

Parson didn't know Dunne well, but he'd flown with him before and was beginning to learn how Dunne operated. When Parson was still a copilot on the C-5, he'd gotten stuck at Manas Air Base in Kyrgyzstan, with a blown starter. The crew, including Dunne, waited for several days for a new starter to come in. When it finally arrived, Parson found Dunne up on a stand with an engine cowl open. The flight engineer had a wooden chock in his hands and he was pounding it against the engine like a battering ram. Parson wasn't a mechanic, but he knew nothing in the maintenance manuals called for beating a jet engine into submission.

"What in God's name are you doing?" Parson said.

"Don't ask, sir."

Parson later learned the old starter had swelled its casing when it blew. As a result, Dunne couldn't get a socket wrench on all the attachment bolts. He'd had to knock the thing around on its shaft to remove it. Unorthodox, and certainly not according to the tech order, but faster and cheaper than changing the whole engine.

What to do now? Parson knew he had several hours' worth of fuel on board. There was no sense squandering it down here at twenty-five thousand now that he knew what he was dealing with. Better fuel economy up high. He waited for Dunne to settle in at his panel, watched him scan his instruments. Good, Parson noted. He's still doing his job.

"Engineer," Parson said, "repressurize us. Then I'm going to request a climb back up to three-four-oh."

"Yes, sir," Dunne said.

"Could it make the bomb go off if we repressurize?" Colman asked.

"No," Parson said. "Remember, it's in an unpressurized section."

"Oh, yeah."

Then Parson made a call to downstairs. "MCD," he said. "Pilot."

"Go ahead."

"Ma'am, we're about to repressurize, if the patients are ready."

"There's not really anything we can to do get them ready."

Parson wasn't sure how to react to that. It seemed simply a fact to which the MCD was resigned. He nodded to Dunne, who twisted the pressurization master switch to FLIGHT. Parson felt the swell begin against his eardrums. Pressing his fingers over the oxygen mask, he held his nose and exhaled against it to equalize the pressure, heard the faint pop. He had to swallow now and then to keep his ears comfortable with the change in cabin altitude. Thought again about what that must do to the inside of a wound cavity. But did any of that matter anymore?

"Tell me when the cabin pressure gets down below ten thousand feet," Parson said.

"Roger that," Dunne said.

Parson turned his wafer switch to VHF. "Control," he said, "Air Evac Eight-Four requests climb to flight level three-four-zero."

A voice responded with the exaggerated *l*'s of a Slavic accent: "Air Evac Eight-Four, climb and maintain flight level three-four-zero. Contact Bucharest on one-one-niner-point-five."

Colman was flying the plane now. He set the altitude alerter, advanced the throttles. The nose pitched up slightly, and the aircraft began a gentle climb. Parson noticed Colman kept his hand on the throttles: a good technique to remind yourself to pull off some power after the aircraft leveled. This new copilot did everything methodically, like most new guys. He moved switches one at a time, not in a quick flow. He seemed to work from memory and procedure rather than instinct. That was okay with Parson. Better to do the right thing slowly than screw up fast. But this kid would have to learn that the flight manual's index would not give him all the answers.

After several minutes, Dunne said, "Cabin's below ten thousand."

"All right, everybody," Parson said. "You can come off oxygen now."

Parson pulled the sweep-on mask away from his mouth and nose, placed it back in its holder. He adjusted the boom mike on his headset, inhaled the cabin's air. It always felt good to take off that mask. His face had gone numb.

He checked in with Bucharest, then switched to HF and called the Tanker Airlift Control Center. The flight manager put the DO on the line.

"Sir," Parson said, "we have a bomb on board. We depressurized so the engineer could check the empennage and he found a device up in the vertical stabilizer."

No response for a moment. Then the colonel said, "We copy

your situation, Eight-Four. Maintain altitude while we get some answers from EOD. We'll gas you up again if we need to."

"Eight-Four wilco," Parson said. "But there's more." Parson told him about the boxes and bags of unidentified material.

Another long pause. Then only: "Hilda Contingency Cell copies all."

As the aircraft climbed, it passed through a thin cirrus layer like punching through a white shroud. After several minutes, the autopilot leveled the plane, the altimeters reading thirty-four thousand. Heavier now with fuel, the C-5 had reached the ceiling for its weight. It did not so much fly as wallow through the air. Parson felt the right wing dip a few degrees, a touch of Dutch roll. Then the flight augmentation computers corrected, and the ship settled into straight and level flight. At least that's working, Parson thought. Hell, we don't need any more problems.

"So what do we do now?" Colman asked. Voice steady, but his face very white. So were his hands, purple veins visible under the skin as he gripped the yoke.

Parson stared out into the blue. "I don't know," he said. Then he chided himself for saying that. The aircraft commander always knows. Or at least he knows who to ask. The crew members, the whole damned Air Force, expect you to suck it up and deal with it. No matter how much you might doubt yourself, he thought, you don't have the right to show it.

The radio interrupted the flight deck conversation: "Air Evac Eight-Four, Hilda. You still on frequency?"

"Hilda, Eight-Four," Parson called. "Go ahead."

"Dip shop needs to talk to you. Stand by."

What now? Parson wondered. Like I have time for their paperwork.

Then another voice on the radio: "Air Evac Eight-Four, Hilda. Be advised Germany has revoked your diplomatic clearance. We're working on a reroute to Rota or Sigonella."

Parson slammed his fist onto his armrest and swore. Pressed his TALK switch.

"Why the— Why would they do that?"

"Word has gotten out. They don't want an at-risk plane over their territory."

Well, word had to get out eventually, Parson thought. Hard to keep a secret about airplanes blowing up. "What about the patients?" Parson asked. "We have some critical cases on board."

"We're working that. The base hospital wherever you land will do what it can."

Didn't sound like much of a solution to Parson. Some base hospitals were little more than walk-in clinics. Maybe they don't expect us to make it that far, he thought.

"Air Evac Eight-Four copies all," Parson said. "We'll maintain a listening watch on this freq until you come up with a new destination."

Now it no longer made sense to follow the flight plan to Germany. Parson looked down at the screen on his FMS, set to a page listing familiar waypoints to Ramstein, a destination now denied him. Wherever the plane wound up, assuming it landed at all, no place could handle the patients as well as the Landstuhl hospital, just a few miles from Ramstein. No doubt more of them would die. If my dip clearance has been revoked, Parson thought, that means the bureaucrats and politicians know what's going on and they've all come in to help. Fuck you very much.

But Parson could do nothing about that now. And there was no point going fast in the wrong direction.

"Control," Parson called, "Air Evac Eight-Four needs to cancel flight plan to Ramstein. We'd like a partial route clearance anywhere more toward the west-southwest. Our destination will probably change to Rota or Sigonella."

The Romanian controller asked Parson to stand by, then called him back:

"Air Evac Eight-Four, you are cleared Belgrade, Split, Aviano. Maintain flight level three-four-zero. We will give you further clearance when you confirm destination."

"Air Evac Eight-Four copies," Parson said.

He entered the new route's waypoints, pressed the INAV button on his navigation select panel. The GPS receivers and the central air data computers fed their inputs to the autopilot. The autopilot deflected the ailerons and flight spoilers, and more than six hundred thousand pounds of steel, fuel, and humanity began a slow roll to the west.

GOLD RETURNED TO HER SEAT AT THE NAV TABLE, buckled the harness, plugged in her headset. She heard the crew talking, but she could not bring herself to follow the discussion. So she only stared out the flight deck windows at clouds scudding below like ragged patches of cotton.

She tried to control the brimming in her eyes. Lost the battle, wiped a tear. Hoped she'd managed it without anyone noticing. Probably; the crew appeared busy. Across the flight deck from her, the engineer tapped on what looked like a laptop computer at his instrument panel. The copilot was poring over some kind of chart, just lines and circles, not like any terrain map. Gold could read nothing on it except the labeling: EN ROUTE HIGH ALTITUDE—EUROPE, NORTH AFRICA, AND MIDDLE EAST. She supposed the crew was following highways that existed only as electrons, identified by patterns of dots and dashes, ones and zeros, pulses from satellites. Parson was talking on the radio, mainly a jumble of numbers she did not understand. Sounded ticked off.

Gold almost envied his annoyance. It focused him, gave him something to do. She wanted to take some kind of action, too, but she could not imagine what that might be. Ultimately, her job and most of her training came down to communicating. But there was nothing more for her to communicate, nothing except to wait and hope. And hope seemed so absurd right now. Perhaps, she thought, this is where hope trails off and faith picks up.

The old instruments on the nav panel in front of her still seemed to work. A needle twitched on a gauge marked TRUE AIRSPEED read something well over three hundred knots. The pointers on the altimeter were a little confusing, but Gold eventually deduced their meaning: thirty-four thousand feet.

Given the situation, she could imagine no way to come down from that altitude except a disintegrating plunge, a wild ride into the hereafter. She remembered an instructor at the jump school at Fort Benning, a veteran of the 1989 airborne assault in Panama. His favorite expression: "Gravity is a bitch."

From that training, Gold knew terminal velocity with a failed parachute was about one hundred and twenty miles per hour. Judging by that old analog altimeter in front of her, if the airplane blew up now it would take more than three minutes for its parts and people to hit the ground.

Who would have thought her career choices would bring her to this? As a translator/interpreter in the airborne division, she knew she could meet her demise in any number of violent ways. Snipers, IEDs, airdrop accidents. But she had never imagined anything like this: to sit in an aircraft seat, perfectly healthy, yet with a terminal condition.

Her memories of jump school drifted to the long runs in the Georgia heat, the heavy packs. The jody calls—songs and chants to keep the pace and pass the time. Many of them infused with wry humor, irony, or fatalism:

C-130 rolling down the strip,
Hauling paratroopers on a one-way trip.
Mission top secret, destination unknown.
Don't know when we'll be going home.

If a platoon ran for long enough, the songs became more than jody calls. Put the calls in the right order and they became a story of battle, an epic poem. Literature in its earliest form, a legend chanted by elders, now called NCOs, repeated back line by line by young warriors so they could learn its lessons. Near the end, the soldiers drenched in sweat, the call would change to the minor flats of a dirge:

I hear the choppers hoverin'
They're hoverin' overhead.
They're coming for the wounded.
They're coming for the dead.

A tale of victory, but with an elegy for the lost. A reminder of the price paid.

And now we're all just a price to be paid, Gold thought. Waiting for the bill to come due somewhere in this endless sky.

7

Parson watched the miles roll by on his CDU display, saw he was nearing the last waypoint on his route clearance. An airway intersection near Aviano, Italy. Beyond that, nothing on the flight plan page but a discontinuity.

Apparently, the copilot was thinking about the same thing. "What do we do when we get there?" Colman asked.

"We're going to have to hold until they decide what to do with us," Parson said.

He pressed a button to bring up the edit page on his FMS. Touched a LINE SELECT key to start building his holding pattern. Right turns. Ten-mile legs. Teardrop entry from this heading. ENTER.

When the autopilot turned the aircraft into the teardrop, Parson placed his hand on the throttles and nudged them back to slow the plane to holding speed. At this altitude, two hundred and sixty-five knots indicated. After five racetracks around the holding pattern, TACC called again.

"What you got for me, Hilda?" Parson asked.

"We're sending you to Rota," the flight manager said.

That worked for Parson. Rota Naval Air Station had a nice long runway. In southern Spain, near the Strait of Gibraltar. Small base hospital, but maybe the Spanish hospitals in Cádiz and Seville could help. That is, if the plane landed in one piece.

"What about some advice from EOD?" Parson asked. "Is there any way to defuse this thing?"

No answer for long seconds. Then the flight manager said, "Ah, Air Evac Eight-Four, there's still no consensus on that. Sometimes these fancy bomb triggers fail. A few of the EOD techs think your best bet might be to leave it alone. If you screw around with it and don't know what you're doing, you could set it off. But sometimes these bombs don't work."

Just hope for a miracle? Didn't sound like much of a solution to Parson. They're writing us off, he thought. They're giving up.

"I need something better than that," Parson said. "Tell them to think harder. Or find somebody who knows more."

"Air Evac Eight-Four, we'll work on it," the flight manager said. "Hilda Contingency Cell out."

There were times to leave well enough alone, Parson realized. He recognized his own tendency to tackle trouble rather than avoid it, perhaps to a fault. While in high school he'd run into a diamond-back rattler during a summer hike. The snake lay outstretched across a swatch of sunlight in the trail, but it coiled and rattled when Parson approached. He knew the smartest thing would be to go around it. But a group of hikers was coming behind him. He'd passed them on the way up and he didn't want to leave the snake there for them to encounter. He threw a fistful of pebbles at the rattler, but instead of slithering away, it only coiled more tightly and buzzed with a higher note. He found a four-foot stick and jabbed at the reptile. When the snake struck at the stick, one of its fangs held fast in the wood for a moment, and Parson saw venom drip into the dust. He raised the stick to throw the whole thing, snake and all, away from the trail. But the rattler fell off, thudded at Parson's feet, and struck his leg. The bite hurt but did not swell. The enraged rattler had injected all its poison into the stick. The ER doctor told Parson he'd not been envenomed. His father told him he'd been protected by the god who watches over fools and children.

Well, then, Parson thought, maybe I'll need the same kind of protection now. He coordinated his new flight plan to Rota with Air Traffic Control. The controller cleared him direct, so he entered the airfield identifier, L-E-R-T, into the FMS. With the touch of a LINE SELECT button, he activated the new course. The jet exited the holding pattern and pointed its nose toward Spain.

Piloting duties complete for the moment, Parson looked outside. Beautiful day over Italy. Wisps of stratus like smears of sea-foam. On the ground, greenery in the ordered lines of cultivation. Orchards and vineyards. Food and drink. Life.

He could not believe his existence was so temporary and fragile, like that of the stone flies he'd seen in trout streams or the fuzzy seed heads of foxtail grass along field borders where he'd hunted doves. And the younger people on this plane had their whole lives ahead of them.

The EOD guys will just have to come up with a plan, he thought. Tell us to look for a wire to cut, a battery to disconnect. Even guessing would be better than just praying the bomb turns out to be a dud.

Parson doubted an amateur could make this kind of bomb. If it really was triggered barometrically, and on descent rather than climb, it might require some kind of complicated circuit with a latching relay. Parson knew little of bomb making, but he knew aircraft systems, and they used electricity, too. No, whoever had designed this thing knew what the hell he was doing, and he probably didn't make any mistakes.

A warning from the flight engineer broke into Parson's thinking: "Gentlemen," Dunne said, "don't move the throttles."

"Shit," Parson said. There was only one reason an engineer told you to stay off the throttles. "Which one is it?"

"Stand by," Dunne said. Tapped on his computer. "Abnormal vibration in number four."

Parson thought he noticed a different sound from his aircraft, a chord change in the thrum of the engines.

"That one again?" he said. "How bad?"

More keystrokes. Dunne brought up a waveform display. "Fifteen mils," he said.

"So we can keep it running," Parson said.

"For now."

"Son of a bitch."

General Electric built a damned good engine, Parson knew, about as reliable as they came. But he had heard that in the rare cases when these big TF-39s failed, they failed in spectacular fashion. He knew an old-school engineer who called it the Jerry Lee Lewis phenomenon: Whole Lotta Shakin' Goin' On followed by Great Balls of Fire. Parson pulled off his right glove, touched the stem of the number four throttle with the end of his little finger. Sure enough, he felt vibration, transmitted through the control cables from all the way out there in the rightmost engine pylon.

"What's our three-engine ceiling?" he asked.

Dunne flipped pages, looked at his outside temp gauge, consulted a chart. "Just over twenty thousand."

"Good." So if we lose that engine, Parson thought, we can stay high enough not to trigger the bomb. Well, at least high enough to stay above the altitude where that C-130 blew up.

Much of Parson's simulator training had included compounding malfunctions. Difficulties that cascaded until he found himself wrestling with an airplane trying to go in every direction except the one he wanted. And forcing him to think hard at the same time: *This landing gear problem means we've lost some brakes, which means we need more runway, which means Martinsburg is too short, so we'll go to Andrews, where the weather just went below minimums, so we'll go to Dover, if we have the fuel.* And over his headset, a taunt from the instructor: "If you fuck this up, you're buying the beer."

But even the most sadistic sim instructor could not have come up with anything like this. And now there was no freezing the motion, no taking a break.

Parson remembered some advice his father had given him when he was still an ROTC cadet. "Some situations require you to think past the books," the old man had said. "They can't write a procedure for everything."

He spoke from experience, two Vietnam tours in the backseat of an F-4. And while Parson was still in nav school, his father got activated for Desert Storm. One night during a Wild Weasel mission, the old man's luck ran out.

Parson wondered what his dad would have said about this. In the old Air Force, they used to say the flight manuals were written in blood, results of lessons learned the hard way. But the books had no guidance whatsoever for something like this.

The F-15s still shadowed Parson's Galaxy, piercing the sky with their honed edges. He doubted they had the range to accompany him all the way to Rota, even though they'd just topped off their tanks. He hoped not. They couldn't do him any good, and they were getting on his nerves. He decided to give them a hint.

"Gunfighter, Air Evac Eight-Four," he called.

"Go ahead, Air Evac."

"We have things as under control as they ever will be," Parson said. "If you're low on gas, you can RTB."

"Roger that, Air Evac. We'll drop into Barcelona if we have to, but they want us to stay with you as long as we can."

Wonderful, Parson thought. And if you keep flying that close to me, you're gonna suck shards through your intakes when we get blown into scrap metal.

GOLD STARED OUT THE COCKPIT WINDOWS, tried to think of what to tell Mahsoud and the others. She could offer little hope now. About all she could say was that the flight engineer had found a bomb and that the aircraft commander was pushing for help. At the moment, Parson was still fiddling with radios. To what end, Gold wasn't sure.

She watched Parson turn a knob, press a switch. He wasn't much of an intellectual, she thought, but the force of life burned strong in that one. He could not seem to accept his situation, or at least he hadn't yet. If someone told him he'd used up all his nine lives, he'd go to supply and put in for nine more. At the moment, he seemed to want information.

"Hey," he said. "I found the BBC's shortwave service."

The crew seemed to be listening intently, so Gold pressed her interphone switch and asked, "How can I hear it?"

"Pull up HF2 on your comm box," Parson said.

Gold hunted for the knob, then pulled it out and turned up the volume. Heard a woman broadcaster with a lilting Scottish accent:

> *The U.S. military confirms two of its transport aircraft have been destroyed by what appear to be terrorist bombs. Officials say at least fifteen lives were lost. There are unconfirmed reports that other American aircraft may still be aloft with bombs on board.*
>
> *The aircraft bombings follow this morning's massive truck bombing at the Afghan National Police training center in Kabul. That attack left ninety people dead and more than twice that many injured. In a video released to Pakistani news agencies, a Taliban spokesman claims credit for both the police center bombing and the aircraft incidents. The Taliban says conspirators within the police helped get the truck bomb past checkpoints.*

The last sentence of the news report sickened Gold. Corruption had long been rife within the ANP, but she had wanted to believe things were getting better. She wondered if the Taliban had enough hard-core supporters within the ANP to pull off something like this. It was possible, but more likely they just bribed people. The U.S. and UN had poured millions of dollars into building up Afghan security forces. Advisers, mentorship teams, equipment, training. And some Judas takes it all down for thirty pieces of silver.

Gold noticed Parson looking at her. When she met his eyes, he shook his head, glanced down at the flight deck floor as if he'd just learned of a death in her family. Except for Gold, this was worse.

"I wonder if anybody downstairs had a hand in any of this," Colman said.

"Good question," Parson said.

"Does it matter?" Gold said.

"How do you know which of these Afghani types to trust?" Colman asked.

Gold didn't know whether it was a rhetorical question and she didn't care. She didn't answer, either. Just took off her headset and went down the ladder to the cargo compartment.

The aeromeds looked busy. Four of them tended to an Afghan patient, a newly qualified police officer. Gold remembered him from class, though she didn't know him well. The man had one eye bandaged, and he was crying out in Pashto.

"What's wrong?" Gold asked the MCD.

"We're not sure. Did I hear that you speak his language?"

"Yes, ma'am. I'll talk to him."

Gold stood by the man's stretcher, touched his shoulder, whispered in Pashto, "Officer Fawad, I am Sergeant Major Gold."

Fawad exhaled, gave a weak smile. "Teacher, it is good to see you here. Are you injured?"

"Not badly. What is wrong, Fawad?"

"My eye hurts."

"I am sorry, Fawad," Gold said. "I will inform the nurses."

Gold turned to the MCD and told her what Fawad had said.

"That doesn't surprise me," the nurse replied. "Pressure changes can worsen eye injuries the same way they aggravate head injuries. We're trying to save his eye, but it's doubtful."

"How bad is it?"

"Lacerated cornea from grit and splinters. Hyphema. He was outside the building and got hit by flying debris. Just bad luck."

"That sounds painful."

"I'm sure it is, even without pressure issues. We're giving him what we can, but the meds probably just keep the pain down to a dull roar."

And it will probably get worse, Gold thought. She wasn't sure what Parson was planning, but she assumed he would try to deactivate the bomb as soon as EOD could tell him how. To get to it again, the crew would have to depressurize once more.

Mahsoud was awake now. He looked at Gold with a questioning expression. When she went to his side, he asked, "What is wrong with Fawad?"

Gold told him, and he said in Pashto, "That is a shame. He would have made a good police officer. Now perhaps he and I shall sell kebabs on the street if Allah allows us to live."

"You must stop this kind of talk," Gold said. "Your body is injured, but your mind is strong. You will use it to serve your country."

Mahsoud adjusted the oxygen cannula in his nose, raised himself on one elbow. He seemed unable to find a comfortable position, and he winced when he breathed. He looked outside.

"What is the pilot doing about our situation?" he asked.

Gold hesitated, then decided not to mislead him. There was no way to sugarcoat this set of facts. "The crew has located the bomb. The pilot is trying to get information on how to deal with it."

"Where is this bomb?" Mahsoud asked, switching to English. His courtesy touched Gold. Whenever he spoke to her, he seemed to use his own language only when he could not express the thought in English.

"In the tail of the airplane."

"Have you seen it?"

"No, but the flight engineer has."

Gold worried about how he would take this news, but he did not appear to react at all. Tragic, she thought, that someone so young was so used to death and violence. Mahsoud shifted his eyes from the window to the floor, like he was thinking about something.

"Rest, Mahsoud," Gold said. "Do you want me to find something for you to read in English?" Maybe someone had a sports magazine or something.

"No, thank you."

Gold wanted to offer some kind of hope, but there seemed so little reason for it. Still, she tried.

"I know this pilot, Mahsoud. If there is a way out of this, he will find it."

"How do you know him?"

"Four years ago, I was escorting a Taliban mullah to be interrogated in another country."

"In Guantánamo Bay?"

"I cannot say. But soon after we took off from Bagram, we were shot down."

"With this pilot?" Mahsoud asked in Pashto. "And you evaded capture?"

"We did not evade for long. We were captured by a Taliban militia."

"But they did not behead you, obviously. Allah be praised."

"Indeed. I have no doubt they would have killed us eventually. American and Afghan soldiers tried to rescue us. They freed Major Parson, but not me."

"How did you survive?"

"I do not tell this story to everyone, Mahsoud. Please keep it between us."

"I am honored by your trust, teacher."

"My captors tortured me, tried to get me to talk. All by himself, Major Parson came for me."

"Then he must be a formidable warrior."

"When he needs to be," Gold said. "But I believe he would rather catch fish and hunt deer."

"That is to be admired, if he is capable of violence but does not relish it."

True enough, Gold thought. But she wondered if, in the end, it really mattered who commanded this airplane now. Life itself was a flight whose destination you could not know. She looked outside, and her eyes focused on nothing.

Mahsoud looked out, too. Gold imagined his thoughts were running in the same current as hers.

"We are trapped between heaven and earth," he said. "For now, we belong to neither."

8

Parson let his boots rest lightly on the rudder pedals. He peeled off his flight gloves, stretched his fingers wide, and looked at his hand. He thought it almost odd that his body, though very probably doomed, was still healthy and alive. Like a well-designed machine, to his aviator's mind. Nerves transmitting signals like electrical wiring. Blood vessels carrying fluid set to a precise temperature. His heart a variable-speed, variable-pressure pump. FMC. Fully mission capable.

Corsica lay beyond the left wingtip, surrounded by a rippling blue Mediterranean. Dots of white in the Bay of Calvi, the sails of pleasure boats. Across the airways up ahead, and getting closer by the minute, was Rota Naval Air Station, Spain. Parson already had his approach plates open to the ILS for Runway Two-Eight. He wondered if he'd ever live to intercept that approach course. And if EOD didn't hurry up and get back to him with some kind of plan, he'd have to figure out a place to enter holding again.

He'd also have to shut down that number four engine before descending. Dunne had found a power setting that kept its vibration within limits, so it was okay for cruise flight. But you couldn't trust it to handle rpm changes while you jockeyed the throttles during an approach, so this would be a three-engine landing. Technically, an emergency by itself, but it was the least of Parson's problems.

Before things got busy again, he wanted to speak face-to-face with the MCD. "Your airplane, your radios," he told Colman. "I'm going downstairs."

"Got it," Colman said.

In the cargo compartment, the aeromeds fussed over their patients—an Afghan in particular, a bandage over one eye. A little farther aft, Parson noticed a litter that appeared only as a mound of green blankets, the patient's face hidden. All monitoring equipment turned off and disconnected.

Parson felt a cold twist in his stomach. He thought he'd made the right decisions with the information he had, but it still hurt to see the consequences right there in front of him. Even if he somehow managed to get this airplane on the ground in one piece, it would mean little to that man's family.

The MCD turned away from the Afghan with the bandaged eye, stripped off her latex gloves.

"Ma'am," Parson said, "how are things down here?"

The flight nurse regarded Parson through her glasses, then took them off and let them hang by a beaded silver lanyard around her neck.

"I shouldn't have been so hard on you," she said. "You have a lot on your shoulders."

"I appreciate that. So do you."

The MCD sighed. "These guys need to get to a real hospital."

"What about that patient you had to restrain?" Parson asked.

"He's quiet at the moment." The MCD pointed to a man Flex-Cuffed to a litter. He seemed to be sleeping.

"Lieutenant Colonel," Parson said, "I guess you realize when we figure out what to do with that bomb, we're going to have to depressurize again."

The MCD put her hands on her hips, stared as though she were watching something far outside the airplane.

"Do what you have to do," she said.

Parson nodded. He looked at the rows of wounded, wondered which of them he'd have to hurt next. Across the cargo bay, Gold sat talking to that Afghan friend of hers. Parson stepped over cables, around Pelican cases, to get to them.

"How is he?" Parson asked.

"I am well, sir," the man said. It surprised Parson to hear the Afghan answer in English. And he clearly was not well.

"Major Parson," Gold said, "this is Mahsoud."

Given the man's injuries, Parson wasn't sure whether to shake his hand. So he just said, "Nice to meet you. Sorry about the circumstances, though."

"A pleasure to make your—" Mahsoud paused.

"Acquaintance," Gold said.

"Acquaintance," Mahsoud repeated.

"Your English is coming along," Parson said.

Mahsoud looked puzzled at that, but he said, "I have a good teacher." Then he said something in Pashto. All Parson understood was Gold's name.

"He says if you are my friend, then you are his friend," Gold said.

"Likewise," Parson said. He was trying to think of something else appropriate to say to Mahsoud when he heard his own name called.

"Major Parson," shouted a loadmaster wearing a headset. "Lieutenant Colman says he needs you upstairs, sir."

Damn, Parson thought, can't he handle ten minutes of straight and level flight? On autopilot, no less? Maybe he should have spent less time at the Air Force Academy playing with falcons and going to football games and more time learning something useful.

"Talk to you later," Parson said. He tromped up the ladder, lowered himself into his seat, put on his headset.

"What you got?" Parson asked.

"I think you need to hear this," Colman said. "There's a C-17 on the way into Rota. They haven't been able to find a bomb on board, but they took off from Bagram ahead of us. They're talking to Rota command post on UHF2."

Parson pulled up his VOLUME knob for the number two UHF radio.

"Reach Eight-Two Yankee, Matador," the command post called.

"Go ahead, Matador."

"Say again your download requirements."

"Reach Eight-Two Yankee will need a pax bus for thirty-one passengers," the pilot said. "Also request a K-loader to off-load three pallets." The voice sounded almost routine.

"And your aircraft status, sir?"

No answer for the moment. Then: "Ah, let's call it Alpha Three."

That's what I'd say, too, Parson thought. Alpha Three, a grounding condition. Even if they land safely, that airplane needs to be inspected nose to tail with a magnifying glass. With dogs and Geiger counters, too, for that matter. It'll likely involve every organization from the International Atomic Energy Agency to the Centers for Disease Control.

"They sound okay so far," Colman said.

"Have you heard them say their altitude?" Parson asked.

"No, but just before you plugged in your headset, they said they were fifteen minutes out."

"So they're descending."

Parson imagined the scene on the flight deck of that C-17. Both pilots watching the altitude scroll down on their PFDs. Probably holding their breaths at each ten-thousand-foot increment.

"Let's see what they're saying to ATC," Parson said. He checked his approach plate, entered the approach control frequency for Rota.

"Reach Eight-Four Yankee, Rota Approach," a controller called. "Expect the ILS, Runway Two-Eight."

"We'll look for the ILS to Two-Eight," the pilot acknowledged.

A few moments later, the controller called, "Reach Eight-Four Yankee, fly heading two-four-zero and intercept the localizer. You're cleared for the ILS to Two-Eight."

No answer.

"Reach Eight-Four Yankee, fly heading two-four-zero for the localizer."

Static.

"Reach Eight-Four Yankee, Rota Approach. Radar contact lost. Squawk ident, please."

Nothing.

"Reach Eight-Four Yankee, do you read?"

Parson looked across the console at Colman, who stared back. The copilot looked shaken. Dunne leaned back in the engineer's seat, clicked a ballpoint pen, slapped a clipboard down on his table. The sky outside seemed to burn, the richest blue Parson had ever seen.

A call on interphone interrupted the silence in Parson's headset: "Pilot, MCD."

"Ma'am?" he said.

"I heard that radio traffic. Let's just keep this quiet."

"That's a good idea," Parson said. Then he added, "All right, crew, you heard the lieutenant colonel. If you were on headset for what just happened, don't spread it around. There's nothing anybody can do about it now, anyway."

MAHSOUD WAS SLEEPING AGAIN. Gold took the blanket that covered his good leg and pulled it up farther, across his chest.

She pondered that news report about how the Taliban said it had infiltrated the police. Such a bitter disappointment to hear the attackers might have had help from the inside, but Gold knew she shouldn't be surprised. Her literacy classes were part of a larger program to professionalize the National Police. However, she sometimes wondered if the culture of corruption and incompetence was just too pervasive. How much good could a recruit like Mahsoud do if no one else cared? And even if you made some progress, as she thought she had, it was so easy for the enemy to destroy it. The work of years set back by the flip of a switch.

Out the window, sunset smoldered on the horizon. Gold felt the plane turn, and she hoped that meant they were getting close to Rota. Maybe Parson would get some instructions from EOD and this thing would be over. The wings leveled for a while, banked, leveled.

The sunset drifted by again. So we're flying in circles, Gold surmised. Dear God, will this never end?

Mahsoud stirred, opened his eyes. "Hello, Sergeant Major," he said in English.

"Hello, Mahsoud."

"You look troubled, teacher."

"I will be all right."

"Has your friend, this pilot—" Mahsoud switched to Pashto. "Has your pilot friend let you tour the aircraft?"

"He has."

"I wish I could see it. I have never flown before."

What an awful shame he can't go upstairs, Gold thought. He'd be so fascinated. Mahsoud seemed to be interested in everything.

That gave her an idea. She went to the baggage pallet, found her backpack, took out her digital camera. If she couldn't bring Mahsoud to the cockpit, she could bring the cockpit to him. A weak gesture, but maybe it would give both of them something to think about, something to put into their minds to dilute the dread. Parson had already said it was all right to take pictures. There was probably not much classified equipment in an airplane this old.

Up on the flight deck, the crew seemed intent on their tasks, but their motions conveyed little urgency. Without hearing the conversations on headset, Gold considered, one might think this all looked routine. Parson was talking on the radio, looking back at Dunne's panel. Dunne scanned gauges, read from a manual the size of the Boston phone book. Colman sipped water from a bottle.

Gold didn't want to interrupt them, so she just raised her camera and took a photo. When the shutter clicked, Dunne looked at her as if she had lost her mind, but he did not object. He was probably wondering why anyone would take photos at a time like this, Gold thought.

The aircraft was over land now. On the ground below, Gold saw a black ribbon of highway. Cars like ants. A train inched along, a brown caterpillar on rails.

Gold snapped another photo, then another and another: the view out the windscreen. Parson, with his hand turning a knob on the center console. Colman, backdropped by cockpit windows. Dunne at his flight engineer panel, with its scores of switches and indicators.

As long as they don't mind, Gold thought, it doesn't matter if they think it's weird. Mahsoud would enjoy seeing the photos if he felt like sitting up. But Gold was starting to worry about the pain he sometimes had breathing.

He'd probably have to talk about the photos in Pashto, since his English wasn't yet fluent enough to cover higher concepts and unfamiliar objects. It always amused her the way he'd switch between English and Pashto in the middle of a conversation. He'd pause to reset his mind, then continue. It was like watching the hourglass symbol on a laptop screen as the computer searched its files. Gold understood why he did that. A foreign language wasn't just a different set of words; it was a different way of thinking.

Back downstairs, Gold found Mahsoud raised up on his elbow. Wide awake apparently, perhaps feeling better. She pressed the REVIEW button on her camera and showed him the shot of the ground.

"That's what Spain looks like," she said. "Or maybe it's southern France."

"Beautiful," he said in English.

Gold advanced the camera and showed him the photo of Parson. Mahsoud studied it with interest. Then the photo of Colman and his side of the cockpit.

"A marvelous piece of machinery," Mahsoud said. Pashto now. "But can you go back to that photograph of the earth?"

Gold returned to the first photo.

"It is so very green," Mahsoud said. "Is it always this way?"

"No. In the winter it is brown, but before that comes the fall. The leaves turn red and orange. It is even more beautiful. My home, called New England, is known for these colors."

"I cannot imagine anything finer than this green."

At first, Gold was surprised that Mahsoud showed more interest in the photo of the ground than the pictures of the cockpit. But she remembered he was from Helmand province. Though northern Afghanistan was mountainous and somewhat green in summer, southern Afghanistan's desert, including parts of Helmand, could look like the moon.

"This place you are from in America," Mahsoud asked, "why is it called New England?"

"The first settlers came from England and that is what they named it."

"And your pilot friend. Where is he from?"

"Major Parson is from the American West. A state called Colorado."

"Ah," Mahsoud said, "a cowboy."

"Exactly."

"And what about the other fliers? Where are they from?"

"I do not know."

Mahsoud looked at her strangely. She thought she knew why. To an Afghan, home and tribe defined you. Anyone you met on friendly terms would tell you about his home. Mahsoud could no more imagine American rootlessness than she could imagine a life of illiteracy spent under a burka.

The sunset came around again. Mahsoud looked out at it and said, "It is time to pray." Then he added, "May I ask a favor, Sergeant Major? Could you bring my Quran?"

"Certainly."

Gold found Mahsoud's duffel bag and brought the silk-wrapped book, careful to hold it with her right hand. She knew Mahsoud could read only a little of its Arabic, but he seemed to enjoy merely running his eyes and fingers over words given to Muhammad directly from God. Perhaps now he might find in its suras something he could understand well enough to bring him comfort.

Gold gave Mahsoud a few feet of space for privacy and watched him while he prayed. She had no trouble reconciling her own religious beliefs with her admiration for traditional Islam. God revealed himself to different people in different ways. Gold loved the English prose of the King James Bible, translated from Greek and Hebrew. And though she was not fluent in Arabic, she knew enough to grasp some of the Quran's poetry. How marvelous it must be to a native speaker.

When Mahsoud finished praying, he began to leaf through the Quran. Then he stopped, looked down, and picked up Gold's camera. He began reviewing the photos again, and Gold moved closer to see. Now he was looking at the cockpit shots. He stopped on the one with Dunne at the flight engineer's panel.

"What is that on his table?" Mahsoud asked. "It looks like the portable computers all you Americans carry."

"I do not think it belongs to Sergeant Dunne," Gold said. "It is part of the airplane, and I believe it is affixed to that table."

"Can it send and receive things on electronic mail?"

"It can. It has brought us a lot of bad news today."

"Teacher," Mahsoud said, "I have an idea."

9

The fighters flew above and ahead of Parson now. They appeared so small he could hardly distinguish them from blemishes on the windscreen until they turned in their own holding pattern. Then their wing flash revealed them as a pair of scythes arcing through the sky.

"Air Evac Eight-Four," the lead fighter called. "Gunfighter's bingo fuel again. We're going to have to drop into Rota for gas. Somebody will catch up with you later. Best of luck, sir."

"Copy that," Parson said. "Thanks." For nothing.

The F-15s began to descend. To Parson, it seemed they were dropping to an ocean floor he could never reach.

He wondered if they would see anything of the C-17 that had disappeared. A column of smoke or dark smears on the ground. All that remained of thirty-one passengers and the crew. Rota command post interrupted his thoughts.

"Air Evac Eight-Four, Matador," called a voice on the radio.

"Go ahead, Matador," Parson said.

"Sir, I'm sorry to tell you this, but the Spanish authorities don't want you landing here. TACC is working on a reroute."

Parson shook his head, muttered, "Son of a

bitch," before pressing his TALK switch. Then he said, "Do they understand we've already diverted from Germany?"

"I think they do, sir."

"Do they understand this airplane is coming down somewhere sooner or later? Or are they going to revoke gravity, too?"

"Our base commander says he's doing all he can. He's even contacted the embassy."

Parson looked across at Colman, back at Dunne. "Can you believe this shit?" he said over the interphone. Then he transmitted: "Air Evac Eight-Four copies all."

What is wrong with these people? Parson wondered. Fifty-six lives on the line up here, and all those suits can think about is how to make the problem go somewhere else. That's why the world is so fucked up.

Parson switched over to HF and called Hilda. The latest dip clearance problem wasn't TACC's fault, but he was annoyed enough that he dropped the "sirs" when the DO came on the air.

"Where do you want us to go?" Parson asked.

"We've found you a good place not too far from where you are now. We want you to divert to the old space shuttle abort landing site in Morocco."

"Isn't that field closed?" Parson asked.

"It is, but the runway's still there, and it's nice and long."

Parson reached down into his publications bag and thumbed through a listing of airfields. "It doesn't seem to be in the IFR Supplement," he said. "Can you get us any data?"

"We'll send you something on satcom," the DO said.

Parson looked out at the sinking sun. He took off his aviator's glasses. The horizon glowed red like a bar of iron heated on a forge.

"Do you at least know if the runway lighting there is still operative?" he asked. "It'll be getting dark soon."

"The flight manager is checking on that."

"What about some guidance from EOD?" Parson said. "We can't descend for landing until we deactivate this thing."

"They're still working on a course of action. We'll get something to you as soon as we can."

"Understood," Parson said. He shook his head. Check's in the mail, he thought.

Parson called ATC and received a clearance south toward Morocco. The Spanish controller sounded glad to be rid of him. The coastline glided past underneath, and the late-day sun turned the water to a rose color. A cutter plowed a pink wake toward Africa. It felt to Parson that the world outside the windscreen was already something apart from him, a world that would very likely go on without him before that sun came up again.

A rattling noise caught his attention. He turned to see that Dunne had thrown down his pen onto the flight engineer's table in frustration.

"What's the matter?" Parson asked.

"Computer trouble," Dunne said. "Again."

Parson squinted to read the message across the top of Dunne's screen: COMMUNICATIONS CONTROLLER FAILURE. "I'll see if I can get it back," Dunne said.

Parson hoped he'd do it quickly. The crew needed that computer to receive satcom messages, among other things. He started to remind Dunne of that, but decided not to state the obvious.

Dunne shut down the computer, then pressed buttons on the panel behind it to depower the processor. After it all went dark, he turned the system back on. The screen remained blank for more than two minutes, but it finally booted up.

"Got it working?" Parson asked.

"For now, I reckon," Dunne said. "Last mission I flew this plane, I fought with the communications controller all the way over the Atlantic. I wrote it up and it got signed off, but it's doing it again."

The computer restart came just in time for a box to appear in the middle of Dunne's screen: YOU HAVE 1 NEW MESSAGE. Dunne opened it, printed it out and passed the strip of paper to Parson. It was what fliers called the Giant Report, for the former Ben Guerir Air Base, Morocco.

Parson skimmed through the data: Runway 36, 13,720 feet long, with more than two thousand feet of dirt overrun. Built for the old Strategic Air Command with its Stratojets standing alert for World War III. General Curtis LeMay had left his mark on the world permanently, with runways more than two miles long for launching bombers armed with nuclear weapons. Perfect for catching a space shuttle that had to make a transoceanic abort. And it would have been perfect for catching a C-5, even heavier than the biggest bomber.

But the Cold War was over and so was Ben Guerir, deactivated in 2005. Not used anymore by NASA. The Giant Report said negative ATC, negative weather services, negative runway lighting. EOD will have to come up with a real quick solution for this to work, Parson thought. Even during the day, a disused runway dusted by grit could be hard to pick up visually if the light came from the wrong angle.

They aren't trying to find me a landing field, Parson thought. They're looking for a good crash site.

As the aircraft flew south, the Mediterranean yielded to the Sahara and its waves of dunes. Past the coastline, Parson noticed something in the fading daylight on the earth below. Though the air at altitude was clear as branch water, a dust storm was making its way across the ground, the leading edge so distinct it looked like a taut rope being dragged over the sand, whipping it aloft.

Parson knew these wild desert winds had several names, depending on their location and direction: the Scirocco, the Simoon, the Haboob. Like different names for the devil in various cultures, depending on the form he took. And whatever the name, it always meant bad news. Visibility at Ben Guerir was about to go to shit.

The moon began to rise behind a veil of dust low on the horizon. It glowed red like torchlight, near to full. In an optical illusion created by the high altitude, it appeared the C-5's flight path would take it over the moon. Parson looked down at it as if it were some final gift, like the cigarette and shot of rum for the condemned man facing a firing squad.

THE WOUNDED AMERICAN SERGEANT was sitting up now. The aeromeds had cut loose his Flex-Cuffs so he could visit the lav, escorted by a medic. He seemed calm enough. Gold kept an eye on him, mainly out of instinctive wariness. But she was more interested in what Mahsoud had to say.

"If someone can get close enough to this bomb to photograph it," he said in Pashto, "then perhaps that computer in the cockpit can send it to your bomb experts."

"That is an excellent suggestion," Gold said. "I will tell Major Parson."

Mahsoud smiled. "Thank you," he said. "IEDs have many configurations. They are limited only by the imagination of the evildoers."

"And by the imagination of those fighting them," Gold said, "such as yourself."

"That is kind of you, teacher. I wished to train to become a bomb technician, but it will never happen now."

"You have studied IEDs on your own?"

"Only a bit. I found little about ordnance disposal in my own language."

"But you learned enough to offer intelligent advice," Gold said.

Mahsoud nodded, pressed his lips together. Gold couldn't tell whether that was a look of satisfaction or resignation. Maybe both.

Gold climbed the ladder to the flight deck. She had left her headset on the navigator's table, and when she put it on, she found Parson in the middle of radio conversations. She didn't understand all of it, but Parson kept moving a switch, apparently talking to different people on different frequencies. One voice was clearly that of an American; the other sounded Arab, perhaps an air traffic controller. Gold didn't know where they were now, but the short trip over the water suggested somewhere in North Africa. During a break in the radio chatter, Gold spoke up.

"Major," she said, "my student has a suggestion you might want to consider." She told Parson about Mahsoud's idea.

"That's worth thinking about," Parson said. "I got my hands full right now, but let's talk about it in a few minutes."

Gold felt gratified that Parson took the suggestion seriously. She hadn't been sure he'd want to listen to one of the Afghans. He was hardly the most politically correct officer she knew, but he seemed to respect anyone trying to help. She remembered an old joke about how to handle officers: Talk them into doing the right thing and let them think it was their idea.

For a few minutes, Gold watched the crew work, with Parson communicating, Colman flying the plane, Dunne monitoring instruments. One of the things she loved most about military service was teamwork, like that of parachutists checking one another's rigs, executing the drop, securing the DZ together. She had never watched a flight crew this closely before, but it was a variation on the same theme—if everybody did their jobs and put egos aside, they could accomplish the difficult immediately. The impossible would take a little longer.

Gold took off her headset and descended the flight deck steps. Fawad waved to her as she returned to the cargo compartment.

"What is happening?" he asked in Pashto.

"Recruit Mahsoud has an idea that can help us. To take a digital photo of the bomb and transmit it to the experts. I have been discussing it with the aircraft commander."

Fawad looked over at Mahsoud, then back at Gold.

"Mahsoud is a fine recruit," Fawad said. "It is a pity he cannot serve."

"I am trying to convince him he can serve in other ways," Gold said. "He should go to university and become a teacher of literature."

"If Allah wills."

"How is the pain in your eye, Fawad?"

"It endures, but so do I."

Gold smoothed the blanket over Fawad, grateful he at least had all of his limbs. Through Mahsoud's window she could see the day was dying. It was getting dark. She figured that would concern Parson; on the radio earlier, he'd been talking about visibility somewhere.

When she moved closer for a better look, the earth had turned black, though some blue remained in the sky. As evening fell, scattered lights appeared on the ground like vesper candles representing prayers of congregants. Isolated homes, Gold supposed, or perhaps the fires of nomads.

Mahsoud raised himself higher. He grimaced as he moved, but he seemed determined to view the ground. From his resting position, he could see only sky. He steadied himself in nearly a sitting position and looked out.

"The lamps are lighted for us," he said in his own language. "The wicks are trimmed, and the oil burns. Some pray for our salvation, and some for our destruction."

Not necessarily a comforting notion, Gold thought. But if Mahsoud could speak so eloquently, maybe his pain wasn't too bad.

A few litters aft of Mahsoud, the American sergeant was eating from an MRE pouch. Another good sign, Gold hoped. Little victories in the midst of a crisis. But it was a bit unnerving the way he kept eyeing everyone, scanning the whole cargo compartment. Someone hungry should be looking at his food. No telling what that head injury had done to him, and the pressure changes couldn't have done him any good.

Gold was helping Mahsoud ease himself onto his back when she heard a scream. It hardly sounded like a person, more like an animal being slaughtered. When she looked up, the sergeant was running down the cargo compartment, back toward the troop doors.

An aeromed and a loadmaster chased him. The wounded man grabbed the handle of the left troop door and pulled hard.

"I'm getting out of here!" he shouted. He yanked the handle again, but it did not budge.

"Stop him!" the MCD yelled.

The aeromed tackled him, slammed him against the door. The loadmaster tried to pin his legs.

"Take it easy, dude," the loadmaster said. "As long as we're pressurized, Mike Tyson couldn't turn that handle."

The man kicked, arched, fought with the loadmaster and

aeromed. Another medic joined the struggle. It took all three of them to subdue the sergeant. Gold had heard that people suffering fits of mental unbalance could have seemingly inhuman strength, and it was frightening to see.

He finally lay still, and the men who'd held him down helped him to his feet. They gripped him by the shoulder and upper arms to keep control of him. But it seemed the ballast of the sergeant's mind had shifted back into place. He appeared calm, even apologetic.

"All right," he said, a slight smile on his face. "I guess that didn't make a lot of sense, did it?"

"Can't say that it did," the loadmaster said.

"I just want to stretch out somewhere that's not moving. Know what I mean?"

"We all do, Sergeant."

The loadmaster and aeromeds walked him back to his litter. He began to lie back, but when he saw an aeromed pull out a Flex-Cuff, he let out a shriek.

The sergeant sprang from his litter. He grabbed a pair of scissors from a medic's pocket, elbowed the loadmaster in the mouth.

The loadmaster stumbled backward, spat teeth and blood. The sergeant slashed at the air with the scissors, forcing the nurses and medics to retreat, then he ran down the cargo bay again.

He began to hack at the wall, raking the scissors through soundproofing blankets. Long rips appeared in the fabric. The man stabbed as if fighting for his life. The scissors clanged into something metal.

A jet of red fluid spewed from behind the soundproofing. The spray struck the sergeant in the neck, and he dropped the scissors. He clutched at his throat and fell to the floor as if he'd taken a bullet to the throat. Blood poured from between his fingers. At first Gold could not understand what had hurt him. But then she remembered the red liquid she had seen on the floor earlier during the initial search for the bomb. That was hydraulic fluid. The sergeant must have ruptured a hydraulic line—a line containing such great pressure that the fluid had cut into him like a laser scalpel.

The spurt of fluid shot across the cargo compartment and sliced into the soundproofing on the other side. Oily smoke boiled from the source of the leak. Gold expected to see flames. But then she realized what looked like smoke was more hydraulic fluid, particulated under intense pressure. Some of it fogged into the air, and what did not atomize injected itself into the opposite wall. A smell like that of auto mechanic's grease filled the airplane.

"Fucking nutcase," the loadmaster shouted. Blood and saliva streamed down his chin.

Two of the aeromeds ducked under the spray and grabbed the sergeant. They dragged him forward, left smears on the steel floor. As they lifted him onto his litter, his hand fell away from his throat. Gold saw blood drip from his fingers onto the floor plates. The MCD pressed a gauze pad against the wound. Dark flecks appeared on the front of her flight suit, spattered the wings on her name tag.

"Did it get his jugular?" a medic asked.

"Might have," the MCD said.

"If that shit's in his bloodstream, he's had it."

"I know it."

An aeromed wiped the loadmaster's mouth and chin. Gold helped him sit down on an empty stretcher.

"Are you okay?" she asked.

"I'm gonna need a dentist if we live through this," he said. His injury slurred his words as if he were drunk.

"Why did it cut him like that?"

"Three thousand psi, that's why."

Another loadmaster was talking on headset. Sounded urgent. Gold had no idea how this would affect the airplane, but it couldn't be good.

She surveyed the scene around her. The spray of fluid seemed to be losing force, but it had soaked the blankets and clothing of two patients. The sergeant struggled with medics, his blood on their latex gloves. Gold couldn't tell whether he was fighting or in the spasms of death. Some of the wounded began to cry out. Mahsoud looked on in silence, then began to cough. Hydraulic fluid slicked the floor and mingled with bloody swirls of a deeper crimson.

10

Warning indicators flickered on Parson's annunciator panel in front of him. They also lit up overhead. He saw a light labeled AILERON POWER, then LAT AUG FAULT, then more.

"What's wrong?" he asked.

"I got quantity loss on system four," Dunne said. "Pressure's dropping, too."

"Pilot," a loadmaster shouted on interphone. "Bad hydraulic leak down here in cargo. A psych case chopped into a line with a fucking pair of scissors."

"All right," Dunne said as he flipped toggle switches, "I have that system isolated."

"Still see the leak?" Parson asked.

"It's slowing down," the loadmaster said. "But we got a compartment full of hydraulic mist."

"Son of a bitch," Parson said. "Smoke and fume elimination checklist."

"Do you want us on oxygen?" Colman asked.

"Negative. That mist is explosive. The last thing we need is to add oxygen to it."

Parson wanted the mist gone right now. Not many things were more toxic, or more flammable, than hydraulic fluid turned to aerosol. He glanced back at Dunne and saw him turn the pressurization master switch to MANUAL. Then the flight engineer twisted a rheostat. Parson felt his ears pop.

"Cargo, this is the engineer," Dunne called. "Still got the mist?"

"It's dissipating. Looks like it's getting sucked through the outflow valves."

"Are you depressurizing?" Parson asked.

"Not all the way," Dunne said. "Not if I don't have to."

Parson waited a few moments to give Dunne's procedure time to work. He looked outside, and the moon was higher. He could no longer fly over it. At altitude, the evening sky was so clear it seemed the cockpit windows were lenses with an infinite depth of field.

"How's it look down there now?" Parson asked.

"It's about gone," the loadmaster said.

"What about the patient with the scissors?"

"The aeromeds are working on him. A spurt of that fluid cut right into his neck."

"That guy's fucked," Dunne said.

"Looks that way," the loadmaster said. "He ain't even moving now."

"Okay," Parson said. "Can you still smell the mist?"

"Not much," the loadmaster said. "It's all over the floor down here, so you're still going to have a little odor."

"I'm back in AUTO now," Dunne said.

That relieved Parson. Dunne had managed to get rid of the mist without completely depressurizing. Otherwise, Parson would have had to dive back down to twenty-five thousand feet. Might have killed another patient. He knew he'd have to descend and depressurize at least one more time to deal with the bomb, but he wanted to keep pressure changes to a minimum.

He took a deep breath, considered his situation. The plane's mechanical condition was deteriorating. No one wanted to let him land. Still no specific guidance about that bomb. Patients were losing their lives and losing their minds.

The cascading problems threatened to overwhelm his know-how and his situational awareness. When he'd gotten shot down with Gold back then, he'd faced the basic challenge of survival on the ground in a winter storm. It had been difficult, God knew, but in a way uncomplicated. Just him and the elements and the enemy. Now he juggled all kinds of technical problems while flying what amounted to a chess piece in some global game. And, oh yeah, the chess piece was rigged to explode.

Parson felt his consciousness on the edge of a survival knife, the membranes of his sanity about to sever. Think straight, he told himself. All these people got nowhere to turn but you.

"Listen up," he said. "Let's go over the status of the aircraft."

Dunne lifted the flight manual from his pubs bag and opened to Section Three. Parson could tell he was in the emergency section because of the crosshatched page margins.

"We've lost an aileron actuator and half the ground spoiler actuators," Dunne said, index finger on a chart.

"I see the warning lights," Parson said. They foretold of control problems: less roll response in the air—and, after landing, less help getting the jet stopped.

"Go ahead and take the POWER switches to OFF where you've lost hydraulics," Dunne said.

Parson reached overhead, flipped a switch everywhere he saw a SYS OFF light. There were several of them.

"We've lost normal brakes," Dunne said. "Give me alternate brakes, please."

Colman moved the BRAKE SELECT switch, and Parson watched the brake pressure needle rise. A hopeful gesture, he thought. We're assuming we're going to get as far as needing brakes.

"The air refuel door won't work now," Dunne said. "If we need gas again, I'll have to crank it open manually."

"Let's hope that's not necessary," Parson said. "Anything else?"

"The reverser on the number four engine won't work, either," Dunne said, "but it doesn't matter. That's the one with the vibe, and we'll have to shut it down before we land."

"How's it doing now?"

Dunne pressed keys on his MADAR computer. "Eleven mils," he said.

"Borderline," Parson said. He rested his right palm across the throttles. Come on baby, he thought. Keep it together for me a little while longer.

The precarious condition of the aircraft reminded him of another emergency he'd experienced three years ago. He'd rented a single-engine Cessna to scout some hunting territory from the air. On the way back into Colorado Springs, he ran into unforecasted icing. The mist over the mountains consisted of supercooled droplets: water below freezing temperature but still in liquid form. It froze instantly when it touched his wings, spoiling their aerodynamic shape and making them heavier. Much heavier. Even at full power, the aircraft began to descend. Unlike larger aircraft, the Cessna had no anti-icing system. Parson expected to impact a ridge; he could only hold the wings level and hope for the best. But as he dropped out of the cloud layer and into warmer air, the ice began to sluff off, and the aircraft handled better. He still had to carry extra rpm on landing, and when the Cessna smacked onto the airfield, the remaining ice shattered like crystal. The shards bounced and jangled along the pavement, left a spill of granules to mark Parson's touchdown point.

He realized he'd made it because he'd kept flying even after his wings had lost their grip on the sky. His life's mission had continued from that scattering of white along the runway centerline at Peterson Field. And now he flew on into nightfall over Africa, with options narrowing by the moment.

Landing at Ben Guerir in the dark was out of the question, even absent a dust storm. Parson called ATC and set up another holding pattern. He requested clearance for landing at Marrakesh or Rabat. Before the answer came, the MCD called up on interphone.

"Major Parson," she said. "I don't know how much damage the patient did to the airplane, but we shouldn't have let it happen. I take full responsibility."

Parson thought for a moment before responding. The MCD had been quick to point a finger at him when he ordered the plane depressurized, but she'd come around when she saw the big picture. And now she was stepping up to take the hit for her own mistake: not blaming her troops, not making excuses. That's what officers were supposed to do. She was all right.

"It's not your fault, ma'am. It's nobody's fault. It's just our little corner of the war."

There came a pause before the lieutenant colonel pressed her TALK switch again. Then she said, "Roger that."

Parson scanned his instruments, some almost too dim to read. He turned up the panel lighting just as Dunne brought up his own instrument floods. A yellow glow bathed the faces of the crew. After three more turns in holding, the controller called.

"Air Evac Eight-Four," he said. "Negative on landing at Marrakesh at this time."

Parson muttered curses, pressed fingers to the bridge of his nose. But he waited before using the TALK switch. If diplomatic clearances were the problem, diplomacy was the solution. Not Parson's strong suit.

"What about Rabat?" he asked. "Or any of the Moroccan military fields?"

"Stand by," the controller said. "Call you back."

"I swear, I believe that's the first thing they learn in English," Parson said to his crew on interphone. "'Stahndbye. Callyoobahk.'"

He thought he could see Marrakesh in the distance. The city's reflected light illuminated dust clouds from below as if the air itself were electrified. The billowing sand occasionally obscured part of the glow completely, and the effect made the town seem to pulse and shimmer. For all intents, Marrakesh had become a mythical place to Parson, of no more use to him than Atlantis.

"Guys," Dunne said, "we got another satcom message." He pressed keys on his computer.

"Good," Parson said. "Maybe it's instructions from EOD."

"Ah, I'm afraid not," Dunne said. He tore paper from his printer and frowned at it, as if he couldn't quite believe what it said. Then he passed it to Parson. It read:

AIR EVAC EIGHT-FOUR—
MOROCCAN AUTHORITIES HAVE DENIED LANDING.
DUE TO THE UNKNOWN NATURE OF THE MATERIAL
PLACED ABOARD YOUR AIRCRAFT, YOU ARE DIRECTED TO
PROCEED TO JOHNSTON ISLAND. WAIVER GRANTED TO
LAND ON CLOSED RUNWAY.

Parson let the paper slip from his fingers. It fluttered onto the center console. Colman picked it up.

"They have got to be bullshitting me," Parson said.

"What's the matter?" Colman asked.

"Do you know where Johnston Island is?"

"No, sir."

"It's on the other side of the fucking world."

GOLD WATCHED AS TWO LOADMASTERS and that crew chief, Spencer, cleaned up the mess. They unrolled absorbent pads across the floor to soak up the hydraulic fluid and blood. All of them wore gloves, and they seemed careful not to let the liquid touch their skin.

Mahsoud kept coughing, and that worried her. If the crew members didn't want that stuff on their hands, what would it do to the inside of your lungs? And though Gold was no doctor, she knew Mahsoud's respiratory system was already in rough shape from the smoke, dust, and heat of the explosion. He'd complained of painful breathing even before the hydraulic leak.

"How do you feel?" she asked in Pashto.

"I will recover," Mahsoud said. But with the rasp in his voice, Gold was starting to wonder. She wanted the head flight nurse to look at him, but she was busy talking on headset.

One of the aeromeds began performing CPR on the injured sergeant. Gold could see his life was ebbing away, either from blood loss or from the poison intermingled with what blood he had left. His head injury, perhaps worsened by the depressurization, had brought him to what amounted to suicide. And the damage he'd done to the airplane could have killed a lot of people, despite whatever good intentions he may have once had.

Gold thought there should be some lesson here about how people come to do evil things, but she could not quite wrap her mind around it. Because of what had happened to this sergeant, no one would hold him responsible for his actions. But what about people with other kinds of wounds, scars on the soul? At what point does wickedness become an act of will?

The MCD checked the sergeant, then shook her head. She pulled a blanket over his face.

The aircraft banked, and the stars shifted in Mahsoud's window. Gold wondered what the change in direction meant. She looked outside and saw the coastline as the C-5 headed out over the ocean. Breakers in the surf shimmered in the moonlight like lines of gold inlay along the shore. No landing in Morocco, presumably. And if Gold's mental map was correct, this heading meant no landing anywhere in Africa. She wanted to know what was happening, but she thought she should leave Parson and his flight crew alone for a while.

Mahsoud began to cough again, in spasms of hacking he could not seem to stop. The head nurse listened to his chest.

"What's wrong with him?" Gold asked.

"Pulmonary edema," the MCD said. "He had it to begin with, and now it's worse."

"What can you do?"

"We'll try some albuterol sulfate."

The MCD went to a roll pack hanging on the wall. From one of its pouches she took a nebulizer. The device had a mouthpiece with a small bottle attached to it. The MCD connected an oxygen hose to the nebulizer and brought it to Mahsoud. He looked at Gold with a puzzled expression. She realized he had no idea what to do with it.

"Place it in your mouth," Gold explained in his language. "Breathe through it."

Mahsoud followed her instructions, inhaling and exhaling with his eyes closed.

"I wish to goodness we had a CCAT team with us," the MCD said. "Then we'd have a doctor and a respiratory therapist, but the CCATs were all tapped out on other flights." She went to a cooler and took out a bottle of water. "Let's at least keep him hydrated," she said.

Gold took the bottle and opened it for Mahsoud. He put down the nebulizer and drank. At first, the act of swallowing seemed to make his coughing worse. But then the hacking eased, and he tried to clear his throat with what sounded like deep growls. His eyes watered with the effort, and Gold placed her hand on his shoulder.

"Take care not to strain your voice," she told him in his own language. "One day you will need it to speak in your classroom."

"God willing," he said.

Gold wanted somehow to distract him from his discomfort, so she went to her books and picked up the Falnama again. As she flipped through it, she finally found something appropriate:

No matter how powerful your enemies may be,
Do not let the whisperings of Satan
Cause you to worry.

When she read it to Mahsoud, he said in English, "I like that one." She liked it, too. It reminded her of the Twenty-third Psalm, something she had often recited to herself.

She hoped Mahsoud would focus on positive thoughts. Otherwise, his physical and mental wounds might lead him into some unrecoverable spiritual fatigue. And if that happened, who could blame him? Suffer enough, and events leave a residue on your mind that never comes off.

Gold knew about that firsthand. Four years ago, when she'd been captured by jihadists after the shoot-down, her captors had come up with the idea to remove her fingernails. One by one. All ten, over a period of hours. They used a tactical knife and a pair of pliers. They asked questions, some of which she could not possibly answer: How do your planes find us? When will your president visit Afghanistan, and where?

The ridiculous nature of the interrogation, along with their initial laughter, suggested they sought entertainment more than intelligence. They got from her screams, curses rare for her, the Psalm, the Code of Conduct, the Soldier's Creed.

Whenever she uttered any line or verse that gave her strength, it angered them, and the blade went in again. They seemed unsure what to expect of her, but they certainly didn't expect faith. When they found her belief system at least as strong as theirs, it confused them. Their response was greater cruelty, and another fingernail would come off. It was as if their knife could penetrate nail and flesh pretty easily, but then it hit tungsten.

Her tormentors apparently wanted to break her for the sake of breaking her, and she did give up a little information: when she had arrived in country, her assigned unit, its home base. But those weren't things they could use to do any damage.

She wondered if they'd resort to rape. A committed Islamist probably wouldn't do that, but a criminal using religion as an excuse wouldn't hesitate. Before they got around to it, though, Parson arrived.

He did it by himself, too, without support or authorization. Just a downed airman alone in a blizzard. Sometimes when she remembered Parson, she thought of an essay by her fellow New Englander Emerson. She doubted Parson had ever read "Self-Reliance," but he certainly lived it.

After her ordeal, it surprised her how quickly her nails grew back. Just a matter of weeks. Little visible scarring remained. Although Gold had dressed modestly all her life, now sometimes when she wore civilian clothes she would paint her nails a deep glossy red. At the moment, however, they were unpolished and clipped short.

In the months that followed her capture and rescue, she had needed as much strength to resist falling into despair as she'd needed to resist the torture itself. But the same values she had called on at knifepoint gave her perspective, and eventually even a start at forgiveness. That, however, she was finding to be a process rather than a single act.

Gold glanced at her fingertips, rubbed them with her thumb. Then she looked outside. On the ocean below, she saw the lights of ships like diamonds glittering on black velvet.

11

Parson steered his aircraft out over the water, two fingers of his left hand curled around the yoke. Then he decided to let the flight director and autopilot take over, so he reached down to his right and pressed two push buttons labeled PITCH and LATERAL. The first thing he needed was a clearance, to set up part of the route to Johnston Island. He needed a lot of other things, too, including at least one more aerial refueling. It would be a long night now literally, flying west as darkness moved west. The stars spread before him, a host of trembling silver points.

"Take the airplane," he told Colman. "My radios."

Parson detached his utility light from over his head. He pulled on its coiled cord and shone it onto the pages of the Flight Information Handbook. He looked up a frequency and rolled it into the number one HF radio.

When he pulled up HF1 audio, he could hear the shifting crackles of radio waves bouncing across great distances of atmosphere. He pressed his TALK switch and called, "Santa Maria. Santa Maria. Air Evac Eight-Four." In sidetone through his headset, his own voice sounded far away. After just a few seconds, a woman answered him from an oceanic air traffic control center in the Azores.

"Air Evac Eight-Four, Santa Maria," she said. "Say your request."

Parson told her his coordinates, then said, "New destination is Johnston Atoll. Yes, the one in the Pacific. Request oceanic clearance, ma'am."

"Santa Maria is aware of your situation," the controller said. "You are cleared to three-three degrees north, two-two west, then two-four degrees north, three-seven west. Rest of route to follow later. Maintain flight level three-four-zero. How copy?"

"Air Evac Eight-Four copies all," Parson said, "but we'd like to amend that altitude. We'll need to descend for aerial refueling and some other things. May we have a block altitude between two-five-oh and three-four-oh?"

Static hissed for just a moment, and then the Portuguese-accented woman said, "That's approved."

"Well, at least somebody finally wants to cooperate with us," Parson said on interphone. Then he flipped his TALK switch the other way and said, "Thank you, ma'am. Do you have any weather information for our route of flight?"

"Ah, Air Evac Eight-Four, we expect widely scattered convective activity across that region of the Atlantic."

Parson would have liked more detail, but for an area not covered by land-based radar it was the best he could expect. "Understood," he said. "Air Evac Eight-Four will maintain a listening watch on this frequency."

"Roger that, Eight-Four," the controller said. "Godspeed."

Parson brought up the flight plan page on his FMS, then entered his new waypoints.

"So where's this place we're going?" Colman asked.

"Johnston Atoll is several hundred miles west of Hawaii," Parson said.

"Oh, man."

"Yeah. We used to use it as a place to burn up chemical weapons."

"Sounds like what's in store for us."

"Exactly."

"I've been there in a C-141, back before they shut it down,"

Dunne said. "Sometimes when you flew in, you'd see this great old big column of smoke, and the controllers would warn you not to fly through it."

"How long is the runway?" Parson asked.

"It's been a while," Dunne said, "but I want to say it's nine thousand feet."

"Sounds like a hellhole," Colman said.

"It's a pretty place, actually," Dunne said, "but it's gotta be contaminated to a fare-thee-well."

"Wonderful," Colman said.

Parson pressed some buttons on his center console, looked at his CDU screen. "Well," he said, "the FMS says it's only sixteen hours away."

"And we got five hours' worth of gas," Dunne said.

"All right, let's prioritize," Parson said. "First we need to get fuel again. Then we're going to make a decision about what to do with that fucking bomb. And we're *not* just going to hope it's a dud. You heard what happened to that C-17."

"What did the sergeant major say about her friend's suggestion?" Dunne asked.

"I don't know exactly what he has in mind," Parson said, "but after we refuel, we're going to find out."

Instinctively, Parson checked his aeronautical charts for places to land if the aerial refuel didn't happen for one reason or another. The Madeira Islands lay ahead and a bit to the south. Normally, he would never plan a mission in which his crew's lives depended on an aerial refuel. The tanker could abort for its own emergency. The aerial refuel door might fail closed. Valves might not open. So he'd always have a divert location in mind; he never left himself without a backup plan.

But that was normal ops. He slapped the chart down onto his side console, set a frequency in HF number two, and made another radio call.

"Hilda," he said, "what's the status of an AR for Air Evac Eight-Four?"

"We have a KC-135 launching from Lajes any minute now," the flight manager said. "Texaco Six-Eight should reach you in about three hours."

Parson looked back at Dunne and said on interphone, "Let me see that fuel sheet again." Dunne handed him the Form 4054, with its columns of numbers. Parson scanned the form, checked his watch, looked at the fuel flow gauges.

"All right," Parson said over the air, "that's closer than I'd like, but it'll work."

Parson imagined the Stratotanker lifting into the air from Lajes Field on the island of Terceira, near Santa Maria, in the Azores. The thunder of its engines rolling across Terceira's windswept pastures. He hoped it wasn't late.

Setting a course across the water with this fuel situation ran against all his training and instincts. The ocean had never seemed so vast. He wondered if this was how the early navigators felt when they sailed into the unknown, with all the experts telling them they'd reach the edge of the earth and fall into the void, ship and crew plummeting forever.

With a few hours to sweat before the tanker rendezvous, Parson told himself to turn his thoughts to something more useful than pointless worry. He decided now was a good time to find out what Gold's friend was suggesting.

"Cargo," he called. "Pilot. You can tell Sergeant Major Gold she can come up here if she wants."

"Yes, sir."

"What do you know about this sergeant major?" Dunne asked.

"Mainly that she's a mystery," Parson said. "I don't get how she does what she does, but I'm glad she's there."

"How's that?"

"Shooting people who don't like us is the easy part. Understanding them and getting them to understand us is a lot harder. That's where she comes in."

"I wouldn't want that job."

"Me, neither."

When Gold appeared on the flight deck, she sat again at the nav table. She donned her headset and said, "What can I do, sir?"

"Tell me about your friend's idea," said Parson.

"I have a digital camera. Mahsoud says the EOD people can better help us if they can see the bomb. He says we should take a photo of it and send it to somebody. Can you do that with the computer over there?" Gold pointed to Dunne's panel.

"Probably," Dunne said. "I've never done that with satcom, but this thing does have a USB port."

"So we need a way to get the image from the camera into the computer," Parson said. "Anybody got a card reader?"

"Not with me," Colman said.

"I'm afraid I don't have one, either," Gold said.

"I didn't bring mine," Dunne said. "But on a plane full of military people, I know somebody did."

"I'm on it," Parson said. He turned the wafer switch on his comm box to PA and told his crew and passengers what he wanted. From downstairs he heard the bustle of baggage being unstrapped and passed around. Boot steps and thuds. After a few minutes, a loadmaster climbed the flight deck ladder. When he slid open the door, he had a cord dangling from his fingers.

"Got it," the loadmaster said. "It belongs to one of the aeromeds." Gold took the card reader and passed it to Dunne.

"Tell whoever it is I said thanks," Parson said. "Sergeant Major Gold, tell your friend the same. What's his name again?"

"Mahsoud."

This development put Parson in a better mood. Progress, he thought, or at least something like it. Our chances are still a million to one, but at least we won't ride it down without a fight.

All his career, the Air Force had sent him to classes on something called CRM, crew resource management. The idea was to encourage aircraft commanders to listen to the rest of the crew and to encourage crew members to speak up. You never knew who might have the nugget of information—or inspiration—that solved a problem. Parson considered it the Air Force's effort to teach and institutionalize what a good leader would do naturally.

He didn't know how useful this particular nugget would become, but he intended to find out. As far as Parson was concerned, Gold and Mahsoud had just got promoted from passengers to crew.

GOLD LOOKED FORWARD TO TELLING MAHSOUD how Parson had taken his suggestion. For the moment, though, she decided to let him rest. She sat at the nav seat and watched the crew. At the moment, they didn't seem as busy as before. Eventually, Parson turned to her.

"I guess we never got around to telling you our new destination, did we?" he said.

"No, sir."

"They're sending us all the way across the Atlantic, over Central America, and into the Pacific, to a place called Johnston Island."

"Oh, my God. Why?"

"They're worried about that stuff on board. If we roll the airplane up into a ball on Johnston, we won't hurt anybody but ourselves."

Gold pondered that for a minute. The thought of that much more flying sickened her, but she had to admit it made sense. The needs of the many outweighed the needs of the few, and if you were one of the few, you were just out of luck. A military concept she knew quite well.

"Will you need to get more fuel?" Gold asked.

"Oh, yeah."

Parson made a PA announcement to inform everyone else. Gold heard the groans from downstairs. She looked around the flight deck, dreading the hours ahead. Then she wondered if she should take those hours for granted. Apparently, the bomb was not supposed to go off until the plane descended to a certain altitude, but how stable was it? With an armed high explosive in the tail, she thought, our lives could end at any moment. But wasn't that always true? She knew a colleague struck in the temple by a sniper's bullet, dead before he hit the ground. A teacher who suffered an aneurysm in her sleep, never to wake. Friends killed by traffic accidents, drunken drivers. Mortality was a silent enemy, invisible but ever present and ever patient.

She knew of wise people who said, "We are not promised tomorrow." But, dear God, we're not even promised the next five minutes.

Up ahead, through Parson's side window, lights gleamed in the distance like swirls of ocher in a sea of ink. Some shone from above the waterline, illuminating hillsides.

"What's that?" Gold asked. She didn't really feel like talking, but she forced herself. Better than sliding into quiet depression.

"The Madeira Islands," Parson said. "Portugal owns them."

"Where the wine comes from," Gold said.

"How's that?"

"Madeira wine. It's a long-lived red. Back in the days of sail, traders could ship it because it wouldn't spoil at sea."

"Oh."

It figured Parson wasn't a wine drinker. The one time she'd seen him drink came right after their medal ceremony, when he had a Scotch. It was at an outdoor reception with a cash bar, at Fort Myer, next to Arlington National Cemetery. At least he'd bought good stuff; he'd splurged on Johnnie Walker Blue Label. Parson tried to order one for her, but she couldn't stand the scent of it. He took two sips of his own, then said, "For those who can't be here," and poured the rest into the grass.

Gold sat in the darkness of the flight deck for a while, until the lights of Madeira receded under the left wing. She decided to check on Mahsoud again.

The aeromeds were working on him when she returned to the cargo compartment. He looked pale, and the medics had attached some sort of clip to his finger. The clip glowed from the inside with a red light, and it was connected to a cord that led to an electronic monitor.

"What's all this?" Gold asked.

"A pulse oximeter," one of the medics said. "That LED shines through his fingernail and tells us the oxygen content in his blood."

"What's wrong with his oxygen content?"

"His system isn't processing oxygen efficiently because of the damage to his lungs."

Gold felt something turn cold inside her chest. If the medical people were this concerned about Mahsoud's vital signs, then his hold on this world must have loosened some.

"How are you, my friend?" Gold asked.

He smiled, drew a long breath, and said, "Fine," in English. Almost turned it into two syllables.

"The aircraft commander likes your idea," Gold said in Pashto. "They are going to take and send a photograph. They have already found the equipment they need."

"I am glad to be of assistance."

"There is something else I should tell you," Gold said. "We have a long way to go." She explained where and why.

"I heard Major Parson's announcement," Mahsoud said. "I could not understand it all, but it seemed to make the Americans very unhappy. I knew it was not good."

Gold tried to judge Mahsoud's reaction, but he gave little by way of cues. He's probably received worse news in his young life, Gold thought. She knew his mother and two brothers were dead, but she did not know when and how they'd died.

"Very few people from your village have seen a tropical island," Gold said. She regretted the words immediately. Worried that they sounded patronizing.

"None that I know of," Mahsoud said. "Few have seen even Kandahar."

Gold admired his strong front, but she felt heartsick. Mahsoud needed a real hospital. Not some sandy strip of pavement on a dot in the Pacific. She hoped somebody was thinking far enough ahead to send doctors and medical gear to meet the C-5 at Johnston.

She decided to ask Parson about that. To his credit, he seemed to be in a mood to listen to people. Gold climbed the flight deck ladder, thinking how to frame the question.

In the cockpit, the crew looked busy again. She could hear what sounded like urgent crosstalk on the interphone, but without her headset, she could not make out the words. The trouble seemed to have something to do with a message on Dunne's computer. She looked over his shoulder:

> AIR EVAC EIGHT-FOUR—
> TEXACO SIX-EIGHT CANNOT REFUEL YOU. IT ABORTED WITH AN ENGINE FIRE ON TAKEOFF. CONTINGENCY PLANS IN PROGRESS.

12

So this is how it will end, Parson thought. For all my efforts, I could change nothing but the coordinates of the crash site, the location of the last-known position. A burning oil slick for an epitaph.

Of course the tanker aborted, he realized. It rolled out of the factory during the Eisenhower administration, and it belonged in the boneyard, not in the air. And now it probably sat on the hammerhead at Lajes, surrounded by fire trucks and wrapped up in foam.

Parson felt no panic. He found himself in an emotional netherworld he'd visited just once before, in the snows of the Hindu Kush. He remembered the cold of the Afghan mountains, so bitter it sapped away not just body heat but reason itself. The snow falling so heavily the air seemed fibrous with it, covering the tracks that were leading him to Gold. The prospect of finding her alive so remote and his own imminent demise almost certain. Each breath of that frigid air scorching his lungs. Darkness coming on, so that he could barely read his compass.

Like then, death was not a risk now but an apparent certainty, and it brought a strange calm, a clarity. He felt he'd already used up his quota of luck and now lived in some cosmic debt. But his passengers and crew—they were another matter. So many of them so young. And Parson could *not* lose another crew. The best friends he'd ever known had died in the shoot-down of his C-130 years ago or had been slaughtered by terrorists shortly after the crash. The thought of something like that happening again turned his stomach, brought bile to his throat. So he'd fight the inevitable, past all realistic hope, against logic itself. Somewhere outside hope and logic, he made a call on HF:

"Hilda," he said, "Air Evac Eight-Four received your L-band message. Tell me about these contingency plans."

"We have another tanker coming to you from Mildenhall," the flight manager said.

All the way from England, Parson thought. They'll never make it in time. "I don't think that's going to work," he said.

"Opec Five-Two is already airborne," the flight manager said.

"What is their position?"

"Ah, I'm afraid I don't have that information."

"When did they take off?"

"Approximately two hours ago. We launched them as a backup for your primary tanker."

Parson tried to do some rough mental math, made difficult because he was starting to get tired. If he stayed on his current course, he'd run out of fuel long before the Mildenhall KC-135 could reach him. The only way to rendezvous with that aircraft would be to turn and go find it. In the vastness of this black Atlantic. Parson switched to the other HF radio.

"Santa Maria," he called. "We have another problem." Parson explained his situation, how he needed a turn toward the northeast to go off track and look for the tanker. He knew that would play havoc with transatlantic flights. The trouble was that this far out over the ocean, there was no radar coverage. Controllers kept track of airplanes the old-fashioned way, with position reports. Pilots would call in their time, speed, and altitude at a given waypoint, and estimated arrival time at the next. They had to get there within three minutes of that estimate.

With an emergency aircraft cutting north, and no way for

controllers to watch for potential collisions, airliners would have to change their courses and altitudes. That was not figured into their fuel planning. Some would probably divert into the Azores. Those that had not reached the midpoints of their routes might turn back to their departure airports. An international incident all by itself.

After perhaps twenty minutes, Santa Maria said, "Air Evac Eight-Four, that's approved. Turn right, heading zero-six-zero. Cleared for course deviations as needed. Please keep us advised."

"Zero-six-zero," Parson said. "Thank you, ma'am." Then he said over interphone, "We just fucked up a lot of vacations."

"You're breaking my heart," Dunne said.

That encouraged Parson a little. If Dunne could crack a joke, then his head was still on straight. If Parson was going to pull off the impossible, he'd need the flight engineer's input. At the pilot's instrument panel, Parson had nothing to tell him fuel quantity, hydraulic pressures, or the status of the electrical systems. These things he'd get from Dunne or not at all.

The copilot, Colman, was also new, but at least he hadn't done anything stupid. Parson felt he owed these guys his very best, no matter how hopeless it seemed. He remembered an instructor who once said, "Fly it until the last piece stops moving." Well, this machine was still in the air.

Colman turned a knob to set an indicator bug on his HSI, pressed HEADING on his nav select panel. The aircraft banked to the right. Then Parson entered a frequency into his air-to-air TACAN, waited for a signal from the tanker's transmitter. Nothing.

"Still out of TACAN range," Parson said. "Let's see if they'll talk to us." He dialed the HF tanker frequency and called, "Opec Five-Two, Air Evac Eight-Four."

"Air Evac Eight-Four, Opec Five-Two. Go ahead."

Well, at least the damned radios are working right, Parson thought. "Opec Five-Two," he said, "We have turned onto an intercept course. What is your position?"

The tanker pilot read off his coordinates, and Parson began to do the math. With the KC-135 heading southwest at around point-seven-five Mach, the two planes' closure rate had them meeting in about three and a half hours.

Parson told his crew what he had calculated, and he said, "Engineer, what's our burn time now?"

"At cruise speed, about three hours," Dunne said.

"What if we slow it down to max range speed?" Parson said. He knew that by flying more slowly, they could squeeze out more air miles per thousand pounds of fuel.

Dunne opened to a range chart, ran his pencil through the curving lines. Tapped at his calculator. Swore, started over, ran the numbers again.

"Three hours and twenty minutes," he said. "And at that speed, we cover less distance."

Parson looked out at an ocean surface bronzed by moonlight. Our final resting place, he thought, after the engines flame out from fuel exhaustion, we descend through the bomb's trigger altitude and hit the water in pieces like scattershot. This is what it feels like to run out of time and luck. His palms grew slick, his mouth dry. It all came down to the numbers on Dunne's calculator, the negative figure at the bottom of the fuel chart.

To have an airplane full of people die for want of ten or fifteen minutes? Such a short sweep of a watch's hand. If only you could stretch time, Parson thought. Conserve it somehow. But it flowed at a constant rate; always had since the Big Bang.

Parson scanned his instruments, though there was hardly any point. He stopped at the fuel flow gauges. Thought for a moment. He could not control the flow of time, but he could sure as hell control the flow of fuel.

"Engineer," he said. "How much time do we have if we slow it down to max endurance speed? Not max *range*, max endurance."

Dunne recalculated. Then he said, "Four hours, but we won't put enough miles behind us."

"No," Parson said, "but the tanker might if they push it up to barber pole speed. They have a fuselage full of gas. They don't care about their burn rate."

"So you're saying if we slow way down and they speed way up, the numbers will work out?" Colman asked.

"You got it."

"Maybe," Dunne said.

"Will the tanker pilots want to fly that close to critical Mach?" Colman asked.

"Oh, yeah," Parson said. "They live for this shit." He called the tanker crew and told them his plan.

"We'll give it a try," the KC-135 pilot said. "Let us have some coordinates to aim for, and we'll meet you there."

Parson checked his FMS, made some calculations, gave the tanker crew the lat/longs. Then he added, "Opec Five-Two, confirm you're Pacer Crag modified."

"Indeed, we are."

"What does that mean?" Colman asked.

"They have a pretty good avionics suite," Parson said, "and that will help them find us."

"I hope it does," Colman said.

Dunne slewed the N1 marker to the power setting he'd calculated for max endurance. "There it is," he said. "Either this will work or it won't."

Parson knuckled back the throttles until the N1 rpm lined up with the marker. The airplane slowed to what felt almost like a hover. Noise from the slipstream fell off in a decrescendo like orchestral strings hushed by the hand of a conductor. Then Parson waited. There was simply nothing left to do but let the clock and the fuel gauges do what they would. The charts and formulas showed only minutes to spare. And that depended on the wind, the efficiency of the engines, the accuracy of the instruments.

A strange thought came to him then, a memory from nav school. One day at Mather Air Force Base, years ago, he'd picked up his schedule of training flights. Training sorties, they were called.

"That's a funny word," he said to an instructor. "Sortie?"

"It comes from the French word *sortir*," the instructor said. "It means *to leave.* It doesn't say anything about coming back. Remember that."

And so he had. Right up until this moment, over these infinite tracts of water, dark and deep as oblivion.

GOLD SAT AT THE NAV SEAT. She felt honored that Parson seemed to reserve that disused crew station for her. No one else ever sat there, at any rate.

She didn't understand everything she'd just heard on the interphone and radios. But she gathered that the crew needed another aerial refueling, and it would be close. Very close. And they sounded like they were doing things way out of standard ops, improvising. Soldiers in the field did that all the time. But these flyboys, in their world of checklists and rote procedure, normally planned and briefed every move they made.

Gold recalled an excruciating briefing for a paratroop exercise involving Fort Bragg and the adjacent Pope Air Force Base. The aircrews described their flight path to the drop zone, and they seemed to have a slide for every turn and landmark. Death by PowerPoint. One of the pilots taking part in Purple Dragon '99 told her the flying was the easy part. Gold wondered what he'd think if he were here now.

Parson and his crew had been in deep discussion, but at the moment, the interphone was quiet. Parson twisted around and looked at her.

"Hey, Gold," he said. "I didn't see you back there."

"Sorry, sir," she said. "If I'm in the way, I'll go back downstairs."

"No, you're fine. I guess you heard what we're up against."

"Yes, sir."

"Well, now there's nothing to do but wait. You're welcome to stay there. Just keep off the interphone once we start the AR."

"I will, sir."

Parson and his crew looked eerily calm for people under that kind of pressure. But she knew from experience that when Parson was quiet, he was thinking. And that surface calm could end with quick action, even violence.

She watched him, Colman, and Dunne check gauges, tweak knobs now and then. They appeared not to accept the hopelessness of their predicament, and Gold admired that. Every thought, every flip of a switch, every reading of an instrument, seemed an act of faith, a belief in life beyond this flight.

Dunne's checklist lay open on the flight engineer's table. Gold noticed a photo taped to the checklist binder. It showed Dunne wearing jeans and a flannel shirt, along with an INTERNATIONAL HARVESTER baseball cap. He and two boys, maybe twelve and fifteen, leaned on the tailgate of a pickup piled with hay. One boy held a banjo, the other a violin. Dunne held a guitarlike instrument Gold did not recognize.

The cockpit lights dimmed, apparently by the switch Parson had just turned.

"Look at the stars," he said. "Best thing about flying over the ocean at night."

A crystalline canopy of silver dust stretched across the Atlantic. Gold had seen the night sky so beautifully unpolluted by urban light in just one other place, and that was Afghanistan.

"That's Ursa Major," Parson said as he pointed. "And there's Ursa Minor, the Little Bear, and Draco, the Dragon. You can see the Dragon's tail looping around Ursa Minor."

At first it surprised Gold to find Parson so knowledgeable about constellations. He hardly seemed the type for stargazing. But then she remembered he'd spent most of his career as a navigator, not a pilot. For him, the stars probably represented a lot of things: Data points. The beginnings of his profession. Astronomy and mythology, man's first relationship with the sky.

"Have you ever used a sextant?" she asked. She was reaching, but if the crew really had little to do at the moment, maybe conversation would help.

"I've used one in older-model C-130s," Parson said. "But I don't think they even teach celestial navigation anymore."

"Where was Draco again?" Gold asked.

"There," Parson said. "It coils around the northern pole, and it never sets."

"Like us," Colman said, "never landing."

No one said anything for a moment until Gold broke the silence. "This is a little out of my field," she said, "but I think the ancient Egyptians had another name for Draco. And because it never sets, they thought of it as an ever-vigilant goddess protector."

"I'll take all the help we can get," Dunne said.

"That checks," Colman said.

Parson peered up at the heavens for what seemed like a long time. Without taking his eyes from the stars, he asked, "How's your friend doing down there?"

"The nurses are worried about his breathing," Gold said. "I've been meaning to ask—can they send some medical help ahead of us to Johnston Island?"

"They should have already arranged that," Parson said, "but we'll check and make sure."

"Thank you."

Gold wondered what else she could do for Mahsoud and the others and she found it frustrating that the answer was, pretty much nothing. She wasn't used to helplessness. On the ground, no matter what she faced, she could nearly always take action: Return fire. Find cover. Translate thoughts. Resist interrogation. To just sit and ride and wait ran counter to everything in her nature. Parson at least had things he could do, or try to do, right up until the end. And, apparently, he was still planning.

"Guys," he said, "after we refuel, let's depressurize like we did last time. Then we'll go take a picture of that damned bomb."

"All right," Dunne said. "Once we get the checklists cleaned up, I'll go do it."

"Negative," Parson said. "I won't ask you to go through that again. I'll let Colman take the plane and I'll go do it. I want to see that fucking thing for myself, anyway."

"Wrap up good," Dunne said. "It's cold as sin back there."

Gold saw her chance. "Sir," she said, "let me go with you as a safety observer like I did before."

"Okay," Parson said. "Won't be the first time we've had our asses in a sling in a cold place, will it?"

"No, sir."

Gold felt some of her tension release, and she almost smiled. Not so much at Parson's comment but at the prospect of a mission. And the idea that Parson seemed to think of her as part of his team.

She also liked his choice to go himself. If you're in charge, Gold believed, you should never tell someone to do something you wouldn't do.

"So I guess it'll just be Dunne and me up here, then," Colman said.

"You'll manage," Parson said. "If I fall and knock myself out or something, just repressurize, climb back up to cruise altitude, and press on to Johnston."

"Yes, sir," Colman said. He took off one of his flight gloves and twisted it so tightly it looked like a short length of rope.

"We'll make a flinty-eyed airlifter out of you yet," Parson said.

Dunne seemed to be ignoring Parson's pep talk to the copilot. He was working at his calculator again, and Gold saw that he'd brought up a page on his computer with columns of numbers. One of the numbers on the screen was red.

"Fuel reading," Dunne said as he passed a form up to Parson. When Parson took it, he shone his utility light on it, clicked off the light, and looked out again at the ocean and stars. He was quiet for a time. Then he said, "Loadmasters, break out the exposure suits."

"Yes, sir," said a voice on interphone.

Sounds of renewed activity came from the cargo compartment, the rattles of tie-down straps released and dropped.

"You reckon anybody will need an exposure suit if we don't make the refuel?" Dunne asked.

"If the engines flame out from fuel exhaustion and we start descending," Parson said, "we don't know when or how that bomb will go off. I might have enough control left to keep the wings level when we hit the water."

That brought to mind another hazard, one Gold had not considered—the prospect of days or weeks adrift. She'd seen the yellow handle in the aft flight deck, the one marked LIFE RAFT—PULL TO DEPLOY. So many dangers, so many ways to die. Gold had spent little time on the water, but she'd read stories of survival at sea. Burning days and freezing nights. Sailors succumbing to thirst and madness. Survivors envying the dead.

And in the event of a ditching, what would happen to the patients downstairs? Quick drowning, probably; most would never get out in time, even with help. Parson was likely thinking of all this, anticipating awful decisions.

"Major," called a voice on interphone, "we got ten exposure suits. Who do we give them to?"

Silence for a moment. Then Parson said, "Anybody who's able-bodied enough to benefit from it."

"Roger that, sir. I'll bring some up to the flight deck."

"I don't need one," Parson said. "I'll be sweating enough as it is when I plug with the tanker."

"What about when you go back in the tail?" Dunne asked.

"I know it's cold back there, but with that suit over my feet I'd probably fall on my ass."

"Then I don't need one," Gold said. "Same reason."

"Me, neither," Dunne said.

"Same here," Colman said.

"Are you guys sure?" the loadmaster asked.

"Yeah," Parson said. "All you loadmasters, put one on. I need you to be able to help with whatever patients make it out. Same with the aeromeds. I want all those suits worn by aeromeds and loads. If anybody argues, tell them I said it's an order."

Gold looked out the cockpit windows again, not up at the stars but down at the water. She thought of derelict ships with tattered sails and crews dead from plague or typhoid, plying eternal courses set only by currents and trade winds.

13

The MAIN TANK LOW lights had been on for three and a half hours. The MAIN SUMP LOW lights had been on for forty-five minutes. Of the C-5's dozen fuel tanks, eight were empty and four were nearly so.

Parson's FMS screen told him he was nearing the tanker rendezvous point. But he saw nothing on TCAS, received nothing on TACAN, heard nothing on UHF. He began to think about what he'd do at the end. Considered just to go ahead and ditch now while he still had easier control with all four engines providing thrust. But he decided not to give up quite yet. Besides, if the bomb blew the tail off, he'd have no control at all. Without the horizontal stabilizer, the jet would probably nose right over and go straight down. Hit the water in a vertical dive.

The first fatal symptom of fuel exhaustion, he supposed, would be erratic turbine temp and fuel flow. One by one, the engines would flame out, and he'd see the N1 and N2 tachometers creep down. When the third engine failed, the ram air turbine would deploy, a little propeller in the slipstream to drive an emergency hydraulic pump. Like a body dying of lethal wounds, backup systems would trigger to no avail. Warning lights would illuminate and then multiply: LOW PRESSURE. LOW VOLTAGE. LOW TEMPERATURE. LOW ALTITUDE.

He kept glancing at the readout for distance from the tanker. It read nothing—no indication at all. But then it seemed to flicker, as if it caught a whiff of the KC-135's TACAN signal. Numbers appeared: 161. Negative reading again. Then 160, steady. Parson tried a call on UHF.

"Opec Five-Two. Air Evac Eight-Four," he said. "I got a DME reading of one-six-zero miles. Would that be you?"

"Air Evac Eight-Four," called the tanker pilot, "we show you one-five-nine miles off our one o'clock."

Parson felt little relief. He needed to be receiving fuel by now. By half an hour ago.

"Opec," he said, "go ahead and give me a turn for an en route rendezvous. We are critical on fuel. Just a few minutes left." If that.

"Opec Five-Two's in the turn."

Parson had stayed high to squeeze out all he could from every drop of gas, but now he cracked the throttles for a descent to the aerial refueling altitude of twenty-five thousand feet.

"All right," Parson said on interphone, "precontact checklist. We gotta get this right the first time."

"Air refueling door," Dunne called.

"Clear to open," Parson said.

Dunne unbuckled his harness and stood up. He opened an overhead panel, exposing the actuator for the air refueling door. Normally, he could open the door with the flip of a switch. But with the plane's hydraulic loss, he had to crank it open manually. He put a dog bone wrench on the end of the actuator and began to turn it.

"Tell me when you get a READY light," Dunne said.

The slipstream rose from a whisper to a growl as the wind swirled around the partially open AR door. But the green light Parson wanted to see remained out. Dunne strained at the wrench.

"What's the matter?" Parson asked.

"Actuator's binding. It's getting real hard to move."

"Well, you better turn it quick."

Dunne pushed hard. Still no READY light.

"That's as far as I can turn it with my hand," he said.

"If you don't get it open, we're fucked."

"I know, Major. Do you want me to hit it with something?"

That would either open the door all the way or break the actuator, Parson realized. No time to debate the options.

"Do it," Parson said.

"Sergeant Major," Dunne said, "hold this in place for me."

Gold stood up and took the wrench from the flight engineer. She held it on the actuator with her thumb and forefinger. Dunne reached for a shelf next to his instrument panel and pulled out a technical manual in a hardcover binder. He swung the book like a maul and hammered the side of the wrench. Parson heard a sickening crack, but on his overhead panel the READY light illuminated.

"That did it," Parson said. "Good work."

Dunne picked up the checklist where he'd left off. "Continuous ignition," he said.

Parson moved an overhead switch and said, "On."

His instruments told him the tanker was now less than a hundred miles away, and the closure rate had slowed. Apparently, the other aircraft had turned one hundred and eighty degrees so he could approach it from behind.

He just wished he could see it. Parson turned his radar gain control to AUTO, antenna stab switch to ON. Fiddled with the target clarity control.

And there it was, a blip on the screen, dead ahead. Clear on the radar but hard to pick up visually because of shreds of cirrus clouds hanging at precisely Parson's altitude. Inside the cloud vapor, the C-5's strobes reflected back like heat lightning. The flashes distracted Parson, so he reached up and switched the strobes from white to red.

He closed on the blip to within twenty miles, and the cirrus layer opened up to reveal clear sky ahead. Eventually, Parson recognized an artificial constellation, the vaguely cruciform pattern of the tanker's lights as seen from the back.

A nudge on the thrust levers increased the rate of overtake, but Parson tried to be judicious with power. This was nothing like accelerating a car; he couldn't just tap the brakes to slow down. Newton's laws came into stark clarity—an object in motion tended to remain in motion, especially if it weighed hundreds of tons. Now the distance closed to yards, and Parson could discern the green light on the end of the KC-135's boom.

He slid his seat full forward and down. This wasn't comfortable for someone so tall, but it gave him a better view of the boom and the pilot director lights on the underside of the tanker. The C-5 crept toward the other aircraft with agonizing slowness. Part of Parson's mind wanted to hurry up and get the gas, but he tried to limit his closure rate to no more than one foot per second. Anything much faster and the bow wave from the C-5's nose would create control problems for the tanker. He'd have to back off and start all over, and he knew he didn't have the fuel for that.

When he was fifty feet behind the boom and about ten feet below it, he pressed his TALK switch and said, "Eight-Four is stable."

"Cleared to contact position," came the response.

Parson watched the red and green lights on the tanker's belly, made minor adjustments accordingly: Fly forward. Fly aft, Fly up, Fly down. The boom extended . . .

And Parson felt his aircraft yaw, not from anything he'd done.

"Flameout on number two," Dunne said. Instruments for the number two engine, now starved of fuel, began dropping toward their zero points.

A loud thump overhead.

"Latched," Dunne called.

Parson pressed his right rudder pedal and added power on number one to try to stay on the boom. With uneven thrust, the jet wanted to fishtail. Parson's feet, hands, and mind held it steady as if his flesh, blood, bones, and brain were mere systems of the aircraft.

"Approaching aft limit," the boom operator called over the radio. The boom was almost fully extended. If it reached its limit it would disconnect.

"I got pressure and flow," Dunne said.

Parson struggled to stay within the arc of the tanker's boom. He had to keep the nose of his aircraft within a space smaller than his kitchen—with a dead engine and partial hydraulics. If he broke away now, it was all over.

"Flameout on number one," Dunne called.

The pilot director lights flickered between red and green as Parson fought the thrust levers and yoke.

"Ignition on number two," Dunne called.

Out the corner of his eye, Parson saw that engine's rpm spool up as fresh JP-8 fuel found its way to the spray nozzles in the combustion chamber.

"Approaching forward limit," the boom operator called. Parson adjusted his power almost imperceptibly, willing it more than physically moving it.

"Ignition on number one," Dunne called.

Another yaw as that engine relit.

"Left limit," the boomer called.

"LATCHED light out," Dunne said.

Parson tensed for engines to start failing again, and he pressed a rudder pedal with the toe of his boot.

"Reset," Dunne called. As calmly as if he were in a simulator.

Parson pressed a button on his yoke, and the READY light came back on. The boom extended again.

"Flameout on four," Dunne called. Then he said, "Latched. Pressure and flow."

Number four reignited, and now Parson had all four engines back. Sweat dripped from the end of his nose. He realized he'd clenched his abdominal muscles so hard, they hurt. He tried to relax them, took a deep breath. Every tendon in his body stretched tight as a throttle cable. A knotted stomach won't do anything but wear you out, he told himself.

Parson held the aircraft as steady as he could, and he nulled out a little bit of leftward roll with a TRIM knob on the center console. "How much fuel we got on board now?" he asked.

"About ten thousand pounds," Dunne said.

Maybe twenty minutes' worth. "Let's take it up to a hundred and fifty thousand," Parson said.

"Yes, sir."

With fuel flowing and the aircraft stable, Parson decided he could afford a break. "Can you take it for a while?" he asked Colman. The copilot placed his hands on the yoke and throttles, and he nodded. "Your airplane," Parson said. "I got the radios. Don't worry if you fall off the boom. We have enough gas now to take your time latching up again."

Colman did not fall off the boom. He flew formation with the Stratotanker so smoothly there was almost no relative motion between the planes, as if the sky were made of glass and the two aircraft embedded in it.

GOLD WATCHED THE TANKER CLIMB AWAY and disappear above a night ocean the color of amethyst. She didn't know how much hope to allow herself, but the crew had bought some time. And with their lives extended at least by a few hours, they could continue working the problems.

She thought about Mahsoud and the others downstairs. The circle of their existence down to the dimensions of that cargo compartment—a purgatory of bloodstained metal, odors of aircraft fluids, and the sight of corpses.

"Major," she said, "before we go back to the tail, should we put those two bodies someplace where the patients can't see them?"

"Yeah," Parson said, "we need to do that."

"We've placed them in bags," the MCD said on interphone. "Where would you like us to take them?"

After a pause, Parson said, "On the floor in the courier compartment, at the aft end of the flight deck."

That made sense to Gold. Nobody was sitting back there. But it meant pulling the dead up the flight deck ladder.

"I'm going off headset," Gold said. She'd gathered that was something she should say. "I'll help move them."

"You're cleared off," Parson said. "Be careful on that ladder. I'm about to turn the airplane."

Gold unbuckled the nav seat's harness and started downstairs. When she was halfway down the rungs, she felt the aircraft bank to the left, and she held to the handrail. Parson was resuming his westerly course toward Johnston Atoll.

In the cargo compartment, Gold went first to Mahsoud. His breathing still seemed labored, but his color looked better, and he was awake.

"How are you?" Gold asked in English.

"I am well," he said. "What is happening?"

"The airplane nearly ran out of fuel, but we have plenty now. In a few minutes, we will go photograph the bomb."

Mahsoud nodded and gave a thin smile. Then he placed his head back down on his pillow and closed his eyes.

Gold watched some of the loadmasters and aeromeds unzip their exposure suits. No need for them anymore, at least not for a while. The crew members struggled out of the rubber clothing and piled it over an unoccupied stretcher. The hoods had left their hair matted and sweaty, and dark patches of moisture stained the backs of their flight suits.

The medics brought the two body bags to the foot of the flight deck ladder. With both hands, Gold took the end of one of the bags. She noticed smears of blood and hydraulic fluid; this was apparently the sergeant who'd gone mad. The MCD took the other end of the bag.

They lifted it, and Gold led the way up the ladder. She climbed one rung at a time, gripping the body bag in her left fist and holding the rail with her right hand. Why were the dead so unaccountably heavy? Gold wanted to do this with some dignity. She pulled hard to keep her load off the steps, but it scraped along despite her efforts.

When Gold shifted her footing for balance, she glanced down at the cargo compartment. Three loadmasters and one of the aeromeds held a salute, as custom required when moving the fallen.

Gold reached the top of the steps, pushed open the folding door, and she and the MCD hoisted their burden onto the flight deck. Parson and his crew watched in silence. Gold picked up her end of the body bag with both hands and led the way past the galley, all the way aft to the courier compartment. Two aeromeds followed with the second body. They left them on the darkened floor, between the rows of seats.

Too bad we don't have a chaplain on board, Gold thought. Someone to say something appropriate.

She looked out a window just forward of the galley. Nothing visible from this view, neither a ship nor a star. Just glare reflected back from the plane's interior lighting. It seemed the aircraft had become disassociated with the earth and sky—there was just the night, and the aircraft carrying its bomb like a terminal cancer.

Gold felt her ears pop; the crew was apparently depressurizing the plane again. She worried about how that would affect Mahsoud, but she knew it had to be done. She dreaded returning to the noise and cold in the tail, too. Just another thing that couldn't be helped.

Up front, Parson was getting up from the pilot's seat, untangling himself from harness straps and interphone cords.

"You ready to do this?" he asked.

"Yes, sir," she said. "I'll meet you downstairs."

Gold took an oxygen cylinder from its mounting and checked the pressure. She carried the cylinder, an oxygen mask, and her headset down to the cargo compartment. She went to her pack, withdrew her camera, and placed it in a cargo pocket. Then she hunted through the pack until she found a T-shirt. She removed her ACU blouse and donned the fresh T-shirt over the one she already wore. As she buttoned the ACU blouse again, she noticed Fawad staring at her. Maybe I just offended him, she thought. He'll get over it if he lives through this.

The aeromeds were hovering over Mahsoud again. Probably watching him closely during the pressure change. Gold felt the swell in her ears again and she swallowed.

Mahsoud looked at her, and she didn't like what she saw in his eyes. Pain, maybe. Worry or fear. She went to his litter and placed her hand on his shoulder. "We are going to take that photo," she said.

"That is good," he whispered.

"Even while injured, you are fighting for your friends, Mahsoud. With your intellect. That is a fine thing."

"Thank you, teacher."

"There is an English poem," Gold said. "I cannot remember all of it. But it says, *'I am the master of my fate; I am the captain of my soul.'*" She had quoted that line to an Afghan once before—to a teenage girl she'd visited at a hospital in Mazar-i-Sharif. From scars across the child's face and neck, Gold could see how the acid had made her skin bubble and burn: the penalty for going to school. And the girl still wanted to learn.

"I would like to read your poetry when I know your language better," Mahsoud said. "What is this poem called?"

"'Invictus.' It is a Latin word."

"What does it mean?"

"It means 'unbeaten,' Mahsoud. It means 'undefeated.'"

Mahsoud nodded, then raised himself slightly and looked out his window into the vastness of the night. For a better view, Gold put her hand over the glass to shade it from the airplane's interior lighting. Her gesture revealed nebulas and galaxies drifting above, with other worlds and other troubles.

14

In the troop compartment, at the negative pressure relief valves, Parson noticed the placard: EMPENNAGE ACCESS—GROUND USE ONLY. He pulled on the flight jacket he'd borrowed from Dunne, and Gold draped a blanket around his shoulders. It was an awkward process because he had to work around his oxygen mask and the MA-1 cylinder he held by a carrying strap. It felt as though he were girding himself with battle armor.

Gold breathed from an identical mask, and she wore her own oxygen cylinder around her shoulder. She had learned her lesson about touching cold-soaked metal; flight gloves now protected her hands.

Parson eyed the pressure gauge on his oxygen supply. Every breath seemed to pull at the needle. No wonder: At eighteen thousand feet, you had only half of sea-level atmosphere. And here at twenty-five thousand, matters became even worse.

When Gold handed him her camera, he placed it in a pocket of his flight suit on his lower leg. From another pocket, he took his Maglite and turned it on. Gold held open the pressure valve, and Parson crawled through.

The cold hit him like a blast of ice water. His T-shirt was still clammy from the tension of refueling; now it seemed to close on his chest and freeze. He began to shiver almost immediately. This wasn't the worst hypothermia he'd ever experienced, but it was damned sure the strangest.

And the noise just made it worse. The god-awful howl of transonic wind right up against metal. Like the scream of a tornado about to blow apart a car, with the moment stopped and the sound sustained.

Still on his hands and knees, Parson balanced on the catwalk and cradled his oxygen bottle and flashlight. Then he stood carefully, fearful of falling and losing his mask. He knew if that happened, he'd have only minutes to find it in the dark before he passed out.

On his feet now, the vibration of the torque deck transmitted itself up through his boots. As a career flier, he knew well the stresses placed on an airplane in flight. But to feel them with human senses brought a whole new perspective. It reminded him of when he had once put on a protective glove and touched a live wire, felt the pulse and surge. It gave him frightening comprehension of a force he had understood only academically.

Parson took small steps as he made his way aft. At the ladder leading up through the vertical stabilizer, he shone his light on another warning placard: TORQUE DECK SECTION. USE CAUTION WHEN WORKING OR TRAVERSING THIS AREA. So the designers of the C-5 considered it dangerous to be screwing around back here, he thought, and that was with the airplane sitting stock-still in a hangar. What would they think of all this?

A shaft of light streamed from the negative pressure valves. The sight comforted Parson. That meant Gold was holding open one of the valves, watching him, but she was staying out of the tail like he'd told her. Dunne had confessed that Gold had rescued him when he lost consciousness. Parson knew he had to hurry up and finish the job or she'd have to rescue him, too. You could suck the oxygen out of these MA-1 bottles faster than you'd expect.

He hung the oxygen bottle from his shoulder and placed the flashlight in a thigh pocket, still switched on. Then he mounted the ladder and climbed through the cramped space. The ladder twisted and buckled with the movement of the aircraft, as if it were trying to shake him off. About ten rungs up, Parson reached the compartment that held the cockpit voice recorder and the flight data recorder, twin orange boxes.

He aimed his light at the recorders—and there it was, right between them. A green duffel bag, stuffed full with God only knew what. Wiring visible at the open end. Two prominent black wires leading from something—maybe a kind of sensor—taped to the outside of the bag. A cardboard box behind it, with no visible wires. More boxes and bags in the recesses of the tail section. What the hell have Dunne and I breathed in back here? Parson wondered.

It became harder to inhale through the mask. Better hurry, he thought. The resistance meant the oxygen was running out. He would have liked to carry a spare bottle, but even one was cumbersome enough.

Holding on to the ladder by the crook of his right arm, Parson placed the flashlight back in one pocket and withdrew the camera from another. With fingers numbed by cold, he fumbled to turn on the camera. He almost dropped it into sheet metal crevices below him, where it would have been irretrievable. When he finally got it powered up, he snapped a photo of the bomb. The flash hurt his eyes, but he took several more shots. It made him think of muzzle flashes in the night. Then he eased back down the ladder.

As he moved, he thought about the placement of the bomb. It couldn't be much worse. If it exploded where it was, it would almost certainly rip the tail off. He wondered if it would destroy the recorders, too. They were designed to withstand a crash, but what about a bomb right next to them? Not that they would do Parson and his crew and passengers any good. He just hoped the underwater acoustic beacon, mounted on the back of the voice recorder, would still work. It was designed to activate when it hit the water. Then it would send out signals for thirty days so search ships could find the wreckage. At least that way the families might get some closure, knowing what happened and where.

Back down on the catwalk, Parson tried to take a deep breath. But he got only a whiff, and the rubber mask collapsed against his cheeks and the bridge of his nose. Damned bottle is already empty, he thought. That means I got maybe three minutes of useful consciousness.

He stepped forward, walking toward Gold and the light. The cold grew deeper, and Parson realized the blanket had slipped from around his shoulders; it must have caught on some part of the aircraft structure. He took a moment to look around for it. He didn't care about losing the blanket, but he couldn't have a foreign object bouncing around back here, fouling control cables. There were enough problems already.

His light played across the catwalk, and the metal stringers and formers. Nothing. He retraced his steps back to the ladder and shone the Maglite up the rungs. Not there.

The light from the negative pressure valves became brighter. Gold had opened one of them wider, and Parson suspected she was thinking about coming in after him. Maybe she believes I've gone hypoxic, he thought. Just stay where you are, Sergeant Major.

Parson decided to give ten more seconds to his search. One Mississippi. He moved his flashlight beam around a cluster of hydraulic lines. Still nothing. Five Mississippi. He searched around the rack that held the HF receiver/transmitters. Eight Mississippi. He looked toward the stabilizer access hatch and found the blanket there, crumpled over the hatch. Parson bent down and grabbed it, then headed for the negative pressure valves to get out of the tail section.

The light coming through the valves was fading, turning from yellow to gray. Parson could see only directly in front of him; his peripheral vision was gone. He could not recall exactly where he was, and he wanted to sit down and rest. Why was he so tired? It was too damned cold to hunt today, anyway. And where was his rifle?

Some part of his mind told him to keep heading for the light. That's where the cabin was.

He kneeled at the pressure valves and crawled through the lower one. Someone had him by the arms, and he closed his eyes, drifted off into a warm sleep. . . .

Gold's face appeared above him. The sight brought him a vague sense of well-being. This person was someone he loved. And she could help him fix the problem. She would know—know what? Parson tried to remember this thing, this trouble he had to deal with.

He lay on his back and saw Gold's hands around the refill port of his MA-1 cylinder. In one breath, all his responsibilities came flooding back. He felt embarrassed that he'd let himself pass out; he'd thought Dunne careless when it happened to him. We've been to the altitude chamber, he thought, and we should know better. But that was a controlled environment and this was a real emergency.

"Thanks," he shouted through his mask. "I guess you're two for two now."

"Sir," she said, "this isn't working. Next time, we need to set up a firemen's relay to hand fresh oxygen bottles back there to you."

Parson nodded as he got to his feet. She had a point. We have plenty of oxygen, he considered. And some of the crew and passengers are offering decent ideas. Those are about the only things in our favor, he thought. Might as well use them.

GOLD ACCOMPANIED PARSON BACK TO THE COCKPIT. She wanted to keep an eye on him since he had just passed out, but he appeared sure-footed enough as he climbed the flight deck ladder.

He lowered himself into the pilot's seat, picked up his headset, and exchanged the portable oxygen mask for the one at his crew station. He and Colman seemed to confer about something, and Gold put on her own headset just in time to hear Parson say, "Oh, shit."

He was looking at his radar screen. Colorful blotches spread across it: greens, yellows, and reds. The green and yellow smears encircled red cores, except in a couple of places where the reds stood apart and took on an odd fishhook shape. To Gold, it seemed a high-tech Rorschach test, and the crew interpreted every pattern as a threat.

"What's all that?" Gold asked.

"Thunderstorms," Parson said. "Strong motherfuckers."

"Oh."

"Let's repressurize and start climbing," Parson said, "so we can get our asses over and around these things."

"Cabin's coming down," Dunne said as he turned a knob.

"Did you get the photo?" Colman asked.

"Yeah," Parson answered. "We'll send it once we make sure these storms don't tear us apart."

Colman advanced the throttles just as Gold felt the aircraft rock with the first jolt of turbulence.

"Everybody strap in tight," Parson said. "MCD—ma'am, you probably want to secure the patients."

"In progress," came the answer over interphone.

Parson moved a selector on his comm panel, keyed his mike, and said, "Santa Maria, Air Evac Eight-Four needs deviations left and right of course for weather."

"Air Evac Eight-Four," the controller said, "approved as requested."

Gold looked outside at utter darkness—no moon, stars, or ships. Then a golden vein of lightning arced between two clouds. Daylight for an instant. And in that instant, Gold saw thunderheads like canyon walls. Mountains of cumulonimbus, roiling with energy. Weapons of angry gods.

She didn't know weather like an aviator, but she had heard of these oceanic clusters of storms. They raged in low-pressure areas, and if they lasted long enough, air would begin to swirl around the low's center, gathering speed, moisture, and strength. The birth of a hurricane.

An eerie blue glow began to dance on the windscreen. It spilled across the side windows, behaving more like liquid than light. Sheets of it pulsed and shimmered like a miniature aurora borealis.

"What the hell is wrong with the windscreen?" Colman asked. "Should I turn off the heat to it?"

"Nah," Parson said. "It's just Saint Elmo's fire. Don't worry about it."

The ride grew rougher, and the shoulder straps of the nav seat's harness dug into Gold's shoulders. The airplane seemed to hit unseen obstacles, rocks in the sky.

"Are we going to make it over this stuff?" Dunne asked.

"Not all of it," Parson said.

Rain started to lash the windscreen, adding a deeper roar to the hiss of the slipstream. Then the sound changed to something like that of gravel thrown against the aircraft. Hail, Gold realized.

Another lightning bolt stabbed into the sea, so bright it hurt her eyes. The flash revealed whitecaps on a heaving ocean, with skeins of foam stretching between the crests.

Gold began to hear the electrical storm as well as see it. Blasts of static fried in her headset. The crackles erupted far more often than she actually saw lightning. She supposed she was hearing the strikes of bolts obscured by clouds.

"Give me continuous ignition, please," Dunne said.

Parson moved an overhead switch and said, "On."

With the next rip of lightning, Gold saw a tremendous cloud mass ahead, its top shaped like an anvil from hell's own forge. She wasn't used to judging distances in the air, but it looked like the C-5 would never clear the top of it. But no turn in any direction looked like a better option. The radar showed a phalanx of similar monsters on all sides.

Parson moved something on his console, and the plane banked a few degrees left. Perhaps he was trying to avoid the very worst of it. Gold wondered if the turbulence and electrical interference might set off the bomb. Everyone else had to wonder the same thing, she thought, but there was no point in discussing it because no one could do anything about it. As it was, the crew had their hands full in the tormented air with a plane trying to go anywhere but where they wanted it.

The hail's pounding grew worse, so loud that Gold turned up her interphone volume just to hear the crew talk. At that moment, something popped like a gunshot.

"What was that?" Colman asked.

"Hail just cracked the windscreen," Parson said.

"Did it get both layers?" Dunne asked.

Parson scratched at the glass with his fingernail. He had to try it a couple of times because the turbulence made his arm flail.

"No," he said, "just the outer ply."

"It'll hold, then," Dunne said.

Another fire stream of lightning. Closer this time. It exposed the building storms in ominous relief: gray walls closing in, hurling stones of ice and spears of fire. It occurred to Gold that in these remote reaches of the Atlantic, she was encountering air, vapor, and water in their most powerful forms. The elements could become an enemy for ground troops, to be sure. But she was learning that for fliers, the weather presented a constant threat, sometimes more dangerous than missiles or tracers.

A laptop that Parson had placed on the nav table nearly slid off. Gold held on to it to keep it from crashing to the floor. Unlike the engineer's computer, this one wasn't bolted down. Gold had paid little attention to it before, but now, protecting it, she saw it was apparently some kind of navigational backup. On the screen, a miniature airplane inched along a green course line, steady and unmolested. The moving map display showed a serene sea marked by waypoints and jet routes. This computer program evidently knew exactly where they were, but had no idea what was happening to them.

Saint Elmo's fire enveloped the windscreen entirely, as if a translucent blue shroud had been draped over the plane. The starts and fits of static in Gold's headset joined one another in a constant cacophony, a wall of white noise. The storms outside attacked all her senses at once, with neon in her eyes, overload in her ears, and nausea in her gut.

The aircraft lurched to the right like a hammer blow had come down on the wing. A cracking sound came from overhead.

"What was that?" Colman asked.

"Probably hail taking one of our antennas," Dunne said.

"Which one?"

"We'll find out soon enough."

"All right, copilot," Parson said to Colman, "give me two hundred and forty knots. Thunderstorm penetration speed."

Colman pulled back on the control column. Gold wondered why, until she realized the crew was *slowing* to a speed at which the plane could better withstand turbulence. So Parson had given up on powering over all the storms and accepted that he must go through part of them.

Blazes of lightning came more frequently now. Diffused by the rain and mist, the streaks appeared more like explosions, as if the sky were filled with gunpowder.

Another hard jolt came as if something had kicked the airplane. The blow slammed Gold against her harness, and her cracked ribs burned with pain. Then the plane dropped as if it had simply ceased to fly. The laptop levitated into the air as the nav table dropped away from it. It slammed back down onto Gold's fingers, and she nearly cried out. Bile rose in her throat from airsickness. Helmet bags, pens, and manuals bounced against instrument consoles and clattered to the floor.

"Damn, that hurt," Dunne said. He began tapping at his computer, and Gold wondered what information he could possibly want from that thing at a time like this. "I got a g-limit fault code," he said. "Two negative gs."

"Felt like about ten," Parson said.

Gold wasn't sure what that meant, but she knew it was bad. She guessed the storm was slamming the airplane beyond its proven capabilities.

The next lightning bolt did not appear as an arc. It lit up the whole sky. The noise made it seem it had ignited all the fuel in the airplane, all the fuel in the world. Sparks bounced from Dunne's panel. The boom sounded to Gold like a mortar round; only her harness kept her from diving for cover. She smelled an odor like burned popcorn.

The airplane went completely dark.

15

Parson heard screams downstairs from people who thought they were about to die. In the darkness, he felt for his flashlight. He switched it on, swept the beam across the dead instrument panel. The N2 tachometers came alive as backup systems activated. He groped for the INSTRUMENT POWER switch and placed it on EMERGENCY.

"Did we flame out?" Colman asked, a catch in his voice.

"Negative," Parson said. "We still got all four engines."

"That lightning strike tripped the generators," Dunne said. "I'll see if any of them will come back on line."

Parson turned and shone his light back toward the flight engineer's panel. Dunne had his own penlight in his mouth while he worked his switches with both hands. He moved a generator control to the TEST position, looked at its frequency and voltage. Apparently, he didn't like what he saw, because he left it off. When he moved to the next switch, the same thing happened.

This airplane has four main generators, Parson thought. Dear God, please give me just one back.

A jolt of turbulence knocked Dunne's hand off the number three generator switch. But when he moved the voltage selector, Parson heard him off mike as he said, Cool, to himself. Dunne moved the switch back to ON, and the airplane lit up. That brought a cheer from downstairs, something about Allah. Dunne checked number four, and that one showed good, too.

Whines and buzzes rose as radios came back to life, gyros resumed spinning, computers rebooted, processors reset. The annunciator panel showed a few more warning lights than before, but at least the damned thing had power to show warning lights.

"We're going to have some damage," Dunne said. "I smell fried wires."

"Me, too," Parson said.

Dunne pressed in circuit breakers that had popped, and OFF flags disappeared from the glass faces of gauges. Parson scanned the panel and took stock of his situation. The attitude indicators rocked with each bump of rough air. The airspeed indicators told him Colman was still holding thunderstorm speed. The flight augmentation computers all showed INOP lights. Parson pressed three buttons to reset them and give Colman an easier time handling the plane. Whatever damage the lightning had done, the aircraft remained flyable.

Rain still whipped at the windscreen, but it sounded like the hail was gone. Flickers appeared in the sky like artillery flashes. Distant lightning, Parson supposed, obscured by clouds. The more distant, the better.

"Go ahead and keep climbing," Parson told Colman. "I think the worst is behind us. Just hand-fly it until we get into smooth air and then we'll put the autopilot back on."

"Yes, sir," Colman said.

The copilot hadn't done too badly. We just got our asses kicked, Parson thought, and Colman was obviously scared, but I never had to take the plane from him. Now we just need to get away from this tropical depression before it strengthens into a tropical storm.

As the aircraft gained altitude, it emerged into clear air as if spat from the maw of some leviathan. Free of the storms' updrafts and downdrafts, it settled into smooth flight. Rain and vapor vanished to reveal a silver panoply of stars. As an old navigator, Parson had always loved the night sky and the order it implied. For all time, mariners and airmen could know their position based on the angle of Rigel, Antares, or any of the fifty-seven navigational stars in the Air Almanac. To Parson, that meant that, from the beginning, somebody was keeping an eye on business.

During better times he had taken pleasure in ocean crossings. He felt he had his own small place in a history that included Columbus, Vasco da Gama, Lindbergh. In those peaceful missions he'd taken his Kollsman Periscopic Sextant from its case and attached it to the sextant port in the cockpit ceiling of the C-130E. He'd find the star, place it in the crosshair, and keep the bubble centered. Then he'd measure the angle and figure a line of position. Usually, when the aircraft began receiving navigational beacons on land, his spherical trigonometry turned out to be dead-on.

A shooting star cut across the horizon like a topaz dropped from the heavens. It burned out and continued its plunge invisibly, followed by another, then another.

"Look at that," Colman said.

Parson thought for a minute, considered the time of year. "It's the Perseid meteor shower," he said. "You'll never get a better view of it than this."

Meteors fell in streaks like electrified needles. Briefly, Parson wondered if they dwindled to ash after they burned out or if something solid remained to make an unseen splash.

Sights like this were part of why he loved his job. In normal circumstances, he might enjoy the scene for hours, sipping coffee and monitoring his instruments and radios with little to worry him. While flying, especially in untroubled night air at high altitude, he could feel he had escaped the ugliness on the ground. To Parson's mind, gravity kept the worst of man's inclinations held down to the surface of the earth. But now, with this bomb on board, hatefulness had reached up and found him in the stratosphere.

"So how bad off are we?" Parson asked.

"I got a couple of fuel pump breakers still out," Dunne said.

"Leave those alone."

"Oh, yeah."

The last thing Parson wanted was to reenergize a torched fuel pump in a tank full of fumes. We already have enough reasons to blow up, he thought.

"Can you work around the bad pumps?" Parson asked.

"Affirmative," Dunne said. "I can still transfer fuel. But I got other issues."

"Like what?"

The flight engineer pressed keys on his computer, scratched at the cursor pad. "We have another controller failure. This computer won't talk to *anything*."

"Reboot it."

"I will," Dunne said. He pressed POWER switches next to the screen. "This makes the third time."

Parson looked aft, watched the screen go through its restart sequence. He needed that thing to work because it was the only way to send a satcom message. The only way to send the photos of the bomb. The problem wasn't the laptop itself; the problem was its link to everything else. Without it, he had no satcom and no text data from the Tanker Airlift Control Center. Nothing left but radios, with antennas torn up by hail. He'd also have no monitoring of engine vibration, no way to know if number four went bad again until it was too late.

Gold still sat at the nav table, eyes alert, watching everything with what looked like professional interest. She had not spoken since the lightning strike. When she finally pressed her TALK switch, she said, "I still smell something."

"I think I do, too," Parson said. "I thought it went away, but now it's back."

"I don't—" Dunne said. Parson looked back to see why the engineer had paused. A red light glowed on Dunne's panel. It said SMOKE.

Parson held his breath. Please, not an electrical fire, he thought. Better to have a burning engine than that. He knew of planes that had filled with smoke and plunged to the ground while choking crews struggled to find and control electrical fires. The damned things had a way of hiding, like a forest fire spreading underground through a peat bog. You could stop it, maybe, if you knew what was burning and you killed its power source. But the fire could lurk behind access panels, underneath soundproofing, inside insulation.

Dunne moved a selector marked LOCATE, turned it through several clicks. He stopped when a second red light came on, and he said, "It's in the avionics compartment. Engineer's going off headset."

Without waiting for Parson's acknowledgment, Dunne dropped his headset onto the engineer's table and unbuckled his harness. He stood, moved aft to the avionics bay door, and pulled it open. Smoke rolled through the doorway and mushroomed against the ceiling. It filled Parson's sinuses with a chemical tang, and his eyes watered. Dunne ducked inside the compartment despite the smoke.

"Everybody on oxygen," Parson ordered as he donned his sweep-on mask yet again. He checked to make sure Gold had hers on and she did. But he worried about Dunne, who would not have heard the order over interphone.

A shout came from inside the avionics bay. Dunne was either calling for help or cursing in pain. Parson rose from his seat.

Dunne emerged from the avionics compartment coughing, holding some sort of electrical box in his hand. The smoke seemed to be dissipating.

Parson removed his mask and said, "You all right?"

"Yeah," Dunne said, "but it shocked the piss out of me."

"What is that?"

"I just yanked it out of the rack. It's the MADAR power supply."

The electrical junction for the flight engineer's computer. For the satcom, and so many other things. Parson glanced at the screen. It no longer said COMMUNICATIONS CONTROLLER FAILURE. It said nothing at all.

WITH THE STORMS BEHIND IT NOW, the airplane flew smoothly enough that Gold put down the airsickness bag she had clenched in her fist. The bag remained empty, though several times she had nearly retched into it. People downstairs must have thrown up, though. She noticed the odor of vomit all the way from her seat at the nav table.

The welcome end to the jet's tossing and rolling made her think of a line from both Scripture and song: . . . *the rough places plain.* If she ever lived to hear Handel's masterwork once more, that phrase would have special meaning. But then she tried to put the idea from her mind; she knew she might never again experience the pleasures of music, reading, culture. Concert halls and libraries, some of her favorite places, seemed worlds away from this ill-fated ship of war and its cargo of wounded, maimed in both body and spirit.

Perhaps she could help clean up whatever mess there was downstairs. She checked off headset and opened the flight deck door. A wave of foul smell hit her, and her stomach heaved. When her gut settled again, she descended the ladder.

Aeromeds and loadmasters were already on their hands and knees, wiping up vomit with thick paper towels. Gold nearly slipped on the slickened floor. She took a pair of latex gloves from a dispenser, then unrolled a wad of the towels. One of the flight medics began to spray disinfectant, and a medicine smell mingled with the stink of bodily fluids. Gold got down on the floor and helped clean up what was left.

Some of the liquids soaked into the knees of her ACU trousers, and the odor made her mouth flood with saliva in a final warning from her stomach. She tried to force it down, gave up, vomited onto the floor. She had not eaten much, though, and she lost little but clear phlegm. An aeromed gave her another paper towel, and she wiped her mouth, then cleaned up the rest.

None of the patients slept now. Mahsoud gazed out his window. Fawad sat up, watching her with his unbandaged eye. She got to her feet and steadied herself against a litter stanchion.

"How do you feel, Officer Fawad?" Gold asked in Pashto, voice still gravelly.

"I am better," he said. "Perhaps better than you at the moment. But I am terribly cramped. Can you help me walk to stretch my legs?"

"I will," Gold said, "as soon as the nurses allow it." As she spoke, she peeled off the latex gloves and dropped them into a trash bag. The black plastic bulged with discarded gloves, bloody bandages, syringes, and other medical waste.

Fawad did not look better. His face appeared grave and ashen. But Gold took it as a good sign that he wanted to move around. The MCD and the other medical people seemed busy at the moment; she'd ask them at a better time. She doubted security concerns would prevent letting the patients walk. Each of the wounded had been searched for weapons before boarding, and searched again in flight.

"That was an awful storm," Gold said, thinking it would do Fawad good to talk.

"Were you frightened?" he asked.

"I certainly was. When the lightning struck, I thought we were going down." And I'm still frightened, Gold thought.

"Allah is mighty," Fawad said. "The airplane is in his hands."

True enough, Gold thought, though she wished she could offer more concrete hope. Fawad was in pain and facing an uncertain future—assuming anyone on board had a future.

Mahsoud motioned to her, and she joined him at his window. "Have you seen the shooting stars?" he asked. He wheezed as he spoke, but his eyes were bright.

"Yes," Gold said. "Major Parson pointed them out."

"Perhaps Muhammad saw something like this on his *Mi'raj*, his Night Journey."

"It is a wondrous sight." Gold did not add that the flight seemed more like a tour of hell than the Prophet's Night Journey to heaven on a winged horse.

"I saw you and Major Parson go by earlier," Mahsoud said. "Did you take photos of the bomb?"

"We did, but I do not know whether we can send them now." She hated to tell him that, but she had too much respect for him to hide important information.

"Why not?"

"When lightning hit the airplane, it damaged some things. There was a fire."

Mahsoud's face fell. "We must send the photos," he said. "The bomb technicians can hardly help us if they cannot see what we are dealing with."

"Major Parson and his crew will do the best they can," Gold said. "I know him to be resourceful. With another pilot, we might be dead by now."

"If God wishes us to live, we will."

I'm hearing that a lot tonight, Gold thought. But she liked the way Mahsoud put it a little better. She kept to herself her own New England version: God helps those who help themselves. Well, we're working on it, she considered. At least if we don't survive, it won't be for lack of trying. We will not go quietly into this night.

She looked out Mahsoud's window. On the water's surface, the flood lamps of a lone ship burned like a single dying ember. A meteor streaked toward the ocean as if to join the vessel. And above, stars blazed as if all glory were shining through pinpoints in the blackness. Gold felt she should draw some meaning from this visitation of lights. But she could not quite work her mind toward what that might be.

Mahsoud turned his face from the window. He coughed once, then again, then began a convulsion of hacking that seemed to tear at his lungs. Unsure what to do, Gold placed her hand on his back and patted gently. His shirt felt damp and clammy. She looked around for help, and the MCD came over.

"Ma'am," Gold asked, "can you give him something else?"

"I'm not sure there's much else we can do now," the MCD said. "I'm going to try to talk to a doctor."

The MCD put on her headset, went to a comm unit on the wall, and turned the selector switch to HF2. So maybe there's some on-call flight surgeon, Gold realized. Too bad not to have one on board, but these Air Force types always seemed to be able to reach whoever they needed. That stood to reason, since they were calling from a thirty-four-thousand-foot antenna. Gold had been on Army patrols so deep in Afghan valleys that line-of-sight radios had little use except as clubs.

The MCD seemed to swear under her breath, and she took off her headset.

"What did he say?" Gold asked.

"I couldn't get through," the MCD said. "Even if I did, the doctor would probably say the patient needs dexamethasone, but we don't have it in our kit."

"Can we do anything else?"

"Just tell him to breathe through the nebulizer for a while."

Mahsoud followed her instructions and then took the device from his mouth and shut his eyes. He exhaled, coughed some more, and said, "Can you bring me your camera? I wish to see that bomb."

"You should sleep," Gold said.

"I cannot. Please, let me see the photographs."

"Major Parson has my camera."

"Well, if he cannot transmit the photographs, he does not need it."

Gold had never heard Mahsoud speak rudely before. His tone stung that much more because it came from someone so unfailingly polite. He really wants to see those pictures, she thought. All right, he's earned it.

"I'll be right back," Gold said.

She climbed to the flight deck, retrieved her camera and headset, and turned on the camera for Mahsoud. As she handed him the camera, he said in English, "I am sorry I snapped at you, teacher. Please forgive me." A tear slid down his cheek. "I am so afraid," he said.

His expression of fear surprised her. He'd wanted to be a bomb technician; he'd have faced this threat all the time. But then, Gold realized, he'd have been in a position to take action. Here, he could only wait, with dread worming its way into his psyche. Perhaps looking at the photos would give him something to do, a way to take part.

When he looked at the first photo, he stared at it for a full minute. Then he advanced the camera, examined the next shot.

"Sergeant Major," he said, "please use your headphones and call the cockpit."

"What is it, Mahsoud?"

"I do not have the words in English. But I need to talk to Major Parson."

16

The airplane did not want to stay trimmed. Parson was flying it now, and he kept pulling back on the yoke to prevent it from descending. But when he used his thumb switch to put in the slightest degree of nose-up trim, the jet tried to climb. The old girl's bent, he thought. We know we exceeded our g-limits in those storms. And the plane probably had a history of rough landings from Saigon to Baghdad.

He gave up and engaged the autopilot. The autopilot servos and the flight augmentation computers made their constant minute corrections, finer than those of any human hand, and the aircraft held its altitude as if on rails.

Parson hardly counted himself a philosopher. But he marveled that man could do something as ingenious as digging minerals out of the ground and fashioning them into a flying machine or as base as constantly finding reasons to kill one another. Our fallen nature, Gold might call it. Parson knew only that it happened, it sucked, and you had to be ready for it. And here we are, he thought, on the receiving end at thirty-four thousand feet.

Out the cockpit windows, he could discern the horizon easily despite the darkness. The stars ended along a distinct line. Beneath that line, an ocean black as oil. Parson tried to mull over his options.

They seemed to diminish as weather and long hours in the air took their toll on the plane.

The hours were taking their toll on Parson, too. His eyes grew so tired the numbers blurred on the dials of his instruments. Just as he most needed good judgment and quick reaction time, fatigue sapped his mind and muscles. He wondered if he—or any pilot—could get crew and passengers through this alive.

Gold's voice came over the interphone. "Major Parson?" she called.

He reached for his TALK switch and said, "I'm here. What's up?"

"I'm downstairs with Mahsoud. He's looking at the photos you took and says he has something to tell you."

"Does he know what he's looking at?" Parson asked.

"Maybe. He wanted to be an EOD guy before he got hurt. He's read everything on the subject he could find in Pashto."

"That can't be much," Colman said.

"Shh," Parson hissed. "Let her talk."

"He says his English isn't good enough for technical stuff, so I'll interpret for him."

"Shoot."

"Okay. Stand by."

Several seconds passed. Then Gold pressed her TALK button without saying anything for a moment. Parson heard only the background noise of the cargo compartment. She seemed to be gathering her thoughts.

"All right," she said finally. "He's saying something about a switch of liquid metal."

"That doesn't make a lot of sense," Parson said.

"I know it. I'm sorry, sir. I'll see what else he says."

"Maybe he's just delirious from his pain meds."

"No, he's not," Dunne said. "He's talking about a mercury switch."

"A what?" Parson asked.

"A mercury tilt switch. It triggers when you move it because mercury conducts electricity. If you have a car alarm, you probably have one on your trunk lid. Somebody opens the trunk, the alarm goes off."

"So if somebody moves the bomb," Parson said, "the son of a bitch explodes."

"Yeah," Dunne said.

"So we're fucked," Colman said. "We can't even touch it."

Parson stared outside. The meteor shower seemed to have played out for tonight.

"Bring me that camera," Parson said. "I remember noticing something on top of that duffel bag. And tell your friend I owe him a case of beer if we get through this."

"I don't think he drinks, sir."

"Oh, yeah. Sorry."

"I'll be right up."

When Gold brought the camera back to the flight deck, she had it set to the first photo. Despite the washed-out glare from the flash, Parson could see some type of sensor taped by its wires to the outside of the duffel bag. It showed up better in the next shot. Whatever it was, it looked pretty simple. Just a black rectangle about the size of a cigarette lighter, with two wires leading from it. Presumably, those wires led to a battery and more circuitry for an ignition source. He had not thought much about it when he'd taken the pictures, given the cold and the depleting oxygen.

"So tell me about these mercury switches," Parson said to Dunne. "How much tilt does it take to set one off?"

"Depends on how it's configured," the flight engineer said. "A lot of them are set to ten or twelve degrees. And then it's a question of how many degrees from what starting point."

A chill ran through Parson's core. He looked at the pitch reference scale on his attitude indicator, with a line at every five degrees. It would have been an unusual maneuver for him to pitch up twelve degrees, but certainly nothing outrageous. And he'd been banking up to thirty degrees. He supposed the only reason that hadn't set off the bomb was because he, Colman, and the autopilot had made well-coordinated turns with just enough load factor to keep the mercury from shifting inside the switch. All the while, he'd held his own destruction by his fingertips.

And the storm was another matter. Every jolt might have brought them within a degree or two of annihilation. But for whatever reason, the mercury never bridged its contacts.

"May I see that?" Colman asked. Parson placed the camera on the center console, and Colman picked it up. "What are you thinking? If we disconnect that switch, the bomb won't go off?"

"No," Parson said. "I'm thinking if we get rid of that switch, we might be able to move the damned thing. It'll still go off when we get below a certain altitude."

"So what's your plan?"

"I'm working on it."

Parson thought he sensed some hope in Colman's voice, more than he felt himself. So they'd identified one mercury switch. What if the bomb had other antitamper devices? Whoever built it knew enough to keep it from exploding due to normal flight maneuvers and even turbulence. The bomb maker apparently wanted detonation only on descent—or if someone actually picked up the device. The bastard had talent. When it came to terrorists, Parson worried more about their competence than their fanaticism.

So what *is* my plan? Parson wondered. Everybody on this jet expects the aircraft commander to fix this, he thought. To fix anything. A burden of responsibility with infinite density, like the inside of a black hole. Something that admitted of no excuses, no alternatives, no delays, no second chances, no way out. Nothing but to face the problem and deal with the consequences.

At least now he had a little more information. Maybe the EOD people on the ground could give him some specifics. He turned his comm switch to HFI.

"Hilda," he called. "Air Evac Eight-Four."

Nothing came back but static. He tried again and still got nothing.

"I bet the antenna for that radio is at the bottom of the Atlantic," Dunne said.

Parson switched to HF2. He got the same result.

"I hope to hell we haven't lost both HF radios," he said. "We'll be deaf and dumb until we're close enough to land for the VHFs to work."

"I'll check the circuit breakers," Dunne said. Parson knew he was just going through the motions. Since the lightning strike and electrical fire, Dunne had been checking the breakers constantly. Parson decided to try a different frequency, using a call sign for any global Air Force station.

"Mainsail, Mainsail," he said. "Air Evac Eight-Four."

No answer.

"Mainsail," Parson repeated. "Air Evac Eight-Four. Emergency aircraft."

A woman's voice came back, barely audible through the hiss: "Air Evac Eight-Four, Yokota. Go ahead."

That wasn't the answer Parson expected, but if nobody heard him except an air base in Japan, he'd talk to Japan. The radio operator sounded like a fourth grader. Parson didn't care if he'd reached a teenage two-striper or a four-star general; he just wanted a phone patch.

"Good to hear you, Yokota," he said. "Air Evac Eight-Four would like a patch to a DSN line at Scott Air Force Base."

"Yokota's ready to copy the number, sir."

Parson read her the phone number. While he waited for the call to go through, he said over interphone, "They can't hear me at Lajes, but we get an answer from the Far East?" It was a rhetorical question. Shortwave radio could work strangely, with its signals bouncing off the ionosphere. And it probably got even weirder if you were working with half an antenna.

When the radio operator spoke again, it sounded as if her voice were warbling through waves of interference, like a Cold War propaganda broadcast punched through a jamming signal. "Air Evac Eight-Four," she said, "the Tanker Airlift Control Center is on the line."

Parson identified himself and asked the flight manager to put ordnance disposal on the phone. A senior master sergeant picked up.

"Please tell me you know something about bombs," Parson said.

"I'm a bomb tech instructor. But I can barely hear you, sir."

"Yeah, we just came through a hailstorm and we also got hit by lightning."

"You're weak but readable," the sergeant said. "How can I help you, sir?"

"We took some photos of the bomb in our tail section. We wanted to send them to you, but the lightning strike knocked out our satcom."

"I'm sorry to hear that. It would help if I could see what we're talking about."

"What we think we have is a mercury switch on an antitamper circuit. We're thinking about cutting the wire to that switch so we can jettison the bomb."

"How did you determine all that?"

"We have a passenger who knows a little bit, but he's not EOD." Parson described the black rectangle and the two wires. Static hissed and roiled as Parson gave the bomb tech time to think.

"You say the bomb is in your tail section?"

"Affirmative."

"Do you have a door nearby where you can pitch it out?"

This guy was thinking of a much smaller aircraft. But a bomb tech would have no reason to know the architecture of a C-5 Galaxy. Parson explained how he'd need to carry the bomb down a ladder, through the tail cone, into the troop compartment, then down another ladder to throw it out a paratroop door. He'd considered jettisoning it through hatches in the troop compartment, but from there it could impact the elevators or rudder.

"Sir," the bomb tech said, "the problem is we don't know if there are other antitamper measures you can't see."

"We've wondered about that, too."

"I don't like the idea of you toting that thing all over the airplane."

"Do we have a choice?"

Another pause, unbroken static. Dunne spoke up on interphone. "What about the stabilizer access hatch?" he said.

"You can't open that from the inside, can you?" Parson asked.

"You can if you drill out the bolts," Dunne said. "It's right by the tail ladder. If we can kick that thing open, all you have to do is pick up the bomb and drop it."

"Do we have a drill?"

"In the crew chief's toolbox."

"Sergeant Dunne," Parson said, "you might be the first guy I know to get a medal for destruction of government property." Then he pressed his TRANSMIT switch and said, "I think we have a plan."

STILL AT MAHSOUD'S SIDE IN THE CARGO COMPARTMENT, Gold listened to Parson's radio calls. She wasn't sure she'd heard right, but it seemed that from over the middle of the Atlantic he'd reached a radio facility in the Pacific, which transferred him to a telephone in Illinois. Some Army troops considered the Air Force a technogeek's alternative to military service, but zoomies could communicate; you had to give them that.

Through her headset, she followed the conversation until Parson signed off. "They talked to a bomb technician," she told Mahsoud. "He believes you are right about your switch of liquid metal."

Mahsoud nodded, and said in English, "I am very happy that I could help." He spoke methodically. Gold noted that he never used broken English. He either said it right or switched to Pashto.

"So am I, my friend," Gold said.

She did not know how much relief she should feel, certainly not how much to convey to Mahsoud and the others. Parson sounded encouraged, but he clearly had no guarantee this would work. Like a platoon commander in the middle of a firefight, he had to make decisions without complete information. And he'd have to live with the results of those decisions for the rest of his life, whether that was forty seconds or forty years.

At least they still had some chance, however small. To Gold, their lives were like guttering flames of candles not yet extinguished.

She kept her headset on, expecting instructions from Parson.

He'd likely carry out his plan right away; she knew he tended toward action, perhaps to a fault. So it surprised her when he announced he'd hold off for a few hours.

"Why's that?" Colman asked.

"Because that thing might go off," Parson said. "If it does, it'll probably just take us down. But what if you still have some control? I'd like to be closer to Johnston Island if that happens."

"I see," Colman said. He seemed nervous, and Gold understood why. Parson was describing a scenario unfolding after his own death. With Colman a brand-new lieutenant, left in command of a crippled jet. So Parson intended to move the bomb himself, and he didn't necessarily expect to survive it.

In the meantime, other matters needed attention. Gold had promised Fawad she'd help him walk around, and he looked restless. She checked with the MCD, who gave her blessing. The aeromeds thought it would do him good. The air was smooth now, so it seemed fairly safe for patients to get up. Gold offered her hand to Fawad, and he pulled himself to a sitting position.

"How is your eye?" she asked in Pashto.

"Still painful," he said.

"It is fortunate you were not inside the building."

He swung his legs over the litter and placed his feet on the floor. Instead of his usual combat boots, he wore white socks with sandals. Fawad took a few shuffling steps, leaning on Gold. The eye wound was his only injury; Gold supposed his legs had fallen asleep. They walked aft down the cargo compartment.

"This airplane is so big one can go for a stroll," Gold said.

Fawad did not respond to her attempt to make conversation. But then he said, "Is it true that the pilot has a plan to save us?"

"It is. He may or may not succeed, but he will most surely try."

"The will of Allah shall be done."

"Certainly."

At the back of the cargo compartment, they came to the troop compartment ladder. "May we go up there?" Fawad asked.

"Can you manage the steps?"

"I can."

"Then be careful. I will be right behind you."

Fawad climbed the ladder a rung at a time. At the top, he stepped into the troop compartment near the galley and the negative pressure valves. It was empty now, with all the patients and aeromeds downstairs.

"The bomb is here?" Fawad asked.

Gold pointed to the pressure valves. "There," she said, "in the tail. Do not think of it."

Fawad looked around, walked down the aisle of the troop section. When he came to the two restrooms, he asked, "Is this a lavatory?"

"Yes," Gold said. The odor of blue lav fluid hung in the air; it had evidently sloshed out of the toilets during the storm. Despite the smell, Gold thought how the airplane probably had more luxurious facilities than any home Fawad had ever known. He opened the door to one of the lavs, entered, and locked it behind him.

Gold heard him urinate for several seconds. Then he washed his hands. After a minute or so, he recited, *There is no god but God, and Muḥammad is His Messenger.* Not in Pashto but in Arabic. Gold thought it was probably all the Arabic he knew.

He opened the door and stepped out. They went back down the aisle toward the ladder, and Fawad paused to peer out the window of the service door. He said nothing, and then he began descending the ladder.

As Gold followed him down, she looked forward across the cargo compartment. From above, she could see all the wounded, with the medics and nurses. She considered what might remain of everyone on board. Some had spouses and children who would be left behind—perhaps dozens of personal tragedies. Those without families would be forgotten more quickly. Their names would be listed on a memorial somewhere, unrecognized. Footnotes in history. Numbers and ranks in Pentagon records stored on disks that would eventually become obsolete and unreadable.

Fawad reached the bottom of the ladder and returned to his litter, but he did not lie down. "It is comfortable to walk," he said. "May I see the cockpit, too?"

If he felt like more exercise, Gold thought, maybe that would improve his mood. Then he'd be less likely to bring everybody else down. She called Parson on interphone, and he said they could come on up.

When they reached the flight deck, Fawad looked in apparent wonder at the hundreds of switches and gauges. A dim yellow glow backlit all the instrumentation. Though Gold knew most of the technology was forty years old, she supposed Fawad was astounded.

"You Americans and your machines," he said.

Dunne looked up when he heard the words in Pashto and he waved a greeting. "Is this Mahsoud?" he asked.

"No," Gold said. "His name is Fawad. He's a new police officer. Not from my class, though."

Fawad looked closely at Dunne's panel, as if he were trying to read the instruments. Then he looked up at the pilots' panels. Gold hoped it was taking his mind off his pain and his situation. It was good of Parson to let him visit like this.

"Would you like tea?" Gold asked him.

"No, thank you," Fawad said. Then he changed his mind. "Actually, yes."

Gold went aft to the galley. As she poured water, she heard commotion, and turned.

Fawad had fallen onto the pilots' center console. What was wrong? Could it be a seizure? She ran forward.

But it wasn't a seizure.

"What the fuck?" Colman shouted.

Fawad was clawing at the switches around him. He seemed to be trying to hit all of them.

Parson wasted no time: he pulled his heavy flashlight from his helmet bag, and he swung hard. But the angle was wrong. The blow glanced across Fawad's shoulder.

Fawad raised himself and yanked at the throttles, then he grabbed two of the four plastic T-handles on the center panel in front of him and pulled them.

Parson twisted in his seat and swung the flashlight again. This time he hit Fawad in the head. The Afghan screamed and lunged at Parson.

Dunne pulled his Beretta from underneath his flight suit. He grabbed Fawad by the hair, pressed the pistol against his temple, and pulled the trigger. The shot's report slammed through the confined space of the cockpit. Gold felt it more than heard it.

Blood and brains spattered into Parson's face and against the windscreen. The spent casing ricocheted off the instrument panel, bounced against the throttles, and spun across the floor. Fawad slumped over the center console. As his nervous system shut down, his left leg kicked as if he were trying to expel a rock from his shoe.

"That motherfucker killed the inboard engines!" Colman said.

Horror overcame Gold in waves. It had an almost physical force, a noxious liquid poisoning and drowning her at once. She could not process the scene before her. Emotion blocked reason; this simply could not happen.

But as she heard Parson issue commands and watched the crew push levers and flip switches, what logic she had left registered two facts: The airplane was in a rapid descent. And it was her fault.

17

With the engine noise quieter by half, Parson wiped blood from his eyes and jammed in the two inboard fire handles. "Airstart checklist on two and three," he ordered. "Now!"

Parson knew everyone would have to do everything right to keep the airplane out of the water, even without the bomb.

He looked at the throttles. Colman had already pushed the outboard engines up to max continuous power. But that was not nearly enough to stop the descent. With the current fuel load, the airplane was too heavy to fly on two engines.

Parson felt his own pulse throbbing in his temples like a pump. The star line that marked the horizon rose higher in front of him. He could not see the ocean below, but he felt it coming toward him.

To set up for a restart, Parson shoved the inboard throttles to the START position. That's when he noticed the EXTEND light for the number two thrust reverser. The terrorist son of a bitch had yanked that throttle back far enough to deploy the reverser and the damned thing was stuck. No wonder the plane was losing altitude at six thousand feet per minute. Because that bearded jihadi bastard invaded my cockpit, Parson thought. *My* place.

The aircraft dropped through thirty thousand

feet as Parson punched the number three START button. He held its ignition switch to AIRSTART.

"Come on, baby," he said, "light off."

He heard clicks and snaps behind him as Dunne's hands played across the flight engineer's panel. Colman pitched the aircraft for two hundred and fifty knots to get the best glide angle. But the jet was still descending way too fast.

The altimeter scrolled past twenty-five thousand feet. The tone of the slipstream changed from its usual rumble of high-speed cruise. Now it seemed to whisper threats, like the murmur of a tide race drawing sailors to grief.

With his free hand, Parson grasped the emergency RETRACT switch for the stuck thrust reverser. Please, God, let this work, he thought. He held the spring-loaded switch in the RETRACT position as the jet neared twenty thousand feet. Until the reverser retracted, he could not even attempt to restart number two. Meanwhile, he scanned the instruments and saw fuel flow indicated on number three, but no sign of that engine spooling up.

"What's wrong with number three?" he asked.

"I'm checking," Dunne said. "Pull out the button before you burn up the starter."

Parson took the START button by his thumb and forefinger and pulled until the holding relay let go. The starter had to cool down for thirty seconds before he could try again. A loss of another three thousand feet.

The number two EXTEND light winked out. The thrust reverser had finally retracted. Parson released the RETRACT switch and pressed the starter for number two. The tendons in his arm tensed into cords.

"What's the word on number three?" he asked.

"Ignition control breaker popped," Dunne said. "That lightning strike fucked us good." Dunne reached to his right and whacked the circuit breaker with the heel of his hand. "Reset," he said.

The airplane descended through fifteen thousand feet.

The number two engine started.

"Got ignition on two," Dunne said. "Stable indications."

Colman advanced the number two throttle. With that engine running now, the descent slowed to one thousand feet per minute. The aircraft was still dropping toward the bomb's trip point, only not quite as quickly.

Parson braced for the explosion. Pressed the starter on three. The engine's turbine temp and rpm began rising.

"Ignition on three," Dunne said. Now all the engines were running.

The plane leveled at twelve thousand feet. Parson took a breath deep enough to fill his lungs. "All right, damn it," he said, "we need to climb. Right now."

Dunne pressed a paddle switch, which moved a marker across the N1 rpm gauges. "I got climb thrust on the bar," he said.

Colman pushed up the throttles. As more fuel flowed into the combustion chambers, the engines answered with a glissando from bass to tenor. The rpm tapes rose until they touched the bar set by Dunne. The vertical speed indicators and altimeters registered an ascent.

"Watch your deck angle," Parson said. "Remember that mercury switch."

"Got it," Colman said. The ADI showed a five-degree pitch.

"No more than that," Parson said.

"Yes, sir."

Parson looked down at the corpse. Fawad's torso was sprawled across the center console, knees on the floor as if prostrate in devotion. Blood had begun to congeal across the autopilot panel. A spongy lump of tissue clung to the test switch for the emergency locater transmitter. Parson grabbed a fistful of Fawad's hair and raised the head off the console. Fluid drooled from the mouth and dripped onto the test panel for the cockpit voice recorder. Parson shoved the head onto the floor.

"Somebody get this piece of shit out of my sight," he said.

"Major Parson," the MCD called on interphone, "are we okay?"

Parson held his tongue for a moment. "We are now," he said. "That patient who came up here tried to kill us."

"We heard the shot. What can we do for you?"

You can keep those bastards tied down, that's what you can do, he thought. What the hell were you and Gold thinking? Then he said, "Ma'am, just send someone up here to move the body."

"Roger that."

The odor of gunshot still hung in the air, pistol smoke drifting in the confines of the cockpit. The altitude alerter chimed to tell the crew they were nearing their selected flight level of thirty-four thousand feet. After the rapid descent and slow climb, Parson thought how their flight path would have looked like some bizarre sine wave. If this were a simulator, the instructor might call up the profile view on his screen and point out the nadir and zenith, note how much altitude they'd lost. But the software to replicate this little piece of hell probably didn't exist.

The flight deck door rattled open, and the MCD herself appeared. She took Fawad's body by the arms and pulled him out of the cockpit. The head bounced against the jump seat pedestal and for a moment the open eyes seemed to examine a chart Parson had dropped to the floor.

Gold came forward and helped the MCD drag the corpse to the courier compartment with the other bodies. She did not speak or make eye contact with anyone. Fawad's remains left smears of blood down the aisleway.

When Gold came back from the darkness of the courier compartment, she entered a bunk room just aft of the cockpit. She slid the door shut. Good, Parson thought. Stay in there. But as his heart rate slowed down and his adrenaline ebbed, he realized he had no right to be angry with her. He shouldn't have allowed access to the cockpit. It was his fault, too.

Parson tried to imagine what she was feeling. Probably the worst betrayal she'd ever experienced. Overdoses of guilt. He decided just to leave her alone. I'd want to be left alone, he thought. He didn't count empathy among his strengths. Anything he said would just make it worse.

Nearly an hour went by, and Gold never left the bunk room.

Hell with it, he thought. After all she did for me, I need to at least try, even if I screw it up. In a few hours, we'll all probably be dead, anyway. Doesn't matter if I screw it up.

"You gonna be all right by yourself for a few minutes?" he asked Colman.

"Sure."

"Your airplane, your radios."

Parson took off his headset, climbed out of his seat, and went to the bunk room door. When he slid it open, he saw only blackness. He felt for a reading lamp button and pressed it. The pale light revealed Gold sitting on a lower bunk, arms around her knees, head down. Blond hair loose across her shoulders.

He shut the door and sat beside her. She did not look up. Parson placed his hand on her back. Then he pulled her close, not the way he'd usually embrace a woman but the way he might comfort a grieving relative. Even this was out of order. I'm on thin ice here, he thought. Her hair gave off the scents of conditioner and sweat.

For just a second, Gold let her head rest on his shoulder. Then she sat up and said, "Sir, I'm so sorry. I almost got everyone killed." Parson wanted to tell her to stop saying "sir," but he checked himself. She probably took solace in professionalism.

"It's no more your fault than mine," he said. "I let him on the flight deck."

"You did that because you trusted my judgment."

Parson considered for a moment. Then he said, "I still do, Sophia." Immediately he wondered if he should have called her that. He hoped she realized he used her name for emphasis, not condescension.

"I should have seen the signs."

"You're not a mind reader. You're a soldier. The best one I know. The best one anybody knows."

Gold stared at the floor. Parson reached over her and turned on a dome light. Brighter in the bunk room now. Not for the first time, they both had the blood of a terrorist on their uniforms.

"I'm going to retire," Gold said. "I'll go to personnel and submit my paperwork. I want to go home to Vermont. I'll plant a garden and substitute-teach, and I'll live in that valley for the rest of my life."

"No, you won't," Parson said. Then he realized that didn't come out right and he added, "You're going to stay in the service and do what you do because we need you. The politicians, the suits who send us out here, they're all just fucking political game show contestants. They're all alike, and they come and go. They think they run the world but they don't. The people who really make a difference are the ones like you."

Gold shook her head, gave a weak smile. She stood as if it hurt to move. She straightened her sleeves, buttoned a pocket. Parson noticed the airborne tab, the jump wings, the stack of chevrons. He knew of no rules for this kind of a relationship with a woman—as strong a bond as he'd ever felt with anyone—but she'd always been strictly a colleague. If they managed to live through this, would he want that to change? Or would that just ruin it?

"Thank you for your thoughts, sir," she said. "You won't see me behave this way again."

"Don't worry about it. You've seen worse from me."

Parson hoped she'd say, *Yeah, I have*, or something like that to take a good-natured shot at him. But she just looked at him with what seemed like gratitude.

"I'm going back downstairs," Gold said. "I better check on Mahsoud and the others."

"Take your headset," Parson said as she stepped into the aisleway. "You're part of this crew."

She lifted her headset from the nav table and disappeared down the ladder.

GOLD FELT EVERYONE'S EYES ON HER as she made her way down the steps. By now they must all know what happened. She couldn't tell whether those expressions meant reproach, relief, or something else. She decided it didn't matter.

When she went to Mahsoud, he asked in Pashto, "Is Fawad dead?"

Gold nodded. "I had no idea he was some kind of jihadist," she said. For a moment, she closed her eyes and leaned on a litter stanchion. The combination of fatigue and adrenaline left her exhausted but unable to rest.

"That was not jihad. That was attempted murder. Jihad happens here." Mahsoud placed his good hand over his heart. "It is the holy war against one's own evil impulses. Fawad failed utterly in his jihad."

"He nearly succeeded in killing us, though."

"And yet, here we are."

Gold looked past Mahsoud, out his window into the darkness. "Charlie Mike," she said in English. Not so much to Mahsoud as to herself.

"What is this phrase?"

"Sorry," she said. "It is an expression in my Army. The phonetic for 'continue mission.'"

"Indeed."

The last time she'd heard that phrase was in Jalalabad. She'd accompanied a colonel who needed her to translate as he spoke to new police recruits. As the recruits lined up to sign their papers, one among them produced a Makarov pistol and began firing. He shot six recruits before a German NATO troop killed him with rifle fire. Four of the recruits died. During the helicopter ride back to Kabul, the colonel's only words were "Charlie Mike."

Gold sat on the catwalk that ran along the cargo compartment wall. She thought about lying on the floor and trying to sleep, but she noticed the aeromeds seemed to be in a huddle, looking around. The MCD was talking on headset to the flight deck. Gold found an unused interphone cord and plugged in her own headset. She heard Parson's voice first.

"What do you mean, you're missing somebody?" he asked.

"One of my medics," the MCD said. "Justin Baker. I thought he went to the restroom, but he's been gone for almost an hour."

"All right, we'll check the lav and the bunk rooms up here. I didn't see anybody come up, though."

"We'll search down here."

Gold wondered if the medic might have passed out somewhere. Easy to imagine, given the changes in cabin altitude, along with extreme stress and maybe dehydration. But you'd think a medic would see the symptoms in his own body before it got that far. She unplugged from the interphone cord to help look for him. Part of her wanted just to rest and let the others deal with it, but it seemed wrong not to help.

The aeromeds looked under the litters, behind crates of equipment. The MCD spoke into her headset mike, then announced, "Well, the crew says he's not anywhere on the flight deck."

"I'll check the troop section," Gold said.

She climbed the ladder to the troop compartment. The compartment appeared empty. She kneeled and peered under the seats, saw no one. Gold walked the aisle and knocked at the lavatory door, the same lav where Fawad had performed his final ablutions. No answer. She knocked again.

"Leave me alone," a voice called from inside.

"Are you all right?" Gold asked.

"Yes. Can I get a little privacy?"

"This is Sergeant Major Gold. Is that any way to address an E-9?"

Gold had never thrown her rank around, and she didn't plan to start now. She just wanted to get the guy to talk. If he were just airsick, he'd have said so. Everybody on board was probably near an emotional breaking point, especially someone hiding in a lav.

"We're all about to become E-nothings, so what does it matter?"

"Your friends are worried about you."

"Ma'am, just tell them to leave me alone."

"Why don't you come out here and talk to me?"

The sliding lock on the lav door snicked into place. The indicator flipped from VACANT to OCCUPIED.

Now Gold began to worry. Was he about to inject himself with a morphine overdose? Had dread and fear overcome hope and reason?

"I really want you to come out and talk to me," Gold said. "I'm scared, too. Maybe we can help each other."

No response.

"Airman," Gold said, "don't make me kick down this door."

"Leave me alone. You're not even in my chain of command."

That didn't matter to Gold, especially if the guy was about to kill himself. She stepped back from the lav door and braced herself against a troop seat. Then she raised her right leg and slammed her boot heel against the door. She struck where the slide engaged its latch, and the wood splintered around the lock assembly. After two more blows, she was able to pull open the broken door. She found the man sitting on the floor of the lav.

Gold recognized Airman Baker as the medic who'd been working with Mahsoud early in the flight. Everybody called him Justin.

She looked to see if he had a weapon or a needle. To her relief, she saw nothing in his hands. The next thing she noticed was his youth. With his smooth cheeks, he appeared more like a schoolboy than a serviceman. Until he looked at her. His reddened eyes were those of someone much older. It reminded Gold of young Afghans she'd met, teenagers who'd witnessed things most Western adults would never face. A lot of Afghans started to look old before they were thirty, and the accelerated aging always started with the eyes. It was as if a soul could advance in years well out of sync with the body it inhabited.

"Airman Baker," Gold said, "are you okay?"

"Um, yeah. I mean, yes, ma'am. I just came up here to use the lav, and I guess I fell asleep."

"Funny place to fall asleep, Justin."

He didn't answer for a moment. Gold noticed the EVACISTAN patch on his flight suit. It bore a red cross. Superimposed over the cross was a map of Afghanistan and Pakistan, along with the letters OEF, for Operation Enduring Freedom. The embroidery along the patch's edge bore a rust-colored stain. Gold wondered if it was the grime of a military airplane or dried blood that wouldn't wash out.

"I'm just not—" Justin paused. "I'm just not doing any good down there. Our patients are dying. We don't have the things they need. And we can't even land to get them help."

Gold had witnessed people breaking from stress before. At one of the forward operating bases, she knew a soldier who'd spent a day and a night beside a dead buddy, pinned down by Taliban fire. The trooper seemed all right at first, but later in the same week he lost his hold on reality. One morning he woke and picked up a squad automatic weapon, pointed it at his comrades. He could no longer tell whether he was among friends or enemies. He tried to fire but a round wasn't chambered. His buddies piled on him and took him down, and he was sent home.

Justin didn't seem that far gone, but the strain was clearly getting to him. Perhaps it was all too much for someone probably just a couple years out of high school.

"We're working the problem," Gold said. "The aircraft commander has a plan." Sort of. She decided not to go into detail.

"So is he some kind of bomb expert? I heard that stuff on the radio. Every plane they put a bomb on got blown up when it tried to land."

"We're not dead yet, Justin. And you know your patients need you."

He appeared to think for a moment. Maybe he's listening to me, Gold thought.

"I don't think I'm helping them very much," Justin said.

"Of course you are."

"Let me tell you about the last time I did this."

Justin described a mission he'd flown only three days before. He and the rest of his aeromed crew got alerted after an unarmored Humvee carrying four soldiers hit an IED. Two died instantly. One lost both legs. The other lost a leg and an arm. The two survivors also suffered third-degree burns over most of their bodies, including disfiguring ones on the face.

At the Bagram MASF, the staging facility for wounded, the doctors had to perform escharatomies: They sliced into the leathery burns to relieve pressure on what living tissue remained. At every touch of the scalpel, the charred, swollen flesh split open like a watermelon.

During the flight to Germany, the soldiers' pain was uncontrollable. Morphine didn't seem to touch it. One moaned for hours; the other made no sound but could not stop trembling. The patient who'd lost his legs died en route. As far as Justin knew, the other one remained alive at Landstuhl, and Justin wasn't even sure that was a good thing.

"That's not all," Justin said. "I transported a guy younger than me with his jaw shot away. And you should see the kinds of injuries the CCAT teams bring through, the ones who have to travel sedated and intubated."

Gold thought she understood how he felt. Once you'd seen certain things, you could not make those images go away. They became part of your mind's home page, whether you liked it or not. There was no right-click to delete. As Justin finished his story, the rattle of boot steps sounded from the troop compartment ladder. The MCD appeared at the top of the steps.

"I found him, ma'am," Gold said. She hoped the MCD wouldn't berate him. Gold explained what Justin had just told her. The MCD took off her glasses, kept silent for a while.

"Son," she said finally, "I'd like to tell you it gets easier. But I won't lie to you."

Gold admired wisdom even more than she admired courage. The head nurse's words gave her just a moment of peace. Gold felt you could learn a lot about human nature from situations where one person had nearly complete power over another. Usually, what you learned wasn't good. Maybe this would be an exception.

"If you work in medicine," the MCD continued, "especially combat medicine, you're going to get your heart broken every week."

"I believe it," Justin said.

"You'd have to be inhuman for it not to hurt," the MCD said. "But somebody has to do what we do."

Justin drew his knees up to his chest and buried his face in his arms. Gold wondered if he would start weeping, but he was dry-eyed when he looked up again.

"I'm sorry," he said.

"Just remember it's never about us," the MCD said. "It's about your patients, and then it's about your team." She leaned into the lavatory and extended her hand. Justin took it, and she helped him to his feet. "We need your help down there, Airman," she said. "Let's get back to work."

18

The moon had reached its apogee, hanging high in the night and burning so brightly it hurt to look at it. Cobalt water heaved below. Parson felt as if the ocean were waiting to swallow his aircraft, as it had so many ships and planes. In the impenetrable darkness of depth, an unknown, uncharted international cemetery lay on the seafloor.

He checked his watch. More than twelve hours since takeoff, or was it sixteen and a half? He couldn't remember whether he was keeping track in GMT or Afghanistan time. Then he realized it had to be closer to sixteen and a half; Dunne had run out of columns on his fuel log and started another sheet. When you started getting tired, mental math was one of the first skills to go. And the hardest part of the flight lay ahead.

"You guys need to get some rest when you can," Parson said. Then he told Colman, "Why don't you snooze in the bunk room for a while? I'll take the plane, and we'll switch out later."

"I don't think I can sleep now, sir. You can nap first, if you'd like."

Might as well, Parson thought. The airplane seemed stable enough, and the radar showed no bad weather up ahead. Good a time as any for the newbie to take over. Parson was starting to feel more charitable toward Colman. Some ring knockers right out of the Academy seemed to think they knew better than anybody commissioned through ROTC, but this kid was listening.

"Get me up if anything happens," Parson said. He draped his headset over the tiller for the nosewheel steering, and he slid back his seat.

In the bunk room, he flipped a green toggle to supply oxygen to a regulator, and he took two whiffs from the mask to make sure it worked. Now he had a ready oxygen supply in case a rapid decompression occurred while he slept.

Parson stretched out on a bunk and closed his eyes. He did not expect to rest well, but he drifted off immediately. Sleep took him outdoors, to a wooded lakeshore. He cast a spinner lure with a bucktail and treble hook, and he gave it a quick retrieve. No fish struck, so he cast again and again, watching the ripples emanate from each splash. He had no obligations, nothing to do but enjoy a summer afternoon by the water, watching the ospreys glide. They could soar for so long without a single flap, with their high aspect ratio wings. He watched them for the rest of the day, admiring their precise management of kinetic energy. Always at the perfect pitch angle for max lift over drag. Something he had to study so hard existed purely as instinct in the primitive mind of a raptor. The sun went down and the night music began, the chirring of cicadas and the songs of tree frogs.

But as Parson returned from the depth of sleep and neared wakefulness, his mind recognized the sounds as only the rush of the slipstream and the hum of avionics.

He opened his eyes and checked his watch again. Its luminous hands and numerals glowed like phosphorus in a night ocean. Two hours of sleep. Not enough, but better than nothing. He picked up the mask and inhaled deeply from it. Maybe the pure oxygen would help stave off the effects of sleep deprivation and preserve some of his reaction time and mental function.

Parson returned to the pilot's seat and buckled the lap belt, donned his headset. His fingers fell naturally to the yoke and throttles, and he scanned instruments and switches more familiar than those of his car. A place of awful responsibilities, but where he belonged.

"I got it," he said to Colman. "Go to sleep."

"I'll try," Colman said. "Copilot's going off headset." He unbuckled, unplugged, and went aft.

The radar still showed no precipitation, but Parson worried about what lay between him and Johnston Island. Hurricane season had begun; that had become painfully clear. And there were thousands of miles of warm water ahead. Ordinarily for an ocean crossing, he'd have all kinds of weather information in his mission folder: severe weather outlook charts, constant pressure analysis charts, winds and temperatures aloft data, even satellite photos. This time he had only outdated forecasts for airports behind him, a dead satcom, and damaged radios.

At least the radar worked. In the worst case, he could dial it out to maximum range and pick his way around the edges of a big storm. But that would be dangerous, and a huge pain in the ass. He decided to try for some specifics.

"Mainsail, Mainsail," he called. "Air Evac Eight-Four."

No answer. He tried again and still got nothing. Maybe another frequency would work better. As he rolled the freq selector, he crossed a Voice of America channel. Parson stopped to listen to the broadcast:

The Pentagon confirms the loss of three U.S. Air Force planes to terrorist bombs, all apparently planted at Bagram Air Base, Afghanistan. A Defense Department spokesman says at least forty crew and passengers were killed. That number is expected to rise as details come in. The attacks have resulted in a worldwide grounding of coalition military aircraft until each plane can be searched.

One American transport aircraft remains aloft, and it has been directed to a remote island in the Pacific. Sources say the crew of that C-5 Galaxy has located a bomb on board. No word on any attempt to defuse it.

In other news, border tensions are escalating between Colombia and Venezuela. The Venezuelan president says . . .

Parson switched away from that frequency. Three aircraft lost. And it would probably be four before it all ended. How could this happen? He knew that a lot of TCNs, Third Country Nationals, worked at Bagram. They were vetted, sure. But if they'd never done anything wrong, there was nothing to find. Terrorists, at least the smart ones, were patient. They could tell their people to get the right kind of job and stay out of trouble for years. When the time is right, they'd say, we'll be in touch.

U.S. servicemen planned from deployment to deployment, Parson thought. American politicians planned from election to election. But this enemy thought in terms of the next several centuries. Letting a sleeper cell sleep for a few years meant nothing to them.

We used to call this the Long War, Parson recalled. We don't know from long.

He tried another freq: "Mainsail, Air Evac Eight-Four."

"Air Evac Eight-Four, Ascension Island. Go ahead."

Whatever, Parson thought. If that rock is where they can hear me, I'll talk to that rock.

"I'd like to get some weather data," he said. "My satcom is down, so you're going to have to read it to me." He explained his situation and where he was headed.

"Absolutely, sir," the radio operator said. "Anything we can do for you, just ask. I'll call you back when I have your weather."

He sounds like he's heard of me, Parson thought. Probably not much to do on shift there but watch CNN. Parson didn't mind waiting as long as the guy seemed helpful. At Ascension, they'd have local weather at their fingertips, but not the kind of information he needed. To get Caribbean and Pacific forecasts, they'd need to get on their computers and dig for it.

While Ascension gathered data, Parson dimmed his panel lighting and looked up at the stars. The Pleiades glowed above him. On land, light pollution often made that star cluster difficult to find, but here Parson had no trouble distinguishing it. Something permanent, always there whether you could see it or not.

Unlike us, Parson thought. He wondered what would be left of him and his crew and passengers when this was over. Not much, most likely. He remembered something he'd noticed during his last flight physical, just a couple months ago. His bulging folder of medical records bore a stamp on the manila binder: DNA COMPLETED. That meant somewhere in a Defense Department storage facility there was a card stained with his blood. The same file also contained his fingerprints and footprints. This medical data would do him no good in life but might help identify him after a particularly violent death.

Parson felt grateful when Ascension interrupted his gloomy train of thought. "We don't have a terminal forecast for Johnston anymore because the field is closed," the radio operator said, "but satellite photos indicate fair weather. Your problems are all en route."

Tell me about it, Parson thought.

"In the northeastern Caribbean, you have Tropical Storm Arlene," the radio operator continued. "Maximum sustained winds of sixty-eight miles per hour. We expect it to attain hurricane strength over the next eight hours."

Parson took notes as the operator gave coordinates for the storm's eye and its predicted track. "Is that it?" he asked.

"I'm afraid not, sir. On Montserrat, Soufrière Hills is erupting. You've got an ash cloud building and spreading east."

Son of a bitch, Parson thought. Fire and rain. He wrote down coordinates for the volcanic ash, and he pulled his pocket atlas from his helmet bag. Hardly the ideal nav chart, but it would do for the big picture. He swiveled his utility light over the atlas and found the pages for the Caribbean and South America. With a stubby pencil, he marked the rough positions of the storm and the ash. It looked like he had two choices: Divert south and shoot the gap between them. Or divert even farther south and avoid the whole mess. He'd wanted to fly a more northerly route, perhaps cross over the U.S., and have easier communications with people who could help. But the damned storm was moving northeast.

He tried to think logically, to force a sensible decision through the mental quicksand created by lack of sleep. No matter what he did, he'd need another refueling. And a lot of luck. Parson wondered whether good fortune came in finite supplies. If so, he must have used up his share long ago and gone deep into some cosmic debt.

He looked up again at the Pleiades. The seven sisters, daughters of Atlas. Transformed into stars to comfort their father, who was condemned to hold up the sky.

THE AIR IN THE CARGO COMPARTMENT felt oily and close. Gold wondered if any hydraulic mist remained or if the mere memory of it was making her uncomfortable. Tension fouled the air as well. Some of the aeromeds snapped at one another as they tended the wounded. Everybody was tired and frightened, and getting more so by the hour. A few glared at the Afghan patients with open malice.

Gold looked up at two of the aeromeds. They had their backs to her. One of them placed a fresh bag of IV solution over a patient's stretcher.

"We got only three more liters of this," he said.

"We ought to cap all these fuckers," the other medic added. "How do we know another one won't try to kill us?"

"Hell, yeah. Maybe not all Muslims are terrorists, but damned near all terrorists are Muslims."

"Watch what you say," Gold warned. "Some of the Afghans can understand you."

"I don't give a—" a medic said as he turned, and then he saw Gold's rank insignia. "Sorry, Sergeant Major."

Gold didn't think he was really sorry, but maybe he'd at least keep his mouth shut. She could understand how he felt, given what Fawad had done. And he was trying to do his job while trapped in the world's largest pipe bomb.

Still, Gold expected him to keep a professional bearing. Nobody was pulling out his fingernails.

The other medic looked at her with—what? Suspicion? They keep hearing me speak Pashto, Gold thought. They probably wonder whose side I'm on. All they know is that I talk in the strange language and I led Fawad to the flight deck.

She could do nothing about that now. And she began to feel that all she'd ever done amounted to nothing. Even if everyone survived this flight, what future would her Afghan students have? Perhaps a short one, hunted down by the Taliban. They might live defenseless under a Kabul government too weak and corrupt to protect itself, let alone its citizens.

Gold looked around at the Afghans. Baitullah lay on his litter, gripping the stanchions so hard his knuckles whitened. She went to his side and asked, "What is wrong, Baitullah?" Stares from the Americans.

"My feet hurt, teacher. It is insane, I know. I have no feet. But I pray to Allah to take away this pain."

"You are not insane, friend. Amputees can suffer phantom pain that is quite real. I will ask the nurses to help you."

She found the MCD and asked if Baitullah could have more morphine. The lieutenant colonel examined his chart, checked her watch, uncapped a needle, and filled the syringe.

"Tell him to give me his arm," the MCD said.

Gold spoke, and Baitullah lowered his right arm to his side. With his left, he still gripped the stanchion as if it were his only hold on life. The MCD wiped his right tricep with an alcohol prep pad and gave him the injection. Baitullah let go of the stanchion and closed his eyes.

"We don't have a lot of morphine left," the MCD said. She tossed the needle into a plastic container marked CAUTION—MEDICAL WASTE—SHARPS.

Baitullah's chest rose as he took a deep breath, and he smiled at Gold as he let it out. "Do you remember when you taught me to shoot?"

"I enjoyed that day," Gold said. Not entirely true. She'd enjoyed helping Baitullah, but what she'd seen had disgusted her. She had accompanied a group of police trainees to the rifle range just to provide translation for the American contractors paid to provide small-arms training. When they'd arrived at the range, they could not conduct training because all the ammunition had disappeared. Thirty cases of 7.62-millimeter ammo, a thousand rounds each, just gone. Sold on the black market, no doubt, and probably to insurgents.

The next day, a Black Hawk helicopter had thudded and beat onto the training site and off-loaded more ammo. Finally, the training could begin. An instructor of unknown qualifications, with the physique of a bag of doughnuts, asked her to have the students line up on the range. He passed out magazines, then told them to fire. Not a word about sight picture. Nothing about breath control, trigger squeeze, or follow-through. Just burn through the ammo and get it over with.

At a hundred yards downrange, the safest place to stand would have been in front of a bull's-eye. Most trainees placed few rounds on paper at all, let alone anywhere near the black circle. The instructor passed out more magazines and repeated the drill. No advice, just more bullets. Gold began to wonder if his company's contract measured success in rounds expended.

"Wudregah," she called. Stop. Then she said to the nearest recruit, Baitullah, *"Tupak. Daa maa tah raakrah."* Give me the rifle.

She did not consider herself an expert marksman, but anybody who'd completed Basic Training could give a better class than this lazy civilian. Baitullah hesitated; he probably resented having to surrender his weapon to a woman. But he handed it over.

Gold kneeled, aimed, and pressed the trigger. A puff of dust erupted below the target and to the right, then vanished in the breeze. The rifle wasn't even sighted in. She ordered all the targets moved up to the fifty-yard mark, and she explained how to aim for center and watch where the bullet went.

Then she talked the recruits through adjusting range with the rear sight and drift and elevation with the front post. She gave the rifle back to Baitullah and used him as an example. Round by round, tweaking the sights, he walked his bullets out of the dirt, onto the target, and left toward the center. When he'd shot a respectable group at fifty yards, she moved his target back out to a hundred. He put all of his rounds on paper, and a few within the black. Not exactly Olympic performance, but at least his AK was more dangerous to the enemy than to himself.

Only at the end of the day did Gold realize she'd nearly made an awful mistake. By taking Baitullah's rifle, she'd publicly emasculated him. It was one thing to take direction from her in a literacy class but quite another to defer to a woman about weaponry. But because he'd had the good sense to listen, he became his unit's top shooter, right then and there, and just as publicly. Maybe her very presence on the rifle range was so strange to him that he just went with it. The outcome could have been far worse. The more she thought about it, the more she respected Baitullah. And he seemed to respect her as well.

But look what he's come to, Gold thought. Even if the insurgents left him alone, how would a double amputee make a living in Afghanistan? Sit on a hillside with his Kalashnikov and protect somebody's goats from the wolves? That bomb in the tail section would probably make it all moot, anyway.

She admired the composure shown by Baitullah and Mahsoud. The men had zero control over their fate, and the situation required courage of an unusual alloy. In a firefight, you could at least see the enemy, and the battle normally lasted just minutes or even seconds.

Here, the enemy had already escaped after laying a minefield with no exit. The passing hours scraped like a grindstone at sanity and will.

19

The winds were costing Parson some groundspeed. The FMS screen showed them streaming from two hundred and forty degrees at ninety knots. Flying wasn't levitating from point A to point B; it was navigating a river of air, with all its currents and eddies.

And that tropical storm in the Caribbean was one big-ass eddy. Parson decided to give it the widest berth possible while running between the storm and the volcano. By his calculus, Arlene's turbulence posed more danger than the ash of Soufrière Hills. At this altitude, he hoped he'd remain above most of the volcano's ejecta. He felt like a mariner of ancient myth, beset by monsters and snares thrown in his way by spiteful gods. He just wondered what he'd done to piss them off.

Maybe he'd pissed them off simply by remaining alive at all. In the years since the shoot-down, Parson had been haunted by the loss of his crewmates. Why had he survived when they had not? God knows, he was no more deserving. The only way he could begin to justify his continued presence on this earth was to be a good officer and aviator. And he had no idea if he was good enough to handle all this.

Right now he needed to coordinate a course change. "Ascension Island," he called. "Air Evac Eight-Four for phone patch."

The response came in no form he could understand. Just pops and warbles in the static, nothing discernible as human speech. The Ascension radio operator was trying, but whatever shortwave alchemy had worked before wasn't working now.

"Mainsail," he called. "Air Evac Eight-Four."

Now the static came as pure white noise, no squelch break at all. Like radio astronomy, with signals traveling for parsecs and bouncing off nothing. The C-5 had been aloft now for about seventeen hours; Parson was so tired, he began to doubt his ability to carry out the simplest tasks. He double-checked the radio's frequency and settings. He called one more time and got the same result.

"Both the HFs out now?" Dunne asked.

"Maybe," Parson said.

He considered his problem. If he couldn't communicate, the danger rose exponentially, and it was already off the charts. Air Traffic Control needed to know his plans; the big sky theory didn't work anymore. There were just too many planes in the air, and when he crossed Central or South America, he'd run perpendicular to a lot of jet routes. Even here, he could see the blinking strobe of an airliner off his two o'clock. It appeared on his TCAS, too: a white diamond creeping across a black screen, millimeters at a time, representing an aircraft moving at eighty percent of the speed of sound.

That gave Parson an idea. The airlines had a common VHF frequency just for chatting. He'd heard the crews during long flights updating each other on football scores and contract negotiations. At one company or another, it seemed pilots, flight attendants, or machinists were always on the verge of a strike. Most conversations on that channel Parson found insufferable. But perhaps now the frequency could do him some good. He entered it into his CDU and switched his comm selector to VHFI.

"Any aircraft, any aircraft," he called. "Air Evac Eight-Four."

The answer came immediately and loud and clear. Someone close by, perhaps even the aircraft he'd seen: "Air Evac Eight-Four, Delta Two-One-Eight. Go ahead." Drawl of the Deep South, perhaps one of Delta's old-line captains.

"Good to hear your voice, Delta," Parson said. "We took some hail damage a while back, and we're just about NORDO on high-frequency. Can you relay some information for us?"

"Be glad to, sir. We're talking to oceanic, and we got data link back to company in Atlanta."

Parson explained who he was and where he was going, including coordinates and waypoints for his course between the storm and the volcano. When he finished, the silence ran so long he wondered if he'd lost VHF, too. Finally, the airliner called back.

"Air Evac," the pilot said. "ATC clears you as requested. They want you to squawk four-three-eight-six. Also, our company weather boys are going to get you some data from the Volcanic Ash Advisory Center."

"Copy that," Parson said. "Thanks much." He entered 4-3-8-6 in his CDU scratchpad, then inserted the code by pressing the IFF button. As soon as he came within range of air traffic surveillance radar, that code would identify him.

He pressed his TALK switch again and asked, "Delta, did you have to divert when we went off the airway to find our tanker?"

"Negative. But a lot of traffic did. ATC's still sorting it out. What else can we do for you, son?"

You don't know how old I am, Parson thought. But he knew the guy meant to be sympathetic and not patronizing. "Can you call the Tanker Airlift Control Center for us and tell them we'll need another refueling?" Parson asked.

"Consider it done," the Delta pilot said. "What airframe you flying?"

"A Charlie-Five."

Another pause. Then the captain said, "I flew 141s in Desert Storm."

Parson wondered if the Delta pilot had known his father. Entirely possible. But this was no time for a social call. Before Parson could respond, the man keyed his mike again.

"All right," he said, "we got some weather information for you.

Along your route, all the heavy ash concentration lies below flight level two-five-zero. You're gonna have light to moderate concentrations at thirty-four thousand feet, so you might think about climbing if you can."

"We copy all," Parson said. "Thanks again."

No response came for several seconds, and Parson thought the conversation had ended. But then the captain said, "Those military transports can take more damage than you think. One night a storm kicked my ass all over the Arabian Sea, and I landed at Dubai with three feet of wingtip missing. Son, you fly that thing till there ain't nothing left to fly."

"We will," Parson said. "Thank you, sir."

He entered his new route on the flight plan page. When he activated it, the autopilot made a left turn of about eight degrees. With his course set, Parson could do little else until he came closer to land. Then he'd work on the next refueling and start getting ready to jettison the bomb, or at least try.

Colman returned from the bunk room and plugged his headset into his comm cord. "Copilot's back up," he said.

"You get any sleep?" Parson asked.

"Not much. An hour or two."

Not surprising. Parson hadn't rested much better. He'd have to ask an exhausted crew to do the impossible. All their skill, training, and ingenuity would need to push through a heavy muck of fatigue.

As he watched over his instruments, he thought about the Delta pilot's advice: Just never give up. He wouldn't have, anyway, but he appreciated the thought. A voice of encouragement came as a gift in the midst of this broad Atlantic.

It reminded him of a lecture he'd attended by a retired United captain. Parson thought maybe Colman could benefit from its lessons.

"Ever hear of an airline pilot named Al Haynes?" Parson asked.

"I don't believe I have."

"He brought a DC-10 into Sioux City after his tail engine blew up and took out his hydraulics. He didn't have any flight controls at all."

Parson explained that when the engine shelled out, it turned the aircraft into an unguided missile. No emergency procedure existed for that problem. On his own, Haynes figured out a way to steer the jet with thrust alone. More than half the passengers survived the landing, their death sentences commuted.

"Depending on what happens to me and what happens to the airplane," Parson said, "you might have to do some things you haven't even thought of yet."

"I think I take your meaning," Colman said.

They flew in silence for the better part of an hour. Dunne looked intently at something on his panel. Not a good sign. Parson waited for the explanation until he couldn't stand it anymore.

"Is something wrong?" he asked.

"I got some oil pressure flux on number one," Dunne said.

"Bad?"

"Not yet. Just a few psi."

"What do you mean, 'not yet'?" Colman asked.

"It's not going to get any better, and it might get worse. Temperature's coming up. That means the oil viscosity is breaking down."

"Why?"

"Who knows?" Dunne said. "That engine has a lot of hours on it, and it's not used to running this long."

So now I have two sick engines, Parson thought. Oil trouble on number one and vibration on number four. If they'll just hold out a little longer. . . .

In the moonlight, broken undercast shimmered several thousand feet below like floating clusters of ice floes. Above it, stars encrusted the horizon. Parson considered how far that vision of stars had traveled to reach him. To shine on him at this moment, that light had begun its journey before he'd ever joined the military, before he'd ever been born. Parson found comfort in that somehow, though he could not say why.

A VAGUE WEAKNESS CAME OVER GOLD. She had no appetite at all, but when she thought back over how little she'd eaten since takeoff, she realized she had to be a little hypoglycemic. Most likely everyone else was, too.

In a carton of MREs she found only one left. The box also contained a half-full water bottle and three empties.

"May I take the MRE?" she asked the lieutenant colonel.

"Might as well," the MCD said. "It won't do anyone any good sitting on the floor."

Gold picked it up and read the label. To her disappointment, the main item was pork slices. She took it to Mahsoud, who looked more pale than ever. His oxygen cannula hung from around his neck, unused.

"What's the matter?" she asked Justin.

"We're out of PT-LOX." He gestured toward a green metal box strapped to the floor. A placard on the knee-high unit read: PORTABLE THERAPEUTIC LIQUID OXYGEN SYSTEM. "It had more than enough to get us to Ramstein, but it's empty now."

We're running out of everything, Gold thought. Maybe Mahsoud would feel better if he ate something.

"This is for you," she said in Pashto. "I know you do not eat pork, but it is permitted to preserve your life. You need your strength."

"My need is not great enough for that," he said, "but I thank you."

"Then you can eat one of the side foods." Gold hunted through the inner packets and found corn bread. "Perhaps this, then," she said. "It is a traditional American bread."

"That, I will try."

Gold tore open the pouch and broke the corn bread in half. She handed the piece to Mahsoud. He took a bite and chewed cautiously.

"You don't like it?"

"It is not bad," he said in English, still chewing. Crumbs fell onto his bloodstained uniform.

"You need something to drink with that." Gold turned toward

the box with the water bottle only to see a loadmaster had just taken it.

"That's mine," a medic said to the loadmaster.

The loadmaster uncapped it and took a drink. The medic charged at the other man and pushed him against a bulkhead. He drove a fist into the load's solar plexus. The bottle fell to the floor and spilled.

"Asshole!" the loadmaster yelled. He slammed the heel of his hand into the medic's nose. Blood streamed from the man's nostrils as the two wrestled. Droplets spattered on the floor in dime-sized starbursts.

"That's enough!" the MCD shouted. She pushed the two apart by the shoulders. Gold pulled the medic away by the arm. The loadmaster took one more swing but got only air.

"You two idiots better unfuck yourselves right now," the MCD said. "Does the phrase 'dereliction of duty' sound good to you?"

"No, ma'am," the medic said. He touched his sleeve to his face and the blood left a dark streak. Justin handed him a gauze pad.

"Then get back to work. We'll forget about this, but if it happens again you'll need a proctologist to get my foot out of your ass."

Gold knew the fatigue and stress would only get worse. She thought of a painting she'd seen once while on leave in Paris. *The Raft of the Medusa* depicted a handful of half-dead castaways adrift in a roiling sea. The artist had taken inspiration from an actual event. Nearly one hundred and fifty survivors of the wrecked French frigate *Medusa* had set out on a makeshift raft in 1816. In thirst, starvation, and madness, the sailors and passengers began to kill one another. Others died of exposure or threw themselves overboard. Only fifteen were rescued.

At least we won't live long enough to reach that state, she thought.

Baitullah wouldn't eat the pork, either, so Gold took a few bites of it and gave the rest to Justin and the other medics. One of the medics offered an orange to Baitullah, which he seemed to relish. He wrapped the peelings in a paper towel and held them in his fist. Gold wondered if he planned to eat those, too, or if he just liked the scent.

The citrus smell contrasted oddly with the odors of fuel, oil, sweat, and blood.

Gold gathered up the empty water bottles and took them upstairs to the flight deck. Her hands were full so she didn't bring her headset.

"May I take some water?" she asked loudly enough to be heard without the interphone.

Parson said nothing but turned and gave an OK sign with his thumb and forefinger. Dunne was finishing an apple, and he even ate the core. So they're out of food up here, too, Gold thought.

At the watercooler, across the aisleway from the galley, Gold filled three bottles. From the cooler's slosh, she figured it was nearly empty. Maybe a gallon left.

One pouch of instant coffee remained on the galley table, along with packets of sugar and dry creamer. Gold heated a cup of water and brewed the coffee. Then she stirred in five sugar packets and two creamers. Too sickly sweet, she guessed, but that way it had more food value, if she could get Baitullah to drink it. She stuffed the water bottles in her cargo pockets and carried the coffee in her hand.

On the way back to the ladder, Gold passed the bunk rooms. On a hunch, she looked inside one of them. Yes, she'd remembered correctly. Each bunk had its own oxygen regulator, like the one at the nav table. If the nurses had no more medical oxygen for Mahsoud, could he come up here and breathe from the aircraft's supply?

When Gold returned to the cargo compartment, she offered Baitullah the coffee. He frowned when he took the first sip, but he drank it all while nibbling on the orange peels. His first experience in the care of Americans, Gold thought, and he's hungry enough to eat trash. She gave the water bottles to the crewmen who'd fought, and she offered another one to Mahsoud. He looked even paler.

"How's he doing?" Gold asked the MCD.

"He'll need a respirator if he keeps declining."

"The bunk rooms upstairs have oxygen regulators. Would it help to move him up there?"

The lieutenant colonel's eyes widened. "They do?" she said.

"Yeah, it would help. We should have thought of that, but we don't normally use this airframe."

A loadmaster overheard the conversation. "Due respect, ma'am," he said. "I don't think that's a good idea. Look what happened last time we let an Afghan patient upstairs."

Gold suppressed a surge of anger. She'd say something she'd regret. And she felt responsible for what Fawad had done. "What's he going to do?" she asked. "He has one leg."

"You never know what a motivated terrorist is capable of," the loadmaster said.

"You do if their oxygenation is that poor," the MCD said. "But it's up to the aircraft commander."

Gold plugged in her headset and explained to Parson what she wanted to do. He said nothing for a while. Then he asked, "You want to bring another one up here?"

A knife to her heart. One that she deserved, in her estimation. She looked at Mahsoud, and her eyes brimmed.

"Hell, no," Dunne said. "Sir."

Parson did not answer.

He said he still trusted me, Gold thought, but he didn't expect to have to prove it. He just wanted to make me feel better.

"Major," the MCD said, "this patient's in bad shape. He couldn't hurt you if he wanted to."

"The other one was wounded, too," Dunne said.

So the jury's deciding Mahsoud's punishment for my mistake, Gold thought. Dear God, everything I touch gets destroyed.

"If he wanted to bring us down," Parson said, "he wouldn't have told us about that mercury switch."

"If that's what it is," Colman said.

They're going to sacrifice Mahsoud to paranoia, Gold realized. Why can't they just take it out on me? The interphone fell silent.

"Pilot," the lieutenant colonel said. "MCD. We need a decision."

No sound but the tenor of the engines and the wind. Then the click of a microphone switch.

"Bring him up here," Parson said.

20

A livid dawn materialized as the C-5 flew west. Parson could not see the sun rising behind him, but its rays lightened the sky ahead with a milky colorless glow. Broken stratus formations obscured the ocean surface, and their edges melded with surrounding air in a way that made it hard to identify any cloud's boundaries. In a few places, darker blotches hung suspended like smoke rising through fog. The entire atmosphere seemed a pastel smear, as if viewed through cataracts.

At least I'm not flying through black billows of ash, Parson thought. But as he looked down through a sky heavy with particulates, he realized that *was* the ash cloud, diffused and spreading, far from its source. Motes of silica from deep within the earth, hurled into the sky and drifting on the trades.

Exhaustion dragged on him like a chronic disease. According to Dunne's fuel log, the jet had been airborne for almost twenty hours. Parson had worked with augmented crews kept on duty for twenty-four hours at a stretch; the regs allowed that if you had an extra pilot. Because of screwed-up circadian rhythms, those augmented days could translate into thirty or more hours without real sleep. Flying tired was nothing new to Parson, but he'd never pushed it this far on any single flight. Once, twice, three times sleep overtook him, until his head sagged and he startled awake.

Thuds, boot steps, and curses echoed from behind and below, and the flight deck door rattled open. Someone's fingers wrapped around the doorframe, and then Gold pulled herself into the cockpit. She turned around, kneeled, and lifted, and she backed up holding the front handles of Mahsoud's litter. Gold and her unseen assistants levered him onto the flight deck floor.

"Sir," Colman asked, "are you sure this is a good idea?"

"Look at him," Parson said.

Mahsoud's face wore the gray cast of the dying. His facial muscles hung slack except at the jaw, clenched in evident pain. Eyes open but unfocused, black pools of fear.

Gold, Justin, and the MCD lifted him again and carried him into the forward bunk room. After they had him settled, Justin leaned the collapsed litter against an aisleway bulkhead.

A faint scorched scent permeated the cockpit. Parson began to worry about another electrical fire—no telling what unseen damage had resulted from the lightning.

"How's your electrical panel looking?" he asked Dunne.

"Yeah, I smell it, too," Dunne said. "I got no warning lights or popped breakers. Load meters all look normal."

"It's getting stronger," Colman said.

"I'll look around," Dunne offered. "Engineer's going off headset."

Dunne got up and opened an avionics compartment door. He unzipped a flight suit pocket, removed a penlight, and shone it around. Then he leaned forward and sniffed. The effort put Parson in mind of a suspicious Brittany spaniel checking a hedgerow for pheasants. Dunne repeated the process at the aft avionics bay, shrugged his shoulders, and returned to his seat.

"Find anything?" Parson asked.

"You can hardly smell anything back there."

"Anybody cooking in the galley?"

"There's nothing left to cook."

Parson ran his eyes over his instruments and annunciator panel. No new warning lights there, either. Not that there isn't enough wrong with the airplane already, he thought. His airspeed and altitude readings all made sense, and they all agreed with the instruments on Colman's panel. So the air data computers weren't fried.

Yet the smell grew worse. The flight deck stank of sulfur. The odor of hell.

Dunne leaned back, sniffed again. "It's coming from the gasper outlets," he said. "Do you see any engine damage?"

Parson looked outside, back at the left wing. An engine with a blown duct or a fluid leak might explain the problem: The air-conditioning used purified air tapped off the engine compressors. Any smoke or fluid loosed in an engine could get sucked into the bleed air.

"My side's good," Colman said.

So was Parson's. Two intact engines, humming away. But in the pallid light of dawn, Parson noticed an odd sight: a shimmering luster surrounded the nacelle inlets. Sharp-edged glints sparkled and danced like sunlight reflected off quartz. In all the strange meteorological phenomena Parson had witnessed in almost two decades of flying, he had never seen anything like this. But through the funk of sleep deprivation, he did manage to connect all the signs.

"We need to get the hell out of here," he said.

"What's the matter?" Colman asked.

"We aren't over the ash cloud. We're *in* it."

"I thought the advisory center said most of it would stay below us."

"They forgot to tell the damned volcano."

Parson hadn't expected to need to climb so early. He felt doubly grateful to that airline crew, because the captain had requested a block altitude for him between twenty-five thousand and thirty-eight thousand feet. Now he wanted the top of it.

"I got the plane for a while," Parson said to Colman. "You take the radios."

"Yes, sir. But the radios aren't working."

"Call in the blind on HF," Parson said. "Say we're climbing to three-eight-oh, but you'll probably be talking to yourself."

"Rog," Colman said. When he spoke on the air, no one answered.

Parson set 38,000 in the altitude selector and advanced the throttles. With the tip of his middle finger, he nudged the autopilot pitch wheel to limit the nose's rise to five degrees. He could get no better than a two-hundred-foot-per-minute climb. The jet was near the ceiling for its weight, and it seemed to claw for every inch.

The aircraft finally leveled at the new altitude, and Parson eased the power back slightly to a cruise setting. As he did so, he noticed a buzz in the throttles. Weird. But he thought he knew where it came from. When he touched each throttle stem individually, he found the rattle came from number four. He'd noticed it earlier, but now it was more severe. Whatever was wrong with that engine, it shook hard enough to telegraph the problem along hundreds of feet of throttle cable.

"The vibration on four's getting worse," he said. "I can feel it in the throttle."

"That ain't good," Dunne said. "Wish I could look at it, but my computer's toast."

It really didn't matter to Parson whether Dunne could look at that engine's tormented waveform on a computer screen. Parson needed all four engines to stay out of the ash; he wasn't about to shut one down and descend back into that shit. For all he knew, it was ash damage that had worsened the vibration. To see that engine's problems quantified by mils and scope divisions would just be pointless aggravation.

At least the sky seemed clearer here. The growing brightness forced Parson to dig into his helmet bag for his aviator's sunglasses. He put them on and looked down. The air below bore the color of dishwater, unfit even for machines to breathe.

The sulfur odor began to dissipate, but the ash left a scorched tang in the air almost as if someone had been smoking. From the bunk room, he heard Mahsoud cough. Parson made a mental note to check on him later.

No horizon existed; the ash seemed to have scoured it away. Land remained out of sight, and Parson navigated by an integrated solution from GPS and inertial gyros. As long as those gyros knew where they started, they always knew where they were. Parson could determine his position within feet.

He did not consider himself a student of history, but he counted among his heroes Magellan and Drake. He admired the confidence and courage it must have taken to set out across oceans armed with little but a compass and an astrolabe. In those days, navigators had latitude nailed, but they could not accurately fix longitude until the invention of the marine chronometer, and that led to dangerous errors.

I got problems they couldn't imagine, Parson thought, but at least I know where the hell I am. Headed toward another aerial refueling somewhere near the New World.

IN THE BUNK ROOM, the MCD placed an aircrew oxygen mask over Mahsoud's mouth and nose. As he inhaled, Gold watched the blinker on the regulator flip from black to white, and it held white for long seconds. A deep breath, then an extended sigh. The green pneumatic hose constricted slightly each time Mahsoud pulled the oxygen into his lungs. After he took three strong drags, he raised his good arm and held the mask in place with his own hand.

"Does that feel better?" Gold asked.

Mahsoud opened his eyes, nodded. His chalky pallor began to change, growing more ruddy with each cycle of the regulator. Eventually, he lifted the mask enough to speak.

"If I die up here," he asked, "am I that much closer to heaven?"

"Your faith and your deeds may take you to heaven," Gold said, "but not today." She wasn't sure she believed that, but it seemed the right thing to say.

"Let's get his antibiotic started again," the MCD said to Justin. "Go downstairs and bring me an IV stand."

"Yes, ma'am."

When Justin returned with the chrome rods, he assembled them and placed the stand by Mahsoud's bunk. The MCD hung on to it a small plastic packet labeled CEFAZOLIN INJECTION, USP. She connected it to tubing that ran to a needle taped to Mahsoud's wrist. "We don't have any more of this," she said.

Mahsoud's eyes met Gold's, then he looked at the MCD. He seemed grateful for the treatment he was receiving, and Gold felt the same way. In some Afghan villages, medical care did not exist. Mahsoud had probably never seen anything like this. Gold, on the other hand, had seen aeromeds in action before.

After the ordeal of her torture and trek through the mountains with Parson, the Army had sent her to Landstuhl for a medical and psych evaluation. She'd traveled to Germany on a C-17, along with soldiers suffering from gunshot wounds, blast amputations, and traumatic brain injuries. The aeromeds' compassion and skill had restored some of her hope for humanity at a time when she'd nearly lost it. One female medic spent most of the flight holding the hand of a blinded Marine.

At Landstuhl, doctors pronounced her medically fit. Technically, her torn and lacerated fingertips were minor injuries. But psychologists told her to expect post-traumatic stress disorder. Her commanders let her spend a month at the Edelweiss Lodge in Garmisch. She didn't even have to take leave. They told her to work on her mission and her mission was to recover.

A nice warm beach might have provided better R & R; the looming Bavarian Alps reminded her of the Hindu Kush. But she decided that was fitting. The things she'd experienced would always loom in her psyche.

She spent her days at the military resort eating good German food and working out in the fitness center and her nights by the fire sipping eiswein and reading the Bible, the Talmud, the Quran, and *The Meditations of Marcus Aurelius.* With holy words and the thoughts of Rome's emperor and Stoic philosopher, she hoped to make sense of her pain. The Roman seemed to speak to her from across the ages, especially with his caution about vengeance: *The best kind of revenge is, not to become like unto them.*

The gathered wisdom of prophets and sages seemed to run in that vein—it told her what *not* to do. That was helpful as far as it went, and a thirst for payback ran counter to her nature, anyway. She found little guidance on what *to* do. But she was pretty sure Marcus Aurelius would say, "Soldier on." And so she had, more or less, right up until this moment.

Mahsoud was hanging in there, too. With what looked like a detached scientific interest, he watched the last of the antibiotic flow down the tubing and into his arm. His eyes, which earlier had communicated only fear, now moved about with an intelligent wakefulness. The mask obscured his facial expressions, but those black eyes alone conveyed an acceptance, along with the constant undercurrent of a student's affection for a trusted teacher. The oxygen seemed to do him good. Justin had left the regulator's diluter lever on 100 PERCENT.

Gold remembered the crew had said they had plenty of oxygen, and she hoped that remained true. It seemed the only thing keeping Mahsoud's body and soul in the same place.

She stepped out of the bunk room and, over Dunne's shoulder, examined the flight engineer panel. Maybe something on that wall of instruments would tell her how much oxygen was left. When she couldn't find it, she put on her headset and asked him.

"Right here," Dunne said. He pointed to a pair of gauges at the bottom edge of the panel. "We still got about seventy liters."

"That doesn't sound like much," Gold said.

"It's seventy liters of *liquid* oxygen. That translates to a whole lot more by the time it runs through the heat exchangers and becomes a gas."

Liquid oxygen sounded dangerous to Gold. The only reference to liquid oxygen she'd ever heard had to do with exploding spacecraft. But it seemed the one item on board in sufficient quantity, and for that she was grateful.

Outside the cockpit windscreen, the daylight had an odd creamlike quality. It reminded Gold of looking up through the fog of the Green Mountains. But now she was looking down and she could identify no distinct cloud layer, so she thought it strange that she could not see the ocean.

While Gold stood behind Dunne's seat and watched the crew, Parson tried several radio calls. He never got an answer, and she gathered he was having communication problems. Yet another difficulty. The plane seemed to be falling apart as time went on.

"Guess I'll have to get one more relay on VHF," Parson said over interphone. He entered numbers in an electronic box on the center console, keyed his mike and said, "Any aircraft, Air Evac Eight-Four on guard."

An answer came immediately. "Air Evac Eight-Four, Avianca Six-Two." Hispanic accent.

"All right," Parson said over interphone, "the Colombians are listening up." Then he transmitted, "Avianca, do you have HF or ACARS or some other way to pass along a message for us?"

"Sir, we are an Airbus with HF capability."

"Excellent. Please contact Hilda and give them our location at"—Parson checked his watch—"eighteen past the hour." He gave the Avianca pilot his coordinates, along with the frequency for the call. Then he added, "Please tell them we'll need one more refueling."

"Stand by," the Avianca pilot said.

"Seems funny to coordinate this through foreign nationals," Colman said.

"It does," Parson said. "But we don't have a lot of choice. And the Colombians are our friends, anyway."

As Parson waited, he tweaked a knob on his console, and the plane banked gently to the right. "I'm going to cut north just a few degrees," he said. "This shit looks like it's getting thicker."

"How does number four feel?" Dunne asked.

Parson placed his fingers around one of the throttles. Gold didn't understand why, but she knew this didn't bode well. And *what* was getting thicker?

"It ain't healing itself, that's for sure," Parson said.

Gold sat at the nav table and waited for a break in the conversation. When it seemed okay, she asked, "What's going on?"

Parson explained that the number four engine was vibrating, number one had oil pressure dropping, Soufrière Hills was erupting to their southwest and Arlene was churning to their northeast. "We're running the gap between them," he said, "if there *is* a gap."

Mount Scylla and Tropical Storm Charybdis, Gold thought, but she kept it to herself.

"There she is," Parson said. He pointed to his radar screen. Along its right edge, green and yellow splotches and crescents shifted and reassembled with each sweep of the radar antenna. "Those are the outer rain bands."

Out the windows, Gold could see nothing except more of that weird high-altitude haze that she supposed was the volcanic ash. However, as the aircraft continued along Parson's adjusted course, the sky to the right began to darken. On the radar screen, the greens and yellows took up more space, and some of the yellows turned red. Gold didn't know if that suggested heavier rain or stronger turbulence, but she did know that in an airplane, red indications probably meant bad things.

Eventually, the Colombian airliner called back. "Air Evac Eight-Four," the pilot said, "your Air Force is sending another tanker to meet you." The Avianca captain passed along radio frequencies and coordinates for the tanker rendezvous.

"Avianca, that's good news," Parson said. "We need all the help we can get."

"Our prayers are with you, sir," the captain added. "Oh, yes, and your people also said escort fighters will accompany the tanker."

"Copy that," Parson transmitted. Then he said on interphone, "Bet those fighter jocks are going to get Air Medals just for being a pain in my ass."

Gold understood his frustration. She didn't see what good an escort could do; it would only complicate Parson's flying. The fighters that had joined them earlier seemed just a distraction. But the Air Force had its doctrines, and Gold did not pretend to know them.

"How much gas do we have now?" Parson asked.

Dunne checked his panel and said, "Just under a hundred thousand pounds."

"Good," Parson said. "Maybe this time it won't be so fucking close."

So fuel might not be an issue, Gold surmised. One less thing for the crew to worry about. She could see they had plenty of other problems.

21

By now, Parson thought, the aeromeds would have had enough time to get Mahsoud comfortable in the bunk room. Since the Afghan lay only about five steps aft of the pilot's seat, Parson wanted to look in on him. That would probably make Gold happy, and the guy had been helpful. Or at least he'd tried. Parson figured the odds of a survivable outcome were still slim.

"Take the jet for a while," Parson told Colman.

"My aircraft, my radios," Colman said.

Parson unbuckled his lap belt and slid back his seat, and he saw Gold still sitting at the nav table. He'd concentrated so hard on the radio calls and navigation that he'd forgotten she was right behind him.

"How's your friend doing?" he asked.

"A little better," she said.

In the bunk room, Mahsoud lifted the oxygen mask and said, "Hello, sir," in English when Parson nodded to him.

"Relax," Parson said. "Don't take off that thing on my account." Parson supposed that in the Afghan police force, a major would seldom deign to speak to a new recruit. He didn't want Mahsoud to be intimidated by his rank. "You've been a big help," he added.

Mahsoud looked at Parson blankly for a moment, and then the skin around his eyes wrinkled in the only visible evidence of the smile under his mask. Probably took him a moment to process the phrase "big help."

Gold said something in Pashto, and Mahsoud placed his hand to his heart.

"What are you two conspiring about?" Parson asked.

"Nothing," Gold said. "It's good of you to treat him respectfully."

"I'm starting to like that guy."

Parson had learned in his wartime experiences that bravery was like good bourbon: It came in different blends. People showed courage in different ways, and it didn't always involve running through hails of gunfire. Mahsoud demonstrated his in a quiet way, much like Gold. It really came down to the ability to function under pressure and do the right thing.

As Parson returned to his seat, he stepped into a smear of congealing blood left when they'd dragged Fawad's body back to the courier compartment. It stuck to his boot like creek bank slime, and he scraped his sole against the floor to get rid of it. He didn't want a terrorist's blood on his rudder pedals.

He sat down, put on his headset, and asked Colman, "Any changes?"

"No, but something weird happened. I thought I saw two blips on the TCAS, but then they went away. I'm so tired it could have been my imagination."

Parson looked at the traffic advisory screen superimposed over a vertical speed indicator. A white diamond meant proximate traffic but no threat. A yellow circle indicated another aircraft a little too close. A red square warned of an imminent collision if you didn't do something fast. But now the TCAS showed no other planes at all.

"I wouldn't worry about it," Parson said. "Our avionics are all fucked up, anyway."

Right now, Parson was more concerned about the weather. Tropical Storm Arlene, or maybe Hurricane Arlene by now, lurked to the right. What he had first seen only on radar became plainly apparent out the windows. Sweeps and grandeurs of cumulonimbus reared and heaved, mists at battle with one another. Below them, tumults of rain lashed the sea. Spindrift danced across the whitecaps like phantoms. Winds and wave heights registering toward the bad side of the Beaufort scale, Parson thought.

Somewhere, he knew, a WC-130 crew out of Keesler was deliberately flying through that monster to take meteorological readings, and he envied them. Turbulence would beat the shit out of them, and they might even reach for their barf bags, but they'd live through the day. He doubted he would.

Jolts and bumps began to rock the C-5. So far, nothing as bad as the thunderstorms during the night, but Parson didn't want to take any more chances with that bomb's mercury switch. He turned a heading knob and adjusted his course to the left. The ride settled down some.

To the southwest, the ash cloud seemed lighter now. Parson knew he couldn't accurately measure the concentration by eyeballing it; he had no experience with volcanic events. But he steered a little more to the left, anyway. He could *see* the trouble to the right, so it seemed logical to avoid it.

From a greater distance, Arlene appeared even more intimidating. Shafts of rainfall hung like gray scarves from the storm's feathered edges. Dark walls of vapor seethed across hundreds of miles.

"Never seen anything like that," Colman said.

"At some point, you'll probably see it again," Parson said. Then he thought, no—you probably won't.

Ahead, visibility improved. Parson was pretty sure he was at least getting the ash cloud behind him. The air cleared enough for him to make out waves on the water below. They might have been ten-foot seas, but from altitude they appeared as ripples across the surface of a pond.

It occurred to Parson that the ocean was the only changeless thing he'd ever view. Anything on land could burn, crumble, or wear away. But this spot on earth had looked exactly like this a million years ago. If his aircraft took its final plunge right now, it would leave a white splash, gone in seconds. And the ocean would go on looking the same for another million years.

But the next million years aren't your problem, he told himself. Better focus on the next few hours.

"How's oil pressure looking on number one?" he asked.

"Still fluxing," Dunne said. "And down about ten psi from the mean."

"We'll let it run," Parson said. "Just keep me advised."

Normally, if an engine lost even half that much oil pressure, Parson would have shut it down. But he needed it now, especially given the vibration in number four. If either of those engines failed, his crew and passengers would be in a world of hurt. If both failed, they'd be dead. He could not maintain altitude with only two engines.

As Parson considered his options—or lack of them—he felt a raging sense of violation. Somebody had boarded his aircraft, climbed its steps, and walked its plating with that fucking bomb. He wanted to grab whoever had done it and cut his heart out with a short pocketknife. But he'd never get that chance, and at best he could only channel his anger into foiling the enemy, landing the plane in one piece.

Just then, a strange sight appeared directly outside the cockpit windows. Parson blinked his eyes to make sure he wasn't dreaming or hallucinating.

A jet fighter joined up on his left side, then pulled slightly ahead of the C-5. At first, Parson couldn't place the model of the aircraft. An identical fighter, presumably the wingman, streaked over the top of Parson's plane and banked into a hard turn.

"What the hell is that?" Colman asked. With his lips parted, he leaned forward in his seat and stared at the aircraft.

Parson had to think for a moment. The two-seat fighter had twin engines with rectangular intakes, twin vertical stabilizers, and a set of small winglets just aft of the canopy. Subdued gray-blue camouflage paint, and a flag painted on the side that consisted of three bars: yellow, blue, and red. Semicircle of stars across the blue section. Missiles under its wings—Russian-built Vympels.

"That's an Su-30 Flanker," Parson said. "Venezuelan." The Venezuelans probably called it something else, but Parson knew it by its NATO designation. Russian-built fighters always carried a name that began with an *F*—supposedly random but always something unintimidating: Flanker, Frogfoot, Fishbed.

The Flanker flew so close that Parson could have seen the crewmen's eyes had they not worn smoked visors on their helmets. It rocked its wings and flashed its navigation lights. When Parson made no response, the Flanker rocked its wings harder, flashed the lights with greater frequency.

That indicated something, Parson knew. But it lay someplace in his mind where he stored knowledge he never expected to use. Something from *way* back in his training—international rules of the air, standard signals.

Then he remembered. This one meant: YOU HAVE BEEN INTERCEPTED. FOLLOW ME.

AS GOLD GLANCED FORWARD INTO THE COCKPIT, she sensed something wrong, or at least different. Maybe it was the crew's body language, the way they looked at one another. As she reached for her headset at the nav console, she saw the fighter jet filling the left side of the windscreen. So close it make her gasp.

She had no idea what kind of fighter it was, but she recognized the Venezuelan flag. So this wasn't one of the friendly aircraft that so annoyed Parson. Something worse, then. Gold put on her headset to listen in.

"Why didn't they show up on TCAS?" Colman asked.

"Because the bastards turned off their transponders," Parson said. "I think you *did* have them on TCAS for a minute."

"Oh, yeah."

Gold noticed Parson and Colman were using the plural. Was there another one somewhere?

Then an unfamiliar voice came over the radio: "American aircraft, Bolivar One-One on guard. You are violating Venezuelan airspace. Please come with us. We will land in Caracas."

"Bullshit," Parson said on interphone. Then he keyed his mike and said, "Bolivar, this is Air Evac Eight-Four. We are a medevac aircraft, with a declared emergency, in international airspace. Check your navigation, sir." When Parson released his mike switch, he added, "And you can take those Russian missiles off your wings and shove them up your ass."

"Negative, sir. We have extended our air defense zone because of Colombia's hostile actions. Our intelligence facilities have monitored you in communication with a Colombian aircraft. You must come with us, sir."

The Venezuelan pilot spoke English with confidence, Gold noted. He was so fluent he was probably *thinking* in English. He sounded older, too. Maybe a full bird colonel or their equivalent. You wouldn't send a new lieutenant to threaten an American airplane, she guessed.

"Bolivar One-One," Parson said, "I am an emergency aircraft with multiple malfunctions. I cannot descend now. And you are violating international law."

"You, sir, are violating international law if you are bringing weapons to Colombia. And why else would you coordinate with a Colombian aircraft?"

Parson looked around at his crew and said, "Are you believing this shit?" Then he transmitted, "That was an Airbus, you dumbass. He gave me a radio relay because my HFs are inoperative. If you're going to eavesdrop, at least pay attention."

Still not much of a diplomat, Gold thought.

A long moment of silence passed, and the fighter turned hard to the left. It banked so steeply Gold could see clusters of ordnance under its wings. Where the wings met the fuselage, puffs of mist formed as the jet powered away. Gold wondered what aerodynamic phenomenon created that effect; she'd never seen it before.

"Are they gone?" Dunne asked. He craned his neck to look.

"I hope so," Parson said. "That's the craziest thing I ever heard."

"I don't think the Venezuelans really want to tangle with the U.S.," Colman said.

"Me, neither," Parson said. But then he added, "Hell, maybe they do. Get us and Cuba and Russia involved in their little dustup with Colombia."

"We have enough trouble as it is," Dunne said.

"You got that right," Parson said. He checked his watch. "Our tanker ought to be here soon. Colman, are you too tired to do another plug or do you want me to take it?"

"I can fly it, sir. Thank you."

The crew flew in silence for several minutes. After a time, Gold saw two specks in the distance. At first, she thought they were imperfections on the windscreen; they showed no relative motion from the C-5. But then they grew larger. They were coming head-on.

The specks widened, took the form of fighter jets. They separated from each other at an altitude just above the C-5. The two aircraft swung out wide and flashed by either side with incomprehensible speed. For an instant, Gold could see the bubble canopies and the helmeted pilots.

"What the hell was that?" Dunne asked.

"The Flankers just came back," Parson said.

"What are they doing?" Colman asked.

"They're setting up for a stern conversion, that's what they're doing," Parson said. "Pincer maneuver."

Gold had no idea what that meant, but it sounded like tactics. *Combat* tactics.

"What can we do?" Colman said. He turned in his seat and scanned the sky, but the fighters had disappeared behind the C-5.

"Not a fucking thing," Parson said. "Maybe they're bluffing."

No one spoke for a moment. Was it over? Just a high-speed middle finger from the Venezuelans, perhaps.

An intermittent, staccato beep sounded in Gold's headset. Then it became a steady tone.

"Son of a bitch," Parson said. "Missile lock." He pointed to his instrument panel. A winglike symbol illuminated on a small screen labeled RADAR WARNING RECEIVER.

"American aircraft, Bolivar One-One," called a voice on the radio. "Please accompany us to Caracas. I really must insist."

"Bolivar One-One," Parson called, "*Air Evac* Eight-Four. I have a terrorist bomb on board. Maybe your intel people should try watching the news. Go ahead and fire, asshole. With these winds, it'll probably blow anthrax all over your third-rate banana republic, Cuba-wannabe country."

The radios remained silent for almost a full minute. Gold tried to imagine what the Venezuelans were thinking. Of all the responses they might have anticipated, they probably didn't expect Parson to dare them to shoot.

Finally, the squelch broke on the frequency. Gold heard a sigh, and then the Venezuelan flight leader said, "You give me no other choice."

Gold closed her eyes in unspoken prayer. She braced for the explosion, clawed her armrests.

Seconds passed. Nothing happened.

"What are you doing?" the Flanker pilot asked.

"What the fuck are you talking about?" Parson transmitted.

"I'm talking about your fire control radar."

"I don't *have* that kind of radar, you dumb shit."

"But—" The Venezuelan released his PUSH TO TALK.

"Look at that," Parson said on interphone. He pointed to the radar warning receiver. It showed another symbol, one farther away judging from its orientation on the screen. Something other than the Flankers was getting ready to fire. And it seemed to be moving closer. Rapidly.

"Switch your radar from weather to skin paint," Parson told Colman.

Colman turned some knobs, and his radar screen flickered. But it remained blank.

"Hah," Parson said. "No cross section. You can't see it." Then he pressed his TRANSMIT button. "Do you know what that is, jackass?"

"Perhaps."

"It's an F-22 Raptor, motherfucker. Why don't you roll in on him?"

No answer.

"You better disarm weapons right now," Parson said, "or that thing's gonna scatter your commie ass all over the Caribbean."

The missile tone went silent.

"No need for such rough language," the Flanker pilot said. "We can conclude this matter as gentlemen."

"Go home, bitch," Parson said.

22

The Flankers broke off from Parson's six o'clock and turned for land. He watched them join up in tight formation, lead and wingman, as they fled. The two jets cut a diagonal path downward and away, and vanished as dust motes in the haze. Probably went supersonic, Parson thought. I'd light the afterburners, too, if a Raptor drew a bead on me.

Two Raptors, actually. The pair of American fighters appeared at one o'clock high, gray ghosts spiriting along against a sky of blued steel.

"Air Evac Eight-Four, Shadow Flight," the lead called. "You doing okay?"

"We're all right at the moment, thanks to you guys," Parson said. All right for a flying IED.

The F-22s soared across the top of the C-5 and disappeared.

"Tanker's not far behind us," the lead fighter said. "We'll fly detached escort with you until you're out of range for those bandits."

Parson had always considered fighter pilots overrated prima donnas, but he had to admit he felt safer now. Of all the dangers he'd faced in Afghanistan and Iraq—shoulder-fired missiles, small-arms fire, RPGs—he'd never expected to need air cover to get Flankers off his tail.

"What's detached escort?" Colman asked.

"They won't always be in sight," Parson said, "but they'll stay within firing distance for their missiles."

"Good."

"Where'd you guys come from?" Parson asked.

"Tyndall," the Shadow leader answered.

All the way from Florida? They must have taken a wide detour around the storm.

"Long flight," Parson transmitted.

"Yeah, we tanked on the way, but we saved some gas for you."

Parson checked the radar screen and the TCAS. Both showed a return now, getting closer by the second. He looked out the cockpit windows, strained to see the dot that would become a KC-135. The air was getting clearer, making the ocean visible below and turning it into an expanse of sapphire. Surface winds must have been rough; Parson noted how the wind whitened the swells with streaks of foam. He still didn't have visual contact with the tanker, but he saw its electronic signature moving nearer to him.

While he waited, he decided to make conversation with the only fighter jocks for whom he'd ever had any use. "I'd like to have seen you guys dogfight those Flankers," he said.

"Wouldn't have been much of a fight," the Shadow flight leader said. "We had 'em dead to rights before they knew we were there."

"Sounded like it," Parson said.

"No kidding. I was about to shoot when they turned off their radar."

And it would have been justified, too, Parson thought. Targeting another aircraft with fire control radar was itself a hostile act. He wondered if the Flanker pilots knew how close they'd come to incineration. Now they were safe, but he and his crew and passengers remained at risk for a fiery death.

"I got the plane for a while," Parson told Colman. "I'll give it back to you for the refuel."

"Yes, sir," Colman said. "My radios."

Parson liked the way Colman verbalized the change in duties.

Normally, one pilot flew the plane while the other pilot handled everything else, such as communication. If you traded jobs, you said so out loud to make sure there was no mix-up. Some guys neglected little details like that, but Colman flew by the book. Parson approved, as far that went. You flew by the book until conditions gave you a good reason not to.

At the moment, he wanted to fly the plane just to stay awake. Parson punched off the autopilot and steered by hand. The use of fine motor skills gave him something to focus on other than his fatigue. No matter how much he tweaked the trim switches, he still had to keep some hand pressure on the yoke to hold the C-5 on a heading and altitude. The airplane had been a little bent to start with, but now it was worse. The turbulence and hailstones had done more than break off antennas. Apparently, the storms had torn up some control surfaces and maybe twisted the entire fuselage.

Doesn't matter, Parson thought. In the unlikely event this thing lands in one piece, it'll probably never fly again.

"Air Evac Eight-Four, Sunoco One-Five," called a voice on the radio. "I think we have a visual on you. Do you see us off your two o'clock?"

Parson squinted, adjusted his sunglasses. Colman saw the tanker first.

"There he is," Colman said. Then he pressed his TRANSMIT switch: "Sunoco One-Five, Air Evac Eight-Four. Tallyho."

"How do you want to join up?" the tanker pilot asked.

"Tell him just to reverse course, and we'll catch him with an en route rendezvous," Parson said. This would be the last aerial refueling, and Parson felt glad it would at least take place during daylight. The KC-135 would give Parson and his crew enough fuel to reach Johnston Atoll, or the scene of the crash, whichever came first.

Colman made the radio call as Parson ordered. The dark blemish in the windscreen turned, and as it banked it revealed the profile of its wings and nacelles. Then the Boeing leveled onto the new heading and became a mere dot again. That is, until it slowed to rendezvous speed. Then it grew larger against the glass and took the shape of an airplane once more, this time as viewed from behind.

Dunne read through the checklists for aerial refueling, but it required little setup. The AR door actuator had broken the last time they used it, and the door had remained open ever since.

"Ready to fly?" Parson asked Colman.

"I have the aircraft," Colman said.

"My radios. Just keep your speed up until we're a little closer."

As the distance narrowed, Parson saw that the tanker had lowered its refueling boom. The boom extended from the aircraft's tail like an insect's stinger. Parson could make out the four black circles of the tanker's exhaust cones, and eventually the USAF painted on the underside of the left wing. From his perspective, the letters appeared inverted.

He didn't know the crew of that KC-135; none of their voices sounded familiar. Strangers had flown all this way to risk their asses refueling a flying bomb. Yeah, they did it because they'd been ordered to do it. But they could have found an excuse to abort, if they'd wanted to. Mainly they did it to save comrades-in-arms. They did it, Parson thought, because we all wear the same uniform. If we make it, he decided, I'll get the tail numbers of all the tankers that gave us gas. Dunne will have the numbers in his paperwork. I'll send Scotch to all the crew members, Parson noted. Better yet, I'll take it to them.

The yellow line along the KC-135's belly loomed larger. Colman flew smoothly, and he nearly had the C-5 in the precontact position.

"Good work," Parson said. "Just keep that yellow stripe lined up with your inside leg."

"Yes, sir."

Parson pointed at the tanker as he coached Colman. "Look at that black antenna on the underside," he said. "When it forms a *T* against that crossways white stripe, you're on a good thirty-degree approach."

"Got it."

As viewed through the C-5's windscreen, the antenna met the

white line in a perfect *T.* The join-up went well enough for the tanker's boom operator to call them in closer.

"Cleared to contact," the boomer said.

"Cleared to contact," Parson acknowledged. Then he said to Colman, "You heard the man. Get us some gas."

Colman entered the contact position, mere feet from the tanker. Parson could see the boomer's eyes. The boom latched into the receptacle, and the C-5 took its final load of jet fuel. Just before the boomer disconnected, he looked at Parson, gave a thumbs-up, and saluted. Parson returned the salute, then gave a casual wave.

"Air Evac Eight-Four, Sunoco One-Five," the boomer called. "Off-load complete. One hundred forty thousand pounds."

"Eight-Four copies," Parson said.

The boom unlatched and retracted, and the tanker pulled away. Parson and his crew voiced the terse calls and responses of the post air refueling checklist like some well-rehearsed catechism.

Another voice called from the tanker, this time one of the pilots: "Eight-Four, we have a message to relay from Hilda."

"Go," Parson said.

"Hilda advises you have a diplomatic clearance to overfly Nicaragua, as long as you stay above flight level two-five-oh. Overflight only, no landing permission. Stand by for the clearance number."

Parson slid a pencil from one of the pen pockets on his left sleeve. He looked around for paper and settled for the back cover of a Chart Update Manual.

"Ready to copy," Parson said.

The tanker pilot called out the clearance number. As Parson wrote it down, he was so tired his *5* came out more like a *Z.* He scratched it out and asked the tanker to repeat the number. Then the radios and interphone fell silent, and Parson's ears filled with the song of wind and machine. Now a translucent scrim of cloud hung over the ocean below.

Eventually, the isthmus between the Americas took form in the blue distance. Beyond it lay the Pacific, and the tasks Parson dreaded most.

ON PARSON'S ORDERS, GOLD, SPENCER, and Justin began to gather tools and equipment. They took a half dozen oxygen cylinders from around the aircraft. By now Gold knew how to check the cylinders' pressure; they all showed 300 psi. Full. Inside a storage cabinet in the aft flight deck she found two safety harnesses. The harnesses fitted over the wearer like a parachute rig, but instead of a canopy the straps connected to a lanyard made of heavy-duty webbing. Justin broke the copper safety wire on an emergency exit light and detached it from its receptacle. It contained its own batteries and could serve as a portable lamp. Spencer fitted a steel bit to a battery-powered drill.

The preparations made Gold think of a platoon gearing up to close with the enemy—loading rifles, honing knives. But she'd never faced or even anticipated this kind of battle. The only thing she knew about IEDs was that you never screwed around with them if you weren't trained for it. In this case, though, she knew they had to try. She also knew Parson would err toward action. He'd rather die doing the wrong thing than die doing nothing. For that matter, she thought, so would I.

Gold and Justin placed the oxygen bottles, harnesses, and lamp in the troop compartment, next to the negative pressure valves. The stockpile of gear somehow made Gold feel just a little less vulnerable. We're still fighting, she thought. Parson's still thinking. His crew's still flying.

As she descended the troop compartment ladder on her way back to the flight deck, the overhead speakers crackled and hummed. She heard Parson make a PA announcement:

"This is the aircraft commander speaking," he said. "You all know what we're up against. And I think you all know the odds. But we'll do the best we can. We're going to depressurize the aircraft one more time, and we're going to try to jettison the bomb. If you have any protective gear, whether it's a Kevlar helmet or a flak jacket or an exposure suit, I suggest you put it on. If you don't have a seat belt, get a cargo strap.

"If anything happens to me and the aircraft remains flyable, Lieutenant Colman will take command, assisted by Sergeant Dunne. I know you'll give them your full cooperation."

Parson paused, but the hum continued, as if he still had his finger on the TALK switch, considering. Then he said, "I'll see you . . . when it's over."

On the flight deck, Gold found Parson giving last-minute instructions on interphone. "Your plane, your radios," he told Colman. "Just keep us level at twenty-five thousand." Then he added, "I'll check in on headset from up in troop. That's when you guys can start depressurizing."

"Roger that," Dunne said.

"What would you like me to do?" Gold asked.

"Same as before," Parson said. "Keep an eye on us from the negative pressure valves, but don't go back in the tail unless there's a damned good reason."

"What about me?" Justin asked. Gold had told Parson about the talk she'd had with Justin up in the lav. She couldn't blame Parson if he decided not to trust the young aeromed.

"Are you up for this?" Parson asked.

"I think so. I want to help."

"All right. You're coming with me and the crew chief. You're going to be our oxygen runner. Keep those full bottles coming, and bring the empties back to Sergeant Major Gold. She'll refill them for you. Don't forget to keep an eye on your own oxygen."

"Yes, sir." Justin smiled. Though Gold could see little to smile about, she understood how he felt.

She looked in on Mahsoud in the bunk room. He lay wide awake, and his color still appeared good. The MCD was looking at his vital signs on a Propaq monitor.

"Any change?" Gold asked.

"He's not any worse," the MCD said. "I wish we didn't have to depressurize again, but I realize it's necessary."

Not the diagnosis Gold wanted to hear. "I will be well," Mahsoud said in English. "I worry about you and the major, with what you are about to do."

"Just rest and let the nurses take care of you," Gold said.

"Very well," Mahsoud said. After a pause, he added, "I wonder what the Falnama would say about this."

"We don't have time to check it now," Gold said, "but we will learn what the future holds soon enough." Or whether we have a future at all, she thought. No matter what the Falnama or any other book said, it couldn't guarantee success. You could never have assurance of winning, she thought. You could only deserve it, and the rest was out of your hands.

She stepped out of the bunk room and looked forward through the cockpit windows. Cumulus bloomed down below, rising above jungled hills. With all that had happened, Gold had stopped keeping track of the flight's progress, and the sight of land surprised her. Was that Panama? Maybe Honduras? Twin mountains rose from an island in the middle of a lake. Their conical shape made it apparent they were volcanoes. Inactive, at least for now.

"What is that?" Gold asked.

"Lake Nicaragua," Parson said.

The growing clouds obscured much of the ground and water. Each white mass featured its own terrain relief: white mountains and canyons, valleys and plains. When the west coast of Central America came into view, the clouds stopped at the beach as if fenced. As the strip of sand passed underneath the nose of the aircraft, Gold looked ahead into a new ocean. The turquoise peaks and troughs of waves stretched into the distance, undulating all the way to Asia.

She put the Pacific from her mind and followed Parson down the flight deck ladder. Justin came with them, carrying blankets from the bunk rooms. In the cargo compartment, Spencer pulled on a pair of black non-issued gloves. White lettering across the back of each glove read MECHANIX. He donned a nylon civilian windbreaker. Parson said, "Chief, that won't be nearly enough."

"It's all I got, sir."

"Take one of these blankets," Parson said. "It's cold as the north side of a witch's heart back there."

"Yes, sir." The crew chief took a blanket from Justin and wrapped it over his shoulders. Then Spencer hoisted his drill, along with a ball-peen hammer and a canvas tool bag.

"You look like you're ready to do some damage," Parson said.

"This ain't exactly precision work."

"No, it isn't."

Up in the troop compartment, Parson plugged his headset into an interphone cord, pressed the TALK button, and said, "Begin depressurization."

A few seconds later, Gold's ears popped as cabin altitude rose. The air expanding in her sinuses and eustachian tubes didn't bother her; she'd experienced the same thing before every parachute jump. If only she could escape that way: Wait for the green light, feet and knees together. Don't anticipate the ground. Just roll when you hit it.

But the C-5 carried no parachutes, and even if it did, she wouldn't bail out unless there was a chute for everybody.

Parson removed his headset and picked up a harness. He buckled it—straps over his chest and around his thighs—and he stuffed its lanyard into a flight suit pocket. Then he wrapped a blanket over his shoulders and donned an oxygen mask attached to one of the cylinders.

Spencer geared up the same way, then picked up his tools. Gold and Justin also went on oxygen, and Parson handed the interphone cord to Gold. She plugged in her own headset and heard Colman ask, "You guys all right back there?"

"We are," she said. "Major Parson is off headset now."

"Copy that. We'll let you know when depressurization's complete."

Gold swallowed to clear her ears and nasal passages, felt the familiar pop again. Parson put his fingers around the edge of one of the negative pressure valves and tugged experimentally. It did not budge. Gold thought about the physics, and she realized the valve would never open until outside pressure equaled inside pressure.

Her ears began to hurt a little, so she swallowed once more. Another pop, and the pain stopped. Parson tried the valve, and this time he lifted it with one finger.

"Zero differential," Dunne said over interphone.

Parson gave a thumbs-up, met Gold's eyes. He pointed to Justin and Spencer. Then, without a word, he opened a negative pressure valve and crawled into the tail section.

23

The cold, the wind roar, and the vibration made Parson's abdominal muscles clench. It all seemed worse than before. At first he guessed it was just his nerves. But several hours had passed since his first trip back into the tail. That much longer at high altitude, with the metal getting more cold-soaked, it probably *was* worse.

He knew B-17 crews in World War II flew whole missions at this altitude without pressurization, ports for the waist guns open to the wind. The gunners could not touch their weapons bare-handed or their fingers would stick to their .50 cals. Crewmen wore heavy leather flying suits wired with heating elements that plugged into the bomber's electrical system. When a man got a limb blown off, his buddies could stop the bleeding by holding the stump in the slipstream until it froze.

Parson lacked the protective clothing—and the youth—of those Air Force ancestors. Through storm damage to his airplane, he'd also lost most of the technical advances made since their time. Nothing he could do about it but suck it up and hack the mission.

He steadied himself on all fours, then rose to his feet. One of his foam earplugs dropped from his right ear and vanished in the darkness. The noise volume doubled, and Parson had no spare plugs. He pulled his flashlight from a lower pocket and turned it on.

The beam illuminated the black nonskid material glued to the catwalk. Parson moved in half steps, careful not to lose his footing on the trembling walkway. The aircraft hit a pocket of turbulence that nearly threw him off the walk and into the aluminum ribs of the aircraft. He cursed and shuffled ahead, now keeping both feet planted and scraping along the nonskid.

Behind him, the pressure valve opened, and Spencer emerged. Parson turned and saw him illuminated only by the shivering glow of an overhead lamp vibrating in its mounts. The crew chief's yellow MA-1 bottle hung from a strap around his shoulder, and a hose ran from the bottle to a mask covering his mouth and nose. He looked at Parson and pressed his elbows to his sides in a gesture that could only mean *It's cold.* Parson gave him an *I told you so* nod and made his way to the empennage ladder.

Near the foot of the ladder, the Pacific backlit the louvers of the stabilizer access hatch. Rays of blue neon shafted up through the hatch and danced across sheet metal and control cables. The torsion and rattle of the tail section gave a shimmer to the light as if the ocean itself were flickering. Parson wondered if the effect would distract Spencer, but there was nothing anyone could do about that.

The crew chief kneeled by the hatch, and Parson mounted the ladder to get out of his way. Then Spencer pulled out the lanyard attached to his safety harness. Normally, the lanyard strap would connect to a tie-down ring by a D clip, but back here there were no tie-down rings. The crew chief improvised by looping the strap around the bottom rung of the ladder and tying a square knot. Next, he adjusted the strap's length so if he slipped toward the hatch once he got it open, he wouldn't fall through.

Parson aimed his flashlight at his MA-1 cylinder's pressure gauge. Two hundred psi. A third of it gone already. Where was Justin? Parson wondered if it had been a mistake to use a young medic in an aviator's place. But how hard could it be? Simply bring oxygen bottles down the catwalk and take the empties back like a milkman making rounds. Parson would rather have given the job to a loadmaster. But he wanted the loadmasters downstairs with the passengers in case the plane went down and they had to do a water evacuation.

On the ladder, with his back to the pressure valves, Parson did not see Justin enter the tail section. But he heard the tromping of boots, and then the young aeromed appeared on the catwalk holding two oxygen bottles and the portable lamp. Justin placed the lamp beside the crew chief, who pointed it toward one of the access hatch bolts.

Spencer placed the drill bit against the bolt and pressed the power drill's trigger. A grinding whine rose underneath the torrents of air flowing over the C-5's tail. The aircraft's designers had placed the hatch there so maintenance workers outside, atop a stand, could service components on the ground. Opening it from the outside might take two minutes. Parson didn't know how long it would take to drill out the bolts from the inside.

After what seemed like several minutes of drilling, Spencer opened his tool bag and took out the hammer and a steel punch. He held the punch like a railroad spike and banged it with the hammer. The punch sank a couple of inches, apparently knocking what was left of the bolt out of the hole. Spencer withdrew the punch, looked at Parson, gave a thumbs-up. Then he started drilling out the next bolt.

As the crew chief worked, Justin examined the man's bottle. He tapped at the gauge and handed him a fresh cylinder. Spencer unplugged his mask from the old bottle and inserted the hose into the new one.

Parson looked at his own oxygen pressure. Seventy-five psi. Just a few breaths left. Justin extended a new bottle toward Parson and Parson swapped it with his original. The hose snapped into the receptacle with a click.

The work in the tail section made Parson think of scuba diving, which he'd learned in younger days—constantly watching air pressure, communicating by gestures, moving with effort in an environment not meant for the human body. It reminded Parson of why he preferred hunting and fishing to diving.

Instinctively, he went through his PRICE check for a new oxygen source: Pressure good, 300 psi. Regulator set to NORM. Indicator not applicable on these cylinders. Connections seated properly. Emergency setting, N/A; if you were using this thing at all, you were in an emergency.

Now that he had full oxygen again, he decided this was a good time to get his first task out of the way. He could not move the bomb until he disconnected that mercury switch. Parson climbed a few rungs until he reached the bomb. Then he took his own harness lanyard and tied it to the ladder.

He dug his penlight from his pocket, switched it on, and placed it in his mouth. Even though the light had been inside his clothing, the cold metal burned his tongue. He bit down on the light to steady it and now its beam illuminated wherever he turned his head.

Parson braced his left knee against an aluminum gusset plate, part of the tail's supporting structure. That relieved his cramped legs just a little. He kept most of his weight on his right boot, still on a ladder rung. But when he leaned backward slightly, his hips and shoulders took some of the load as well. Hardly the most comfortable position for a tricky job, but it was the best he was going to get. *Good thing I'm not claustrophobic*, he thought. *Why does it have to be so damned cold?*

With both hands free, he regarded the bomb. In the weak beam of the penlight, it looked so mundane. So harmless. A common duffel bag, with nothing out of the ordinary except the wires leading to the black rectangle of the mercury switch.

Parson unsnapped the sheath for his Leatherman multitool and he opened the tool's jaws. The jaws functioned as needle-nose pliers, but their hinge point doubled as a wire cutter. Moving his head slowly, Parson shone his penlight along the length of the wires. He wanted to find a place where he could get the Leatherman around one of the wires without moving it. If he bumped the wire and shifted that mercury switch, he'd probably have just enough time for a flicker of regret. Then the flash would take him—and everybody else—into the next world.

The wires lay flat against the canvas bag. He couldn't get so much as a knife blade between the wire and the cloth, let alone the Leatherman. Below him, Spencer banged out the second bolt from the access hatch. The crew chief looked up and motioned with another thumbs-up. His effort was pointless unless Parson could disconnect that mercury switch from its electrical source. His airplane's circuits coursed with three-phase high-voltage current—enough to light a small town. But right now his life depended on cutting power from a pissant drugstore battery.

He placed the fingertips of his left hand against the duffel bag, next to the wire. With only the slightest pressure, he felt something underneath the canvas. Whatever it was—Semtex, C-4, or RDX—it gave just a little bit. Now a gap of about a centimeter opened between the wire and the bag. Not quite enough.

Using two gloved fingers, Parson started to press one more time. Just as his hand made contact with the duffel bag, the aircraft hit turbulence. It was only light chop, but it jolted him and made him push the bag harder than he'd intended.

His chest went cold with dread. Parson withdrew his hand and held on to the ladder. He closed his eyes and felt a bead of sweat turned to ice water roll down his back. He stretched out his left leg, then braced his knee as before. The aircraft settled down again.

The penlight nearly dropped from his mouth. But when he opened his eyes and raised his head, he saw he had about an inch and a half of space between the wire and the duffel bag.

Please, God, he thought, give me five seconds of smooth air. Parson placed his Leatherman's pliers around the wire, all the way up to the cutting blades.

Time stopped. Nothing existed but the cold, the shriek of the wind, and the tenor whine of jet engines. Parson closed the tool over the wire—and pressed.

He felt the wire snap. His heart beat once. No flash. Then it beat once more. Parson exhaled. He continued to see, and to live. He inhaled oxygen, pure and frigid, and he looked down at the crew chief. Three bolts gone now. About a dozen to go.

GOLD HELD OPEN THE PRESSURE VALVE and watched the work going on in the tail. Flashlight beams jittered and bounced; they made her think of the headlamps of an Afghan jingle truck laboring up a mountain path.

Cold air flowed through the valve opening as if it were the portal to some frozen hell. She wanted to turn her face, but she didn't dare take her eyes off Parson, Justin, and the crew chief. Gold shuddered, and not entirely because of the temperature.

As she'd recovered from her capture and torture, the counselors warned her that certain things would spark unwanted memories. Any sensation that reminded her of the experience might bring anxiety, sweats, hypervigilance. For her, the main triggers were pain to the fingers and severe cold. Right now, her palms grew clammy, and her stomach churned with nausea.

She fought instinct with intellect. What would the Stoics say? Pain and discomfort exist, but they only color the world in which one acts. Therefore, they are of no consequence.

Justin began plodding up the catwalk toward her. He carried in his arms two oxygen cylinders, presumably empty, and he breathed from a third cylinder strapped around his shoulder. He kneeled at the pressure valves and pushed through the empties. Gold took them from him, then extended her arm and helped him crawl into the troop compartment.

"How's it going back there?" she asked. Though she wore a headset, she had to shout through her mask because Justin wasn't on interphone. No point dragging a cord back into the tail section.

"Slowly," he said. "Crew chief's got less than half the bolts out of that hatch." He stretched out his arms, apparently trying to absorb the relative warmth of the troop compartment.

Gold went to the recharger hose and plugged in the first bottle. The hiss brought the needle from near 0 to 300. She thumbed the hose's latching lever, and the braided steel tubing disconnected with a *pfft*. Condensation dripped from the cylinder as she handed it back to Justin. She refilled the second cylinder, then topped off Justin's and her own.

"Are you all right to head back in there?" Gold asked.

"Yes, ma'am," Justin said.

Gold couldn't get used to these junior airmen calling her ma'am. In the Army, you said ma'am and sir only to officers, but these Air Force types seemed to use those honorifics with anyone of greater rank, commissioned or not. A minor point, but she liked it that Justin was observing his service's protocol. Maybe he had his head back on straight. Without another word, he gathered the refilled bottles, opened the lower pressure valve, and reentered the tail.

Alone again in the troop compartment, Gold became aware of chatter in her headset. Perhaps it had gone on for a few minutes. She'd been so busy talking to Justin and refilling oxygen that she hadn't really heard it. But in the front of the airplane, Colman and Dunne seemed to have their own problems.

"What's three-engine ceiling now?" Colman asked.

"Twenty-nine thousand," the engineer said.

"So we won't lose any more altitude."

"Correct."

"All right," the copilot said. "I wish Major Parson were up here, but I guess we don't have any choice."

"No, we don't," Dunne said.

Gold considered whether to break in and say something. Finally, curiosity got the better of her and she pressed her TALK switch.

"Flight deck, this is Sergeant Major Gold," she said. "The major is back in the tail area, but I can have Justin give him a message."

"No, thanks," Colman said. "The book is pretty straightforward on this. Oil pressure's dropping even more on number one."

Gold wondered how serious it was, but Colman and Dunne didn't seem panicked. They sounded like they were following a technical manual that gave clear guidance.

"We need to stop talking about it and do something," Dunne said. "It's below ten psi. If we keep screwing around, we'll have an engine fire on our hands."

"Okay," Colman said. "Precautionary engine shutdown on number one. Fuel and start ignition switch to OFF."

"Confirm one," Dunne said.

"Off."

A noise came from out on the left wing that sounded like a sigh as the jet engine spun down. Gold felt no maneuvering, no descent. So maybe this didn't put the airplane in any more immediate danger. But losing an engine couldn't help matters.

She looked through the pressure valve and into the tail. The crew chief remained bent to his labor. Justin held a light for the chief, and Parson remained on the ladder. Of Parson, Gold could see only his legs and the dangling strap of his safety harness. From this distance, the three appeared to work with a casual unconcern. An uninformed observer would have no idea that a mistake or a moment of bad luck could touch off an explosion and betray them all to the water below.

More cross talk on headset. This time it was the aeromeds.

"How's he doing?" a voice asked.

"A little respiratory distress," the MCD answered. "I switched his oxygen regulator from NORMAL to EMERGENCY."

That could only mean Mahsoud. God, please let us finish this and land and get him some help, Gold thought. She felt as hollow as the inside of an expended rifle cartridge. There was nothing she could do for Mahsoud now except carry out her little part back here.

Whatever breathing trouble he had, Gold hoped he wasn't in pain. She knew from experience how agony could make time thicken and clot, drag out seconds into minutes and minutes into infinity. If you let it, pain could drive out all thoughts except the desire to make it stop.

And now pain seemed to fill this aircraft from nose to tail. It would have done so even absent this bomb, given the cargo of wounded. Amid terrorism and war, certain people took the pain for everybody else.

Gold wished she could bear Mahsoud's discomfort for him. She wished she could lighten Parson's load of responsibility. But for now, she could only point her flashlight into that crypt of a tail cone and wait for Justin to bring up more empties.

24

Feathers of frost curled across the sheet metal plating where Parson stood on the tail ladder. He guessed the moisture came from his breath, exhaled through the ports of his oxygen mask. Thicker frost, in whorls and spirals, formed on the aluminum structure nearest the crew chief. The shapes reminded Parson of the patterns of ice on rivers where he'd hunted ducks, the moving water having finally surrendered to the cold, changing its state to a motionless solid, but with the memory of when it flowed free.

This was taking longer than he'd expected. The seventh bolt gave Spencer a lot of trouble. Parson even wondered if the drill's battery was running down. The bit seemed to spin more slowly, and Parson heard Spencer's muffled curses from behind his mask.

The noise of the aircraft and slipstream changed in pitch, almost like that of a car downshifting. Parson was pretty sure that meant an engine shutting down, but he wasn't used to the sounds back here in the empennage. From the pilot's seat, he knew the plane by all its tones and vibrations as if he were part of the machine. That's where he wanted to be now if the crew had lost an engine.

Just let them deal with it, he told himself. A

commander has to delegate. Besides, if Colman couldn't handle an airplane, he wouldn't be wearing wings.

A rim of daylight gleamed at the rear edge of the access hatch. That's where the crew chief had removed the first bolts, and there the light shone more brightly than that filtered through the louvers. It was as if Spencer were prying open a door to some brilliant future without that damned bomb.

But it would never happen until he freed those bolts. And now Parson could see the drill *was* running out of power. No doubt the cold sapped the battery. Worse, that cordless drill probably wasn't meant for this kind of work, anyway. Parson didn't know what kind of torque it had, but mechanics normally used it for turning screws, not cutting through metal.

Justin shuffled back down the catwalk with fresh oxygen bottles. He moved like a spacewalking astronaut, as if only Velcro held his boots to the floor. He swapped out the crew chief's oxygen bottle and passed the other full cylinder to Parson. As Parson fumbled with the hoses and straps to complete the exchange, he heard Spencer shouting instructions to Justin:

"Go downstairs and get a new battery out of my toolbox," he said. The chief unsnapped the battery pack from the drill's pistol grip and handed it to Justin. "Bring me a hacksaw, too."

"Yes, sir," Justin yelled. He pocketed the battery, picked up the expended oxygen cylinders, and left the tail section.

Parson fumed while he waited for Justin to return. Until then, he and Spencer could make no progress. Why hadn't Spencer just brought extra batteries? Parson supposed he wasn't used to working in this kind of cold, and in more normal conditions the battery would have lasted longer. Everything about this operation lay outside the envelope of his crew's training and experience.

Parson looked at the bomb, inches from his torso. A device waiting to immolate him and everyone else aboard. What kind of hate lay behind the construction of that thing? The same kind that flew airplanes into buildings, flung acid in the faces of Afghan schoolgirls, stoned people to death.

He remembered the first time he'd encountered that kind of evil. It had happened early in his career, when he was a newly commissioned lieutenant fresh out of navigator school. The old Soviet bloc was coming apart, and Yugoslavia's self-dissolution uncorked hatreds that had remained bottled up for decades. At the height of the Balkans' ethnic cleansing, Parson and the rest of his C-130 crew left Ramstein Air Base, Germany, with a load of relief supplies bound for Sarajevo.

When the Herk began descending over Bosnia, it was early afternoon. Forested valleys of the Dinaric Alps unrolled beneath the wings, and the beauty of the terrain put Parson in mind of his native Colorado. But then columns of smoke began to appear, rising from mortared homes along the Miljacka River.

The pilots did not fly a normal straight-in arrival. They overflew the field at five thousand feet above ground level, then racked the aircraft into a sixty-degree bank to start a random steep spiral down. The crew wanted to avoid small-arms fire from the Dobrinja neighborhood. The area that had once hosted the Olympic Village now provided nests for Serb snipers.

After the C-130 touched down, the front-end crew kept the engines running while the loadmasters pushed off five pallets of aid from the UN World Food Program. Parson studied his charts for departure, but he happened to look up in time to see an airport worker step from behind a fuel truck.

A spray of red erupted from the man's back. Blood spattered the truck's hood and fender as the worker crumpled to the pavement.

"What the hell?" Parson said. "Did you see that? We need to help that guy!"

The man raised himself with both arms. Another round caught him in the head. He fell facedown and did not move.

"There's nothing we can do for him," the pilot said. "And we'll be casualties ourselves if we don't get out of here."

A mortar round exploded in the grass beside the runway. A splinter of steel chipped the C-130's center windscreen.

"They'll have this aircraft bracketed in about a minute," the pilot said. He shoved up the throttles and began to taxi. Propeller blast tousled the dead man's hair.

The aircraft trundled along past sandbags and razor wire. A shell struck the taxiway. Fragments slammed into the Herk's fuselage.

Parson had never seen mortar fire before. As he watched the explosion, he marveled that it left only a pockmark in the asphalt, not a wide crater. Then he realized blasting open a big hole wasn't the point. Those shells were built to throw shrapnel—to sling hot, jagged shards of metal through flesh and bone.

The pilot turned onto the runway and made an intersection takeoff without clearance. After the plane leveled at altitude, the copilot said, "They're killing each other over shit that happened in the thirteen hundreds."

In the years since that flight, Parson had come to find it ironic that he logged his first combat time on missions to help Muslims. And now he clung to a ladder, freezing his ass off, sucking oxygen from an MA-1 bottle, in a part of the airplane where he had no business, because of some jihadi's fucked-up version of Islam.

He checked his cylinder pressure. Ninety psi. Justin better get back soon.

Spencer pounded at the hatch with his hammer and widened the slice of radiance shining from the outside. Parson squinted as he looked through the gap. When his eyes adjusted, he made out the pattern of waves on the ocean far below like a sheet of corrugated steel.

He tried to check his pressure once more, and his daylight-narrowed pupils could not read the gauge. Stupid of me, he thought. He looked away from the hatch, into the dark corners where the bomb and its accompanying packages lay, until he could see again.

Fatigue crept up on him, and his eyes closed. Pressure against his face woke him. As he inhaled, his mask tightened around his mouth and nose. That meant his oxygen cylinder contained nothing but a vacuum. Everything around him went gray, and the light from the hatch dimmed. And there was Justin, just a gray shade, extending a fresh MA-1 toward him.

The tangle of hoses looked so confusing. Which one led where?

Parson disconnected a hose from his empty cylinder and held it. Now where did it go? He felt tugs as Justin pulled at him and the hose. Something clicked.

Parson's lungs filled with oxygen. Colors returned: yellow bottle, blue water, tan uniforms.

"You okay, sir?" Justin yelled.

Parson nodded. Then he thought, All right—let's not cut it that close again. When Justin climbed down from the ladder, Parson saw Spencer drilling out another bolt. The crew chief put down the drill, held the punch in place with his fist, and swung the hammer. One more bolt gone.

Spencer began drilling again, and he repeated the same process of boring and punching until the drill stopped working. One bolt still held the hatch in place. The chief used the hacksaw, pumping his elbows like a woodsman.

When the last bolt severed, the hatch did not fall away. It just disappeared, snatched by the slipstream. The ocean lit the inside of the tail section as if someone had switched on an arc lamp. Spencer kneeled by the open hatch, gave a high five to Justin and a thumbs-up to Parson. With both arms, the crew chief beckoned toward the opening: *It's all yours, sir. Drop that damned bomb.*

Parson drew a deep breath, lifted the duffel bag ever so slightly. No flash, no heat, no anything. Dear God, he could really do this—drop it out and be long gone before it hit trigger altitude. He raised it with one hand; the thing was lighter than he expected. He pivoted on the ladder, held the bomb over the open hatch. Parson gripped it by a handful of the duffel bag's canvas, like something annoying that he'd grabbed by the scruff of the neck . . . and he dropped it.

The bomb cleared the hatch. As soon as the wind caught it, it detonated.

THE EXPLOSION SLAMMED GOLD BACKWARD against the grating around the troop compartment stairway. Debris hurled through the negative pressure valves stung her face. A shock traveled through the frame of the aircraft into the marrow of her bones. The sound of the blast never seemed to stop; a roar like the passage of an unending train came from the tail section.

The aircraft dived, climbed, banked. The wild maneuvers generated forces that lifted her from the floor, then pinned her to it, then slid her sideways across it. The C-5 seemed to writhe in pain. Gold clawed toward the pressure valves to try to see if anyone remained alive in the tail cone.

"Major Parson!" she shouted though she knew he could not hear her.

Her headset had twisted out of place, but its left dome and ear seal remained partially over her ear. She heard Colman and Dunne fighting for control of the jet.

"Losing hydraulics on two and three," Dunne said.

"I can't do anything with it," Colman said.

"You've got only one rudder actuator left."

Gold tore the headset away. The plane's gyrations settled into an oscillating pattern: a steep climb, a moment of stability, then a stomach-knotting drop. At the top of a climb, Gold dragged herself to the pressure valves and opened the lower door.

The blast had torn open the aft end of the tail cone. Blue sky and blue water slid alternately into view, one pushing away the other, as the C-5 pitched up and down.

The wind took forms that Gold did not know existed: rushing high-altitude air nearly too strong to stand against yet too thin to breathe. The slipstream slashed at her with blades of ice. Gritty projectiles peppered her cheek. Red flecks appeared on her sleeves; they were droplets of blood launched with force enough to spatter on her uniform.

Two figures lay alongside the catwalk. Gold knew she couldn't get them by herself. She fumbled for her headset, found the TALK switch, and shouted, "We need some help back here!" Then she dropped the headset, crawled through the pressure valve, and tried to get to her feet.

The aircraft pitched up. The g-forces doubled, then tripled her body weight. Gold's muscles turned to lead and her joints to rubber. An invisible power bore her down to her knees. She knew she faced no danger of getting sucked out of the opening in the tail since the plane was depressurized. But *falling* out was another matter.

She timed her movements by the C-5's flight pattern. At the top of the climb, the unseen magnets pulling her to the floor released her, and she stumbled down the catwalk. The maelstrom of wind assaulted her ears like some chorus of the damned.

Parson clung with both hands to a length of aluminum bracing marked NO STEP. Blood speckled the legs of his ripped and punctured flight suit. Shrapnel wounds, Gold supposed. She wondered if he was conscious until he raised his head and shouted, "Get Justin!"

The aeromed stared upward through sightless eyes rolled back into his head. As Gold tried to assess his injuries, the aircraft began another dive. With nothing to tether him, Justin slid nearer the open end of the tail cone, its jagged edges in a metallic shudder as the wind tore at them.

Gold lunged toward him and grabbed him by the collar of his flight suit, her oxygen cylinder clanging against the flooring as she fell. The fall turned her cracked ribs to razors, and the pain took her breath. Sprawled across the catwalk, she held Justin with one hand and gripped a length of steel tubing with the other. Gold timed the next lurch of the aircraft and let the plane's motion help her pull him away from the opening. The Pacific loomed beyond, a fall through infinity to a sapphire obliteration. The sight brought a wrenching nothingness in her stomach.

Blood soaked the left leg of Justin's uniform, and splinters of bone jutted through the fabric in three places. The points and edges looked like foreign objects, not of the human body, shards of a vessel that had held raw meat until something crushed it. Below the ankle, cords of sinew and torn ligaments were all that remained of his foot. Wind caught the blood as it poured from the mangled knots of tissue and turned it to spray.

The crew chief had simply vanished. The lanyard of his safety harness was still tied to the empennage ladder. The other end of it, frayed and charred, flailed in the slipstream. In a fleeting thought, Gold hoped the explosion had killed him instantly, that his body had plummeted those thousands of feet with no awareness left in it.

Justin and Parson had both lost their oxygen masks. Parson still seemed alert; perhaps in all the maneuvers the jet had descended into breathable air. The C-5 banked, a roll to the right. Where the sky met the ocean, the cerulean horizon tilted across the yawning gap in the tail cone. Gold feared the next lurch might throw all three of them from the aircraft. But then she saw Parson's harness, still tied to the ladder. A measure of insurance perhaps, but someone would have to cut or untie the strap to move him.

Where was her help? Hadn't they heard her call? Gold worried that the crew might assume everyone back here was dead. If they just repressurized the airplane and flew on, she could never get back inside through the pressure valves. Along with Parson and Justin, she'd soon die of exposure or hypoxia.

She looked around the tail section. Its torn interior appeared skeletal to her, a cadaver long dead of a grievous wound. But the airplane remained very much alive, if badly hurt. The climbs and dives continued, though not with the same sickening amplitude. Maybe Colman and Dunne were regaining control. The C-5 seemed to ride gentle swells. She didn't know if they could land it in this condition, but at least the aircraft no longer threatened to plunge straight for the bottom of the ocean.

One of the pressure doors opened, and a gloved hand reached through it. At first, Gold did not recognize the flight-suited figure, face covered by an oxygen mask, as it emerged into the empennage. Loose strands of graying hair tangled around the straps of the face mask. It was the MCD.

She balanced her way down the catwalk. A loadmaster came through the pressure doors and followed behind her. When they reached Gold and Justin, they lifted the wounded aeromed by the arms and pulled him farther from the hole in the tail cone.

"Grab his legs," the MCD shouted. "I'll take his arms."

Gold got up on her hands and knees. She took Justin's right leg.

The loadmaster held him by the calf of his shattered left leg. Arterial spurts from the stump of Justin's foot reddened the loadmaster's flight suit. Justin gave no sign of consciousness. He was dead weight. Gold could find little reason to hope for his life except that the dead didn't bleed.

They carried him forward, dripping spatters of blood onto the catwalk. When they put him down by the pressure valves, the MCD opened the lower door. From inside the aircraft, two medics pulled him through. Exposed veins and tendons dangled from his stump like tentacles. They left red trails as they dragged across the valve seal.

"Stop that bleeding," the MCD yelled to her troops.

"Parson's hurt, too," Gold said.

The MCD nodded, and the three of them took half steps down the catwalk toward Parson. A rumble of turbulence put Gold on her knees again. The MCD and loadmaster pulled her to her feet. It felt a little warmer now. Maybe the aircraft really had descended quite a way, but as Gold looked out through the rip in the tail the water seemed no closer.

Parson stared up at them. So he was still conscious. The dark stains on his flight suit had all widened, but Gold saw no sign of severe blood loss anywhere.

The MCD reached into one of her leg pockets and withdrew a pair of medical shears. She cut through the strap of Parson's safety harness. Wind caught the loose end and sucked it through the opening. Whipping in the slipstream, it beat against the outside skin of the airplane until it frayed into silence.

"Can you stand?" the MCD shouted.

Parson shifted his torso and bent his left knee. He raised his upper body by his arms, and Gold held out hope his injuries were minor. But when he put weight on his right leg, he collapsed and growled through gritted teeth.

"Broken tibia," the MCD said. "He's a big guy. This won't be easy."

The loadmaster grabbed Parson by his armpits. Gold moved to take his left leg, but she hesitated. Could they lift him without hurting him?

"Let's pick him up by the thighs," the MCD yelled. "Don't put any pressure on his lower leg."

The MCD took Parson's right leg. Gold put her hands around his upper left leg. Parson made that growling sound again, and she felt something sharp through her left glove. In horror, she thought she'd found—and worsened—a compound fracture. But then she realized it was a sliver of metal embedded in his flesh. She moved her hand to avoid driving it in deeper.

"You got him?" the MCD asked.

"Yes, ma'am," Gold shouted.

"On the count of three," the MCD said. "One . . . two . . . three!"

They lifted and Parson groaned, but they got him onto the catwalk. The three struggled with him, by inches, until they moved him to the pressure valves.

The MCD opened the lower portal. She shouted a quick diagnosis to the medics waiting on the other side: "Shrapnel lacerations all over. Fracture of the lower right leg."

The aeromeds dragged Parson inside the troop compartment, and Gold, the loadmaster, and the MCD crawled through after him. When Gold put her hand down on the troop compartment floor, it came up sticky with blood. Justin lay beside a baggage closet, two medics working on him. They had scissored the legs of his flight suit, and what Gold saw brought bitter fluid up her throat. She forced it back down.

The medics had placed a combat tourniquet above Justin's knee. One of them tightened it down with the windlass rod and clipped the rod into place. The burned and torn flesh below the tourniquet looked like something a week dead. The bones were so shattered they gave no form to the muscles and left them a bleeding, shapeless mass. Justin would be lucky to live, let alone keep enough leg to walk easily on a prosthesis.

Parson sat up against the galley refrigerator. He clenched his jaw as the aeromeds cut open his flight suit and examined his legs.

"Give me a headset," he said.

"Let us treat you, sir," a medic said.

"Do what you gotta do, but give me a damned headset," Parson ordered.

Gold closed her eyes and offered a silent prayer of thanks. That was the Parson she knew: pissed off and in pain, but still in command.

25

Parson took the medic's headset and plugged it into an interphone cord coiled beside him. His legs felt as if they were bound with barbed wire. Tinnitus rang in his ears continually, like a warning tone for which there was no MUTE button, and he had to turn the headset volume all the way up to hear anything. He adjusted the mike and pressed the TALK switch.

"Flight deck, troop compartment," he said. "This is Parson. Tell me what you got."

A pause of several seconds. Then Dunne said, "Great to hear you, sir. We lost all the fluid out of systems two and three. We have the shutoff valves closed to a bunch of actuators and we're going to try to refill the reservoirs. Maybe we can get those systems back."

"Good work," Parson said. "It feels like you have partial control now. What did you do?"

"I added power whenever we climbed and I wiped it off when we dived," Colman said. "That seemed to civilize those oscillations, exactly like the book says."

"We uprigged the ailerons, too," Dunne said. "I just told him to turn on the LDCS."

"All right," Parson said. "You boys have been studying." Parson had never felt prouder of crewmates than now. They *deserved* to live. He just didn't know if they had a landable plane.

"How's everybody back there?" Dunne asked.

Parson hesitated. Then he said, "Spencer's gone. Justin's fucked up real bad. Gold is okay. I got a broken leg."

"I'm sorry," Colman said.

"Yeah." Parson didn't know what else to say. Could he have prevented the crew chief's death? He'd have to think about it later. "Repressurize the aircraft," he said.

"Yes, sir," Dunne said.

When the medic adjusted Parson's broken leg, pain shot through his body as if his nerves had turned to acid. He cried out, then closed his eyes hard and muttered curses. It was the worst he'd suffered since an insurgent twisted his cracked wrist four years ago when he and Gold were captured. He felt light-headed. So this is what it's like to pass out from pain, he thought. But he remained alert. No such luck as a few minutes of unconsciousness.

Sweat beaded cold on the end of his nose and dropped onto the front of his flight suit. He felt a flutter of panic. For a moment, the agony put him on the ground in the snow in Afghanistan. He forced the memory back down, pushed it into that mental oubliette where he kept all the emotions he could not afford.

The MCD helped remove his boots and secure the plastic splints, and she managed not to hurt him again.

"I want to give you morphine," she said, "but Justin's going to need what little we have left."

"That's okay," Parson said. "We still got problems, and I don't need anything that'll screw up my judgment."

"We have plenty of aspirin."

"It'll do."

The MCD went down the steps and came back with two white tablets and a foam cup filled with water. Parson downed the aspirin and gulped all the water. He hadn't realized he was so thirsty. The aeromeds brought him another cup, and he drank it in three swallows. Part of it ran down the sides of his mouth.

"Once the aspirin kicks in," the MCD said, "we'll get some of that metal out of your skin. What's in deeper might have to stay there."

"Just get me so you can put me back in the cockpit."

"You're crazy, Major," the MCD said. "You're in no condition to fly. Your copilot and engineer have the airplane."

"They do," Parson said. An argument normally would have made him angry, but he was glad to talk about Colman and Dunne. "They did damned good."

"So let them fly the plane."

"I will," Parson said. "I can't fly now. I sure as hell can't push on rudder pedals. But I can think. So I need to be with my crew."

"We'll see, Major."

As Parson spoke with the MCD, he could hear Colman and Dunne on interphone. It sounded like they'd restored some of the lost hydraulic pressure, but not to the control surfaces in the tail.

"So what do we have?" Parson asked.

"Nothing to the rudders and elevators but system one," Dunne said. "It's real sluggish."

Parson knew pilots who had crashed the simulator with lesser malfunctions. He'd thought his crew would be home free if they got rid of the bomb. But now when they tried to maneuver for landing, would the airplane just roll over on its back and die?

"By the way, sir," Colman asked, "what made the bomb go off?"

"Damned if I know," Parson said. "I cut the mercury switch and moved it, no problem. But when I dropped it out, the son of a bitch exploded."

"It went off outside the plane?" Dunne asked.

"Yeah."

"I guess that's why we're still flying," Colman said.

"If it was triggered barometrically," Dunne said, "there's no telling what kind of pressure gradients it hit when it entered the slipstream."

Typical flight engineer to want to know how the fucking thing worked, Parson thought. All that mattered was that it *had* worked. Just not inside the aircraft, thank God.

"Look," Parson said, "you guys keep doing what you're doing.

I'd like to get back up there as soon as I can, but the nurses want to work on me first." At least he felt confident leaving the aircraft to Colman and Dunne a little longer. Despite the Air Force's endless management courses, Parson felt you couldn't teach leadership. It was a natural ability, like hand-eye coordination. Either you had it or you didn't. And those two had enough to get by.

"No rush, sir," Dunne said. "I think the worst is over."

Parson didn't know about that. They needed to take an object weighing hundreds of tons, flying at more than four hundred miles per hour, and get it down to landing speed on a narrow strip of asphalt. That required control they might not have.

"The aircraft's in bad shape," he said, "but at least it's all ours now."

"Roger that, sir," Colman said.

A small comfort, Parson thought. We've traded one crisis for another. He sensed an almost mechanical tightness inside him, something more than muscles tensed by pain. This felt spring-loaded, held by a pawl he could not unlatch. The burden of his duties had become tactile.

"Should we work on him here or downstairs?" the medic asked.

"Let's take Major Parson down the steps," the MCD said. "He can't stay up here forever, and he seems to think he's going back to the flight deck eventually."

"I'll help," Gold said.

"Know how to do a seated carry, ma'am?" the medic asked.

Gold nodded. She kneeled beside Parson and put his arm over her shoulder. Then she and the medic joined their arms under his thighs and stood up with him. That hurt; he felt shards grinding into the meat of his legs. Gold and the medic began easing him down the troop compartment steps one rung at a time. Each step stung, though it was bearable.

By now, Dunne had restored cabin pressure, and Gold had removed her oxygen mask and cylinder. Her untied blond hair spilled over Parson's forearm and hand. For a moment, he let the strands flow among his fingers. Then he forced his mind to a different train of thought.

"Will Justin make it?" he asked.

"I really don't know," the medic said. "He's lost a lot of blood, enough to cause tachycardia. His heart rate's way up, trying to pump up the pressure."

Just like a machine, Parson thought, like the systems in an aircraft. Everything around me seems to be dying for lack of fluid and pressure.

GOLD AND THE MEDIC PLACED PARSON on a litter in the cargo compartment. He winced as he lay back. She hated seeing him hurt like that. She wished she could do more for him, but she could only place her hand on his chest and say, "You did well, sir. Thank you."

"It's not over yet," Parson said.

"I know."

The MCD and another nurse put Justin on a litter beside Parson. The wounded aeromed still showed no sign of consciousness.

"He needs a transfusion," the MCD said. "Right now."

The other nurse checked Justin's dog tags. "He's B negative," the nurse said. "Rare."

"Find out if anybody else on board has that blood type," the MCD said.

The aeromeds checked the dog tags and medical records of the less seriously injured patients. They also polled the crew on interphone. Nobody had B negative. When the nurses asked Gold, she said, "I'm O negative."

"We can work with that," the MCD said. "O negative is the universal donor."

For the second time in twenty minutes, Gold offered a cosmic thanks. She felt useful again, a functioning senior noncommissioned officer. Without another word, she unbuttoned her ACU top and removed it. The T-shirt underneath bore the white arcs and splotches of salt stains from dried sweat.

The MCD tied a blue elastic band around Gold's arm, about two inches above the elbow. Gold felt the pinch of the restricting band, then the cold wet of the alcohol pad and the prick of the needle. The little discomforts gave her a slight glow of satisfaction. Her blood filled the clear tubing connected to the needle and made it look like red cord. The MCD handed her a roll of gauze.

"Squeeze on this," the aeromed commander said.

Gold closed her first around the gauze. She alternately gripped the roll and then relaxed her fingers. At the other end of the tubing, the blood smeared into the folds of a plastic pouch. Slowly, it filled the plastic wrinkles with scarlet. Gold closed her eyes and tried to rest, let the blood flow and her mind wander.

In all of her travels, studying, and reading, she had yet to understand why people did such awful things as place bombs on airplanes. She sometimes doubted the terrorists themselves believed the stated justifications. But philosophy—and her own experience—had led her to one conclusion: Ultimately, evil was the assertion of self-interest over the greater good. So its opposite had to be self-sacrifice. If she could bleed a little for someone else—in this case quite literally—then perhaps she was pulling in the right direction.

From across the cargo compartment, Gold watched the aeromeds work on Parson. They slit open the pant legs of his uniform from ankle to hip.

"Hey," Parson protested, "I don't have another flight suit with me."

"That's the least of your problems," the MCD said.

"You got that right."

Dried blood matted the black hairs of Parson's legs. Despite the well-defined calf and thigh muscles, the bruises, lacerations, and puncture wounds made his limbs look frail and weak. The MCD painted his injuries with an antiseptic tincture. Then she worked at one of his wounds with a set of forceps. Parson swore, and the MCD apologized. In the jaws of the forceps, she lifted a bloody, twisted shard of metal and dropped it into a trash bag of medical waste.

"So how bad is it?" Parson asked.

"I don't see anything real serious, apart from the fracture," the MCD said. "Whenever this is over, a surgeon can get more of this stuff out of you than I can."

The plane still seemed to ride swells. It worried Gold to realize the crew did not have the aircraft entirely under control. As a paratrooper, she understood only the very basics of aerodynamics. But she knew an airplane moved in three axes: pitch, roll, and yaw. Right now, pitch seemed to have a mind of its own.

She could understand why Parson wanted so badly to get back in the pilot's seat. And she hoped the MCD wouldn't give him much of an argument. His body was wounded, but his head remained sound. The more aeronautical minds on that flight deck, the better.

The MCD pulled three more pieces of shrapnel from Parson's legs. He made no noise, but as she worked he gripped the side poles of his litter so hard that the bones of his hands stood out. Gold had watched him swallow the aspirin. Poor medicine for this kind of pain.

The ancient Stoics would have approved of him, she thought. Despite the sting of metal barbs under his skin, he wanted to do his job.

Gold didn't know what it would take to put this wounded airplane on the ground safely, or if it was even possible. She had a feeling Parson wasn't even sure himself. Out the windows, she could see puffy fair-weather clouds dotting the ocean like a field of cauliflower. The Pacific was waiting for the aircraft, whether it touched down intact on an island or plunged inverted into the water. The elements, the sea and the sky—just like the forbidding terrain of Afghanistan—took no sides, made no judgments. But neither did they forgive mistakes.

When Gold had filled the pouch with a pint of her blood, the MCD removed the needle.

"Will that be enough?" Gold asked.

"It'll have to be," the MCD said. "You're the only person who can give him blood."

The MCD took the pint and connected fresh tubing to it. Then she mounted it on a pole beside Justin's litter and inserted a needle into his arm.

"Somebody hack the clock and keep an eye on him for fifteen minutes," she said. One of the medics pressed a button on his flight watch and stood by Justin. The MCD went back to Parson.

"What are you looking for?" Gold asked the medic.

"Hemolytic reaction, anaphylactic reaction," he said. "But if it happens, there's not much we can do about it."

"Why not?"

"We're not equipped to deal with it. This transfusion just has to work. Most people have ten or twelve pints, and he's lost at least four or five."

"Can I give another pint?" Gold asked.

"No," the medic said. "Good of you to ask, but we won't do that. We'll do the next best thing."

The medic inserted a second needle in Justin's other arm. The additional IV dripped clear liquid from a bag marked LACTATED RINGER'S INJECTION USP.

Justin's eyelids fluttered, and he made a long, moaning sound.

"Hold on for us, buddy," the medic said. "You done good."

"I'm sorry your friend got hurt," Gold said to the medic. "Do you know him well?"

"Yeah, he's pretty green. But he doesn't mind working. I can't figure why he cracked up earlier. Seen too much too early, maybe."

"May I talk to him?" Gold asked.

"It won't hurt," the medic said, "but I don't know if he can hear you."

Gold had seen chaplains whisper words of comfort to the wounded and dying. A soothing voice could give strength to someone fighting for life or ease the passing of someone losing that fight. A minister had once told her it didn't even matter what you said. It helped just to keep them company, remind them they weren't alone.

She wanted to be in three places at once. She wanted badly to check on Mahsoud. She wanted to let Parson squeeze her hand while the MCD plucked foreign objects from his body. But for now, she thought she could do the most good here.

"Airman," she whispered, "this is the sergeant major. We're all proud of you. You helped Major Parson do what he had to do."

Justin's eyes opened about halfway. They seemed cloudy and uncomprehending. Gold watched her blood flow into him, and to her relief, he suffered no reaction to the transfusion. The medic checked his watch. "Well, at least that's working," the medic said.

"The transfusion's going fine, Justin," Gold said. "I'd have felt rejected if you didn't like my blood." She tried to think of more to say, just to keep the words coming. "That injury doesn't have to stop you. You can still be a paramedic, almost anything you want. You know the Golden Knights, the Army parachute team? One of those guys has an artificial leg."

Gold continued her monologue. She spoke of the New England countryside, of maple leaves and maple syrup. She asked if Justin liked Bach. She inquired about his favorite subjects in school. She told him hers were history and social studies. After a while, his eyes opened all the way, and he looked straight at her.

"Bomb gone," he said.

26

Parson's legs felt as if they were on fire, reignited with each touch of the MCD's forceps. Finally, she stopped and said, "That's all I can do. You'll still set off metal detectors, though."

The MCD and another nurse bandaged his wounds as best they could. The pain still burned, but the flames flickered down into a heated ache like banked embers. The nurses closed the rips in the pant legs of his flight suit with safety pins.

"Now you look like a punk rocker," the MCD said.

"Country's more my speed," Parson said. "I want to get back to the flight deck."

"If you insist," the MCD said.

Parson raised up on his arms and tried to turn over on his back. The pain hit him again, this time more like lightning than fire. Most of it came from the fracture. "Fuck!" he shouted.

"I guess now you know to let us help you," the MCD said.

Then help me, damn you, Parson thought. He realized that was just the pain talking. She was doing all she could with what she had. She pulled gently on his arms to help him roll over.

"Now sit up very slowly," she said.

Parson levered himself into a sitting position,

taking his time. Every movement hurt, but not with the searing pain he'd experienced a moment ago.

"How about we take you up to the flight deck the same way we carried you down from the troop compartment?" the MCD asked.

"That was pretty uncomfortable," Parson said. "I think I can make it if you just give me one guy to lean on."

"All right. But don't put any weight at all on that broken leg."

"I won't," Parson said. "Can I have my boots back?"

"No. You might experience some swelling in your legs and feet. You're better off without footwear."

So I won't die with my boots on, Parson thought. But at least I'll be in command of my aircraft.

The MCD and one of the medics eased Parson down from his litter. With his arms around their shoulders, he steadied himself on his unbroken leg. Through his sock, he felt the warmth of the under-floor heating system. At least some things on the airplane still worked. Gold watched him as he mounted the flight deck ladder.

"What can I do to help, sir?" she asked.

"Give me a few minutes to get settled in upstairs," Parson said. "Then you can bring me a cup of water and some more aspirin."

"Yes, sir."

Parson hoped she'd come up and stay in the nav seat. Her presence had a calming influence that helped him think clearly. She seemed to have that effect on most people. Except, of course, that bastard who'd pulled the fire handles and tried to kill everybody.

The medic gripped Parson's upper left arm, and Parson held on to the handrail with his right. He picked up his good leg—or at least his less injured leg—and let his weight rest on the medic and the handrail. Then he put his foot up on the next rung. Fortunately, the ladder did not run vertically from the cargo compartment floor. It was essentially a retractable stairway, on an incline, and Parson managed to climb it one step at a time. Each time he put his foot down, the metal structure shuddered.

Eventually, he reached the top step and the flight deck door.

He pushed the door open. Then he stood and puzzled for a moment, holding onto the handrails, trying to figure how to make it to his seat.

From the front bunk room, Mahsoud recognized him. Mahsoud lifted his oxygen mask to speak. "Major Parson," he called. "Sir, are you—hurt?"

"I'm okay, Mahsoud. Thanks."

Dunne and Colman both turned around. Dunne unbuckled his harness, stood up, and said, "Let me help you to a bunk room."

"Bullshit," Parson said. "You can help me to the pilot's seat. I want to see what's going on."

Dunne went to the pilot's seat and slid it all the way left and aft. Then he and the medic helped Parson hobble between the seat and the center console. When Parson's bad leg brushed against a seat adjustment lever, it caused him another blinding jolt of pain.

"Son of a bitch," Parson cried. Then he said, "No, not you guys. It just hurts like a son of a bitch."

"I bet it does," Colman said. "You sure you're up for this?"

"Yeah, I was getting bored downstairs."

Dunne and the medic lowered Parson into his seat. Parson noticed Dunne had a scarlet blotch across the white of his right eye—no doubt a capillary burst during the repeated depressurizations. It didn't seem to bother him. "You ready for me to move your chair?" Dunne asked.

"Yeah, just do it slow."

Dunne moved a lever and slid Parson forward and to the center of the seat tracks.

"Want your rudder pedals cranked closer to you?" Dunne asked.

"No, I can't do anything with my feet. Colman's got the aircraft. I'll just supervise."

Parson reached down into his helmet bag and found his sunglasses and headset where he'd left them. When he put them on, something seemed to click within him like a switch returning to its normal setting. His personality, training, and talents had brought him to this place, and he felt he belonged in it. He still didn't know if he was the best aircraft commander to handle this set of problems. But he was the only one here.

He gathered up the ends of his leather-and-webbing seat harness. Then he connected the steel fittings of the quick-release buckle and closed the locking lever. Parson listened for a moment to the slipstream hissing like river rapids. He looked out at the Pacific, furrowed with swells and dotted by low clouds. Then he got back to work.

A scan of the panels gave little but bad news. Warning lights decorated the cockpit like a Christmas tree. On the engineer panel, he saw GEN OUT, PUMP OUT, LOW PRESS, all from that number one engine shut down for lack of oil pressure. On his own annunciator panel, he noted ELEVATOR POWER and RUDDER POWER. They merely suggested more trouble above, on the overhead panel. The indicators up there illustrated his difficulties in more detail, with hydraulic system warning lights for each individual control actuator: SYS OFF, SYS OFF, SYS OFF, SYS OFF. Colman had all three axes of the autopilot engaged. Parson wondered how hard it was working to maintain some semblance of stable flight, so he decided to see for himself.

"I want to feel how it's flying for a minute," Parson said. "It's all yours after that."

"Yes, sir," Colman said.

Parson placed both hands on the yoke. He put his thumb on a red button marked AP DISC. Then he punched it.

The yoke immediately pressed forward against his fingers as the nose dropped. The vertical speed indicator showed a descent of about six hundred feet per minute. Parson pulled back to regain the lost altitude. For several seconds, the aircraft did not respond. Then the nose came up into a thousand-foot-per-minute climb. The C-5 overshot its original altitude, and again it took several seconds to respond to Parson's control inputs. The delayed reactions reminded Parson of when he'd once fired a replica flintlock rifle: after the trigger pull, the fizz of powder in the pan, then nothing, nothing, and BANG.

"Oh, boy," Parson said. "She's hurt real bad."

"That's the truth," Colman said. "I've had to learn to fly all over again."

Parson figured the depowered control surfaces were free-floating, causing those oscillations. He waited until the nose leveled somewhat, and then he said, "All right, I've had enough. Reengage."

Colman pressed buttons on the center console, and the autopilot and flight augmentation computers took over again. Even they could not hold completely level flight. Parson imagined their servos and EH valves in constant motion trying to stabilize something inherently unstable.

"We're going to have to figure some way to get more pitch control," Parson said.

In the aircraft's current state, there was no telling what it would do at touchdown. If the deck angle dropped, the C-5 would likely slam down nose first and break apart. If the nose cycled up, the plane would climb out of ground effect at low speed, enter an aerodynamic stall, and fall back down like a cinder block. Probably not survivable either way. And at Johnston Island, there were no fire trucks, no rescue teams. Nothing but a ribbon of decaying pavement.

"What can we do?" Colman asked. Parson noted his tone as much as his words. No quaver in his voice now. Just an academic question. As if this were a simulator.

"I'm thinking," Parson said.

As Parson scanned his instruments, he remembered the vibration problem on the number four engine. He placed his thumb and forefinger around the knob of the number four throttle. He felt it trembling, worse than before. Like the rumble of a distant train, sensed by the touch of a rail.

JUSTIN DIDN'T STAY ALERT FOR LONG. He drifted into a morphine trance, for which Gold was grateful. Then he seemed to fall asleep. Some of the color returned to his cheeks, or was it her imagination? She wanted to believe her blood and the saline solution had brought him back from the brink. But she knew his continued survival depended on a safe landing and then a quick medevac from Johnston Island. Both appeared far from likely.

Something burned slow within her, like the hung fire of a cartridge with a bad primer. The feeling reminded her of working with Provincial Reconstruction Teams in Afghanistan. The PRT would enter a village supposedly cleared of Taliban. By then, things should have been safe, the way cleared for the building of a school or a clinic. But the chatter of an AK-47 or the crump of a distant IED would start the war all over again. Eventually, nothing felt secure anywhere. For Gold, it brought to mind more words from Marcus Aurelius: *Our life is a warfare, and a mere pilgrimage.* If safe harbor existed, it was not on this mortal dimension.

Gold looked for a foam cup and she could find no new ones. From the floor of the cargo compartment, she took the cleanest used one, then filled it with the last few inches of water from an opened plastic bottle. The MCD gave her two more aspirin, and Gold climbed the steps to the flight deck.

When she opened the door, daylight assaulted her eyes. The blue ocean reflected the sun's rays as if the water were lit from beneath the surface. All the crew members wore their aviator's shades, and they were deep in conversation on headset. Dunne had two thick manuals open across the flight engineer's table. One of the pages had a multicolored schematic that looked to Gold like abstract art. The caption read HYDRAULIC SYSTEM NUMBER ONE. Colman was looking up at the overhead panel. Parson was talking, pointing to switches.

He looked more than four years older. Pale skin, now shadowed with stubble, stretched across his jawbone like aged parchment. A bloody scratch marked his nose. When he removed his sunglasses to rub his eyes, they were as red as an addict's.

Gold didn't want to interrupt, so she extended her cupped hand silently, holding the aspirin. Parson nodded at her and took them and the water. He cut his eyes toward the nav station and said, "Have a seat. You won't bother us." Then he popped the aspirin into his mouth, took a swig of water, swallowed, and frowned.

"I will, sir," she said, "after I check on Mahsoud."

In the forward bunk room, Mahsoud lay awake, holding the oxygen mask to his face. His eyes widened when he saw Gold. He raised his mask and said, "How are you, teacher?"

"I am well," she said. She didn't say, I am tired. I want this to end. I want to wake up from this bad dream.

For a moment, she wanted to climb into the bunk opposite Mahsoud and pull that green U.S.-issued blanket over her. There, she could imagine herself safe as in the bedroom of her childhood home and forget the speed, altitude, and the damaged state of this machine. But she decided not to indulge in illusory security. Life's only guarantee was death. No point denying it, even for a few minutes.

Gold thought Mahsoud looked better. But then a spasm of coughing racked him. He lifted the mask until his fit of hacking cleared. When he inhaled again, he drew a rasping breath that reminded Gold of a child she'd seen in Herat dying of whooping cough. It didn't take an aeromed to know Mahsoud had fluid in his respiratory tract.

He needed a real hospital right now. Gold did some rough geography in her head. If Parson and his crew managed to land the plane, a miracle in itself, where was the nearest medical facility? Hawaii. Hickam Air Force Base. How far was that from Johnston? Probably several hundred miles east. Not far compared to the distance they'd already traveled.

"Put the mask back on, Mahsoud," Gold said in Pashto. "You need the oxygen."

Mahsoud nodded, coughed once more, and replaced the mask. Gold heard that rasp again, muffled this time.

"Have you ever been on a beach?" Gold asked. "Seen waves breaking on shore?"

Mahsoud shook his head. His eyes held a puzzled look: *Why are you asking me this?*

Gold decided not to pursue the thought further. She told Mahsoud to rest and that she'd be close by if he needed anything. Then she sat at the nav table and put on her headset.

Parson, Colman, and Dunne were still working out their technical problems. Dunne had opened the metal rings on one of his binders, and the three of them were passing around pages.

"So it says to depower the ground spoilers," Parson said on interphone. "Then you override the lockout and use the spoiler handle."

"And that makes the flight spoilers come up together?" Colman asked.

"Yeah," Parson said. "That should give us a nose-up pitching moment."

"It will," Dunne said. "But it'll also dump part of the lift, so you're going to have to add some power."

"And time it all just right," Parson said. Then he noticed Gold in the nav seat. "Welcome back," he said.

Colman shook his head. "Sure sounds tricky," he said.

"You bet it is," Parson said, "but it's all we got."

Gold did not understand everything she heard, but she could tell they were talking about something they'd never done before. And they'd have to figure it out despite their pain and sleep deprivation.

"Have you ever done this in the sim?" Colman asked.

"No," Parson said.

"I don't think it's been flight-tested, either," Dunne added.

"Maybe we ought to flight-test it ourselves at altitude before we try to land with it," Colman said.

"That's a good idea," Parson said.

Gold considered the task faced by the crew. Hundreds of miles of ocean lay ahead that they had to roll up, minute by minute, with a crippled aircraft. And that was the easy part. Then they had to aim this thing at a strip of asphalt probably narrower than the plane's wingspan, using controls that didn't work.

She felt frail as she looked out over the water spangled by slanting light. The sight gave her a chill. Her own life seemed brief and unimportant now that it might be nearing its end. Once at Nags Head, while on leave from Fort Bragg, she had watched a German shepherd puppy walk on the beach, apparently for the first time. The vastness of the sea frightened the animal, and it sat in the sand and yowled and cried. Now Gold understood how the pup felt. It had suddenly faced its own insignificance. The sweep of creation overwhelmed the animal's mind, as it nearly had Gold's.

The crew looked over stray pages from their manuals. Then Dunne gathered up the sheets, placed them back in his binder, and snapped the rings closed.

"So do we want to try this now?" Colman asked.

"No time like the present," Parson said. He reached overhead and flipped a row of switches. At each click, a corresponding OFF light illuminated. Gold didn't quite get this business of turning things off; more than enough parts seemed to have stopped working on their own. But Parson and his crew had clearly done some in-flight research.

"What do you want me to do?" Colman asked.

"Take the control column," Parson said. "When you're ready, punch off the autopilot. I'll take the spoiler handle. You got the throttles."

"All right," Colman said. "Here goes nothing." He placed his hands around the yoke.

"Remember," Parson said, "if it all goes to hell, just put the airplane back in the configuration it's in now. And if we can't control it, we might as well know right here."

"Yes, sir," Colman said. "Disengaging."

Colman pressed a button with his thumb. The nose climbed. Gold watched shadows in the flight deck crawl across the floor as the angle of sunlight changed. She felt a dip in her stomach.

"A little forward pressure," Parson said. The nose continued rising, then reversed itself and fell. "All right, now, a little back pressure."

Parson moved the handle on the center console, and the nose slowed its drop. He moved the handle farther, and the nose pitched up. Gold's stomach lurched again. The sensations made no sense. The nose was climbing yet she felt she was falling.

"Altitude," Dunne said.

"Shit, we lost two thousand feet," Colman said. "I didn't even notice."

"Don't forget," Dunne said. "You gotta add power when you do that."

"Sure as hell can't do this and chew gum at the same time," Colman said.

"Do you want to try it with flaps down?" Dunne asked.

"I don't think so," Parson said. "No telling what this damned thing will do if we lower flaps. I'd rather land fast even if we burn up the brakes."

"Works for me," Colman said.

"I do want to try it at a slower speed than this, though," Parson said. "We can't touch down at three hundred knots."

Gold marveled at their clinical detachment, as if lives, including their own, didn't depend on every decision. She felt herself a patient on an operating table, under the scalpel but completely aware, listening to the banter of surgeons.

"Now?" Colman asked.

"Yeah," Parson said. "Slow us down to two hundred."

Colman eased back on the throttles. He moved only three of them. The other remained out of place like a missing tooth, and Gold remembered the crew had already shut down one of the engines. The undertones of wind and turbines hushed as the aircraft decelerated. The nose fell, rose, fell again.

"Careful on trim," Parson said.

"She's handling different now that we're slow," Colman said. He moved one of his hands, and Gold saw his palm had left a sheen of sweat on the horn of the yoke.

"You got less lift now," Parson said, "and what controls you still have are less effective."

"Altitude," Dunne warned. Gold noticed needles and tapes moving within the instruments, though she could not tell what it meant.

"Let's catch that descent," Parson said.

Colman pulled back on the yoke and advanced the throttles. Parson tugged at that handle on the center console again, and the nose snapped up sharply. The abrupt maneuver startled Gold so that she gripped the nav seat's armrests. In the next moment, she thought she knew exactly how, when, and where she would die.

The aircraft shuddered. The warbling screech of a warning tone sounded in the cockpit. The C-5 stopped flying. It rolled off on its left wing, then dropped its nose toward the ocean. The windscreen showed nothing but blue water straight below.

"Stall," Dunne said. Voice calm but eyes wide.

Pens and manuals clattered against the consoles. Screams erupted downstairs. Gold hugged herself into a tight ball and hoped the end would come quickly.

"Power off," Parson said. "Get it back." His words carried the resin of tension.

Colman slapped the throttles, pulled at the control column. The Pacific began to twist in the windscreen.

"Opposite rudder," Parson said.

Colman kicked, and the sea stopped rotating. Then the ocean seemed to tilt away as the nose began to come up again. Gold's cheeks sagged from some malign form of gravity, doubled and tripled, and coming from wrong directions.

"Airspeed," Dunne said.

The crew seemed to have kicked into some cyborg state, become mere components of the aircraft. Not a wasted motion or word. Not even sparing the breath for profanity.

"Got it," Colman said. Then he put his left hand on the throttle levers.

"Wait," Parson said. "Wait—now gimme some power back."

Colman advanced the throttles. He wasn't wearing gloves, and as he adjusted the power he glanced down at his hand as if something had bitten it. He took his hand off the levers and shook his fingers. Gold saw that one of the throttles—the one to the far right—was shaking so hard it buzzed in its mountings. The aircraft leveled and flew. Gold closed her eyes, exhaled a long breath.

"What's with number four?" Colman asked.

Out on the right wing, something exploded.

27

The aircraft shook so violently Parson could hardly read instruments. But he could see and feel enough to know the number four engine had disintegrated.

"Somebody scan that wing," he said.

Colman turned in his seat and looked out the window. "It's shelled out pretty bad," he said. "And it's on fire."

"Emergency shutdown checklist," Parson ordered. He wasn't surprised the damned engine finally blew. It had been running for about thirty hours.

Parson pulled the number four fire handle, then pressed a button to shoot extinguishing agent into the engine. Colman pushed up the power on the two remaining engines. Dunne's hands played across the engineer's panel; Parson heard the clicks and snaps of switches being turned off. With an engine fire added to their problems, Parson wondered if he and his crew were just going through the motions. But they'd come too far to give up now.

"Two-engine ceiling's nine thousand feet," Dunne said.

Parson tried to interpret the blurred and bouncing needles and indicators in front of him. The C-5 seemed to be descending at around a thousand feet per minute.

"Just hold this attitude," he told Colman. "She'll level off by herself when we get to nine thousand."

No fire warning lights were on, but Parson realized he'd never seen any to begin with. That really meant nothing. An engine coming apart might rip out the sensors and circuitry for fire detection.

"Is it still burning?" Parson asked.

"You bet it is," Colman said.

Parson flipped a switch to direct another bottle of extinguishing agent into the bad engine and he pressed the FIRE button again.

"How about now?" he asked.

Colman peered outside, shook his head. "Still burning," he said.

Dunne unharnessed himself and stood to look out the window. Parson could tell from his expression he was puzzled. The flight engineer looked back at his own panel, then out at the engine again.

"Those aren't flames," he said. "They're sparks."

"What the hell?" Parson asked.

"The fan's still windmilling," Dunne said, "and those titanium blades are scraping against the inside of that fucked-up cowling."

Parson leaned in his seat to see for himself. The effort brought waves of pain from his broken leg, and he cursed under his breath. He cursed again when he saw number four. Sure enough, a fountain of sparks spewed from the engine like those from a knife blade held against a spinning grindstone. The plume shimmered and danced for several yards behind the tailpipe.

"Is there anything we can do to stop it from turning like that?" Parson asked.

"No," Dunne said, "but I imagine it'll quit by itself soon enough."

No telling what that implied. If that TF-39 finally seized up, what further damage could it do? The pylon and wing structure might already be compromised, depending on whatever stresses the engine caused when it let go. The aft end of the cowling looked like someone had fired buckshot through it from the inside. The force of the disintegration had thrown parts, probably turbine blades, through the sheet metal. The technical term was "uncontained failure." Parson wondered that the compressor still turned at all.

He leaned back in his seat and closed his eyes. Tried to think. He drowsed, faded, entered a dark wood infested with copperheads. The only route away from them led through them. When Parson jolted awake, he wondered how long he'd slept. He checked his watch. Only seconds.

Whatever adrenaline had kept him alert was gone now. Just a little longer, he told himself. Hold on just a little longer. He knew that could make all the difference in a combat situation: the guts to hold course, hold position, stay on the target, just a few seconds more. This wasn't exactly combat, but it would sure as hell do until the real thing came along.

Gold had remained silent through the engine failure. Now he felt her hand on his upper left arm. Those thin fingers, with their hints of scars, pressed down ever so slightly, and his anxiety broke like a vacuum, if only just for a moment.

Parson took her gesture as a reassurance, an expression of confidence in him. He looked back at her over his aviator's glasses. She met his eyes, nodded, looked away.

The jet leveled at nine thousand feet, and now Parson needed information. What was the temperature deviation down here? It would affect fuel burn. His finger hovered over the control pad for his FMS on the center console. In his exhaustion, he struggled to remember the keystrokes to give him the data he wanted. He was so tired he had to think about things that should have been second nature. It was as if his brain's automatic functions had shut down and switched to manual.

He recalled, pressed buttons, read numbers. "Temp deviation is plus fifteen," he told Dunne. "What do your charts tell you?"

Dunne ran his pencil through a graph, tapped at his calculator. "We're still okay on fuel," he said.

Parson let out a long breath. Then he said, "All right, the box says we have five hundred seventy-five miles to go."

"What about our pitch problem?" Colman asked.

Parson wasn't sure how to answer that. Given what had happened earlier, it seemed the spoilers would, indeed, help bring up the nose a bit. But beyond some unknown threshold, they'd dump the lift and bring on a stall. Parson and Colman had not practiced with it enough to perfect the technique and they couldn't screw around with it anymore after two engines had failed.

"When we make our approach," Parson said, "just keep it in a level attitude as best you can. You're not looking for a smooth landing, just a survivable one. I'm not touching that fucking spoiler handle again unless I have to."

A disagreeable fact lodged in his mind: He had done all he could. The thought gave him no satisfaction. Rather, it made him realize his limits. He and his crew and passengers remained trapped within this enclosed tube of metal, a certain mass traveling at a certain speed, with a given mix of flammable materials and a set number of system malfunctions. Soon now Parson must allow his decisions to run their course, let physics and gravity do what they would.

He wondered if a dying man might feel this way as he waited for judgment. The sum of his deeds, both good and evil, now closed out and tallied. And on the other side either paradise or damnation awaited, depending on the final calculus.

Parson examined his radar altimeter. Its digital numbers flickered and danced as the radar beam swept the water: 9005, 8990, 9003, 9000. He realized his aircraft had descended below the bomb's presumed trip point. If he hadn't already gotten rid of the damned thing, the people under his command might be dead already.

And he still had work to do. Could he let somebody know his status? He decided to try the HF radios again, just for good measure. Parson turned his wafer switch to HF1.

"Mainsail," he called. "Air Evac Eight-Four."

No answer. He repeated the call. Still nothing. Parson switched to HF2 and tried again. Nothing but static.

All right, he asked himself, now what? The C-5 was no longer on any charted jet route. There might be no one anywhere near here monitoring the emergency channels. But it couldn't hurt to try. Parson turned his wafer switch once more.

"Any station," he said, "Air Evac Eight-Four."

The answer came in grainy UHF: "Air Evac Eight-Four, Reach Two-Zero has you weak but readable. We are a C-17 off Hickam, en route your destination. Please advise."

A rescue bird. Was it possible? Or was this some auditory hallucination? Maybe not. Parson saw Colman, Dunne, and Gold were looking at him. So they'd heard it, too.

"We're about five hundred miles out from Johnston," Parson transmitted. "The bomb's gone now, but it went off when we jettisoned it. Two engines failed, heavy damage, marginal control."

"Reach Two-Zero copies," the C-17 pilot called. "We have a medical team on board. Look, buddy, you just set that thing down on that chunk of coral, and we'll take you home."

Parson leaned back against the headrest, looked out at the Pacific. Glints of sunlight sparkled on the water like drifting shards of silver. Just set that thing on that chunk of coral. Just lay your burdens down. If only it were that simple. But if he and his crew could pull it off, salvation awaited in the form of a C-17 Globemaster and the medics, food, water, and morphine inside it. God, for the morphine.

GOLD BEGAN TO WORRY ABOUT the best-case scenario. What if the crew actually *did* land this thing? How would Parson—let alone Mahsoud, Justin, and the other patients—get out quickly if necessary?

"Yeah, we need to think about that," Parson said when Gold brought it up. "I hate to take away Mahsoud's oxygen hose, but we better get him downstairs so the aeromeds can bring him out."

"Concur," the MCD said on interphone. "If the loadmasters open the aft ramp as soon as we get slowed down, we'll take everybody out the back."

"What about you?" Gold asked Parson.

"Don't worry about me," Parson said. "I don't want to block anybody on the ladder, so once everybody else gets out, I'll climb down."

"With a broken leg?" Dunne asked. "What if the aircraft's on fire?"

"What if it is?" Parson said. "I still want everybody else out first."

"Screw that," Dunne said.

Not how Gold would address a major, but she agreed with the sentiment.

"Just let me drop out the window with an escape reel," Parson said.

"That's tricky even for someone who's able-bodied," Colman said. "We can get you down the ladder quicker than we can get you out a window."

"All right, but if it looks bad, just egress without me."

No one answered.

"I'm serious," Parson said. "If you guys get killed trying to rescue me, I'll kick your asses up one side of hell and down the other."

"Once the airplane stops," the MCD called, "I'm in command. And we *will* get you out."

That's right, Gold thought. Pull rank on him.

"All right," Parson said. "The lieutenant colonel's in charge on the ground."

"That's better," the MCD said. "Now let's see about moving Mahsoud."

Gold didn't like it when the aeromeds took away Mahsoud's oxygen mask and snapped his regulator to OFF. But to have any hope of getting him out after a crash landing, they had to carry him to the cargo compartment. Mahsoud did not protest, but he groaned when they strapped him to a stretcher. And he cried out when it scraped against the flight deck door panel on the way down. The airplane had become a pipe filled with pain, Gold thought. A vessel of hard edges and narrow passageways, reverberating with the moans of the wounded and the curses of the crew. And, surrounding it all, the slipstream's rush like the sound of days slipping away.

The medics latched Mahsoud's stretcher into place at his old spot by the porthole window. Sunlight filtered through the delaminated glass and formed a penumbra around the window's edges. Outside, the Pacific glowed like blue lava.

"It will be over soon, Mahsoud," Gold said. She took out a handkerchief and wiped sweat from his face, careful to avoid burns and contusions.

"One way or another," he said. He wheezed when he spoke.

"A rescue plane is on the way," Gold said. "I heard it on the radio."

Mahsoud showed little joy at that news. He seemed to feel it did not apply to him.

Gold wondered about that herself. Would the aircraft from Hickam arrive only to find debris floating just offshore from Johnston? She could imagine the C-17 circling a rainbow smear of jet fuel, looking for life vests. Then perhaps it would overfly the atoll in a sad low pass before returning to Hawaii.

"What does your Falnama tell us now?" Mahsoud asked.

Gold didn't feel like retrieving the book from her bags, but she decided it was worth it if it would distract Mahsoud. She just hoped he wouldn't take any passage too seriously. To Gold, anything that smacked of fortune-telling ranked as nonsense. Though she respected all religions, she put no value on their stray tendrils of superstition. She read the Falnama as a cultural document, nothing more.

"Open to a page at random," Mahsoud said when she brought the book.

Gold knew that was how people used the Falnama centuries ago. She hoped Mahsoud sought mere entertainment and not serious guidance. For that, he should read the Quran, as she read the Bible. But she opened her translated edition as he asked. At the top of the page, it read:

Accept that you are an instrument of Allah's will.

A sentence filled with merit, to Gold's mind. At least it wasn't something that might raise hopes higher than warranted. She showed Mahsoud the English words.

"True enough," he said in Pashto. "We have reached a point where we can only accept what comes."

"Such as a life of academics instead of a life of action?" Gold asked.

"You chose both," Mahsoud said, "but, yes, I understand your meaning—if life remains for us at all."

Mahsoud closed his eyes, and Gold decided to let him rest. He seemed, if not at peace, at least resigned. The words of the Falnama appeared to remind him he had a proper role in a plan too vast for comprehension.

Around the cargo compartment, a few of the aeromeds and loadmasters tried to sleep. Gold noticed no one slept for long, but when they did, they slept anywhere: lying flat on the floor, sitting up with forehead on knees, in fetal position on a vacant litter.

The crew members who remained awake began to secure equipment. They anchored Pelican cases to the floor with chains and tie-down devices. Loadmasters ratcheted straps tight across mounds of luggage. Aeromeds placed some of their more delicate tools, such as IV pumps and cardiac monitors, into foam-padded crates. Gold wondered how much of the effort was rote procedure and how much stemmed from an expectation that the equipment would ever be used again. At the very least, Gold realized, secured gear would not turn into missiles during a crash landing.

Across the cargo bay from Mahsoud, Justin watched with listless eyes. Gold could not tell how much he understood. He seemed to have drawn blinds within himself, closed off light from outside. She hoped he would come to know what a gift he'd helped give everyone aboard, that pride and satisfaction in his deed might see him through the painful recovery that awaited him if he survived this flight.

For now, anyway, he remained alive. Gold felt light-headed, just a bit tired and weak. She knew why; she realized where that part of her strength had gone. It lay before her, in someone else's veins, her tithe of blood.

28

The pain in Parson's leg twisted around itself, reached ever greater heights. He had to force his thoughts through it, across it, like concentrating with a high fever. The agony seemed to shape-shift: One moment, a thousand needles pricked the broken limb. Next, a single blade ran it through. Then the sharp points and edges went away only to be replaced by a coat of oil lit afire.

His throat felt as if he'd swallowed sand. A strange buzzing annoyed him, barely audible. It didn't seem like the normal whines of avionics. Parson realized it was probably in his head—the sound track of shock. Or maybe hearing damage from the blast.

The number four engine still seemed to want to shake itself off its pylon. Though it no longer ran, the rotors turned with the air forced through the intake. That created drag and vibration more severe than anything Parson had ever experienced. He just hoped the shutoff valves would hold. When he'd pulled the fire handle for number four, it should have cut off fuel and hydraulic fluid to that engine. But given the way the TF-39 had shelled itself out and then begun rattling and spewing sparks, he could not know with certainty. The nacelle contained any number of components and fluids that could burn like hell's own furnace. A generator cased in magnesium. A pylon, connecting the engine with the wing, laced with lines of flammables.

Parson wished he could just jettison the damned thing—press a button and drop it into the ocean. No such system existed. Whatever was going on with that engine, he and his crew would have to live with it.

Gold entered the flight deck and sat at the nav table. "Where do you want me for the landing?" she asked.

"Right there," Parson said. "Your seat has a four-point harness. If you cinch it down tight, that's as safe a place as any." All true, but Parson didn't add that he wanted her there for his own reasons, too. Her voice cut the pain. Her presence helped him think.

He checked the FMS: a little more than two hundred miles to go. "Listen up, guys," he said. "We're still a ways out, but I want to start configuring to land. We know we have to emergency extend some of the landing gear."

"The forward mains, at least," Dunne said. "God only knows how the electric motors will work after the lightning strike."

"Yeah, that's what I'm thinking," Parson said. "Whatever new problems we're going to have, let's go ahead and find out what they are." He needed to make sure the plane was set up for landing well before arrival at Johnston. In its damaged condition, it did not have the power or controllability for a go-around.

"So do you want me to put the gear down now?" Colman asked.

"Gear down," Parson ordered.

"Airspeed," Dunne said.

Parson checked his instruments. The plane was flying at two hundred and fifty knots. Gear operate speed was two hundred.

"Good catch," Parson said. "We're all tired, and I feel like hell. Keep backing me up like that."

"You mean, like always?" Dunne said.

Colman retarded the two good throttles by millimeters.

"That's it, sir," Dunne said. "Don't change speed too quick."

The airspeed crept down a few knots at a time. Parson scanned the panel, then looked outside. The scene before him presented no color except blue, in every possible shade. The sunlight illuminated the water as if to cleanse the whole planet. Aquamarine in the peaks of the waves, deep azure in the troughs. The horizon like a straight line of a fountain pen's ink, and, above it, the lapis infinity of the sky.

When the airspeed indicator reached two hundred, Parson repeated, "Gear down." Colman put his hand on the gear handle and hesitated, as if moving it would lever open a door to realities too harsh to face. Then he placed it in the DOWN position.

As expected, the indicators for the forward main gear continued to show their UP flags. But Parson felt and heard a thunk underneath him as the nose gear unlocked. And the indicators for the aft mains flipped from UP to the barber poles that meant IN TRANSIT, like the barest hint of a promise.

"Pressure holding?" Parson asked.

"So far, so good," Dunne said.

The aft gear extended and locked down. Their indicators displayed the green wheels of safe landing gear.

"Well, that's a little progress," Colman said.

The nose gear now showed red wheels. So at least the doors had opened, but the nosewheels had not fully extended and locked. Parson cursed himself for forgetting to glance at his watch's second hand when Colman moved the gear handle. It shouldn't have taken longer than twenty-five seconds to put down the wheels through normal means. He thought more time than that had passed, but in his pain and exhaustion he couldn't be sure. Blazing nerve endings in his legs sent filaments of madness into his mind. By sheer will, he forced those filaments to retract.

Finally, Parson felt a slight trundle, as if he'd driven over a speed bump. The nosewheels locked green.

"You want me to go ahead with the emergency switches?" Colman asked. He opened the red guards over toggle switches for the forward main gear. They controlled electric motors to drive down the landing gear bogies when the hydraulics failed.

"Yeah," Parson said. "Remember, start counting seconds when

you flip the switches. If the gear don't go from UP to IN TRANSIT in five Mississippis, turn off the switches or you'll burn out the motors."

"Yes, sir," Colman said.

Colman did not look surprised by that information. He knows what he's doing, Parson realized. Just let him do it. The copilot clicked both switches, and Parson saw him mouth the words "Thousand one . . . thousand two." The right forward gear began moving, but its symmetrical opposite remained at UP. After five seconds, Colman snapped off its switch.

"Figures," Dunne said. "I'll check the breakers." The flight engineer rose from his seat to scan a circuit breaker panel in the aft section of the flight deck. When he returned, he said, "All three are popped, and they won't reset."

Those wheels would never come down, Parson realized. Lowering them required either hydraulics or electrics. Unlike smaller aircraft, the C-5 had no means of manually cranking down its landing gear. The hardware was just too heavy for that.

Parson considered his newest predicament: two mains down on one side, only one on the other. Uneven wheels meant uneven braking. Uneven braking meant veering off the runway. Didn't the book address that problem?

"Let's check that configuration chart in section three," Parson said. "I believe we gotta raise the right forward now." It hurt to move. It hurt not to move. It hurt to think.

"We can't, sir," Dunne said. "We have no hydraulics to bring it up. The emergency system will only take it down."

Parson looked out at the ocean for a full minute. Then he said, "Can somebody bring me some more aspirin?"

"I'll be right back," Gold said. She unbuckled and disappeared down the flight deck ladder. When she returned with two tablets, Parson had no more water within reach. He chewed them to a chalky powder, swallowed. Even moving his jaw muscles hurt his leg. He put his thumb and fingers around the manual trim handle and squeezed it without moving it, tried to get control of the pain. If he concentrated hard enough, gripped that handle and focused on a scratch across the windscreen, he could put the torment from his mind for about four seconds.

"I'll just take it real easy on the brakes," Colman said.

The words broke Parson's momentary trance and slammed him back into misery like striking a wall. He drew a long breath and said, "Yeah, but not *too* easy. I'd rather go off the side of the runway at forty knots than off the end at a hundred." He tried to keep his voice even, but its strain betrayed him.

"Yes, sir," Colman said. "You okay?"

Parson nodded. Then he gripped the trim handle again and ground his teeth. How could he have lived most of his life taking the absence of pain for granted? Just not to hurt would be paradise. He stared at the scratch on the glass, hoping to Zen himself just a couple seconds of relief.

Out the corner of his eye, he saw Colman reach up and press the master caution RESET button. Parson found it hard to care why.

"It's the number four pylon," Dunne said. Colman and Dunne began to move switches on their panels, recite checklist items.

Wading through currents of pain, Parson brought his mind to bear on the new task at hand. He checked the light on his annunciator panel: FIRE WARNING.

WHATEVER HAD JUST HAPPENED, Gold thought, it must have been bad. The crew seemed to perform their first actions from memory, as if they'd rehearsed for this moment. No one stopped to explain anything to her. She leaned forward, saw the FIRE light.

She experienced not quite panic, but more a sense of urgent need—like that time she'd exited a C-141 over Fort Bragg. When she'd felt no opening shock, she looked up to see the streamer: a twisted, writhing parachute that would not inflate. She'd pulled her reserve, and its canopy flowed, billowed, and opened just a couple hundred feet above the North Carolina clay. Gold burned it in and turned her ankle, but the jumpmaster called it a textbook recovery from a malfunction.

This time she had no rip cord to pull, no action she could take. She could only hope whatever the crew was doing, it would work.

"I still got a FIRE light," Dunne said. "How does it look out there?"

Colman peered out his window. "In flames," he said.

Dunne pressed a button on a panel over his head. "I'll keep shooting it with nitrogen," he said.

The crew began running some kind of emergency checklist. To Gold, the calls and responses sounded like an incantation or a catechism. She rose from her seat to see outside.

Now, instead of sparks, the aircraft trailed ropes of black smoke. It boiled from the right wing's outboard engine and the structure that attached the engine to the wing. The smoke plume expanded behind the aircraft, marked its progress over the ocean. Orange flames wrapped clawlike around the pylon. Sheet metal buckled and darkened as the fire spread. Gold knew little about aircraft design, but she did know the wing above that burning pylon contained fuel tanks.

"Is it growing?" Parson asked.

"A little," Colman said.

Dunne pressed that overhead button again. "I might be able to keep it off the wing as long as the nitrogen holds out," he said.

On that thread of hope, Gold searched Dunne's panel for anything that looked like nitrogen quantity. She saw no such gauge. Apparently, it didn't exist. So they had no idea how much nitrogen they had.

"If I have to," Parson said, "I'll ditch the airplane. That'll put out the damned fire." And drown anyone not able-bodied enough to get out, Gold knew. Including Parson.

"Let me try to keep it knocked down," Dunne said. He pressed the button again. Gold saw that whenever he did so, the flames weaved as if dodging a blow. Their color shifted and lightened as the spray of liquid nitrogen stole oxygen from the fire. But when the spray stopped, the flames reddened and climbed. The blast of the slipstream did not blow out the fire, only fed it. And then Dunne would press his fire suppression button again.

"Loadmasters," Parson called on interphone, "make sure everybody has an LPU."

That, Gold understood. Life preserver units.

"Yes, sir," came the answer.

"How far out are we?" Dunne asked.

Parson looked down at the center console. Charts and other paperwork littered it like so many dead leaves. He examined a digital readout and said, "About a hundred miles." Then he moved a switch and said, "Reach Two-Zero, Air Evac Eight-Four is on fire. Our position is ninety-eight miles southeast of Johnston. Be advised we may have to put it in the water."

No response came for long seconds. Then: "Reach Two-Zero copies all. We're inbound, about three-zero-zero miles out."

Gold watched Parson, strapped into his seat, prepared to ride it to the bottom of the Pacific. She thought of Mahsoud, Justin, and Baitullah, and her eyes brimmed. So much promise and so much pain. And now it came down to the spread of fire, the supply of nitrogen, the stretch of nautical miles.

"Hey, loads," Parson said on interphone.

"Sir?"

"Give everybody an EPOS, too. Open them up and show the pax how to use them."

"Roger that."

When a loadmaster climbed the steps, he handed Gold and the crew members their LPUs. Then he brought her a vinyl pouch labeled EMERGENCY PASSENGER OXYGEN SYSTEM. He tore off a red strip to open the pouch. Then he withdrew a plastic hood with a narrow oxygen cylinder. A lanyard connected the cylinder to a red knob.

"If it gets smoky," the loadmaster said, "pull the knob, stretch open the neck seal, and place this over your head."

"Got it," Gold said.

"It'll give you just a few minutes of breathing to get out of the airplane."

Gold realized Parson was preparing his crew and passengers for two possibilities: a ditching in the ocean or a flaming landing.

"Is anybody back in the courier compartment?" Parson asked.

"Negative," the loadmaster said. "Just the bodies."

"All right," Parson said, "so it'll just be the four of us up here when we land. If we make it to the island, open the aft ramp as soon as we touch down. Don't waste any time because I don't know how long you'll have hydraulics."

"And if we ditch?"

"Deploy a life raft if you can. But remember, fuel can burn on top of the water. If the fire doesn't go out when we hit the drink, just use the LPUs and swim as far from the aircraft as possible."

The loadmaster looked at his commander, seemed to search for something to say, then only nodded.

"A C-17's on the way," Parson said. "They'll mark your position."

Your position, Gold thought. He didn't say *our* position. Gold looked out at the fire. Flames danced along the length of the pylon and lapped at the underside of the wing. The smoke had thickened. But when Dunne hit the fire with more spray of nitrogen, the smoke dampened enough for Gold to see the exposed ribs of the pylon. Most of the sheet metal had melted away. A dark stain spread into the wing's leading edge.

The smoke erupted once more. Dunne pressed his fire suppression button. Then he pressed it twice again.

"I'm not getting a MANIFOLD light," he said.

"What's that mean?" Colman asked.

"Nitrogen's gone."

Flames enveloped the pylon and flowed across the top of the wing. Gold thought she could smell the fire, a chemical smolder that seemed to have invaded the air-conditioning. The odor grew stronger as the smoke trail widened, like the foul tang of a bonfire.

29

The FMS showed fifty miles to Johnston Atoll. Parson squinted into the distance, tried to find a speck of sand or coral. Twice he thought he glimpsed something solid, only to recognize it as a wave's shadow or a glint of light reflected off a swell. Oceanic mirages. Probably still too far out to see it, anyway. And what if lightning-damaged instruments had him a little off course?

Sheets of flame shimmered farther across the right wing. Smoke spewed at odd angles from underneath the slats, between seams of aluminum.

"I got a fire light for the inboard section," Dunne said.

Parson looked back at the flight engineer's overhead panel. Two red lights now instead of one. Time for a decision. He turned his wafer switch to PA.

"Prepare to ditch," Parson said. On the panel above him, he opened a red guard for the alarm horn's switch. He gave six short blasts of the horn, the signal to stand by to hit the water.

"Sir, are you sure?" Dunne asked.

"If we keep screwing around with this fire," Parson said, "that wing will blow off, and nobody will get out."

Colman regarded Parson, let out a long breath, and placed his left hand on the throttles.

"Try to put it parallel to the waves," Parson said. "It's going to bounce when it first strikes the water. Just hold it in the landing attitude until it comes down again."

Colman closed his fingers around the throttle knobs.

"You're a hell of a pilot," Parson said. "You guys are a hell of a crew. Now ditch this aircraft."

At that moment, Parson became aware of a presence behind him. Gold stood with her hands on the back of his seat. She pointed and said, "Birds."

Four white petrels glided above the water at about two o'clock low. One veered away, and the others held themselves in a broken V pattern, a perfect missing man formation.

"The island has to be close," she said.

"I see it," Colman said.

Parson saw nothing. He removed his sunglasses and still saw nothing. "I don't think so," he said.

"Yes, sir," Colman said. "I have the island."

Perhaps Colman's younger eyes were right. Those birds had to come from somewhere.

"Let me try to make it, sir," Colman said. "Please."

A commander has to trust his crew, Parson thought. If you lead them well, they'll do the right thing. You can't do it all yourself.

Ahead, a shadow on the ocean lingered, became motionless. As the aircraft grew nearer, the shadow turned to a white lozenge in the distance.

"I got it," Parson said. "Eleven o'clock."

"Yes, sir," Colman said.

"You're only going to get one chance at this," Parson said. Then he switched to PA and said, "Disregard the ditching order. Stand by for landing."

The waves flashing by below seemed smaller now. Perhaps the surface winds were calming.

"Give me a nice flat approach," Parson said.

"No steeper than three degrees," Colman said. He's on it, Parson realized. At ten miles out, he should be at three thousand feet.

Colman cracked the throttles just slightly. The aircraft began a descent, its right wing a meteor burning to earth in a fury of smoke and flame. Parson hoped he'd not chosen wrong.

The C-5's descent rate increased. Johnston Island rose higher in the windscreen. Colman pulled back on the yoke. The aircraft did not respond.

"I can't get the nose up," Colman said.

Parson placed his hand on the spoiler handle, hesitated only a moment, then tugged it as gently as he could. The nose climbed one or two degrees, but not enough.

"You're way above approach speed," Dunne said. "And above tire limit speed."

"Fuck those tires," Parson said. "They don't need to work but one more time."

The vertical speed indicator showed a descent of two thousand feet per minute. Far too much. The Pacific rose toward the burning airplane. Parson pulled the spoiler handle harder.

The C-5 pitched up as if launched. Stall warning tones shrieked. The stick shaker rattled the control columns.

"Power, power," Parson said.

Colman shoved the throttles. The jet climbed, leveled. Its nose fell, rose, fell again.

"We've got to make it stop doing this shit," Parson said. "When the nose comes up, give me just a little more thrust."

The jet flew at about three thousand feet above the water now. As its deck angle rose, Colman advanced the throttles. Parson held the spoiler handle, moved it by fractions, more with his mind than with his hand.

The nose stabilized at zero pitch. Not good for landing. Better to have a few degrees up.

"I think we'll have to make do with that," Colman said.

"Yeah," Parson said. "Just hold what you got."

In the clear water rushing by, reefs appeared as if viewed through molten glass. Each coral formation seemed shot through with specks. For an instant, Parson wondered if they were niches in the coral or fish actually visible from the air. Or perhaps a trick of a sleep-deprived mind.

The island widened in front of the aircraft, white sand like a crust of salt. Now Parson made out the disused runway, its cracked pavement with an X painted on the end.

"We're fast," Dunne said.

"Best we can do," Colman answered.

"Come a little left if you can," Parson said. Colman moved the yoke, lined up with the ribbon of asphalt.

"You can use the thrust reversers on the inboards when we touch down," Dunne said.

Parson turned his comm switch to PA. "Brace for impact," he said.

At about one hundred and ninety knots, the aircraft carried far too much speed. Parson knew this would be more a controlled crash than a landing. Just below, the atoll reeled out its breakers, then surf and sand, then gravel and a fallen wire fence. Then asphalt splattered white with bird droppings.

Colman yanked the throttles to IDLE. With its excess speed, the aircraft floated above the runway. The end of the pavement hurtled toward the jet.

"Spoilers," Colman called.

Parson pulled the handle. The C-5 pitched up, lost its hold on the air, slammed to the earth.

Utility lights broke from their overhead mounts and dangled by coiled cords. The nose gear collapsed. Parson felt the fuselage grinding along the pavement. The impact hurt his leg so much, his visioned silvered and darkened. Pain flowed from the broken bone like a liquid, a hot magma that threatened to overcome him. He gripped his armrests, gritted his teeth, and hissed, "Stand on 'em."

Colman stomped the brakes. Parson pulled the inboard throttles into REVERSE THRUST. The jet swerved off the runway and into the sand, mowed down a copse of palm trees. Dust and smoke billowed over the windscreen. When the right wing's main tanks ignited, the land and sky bled orange and black.

THE FLIGHT DECK DOOR JOLTED OPEN, and smoke began to roll into the cockpit. Through stinging eyes, Gold saw that the crew remained in their seats.

"Evacuate to the left and aft," Parson called. "We'll use the slide." He flipped switches on his overhead panel, and the engine noise whined down.

"Negative," a loadmaster reported from downstairs. "You got a brake fire on the left side and it's spreading forward. Your slide will burn right up."

So they'd have to take Parson down the ladder. Gold removed her headset. She coughed, held her breath, pulled the activation knob on her EPOS. She forced her chin through the neck seal and yanked the hood over her head. Now she could breathe, but she could hardly see as the smoke thickened.

Despite the oxygen flowing in the EPOS, Gold felt she was drowning. The hood confined her, brought forth the primal terror of an animal restrained. Part of her wanted just to head down the flight deck stairs and out through the first opening she could find. Only her concern for Parson held her on the flight deck. She admired the military discipline that kept the crew at their stations, completing some kind of shutdown or firefighting procedure.

The myriad of warning lights on the panels around her went dark. Screams and shouted commands emanated from the cargo compartment, over the rumble of flames and the creaks of burning metal. The pops of tortured aluminum sounded to Gold like distant artillery fire. The smoky cockpit grew hot.

She unharnessed and went to Parson. As he donned his own EPOS, she unbuckled his straps and tossed them aside. Dunne stumbled toward them through the smoke. He groped for a lever and slid Parson's seat aft. Colman struggled to slide back his own seat, which was jammed in its tracks. He gave up, opened the quick-release buckle on his harness, and climbed over the center console.

Gold took Parson under his left arm as Colman took his right.

Parson's body felt impossibly heavy to her until he placed a stockinged foot on the center console and levered himself up with his good leg. As Gold helped drag him from the seat, something outside blew up. Through the EPOS hood, she felt a surge of baking heat against her face.

Flames billowed into the hallway by the bunk rooms. Puddles formed on the floor as plastics melted. Through the smoke, Gold saw Dunne lift a fire extinguisher from its wall mount and pull the pin.

She and Colman began dragging Parson down the flight deck ladder. Each step presented a new obstacle: a turned knee, an awkward handhold. Any torque on Parson's broken leg brought shouts and curses of pain, muffled by his hood.

"Leave me," he yelled. "Get out!"

Gold and Colman ignored the command and muscled him down one more rung. From her place on the ladder, above the cargo compartment, Gold glanced toward the patients. She saw little but smoke. She could tell, however, the aeromeds and loadmasters were fighting to get the wounded through the fire and to the open ramp at the back of the aircraft. She did not see Mahsoud or Baitullah. Plumes of white split through the black smoke. The MCD was blasting at the flames with a fire extinguisher, trying to cut a path.

At the bottom of the flight deck ladder, a crew member fumbled with a lever to open the door to the outside. The door unlatched and extended downward until its ladder reached the ground. The crew member turned to help an ambulatory patient stumble out.

Claws of flame raked the walls and ignited a fluid leaking from a ruptured reservoir. The burning ooze dripped fire onto the floor. In the blazing aircraft, the fire did things Gold had never seen fire do before. Flames splashed across the cargo compartment as the fluid reservoir failed altogether. A length of tubing broke open. Whatever it contained ejected, under pressure and on fire, and lunged at Gold in an incandescent spray of vapor. A rivulet of fire torched its way underneath the ladder. Spatters lit the suede and canvas of Gold's boots. Parson twisted free and beat them out with his gloved hands.

She pulled him by the arm again, but Colman held back. Fire blocked both the crew door and the aft ramp.

"Move!" Dunne shouted from higher up the ladder.

Dunne pointed his extinguisher at the flames below and squeezed the lever. White spray battered the tongues of fire enough for Gold and Colman to reach the crew door with Parson.

For just an instant, Gold hesitated, looked around. She wanted to know if Mahsoud needed help.

There wasn't time. She felt a hand grab her by the collar and shove her through the door, onto the steps that led to the ground.

"Out, Sergeant Major," Dunne yelled. "I got it."

Dunne loosed another blast from his extinguisher. It beat back the flames long enough for Gold to see more flames—in the form of a thrashing human enveloped in fire. Gold could not tell who it was. Dunne advanced toward the burning figure, sweeping with his extinguisher.

Then the fire in the cargo compartment exploded as if the air itself had turned flammable. It singed Gold's hands as she held on to Parson. Despite the pain in her hands and ribs, she worked with Colman to hoist Parson down to the ladder's lower rungs.

Parson pushed himself off, tumbled to the ground. Gold jumped after him. She landed hard and scraped the heel of one hand on the coral surface where the C-5 had skidded from the runway. Colman dropped to the ground beside her. Gold took Parson by the legs, and Colman grabbed his arms. They lifted him in a two-man carry and ran.

30

The fire had reached the converters for the liquid oxygen. Parson knew nothing else would make the blaze accelerate so aggressively. His leg hurt so much he felt faint. As Gold and Colman ran with him, each step seemed to pound in a hot spike. They took him upwind of the smoke, across the abandoned tarmac. His own perspiration and breath created an unbearable humidity inside his EPOS hood.

They put him down on a beach, several hundred yards from the burning airplane. His EPOS collapsed against his face, its cylinder depleted. Fighting the panic of suffocation, Parson placed his fingers under the neck seal and tore the hood off his head.

He gasped, filled his chest with sea breeze. Sweat dripped from his matted hair. Colman removed his own EPOS, then helped Gold out of hers. Heat stress flushed her face, which streamed with moisture. Her eyes had that look he'd seen when he rescued her in Afghanistan: like they had peered into an abyss and still saw it. He noticed red wet burns on the backs of her hands.

Parson raised himself to look at his aircraft. It was like asking if hell existed and getting the answer. He could see its radome and wingtips. Fire and smoke blotted out the rest. Flames towered above its tail, and smoke churned a black arc over the water.

He tried to assess the evacuation. An aeromed and a loadmaster bearing a patient on a stretcher ran from behind the aircraft. The stretcher itself was smoking until the loadmaster ripped away a burning blanket and left it in a smoldering heap on the beach. No one else came out the aft ramp or the crew door.

"Where's Dunne?" Parson asked. Hadn't the flight engineer been right behind him?

Colman gazed back at the C-5. He appeared overheated like Gold, and his desert tan flight suit bore dark streaks and splotches. Though the flameproof fabric would not burn, fire could discolor it. Sweat beaded on Colman's face, and he looked as if he were about to throw up.

"Dunne didn't get out," he said.

The realization invaded Parson's body with a physical presence and circulated straight to his pain centers. The edges of the broken bone in his leg sharpened. His eyes scorched from the sun and the smoke, and even his minor burns and cuts deepened and seared. The hurt took up most of his awareness; it became difficult to concentrate on anything else. He tried to direct his consciousness toward only the essential, like narrowing the sweep of a radar to nothing but the storms in front.

"See if you can help the MCD," he told Colman.

"Yes, sir."

Gold looked up. "I'll go help with the patients," she said.

"Good," Parson said. "Can you count the survivors for me?"

Gold shook her head, as if she weren't able to face a final tally. Parson looked back at her, shrugged. What had happened had happened. They might as well know. She sighed and followed Colman down to the beach, where the aeromeds were setting up a makeshift casualty collection point.

The fire found more of Parson's aircraft to devour, perhaps an engine's oil tank or a line full of hydraulic fluid. The blaze crackled like a rifle on full auto, and debris shot skyward. The burning pieces tumbled in seeming slow motion, trailing pennants of smoke. Colman wandered in search of the MCD as Gold stepped from litter to litter.

A SHORT WAY DOWN THE BEACH, in the dry sand just beyond reach of the waves, Gold found Justin on a stretcher, conscious now. He raised his hand in a languid gesture. Baitullah sat up against a hummock of sand and grass. Gold did not see Mahsoud or the MCD.

She went to Baitullah. He wore a stricken look, though he seemed to have no new injuries.

"Are you all right?" Gold asked in Pashto.

"I am, teacher. But we have lost a friend."

It took a moment for his meaning to sink in. When it did, she imagined Mahsoud's final moments with horror.

"We landed hard," Baitullah continued. "I thought the Americans would leave us, but they took me out right away and rushed back in to save more patients. I kept looking for our friend. . . ."

He stopped, seemed unable to say Mahsoud's name. Gold searched for words of comfort but felt only loss. With her handkerchief, she wiped sweat and soot from Baitullah's forehead. When his tears began, she turned away and went toward the water. The surf foamed around her boots, then retreated. She sank to her knees in the wet sand, placed her fingers in the damp coolness, and closed her eyes.

To her, Mahsoud represented his country's potential. But he came from a hard place where bullets, stones, ropes, and bombs made quick work of thoughtful minds and gentle spirits. To build, to educate, came with such great exertion, over such long stretches of time. Destruction came effortlessly, instantly. What was the point?

The combers rolled up the beach again. The water sissed as it advanced, frothed white over Gold's burned hands, held still for one heartbeat, then slid back into the sea. She got up and continued counting the living: fifteen crew, twenty-five patients and passengers, including herself. The MCD was gone.

Cracks and booms reverberated from the flaming aircraft. The tanks in the left wing cooked off. The wing blew up, then crumbled away from the fuselage like ash.

Gold found Parson raised up on one elbow. He shaded his eyes with his hand, still wearing a beige flight glove darkened by fire. He was watching the C-5 burn. Little of it remained recognizable as an aircraft except the tail. Colman was at his side, seeming frustrated, trying to get his attention.

Finally, Parson said, "Look, Lieutenant, the MCD is dead, and I might pass out any minute. You have to take charge, here."

"I don't know how to take care of patients, sir," Colman said. Gold thought he looked frightened, unprepared. He'd handled himself so well in the airplane, but now he was out of his element.

"You can do it," Parson said. "The medics will take care of the wounded. And when the C-17 gets here, you'll have plenty of help. Just don't ever stop leading."

As Parson coached, Gold recalled her first desperate moments with him four years ago: downed in Afghanistan, facing deadly challenges for which they weren't prepared. But he'd seen her through. He'd made mistakes, but he never stopped leading. And now, perhaps, Colman would learn what Parson seemed to understand instinctively. When you took on responsibility for the lives of friends and family, those lives became more important than your own.

PARSON FELT HIS AIRCRAFT HAD BECOME A FUNERAL PYRE. He thought of Dunne, the MCD, Spencer, Mahsoud, the patients who died during the flight, and those who died in the flames. He felt no triumph over the lives he had saved. Parson wasn't even sure he'd really saved any lives, depending on what spores or chemicals drifted in that smoke. His mind drifted back to that time he'd come in from drinking at Ramstein and found Dunne strumming that funny all-silver guitar. As the slide passed over the strings, the instrument seemed almost to cry. Dunne said it was a Civil War song called "The Vacant Chair."

The fronts of tropical trees brushed the sky. Seabirds wheeled and squawked, protested the fiery invasion of their refuge. No structures remained on the island, just the concrete outlines of their foundations. Paved roads led to nowhere.

Parson had begun this flight with fifty-seven crew and passengers. Only forty, including himself, survived. What could he have done differently? How many of the dead might still be alive if he'd commanded better?

The same questions had dogged him four years ago, had dogged him ever since. In war, people lived and died by decisions to turn right or left, to speed up or slow down, to pull the trigger now or to wait.

Parson thought of the friends who had died around him in Afghanistan. He doubted he could ever form bonds like that again. That part of him had sheared away, left behind in the snows of the Hindu Kush. Nothing mattered but the people you loved, and they could be taken so quickly.

He still had bad dreams about having to leave his crewmates behind in their wrecked C-130. Those images even came to him, unbidden, when he was awake: Jordan with a snapped neck. Luke talking to him one moment, shot through the throat the next. Lieutenant Colonel Fisher immobilized with two broken legs, waiting to be overrun.

And then he'd found Nunez with his head sawed off. The aftermath of that medieval execution—the putrefying blood, the decapitated corpse, the stench of death—seemed to decompose Parson's very sanity. The memory moldered inside him, colored everything else in his mind. The scene replayed itself over and over when he saw Nunez's closed casket at a Catholic church in East Los Angeles. After the funeral, Nunez's sister had held on to him and would not let him go. To his surprise, the family held no resentment that he had survived when Nunez had not. To his relief, they'd asked no questions.

Fisher's family wanted to know everything. At the grave site in the Gettysburg National Cemetery, an EC-130 from the Pennsylvania Air National Guard had flown over in tribute. Then Parson had explained how Fisher had ordered him and Gold to take to the mountains with the prisoner they'd been transporting.

Parson had missed Luke's service. But later, at the cemetery by a cotton field in Mississippi, Luke's father gave Parson his old Air Medal from the Vietnam War. And after Jordan was laid to rest in Iowa, the local VFW held a memorial. The VFW post commander offered Parson a salute.

He'd worried about how the families might receive him, whether they'd blame him for leaving the rest of the crew. But they seemed to understand the importance of the mission. He supposed they had to believe in the mission.

This time, he didn't know most of the dead, but somebody knew them. Those dreaded knocks on doors would begin soon. The fire's black smoke mocked him as it rose from the cremating flames. It seemed to signal the futility of his efforts and carry it across the Pacific and around the world.

He watched Gold talking to one of the Afghans, moving among the wounded. At least she was still here. People could still learn things from her, just like he had. Maybe that was worth something.

If she went on with her work, that might bring a little salve to his wounds. Through his years of military service, Parson knew the value of joint effort. When you did your best to help the team, you became part of something more important than anything you could manage by yourself. Perhaps his biggest contribution, the reason for all his skill and training, was to keep her alive to make her contribution.

The breeze freshened, brought with it a hint of salt. Some part of Parson's mind never quit analyzing the wind and sky, and he noted that the zephyrs bent the smoke and shifted it about twenty degrees. Not a big change, perhaps the result of frontal movement two hundred miles out. The odor of blazing jet fuel remained, though not as noxious as before. The flames had already consumed most of the gas, and now they had to content themselves with oil, tires, metals. It might take days, but eventually the fire would burn itself out.

GOLD COULD SEE COLMAN and the aeromeds had things under control, the wounded calm and still. She assured Baitullah and the other patients that an aircraft was on the way. Then there was little left to do but wait. She sat beside Parson in the sand, but she did not look at him. Her eyes were dry now. Gold picked up an amber cowrie shell, smooth and perfect like petrified sap. She wondered about the life that had once inhabited it.

Then she considered some alternate future, one that included Mahsoud. She imagined him an older man, standing on his prosthesis in a lecture hall, expounding on some point of literature.

The tears returned silently. Parson sat up, winced with the pain it caused him. He put his hand on her shoulder.

"I don't know if I can do this anymore," Gold said.

Parson didn't speak for a while. A tern landed in the flat sand left by the tide. It regarded them with apparent curiosity, then flapped across the atoll toward a lagoon.

"What do you think Mahsoud would want?" he said finally.

"I don't know." Gold looked at the cowrie. The sun hit it at an angle that illuminated it like a nugget of opal.

"I think you do."

Gold didn't feel like hearing that now, but she liked it that Parson cared. If Mahsoud mattered to him, then he must have learned something since the days when all he wanted was payback for his dead crewmates.

"We have a long way to go to get to the kind of world Mahsoud would have needed," Gold said.

"There are others like him," Parson said. "You'll find them. Or they'll find you."

Gold looked out at the ocean. On the horizon, a line of distant clouds took the shape of a snow-covered mountain range. A dot appeared in the sky, just above a line of palms. At first it seemed not to move. After a few minutes, it took the shape of an airplane. It expanded until Gold could make out its wings and hear its engines.

"That's the C-17 out of Hickam," Parson said.

Gold knew it would take her to a place of rest, but she despised the thought of getting back on an aircraft. The jet overflew the island, banked into a turn. A loadmaster ran up the beach to Parson, carrying a handheld radio. "They want to talk to you, sir," the loadmaster said.

"Where'd you get that PRC-90?" Parson asked.

"I grabbed a survival vest on the way out."

"Good job." Parson took the radio, pressed a switch on the side, and said, "Reach Two-Zero, Air Evac Eight-Four Alpha."

"Air Evac Eight-Four Alpha, Reach Two-Zero," the C-17 pilot called. "Good to hear you got out of that thing."

"Some of us did," Parson said. "Please tell me you have morphine on board."

"I'm sure we do," came the answer. "We also got a flight surgeon who's going to run a bunch of tests and have you guys starting popping Cipro."

"Copy that," Parson said. "Hey, don't fly through the smoke."

"We won't, Air Evac. Where are you?"

"On the beach, about five hundred yards upwind of the fire. Lieutenant Colman will be in charge down here."

"See you when we get on the ground."

Gold watched the C-17 make its approach. For a moment she could imagine it came from a netherworld, that nothing else existed but this crust of coral and sand and the infinite Pacific that surrounded it. The reverie lasted only a second or two; Gold had experienced too much reality to indulge in fantasy. That jet didn't come from the world Mahsoud would have needed. It came from the one that failed him.

"Sophia," Parson said. "Sit beside me on the ride to Hickam, will you?"

"All right."

She looked at Parson, the bags under his eyes, the scratches on his face, the bloodstains and scorches on his flight suit. Back then in

Afghanistan, she had helped him keep focused on the mission. Now he seemed intent on returning the favor.

She wanted to say more, but the C-17's whistling howl drowned out conversation. Its wheels barked onto the pavement, left puffs of gray smoke. The aircraft shimmered in heat waves rising from the asphalt as it rolled to the far end of the runway. The engine noise hushed with the distance. The jet came to a full stop, then began a slow, ponderous turn. Aeromeds and loadmasters on the beach started standing, collecting gear, talking to patients.

Colman and a medic came over with an empty litter. Parson slid himself onto it, and he grimaced as they lifted him.

"Time to go home," he said.

Gold shook her head. No, not time for that yet. Between here and home, she had much work to do, if she could still find the strength to do it. She took one last look at the cowrie, threw it with a sidearm toss. It struck the water once, twice, three times. Then it vanished into the endless blue.

ACKNOWLEDGMENTS

If not for my wife, Kristen, this book would probably not exist. From her unwavering support during my long absences for military duty to her encouragement through all the frustrations and rewards of an author's life, she has been the beacon that kept me on course. (And she's a pretty darn good writing coach.)

Once this manuscript met Kristen's approval, it went to some fine folks at Putnam. I'm honored to work with publisher and editor in chief Neil Nyren and company president Ivan Held, along with Thomas Colgan at Berkley. Many thanks also to Michael Barson, Victoria Comella, Kate Stark, Chris Nelson, Lydia Hirt, and all the staff at Penguin Group.

My literary agent, Michael Carlisle, made it all possible. His colleague, Lyndsey Blessing, has helped bring my work into foreign translation. And I owe much to author and professor John Casey, as well as Richard Elam, Barbara Esstman, Liz Lee, and Jodie Forrest. Thanks also to old friend and Navy vet Carol Otis for some medical information.

In addition, I'd like to extend thanks to my great friends and squadron mates in the 167th Airlift Wing, West Virginia Air National Guard, for their companionship and inspiration. Kevin Miller, Curtis Garrett, and former commander Wayne "Speedy" Lloyd provided technical help. Special appreciation goes to Joe Myers for his encouragement and editing input, and to the aeromedical section's Bud Martz, who found time to help me with medical details while he was busy helping save the lives of heroes.

THE STORY BEHIND *SILENT ENEMY*

In my previous novel, *The Mullah's Storm*, Major Parson and Sergeant Gold found themselves shot down, trapped on the ground, fleeing an enemy they fought hand to hand and bullet by bullet. In *Silent Enemy*, they meet again for what should be an uneventful flight, transporting wounded out of Afghanistan—but a terrorist bomb traps them at altitude, unable to land. The crisis forces them on a journey more than halfway around the world, beset by danger.

From the Trojan War to the War on Terror, tales of a ship and crew in peril have timeless appeal. We can all relate to the fear of getting lost, the challenge of facing the elements. We can all envy the bonds that form within the crews, and admire the skills they bring to bear, whether they're seamen climbing through rigging or airmen climbing through clouds. We're all fascinated by their leaders, from Odysseus to Captain Kirk. How will he handle *this* problem? What would *we* do in his place?

For military aircrews, these types of questions come up all the time. As an Air National Guard aviator, I've found myself in situations where the worst could have happened if not for the commander's leadership, the crew's airmanship, and a little mercy from the gods of wind and storm.

One morning in 1998, my crewmates and I were in the middle of a long trip home from an airlift mission in Bangladesh. We took off from Kadena Air Base on the Japanese island of Okinawa in our C-130 Hercules cargo aircraft, headed for Wake Island, a tiny atoll in the Pacific. En route, we suddenly encountered unforecasted, unfavorable winds. As the navigator and I made calculations, the cost in groundspeed and fuel became clear, and it became apparent we might not have the fuel to reach Wake. Looking down, the ocean never seemed so vast. We discussed options with the aircraft commander, considered turning around, declaring a fuel emergency, landing at Iwo Jima. . . .

And then the winds shifted to our tail, the numbers improved, and we landed at Wake with fuel to spare.

My logbook also includes about five engine shutdowns, smoke in the flight deck, a couple of hydraulic losses, a brake fire, two pressurization failures, and electrical weirdness not even covered by the flight manual.

In *Silent Enemy*, Major Parson has those kinds of troubles, and they compound as his long flight continues. That happens in airplanes: A malfunction in one system might cause problems with another. What makes it worse for Parson is that he can't land for repairs without triggering the bomb. As you might imagine, there aren't too many things you can fix on an airplane while it's flying.

But Parson *can* refuel in the air. He keeps his aircraft aloft through multiple aerial refuelings. Military fliers practice aerial refuelings so often they become routine, and as a crew member you almost forget the inherent danger of two jets flying within feet of each other. That is why I chose to describe the novel's first aerial refueling from the point of view of Sergeant Gold, one of the passengers.

Throughout the novel, the point of view switches between Parson and Gold so the reader can experience the flight from the perspective of both pilot and passenger. For Parson, the burdens of leadership weigh heavy as he and his crew grow tired, the patients worsen, and the aircraft breaks down around them. For Gold, the journey tests her faith, her endurance, and her belief in the fight for a better world.

This is all further complicated by the fact that this is a medical flight. The most poignant journeys I've ever flown as a military flier have involved transporting troops injured in war. The entire concept of modern combat medicine depends on airlifting the severely wounded off the battlefield almost immediately. In the old days, the effort focused on moving medical facilities as far forward into the combat zone as possible (think of the old MASH units), but now it's the reverse, moving the wounded to state-of-the-art medical centers in Europe or the U.S.

This means transporting people still fighting for their lives: treatment continues almost seamlessly from battlefield to combat theater surgical facility to major hospital, and the wounded fly while still under intensive care. Flight nurses and medics, called aeromeds, specialize in this continuity of care, their equipment and training turning the back of an airplane into a sick bay. *Silent Enemy* puts readers on board an airborne emergency room, where the flight nurses and medics deal with the most heartbreaking of war injuries in a confined space rocked by turbulence and subject to all the other hazards of flight.

One hazard they usually don't have to worry about, however, is a midair explosion. The novel's basic plot element is fictional, and I'd like to think the Air Force's security police will make sure it stays that way. But if a crew ever did take off with a bomb rigged to detonate on descent, the ensuing events might be terribly similar to those described in *Silent Enemy*. As my wife read the manuscript, she noted that I seemed to be retelling every in-flight crisis I'd ever experienced or trained for.

I happened to write a few pages of *Silent Enemy* while stuck with several other aircrews in Rota, Spain. We were waiting out a cloud of volcanic ash that had played havoc with air traffic all over Europe. It seemed appropriate to work on a journey story while I was in mid-journey myself, trapped at an ancient seaport, running into old crewmates I hadn't seen in years. Some were on the way out of Iraq or Afghanistan. Some were on the way in.

As I complete this essay, their travels continue. In even the best-case scenarios, young soldiers, sailors, and airmen will keep going into harm's way. At any moment, service members like my fictitious Major Parson and Sergeant Gold are in the skies above you, headed for wherever their missions take them. When they get there, politics won't matter. They'll care only about doing their jobs, watching their friends' backs, and getting home. I hope *Silent Enemy* offers a glimpse of who they are and why they do what they do.

ABOUT THE AUTHOR

Thomas W. Young, author of *The Mullah's Storm*, served in Afghanistan and Iraq with the Air National Guard. He has also flown combat missions to Bosnia and Kosovo, and additional missions to Latin America, the Horn of Africa, and the Far East. In all, Young has logged almost four thousand hours as a flight engineer on the C-5 Galaxy and the C-130 Hercules, while flying to almost forty countries. Military honors include two Air Medals, three Aerial Achievement Medals, and the Air Force Combat Action Medal.

In civilian life, he spent ten years as a writer and editor with the broadcast division of the Associated Press, and flew as a first officer for Independence Air, an airline based at Dulles International Airport near Washington, D.C. Young holds B.A. and M.A. degrees in mass communication from the University of North Carolina at Chapel Hill.

Young's nonfiction publications include *The Speed of Heat: An Airlift Wing at War in Iraq and Afghanistan*, released in 2008 by McFarland and Company. His narrative "Night Flight to Baghdad" appeared in the Random House anthology *Operation Homecoming: Iraq, Afghanistan, and the Home Front, in the Words of U.S. Troops and Their Families.*

5/18